"You think Darez Fort was a test," Arwa said. She spoke slowly, tasting the words. They were metal on her tongue, bitter as blood.

"Oh yes," Rabia said eagerly. She leaned forward. "All of it is intended to test us—the unnatural madness, the sickness, the blight on Irinah's desert. One day the Maha is going to return, if we prove our worth against evil forces, if we show we are strong and pious. And what happened to your husband, his bravery when the madness came, and your survival, it's *proof*—"

"Thank you," Arwa said, cutting in. Her voice was sharp. She couldn't soften the edge on it and had no desire to. Instead she bared her teeth at Rabia, smiling hard enough to make her face hurt.

Rabia flinched back.

"You've been *very* kind," added Arwa.

Rabia gave a weak smile in response and fled with a mumbled apology. Arwa didn't think she'd be bothered by her again.

Praise for

Empire of Sand

"A stunning and enthralling debut, *Empire of Sand* thoroughly swept me away. With wonderfully lyrical prose, Suri deftly balances fantastic worldbuilding with a nuanced exploration of family ties and the lengths one will go for love. A quiet, powerful and unexpected love story set in a crushing world of magic and tyrants, *Empire of Sand* is a gripping tale of survival I'll be recommending for a long time!"   —S. A. Chakraborty

"A brilliant debut that shows us a rich, magical world with clear parallels to this one: It has a sadistic leader with a cult-like following who warps the world for personal gain, a few individuals with the strength to resist him, and a planet seeking balance. But its core is a heroine defined by her choices, and her journey is absorbing, heart-wrenching, and triumphant. Highly recommended."   —Kevin Hearne

"The best fantasy novel I have read this year. I loved it!"
—Miles Cameron

"*Empire of Sand* is astounding. The desert setting captured my imagination, the magic bound me up, and the epic story set my heart free."   —Fran Wilde

"I was hooked from the moment I began Tasha Suri's gorgeous debut novel, *Empire of Sand*. Suri has created a rich world full of beautiful and powerful magic, utterly compelling characters, high stakes, and immersive prose. I absolutely loved it!"

—Kat Howard

"A darkly intricate, devastating, and utterly original story about the ways we are bound by those we love."　　　—R. F. Kuang

"A lush, atmospheric, and sweeping epic fantasy, a powerful story of resistance and love in the face of terrifying darkness. You'll want to devour *Empire of Sand*."　　　—Aliette de Bodard

"Genuine, painful, and beautiful. A very strong start for a new voice."　　　—*Kirkus* (starred review)

"Complex, affecting epic fantasy....Intricate worldbuilding, heartrending emotional stakes...well-wrought prose."
—*Publishers Weekly* (starred review)

"The desert setting, complex characters, and epic mythology will captivate readers."　　　—*Booklist* (starred review)

"This is the future of fantasy: rich, complex, unflinching. *Empire of Sand* is a stunning achievement."　　　—Mark Oshiro

"Riveting and wonderful! A fascinating desert world, a compelling heroine, and a richly satisfying conclusion. *Empire of Sand* will sweep you away!"　　　—Sarah Beth Durst

REALM
OF
ASH

By Tasha Suri

THE BOOKS OF AMBHA

Empire of Sand

Realm of Ash

REALM
OF
ASH

THE BOOKS OF AMBHA

TASHA SURI

www.orbitbooks.net

Copyright © 2019 by Natasha Suri
Excerpt from *The Throne of the Five Winds* copyright © 2019 by Lilith Saintcrow
Excerpt from *The Sisters of the Winter Wood* copyright © 2018 by Rena Rossner

Author photograph by Shekhar Bhatia
Cover design by Lauren Panepinto
Cover images by Alamy and Shutterstock
Cover copyright © 2019 by Hachette Book Group, Inc.
Map copyright © 2019 by Tim Paul

Orbit
Hachette Book Group
1290 Avenue of the Americas
New York, NY 10104
orbitbooks.net

First Edition: November 2019
Simultaneously published in Great Britain by Orbit

Orbit is an imprint of Hachette Book Group.
The Orbit name and logo are trademarks of Little, Brown Book Group Limited.

The publisher is not responsible for websites (or their content) that are not owned by the publisher.

The Hachette Speakers Bureau provides a wide range of authors for speaking events. To find out more, go to www.hachettespeakersbureau.com or call (866) 376-6591.

Library of Congress Cataloging-in-Publication Data
Names: Suri, Tasha, author.
Title: Realm of ash / Tasha Suri.
Description: First Edition. | New York, NY : Orbit, 2019. | Series: The books of Ambha
Identifiers: LCCN 2019027766 | ISBN 9780316449755 (trade paperback) |
    ISBN 9780316449748 (library ebook)
Subjects: GSAFD: Fantasy fiction.
Classification: LCC PR6119.U75 R43 2019 | DDC 823/.92—dc23
LC record available at https://lccn.loc.gov/2019027766

ISBNs: 978-0-316-44975-5 (trade paperback), 978-0-316-44972-4 (ebook)

Printed in the United States of America

LSC-H

10 9 8 7 6 5 4 3 2 1

For my mother, Anita Luthra Suri.

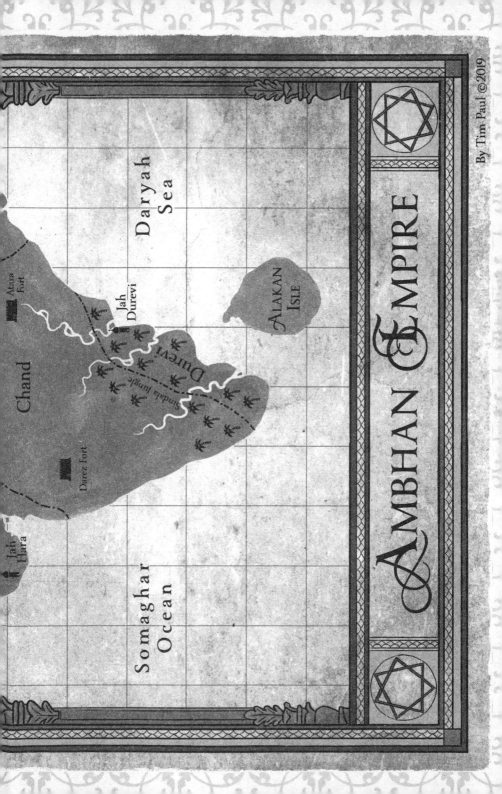

CHAPTER ONE

Don't be sick. Don't be sick.

The palanquin jolted suddenly, tipping precariously forward. Arwa bit back a curse and gripped the edge of one varnished wooden panel. The curtain fluttered; she saw her maidservant reach for it hastily, holding it steady. Nuri's eyes met her own through the crack between the curtain and the panel, soft with apology.

"I'm sorry, my lady," said Nuri. "I'll tie the curtain in place."

"No need," Arwa said. "I like the cold air."

She adjusted her veil to cover her face, and Nuri nodded and let the curtain fall without securing it.

Arwa leaned back and forced her tense fingers to uncurl from the panel. Traveling through Chand province hadn't been so bad, but once her retinue had reached Numriha, the journey had become almost unbearable. A frame of wood and silk was a decent enough mode of transport on even paths, such as were naturally found in the flat fields of Chand, but the palanquin was ill-suited for travel up winding mountain roads. And Numriha was *all* mountains. Here, the disrepair of the Empire's trade routes was impossible to ignore.

Arwa had heard the guards complain of it often enough: the way the once grand passes through the Nainal Mountains had grown unstable from rainfall and avalanche, their surfaces by turns sheer as a knife edge or gouged with deep, ankle-twisting holes. One misplaced step, and a man could easily stumble and fall straight to his death down the mountainside.

"If the roads don't kill us," one guard had said to Nuri, "then the bandits are bound to do it. These Numrihans are like goats."

"Goats," Nuri had said, nonplussed.

"They can climb anything. I once heard of one Numrihan bastard who jumped down right into the heart of a lady's retinue, straight into her palanquin—cut clean through the woman's throat—"

"Don't scare her," another guard had said. "Besides, what if *she's* listening?" She, of course, being Arwa. Their fragile, silk-swaddled package, silent inside her four walls. "She doesn't sleep as it is. Girl," he said to Nuri, "you tell your lady she needn't fear these people. They're not Ambhan, not proper, but they're no blood-worshipping heathens either. They'll leave us be."

"It's not fear of bandits or Amrithi that keeps my lady awake," Nuri had said coolly, and that of course had been the end of *that* conversation.

They all knew—or thought they knew—why Arwa did not sleep.

For four days, Arwa's nausea had ebbed and flowed along with the shuddering movement of the palanquin, as she was carried slowly up the narrow and treacherous pass. She could not see the road from her veiled seat, but her body was painfully aware of the truth of her retinue's grumbling. Once that day already, she'd stopped to heave up her guts by the roadside, as her guardswomen milled close by and her guardsmen waited farther up the pass, respectful of her dignity. Nuri had stroked her hair and given her water to drink, and told her there was no need for shame, my lady, no need. Arwa had not agreed, and still did not, but she knew no one expected her to be strong. If anything, her weakness was a comfort to them. It was expected.

She was grieving, after all.

Arwa sank deeper into her furs, her veil a cloying weight against her skin, and tried to think of anything but the ache of her stomach, the heat of nausea prickling over her flesh. She turned her head to the faint bite of cold air creeping in through the narrow gap between the curtain and the palanquin itself, hoping its chill would soothe her. Even through the rich weight of the curtain, she could see the flicker of the lanterns carried by her guardswomen, and hear her guardsmen speak to one another in low voices, discussing the route that lay before them, made all the more treacherous by nightfall.

The male guards were meant to walk in a protective circle around her guardswomen, close enough to defend her, but far enough from her palanquin to ensure she was not directly at risk of being visible to common men. But the narrowness of the path and the dangers posed by following a cliff-edge road in darkness had made following proper protocol impossible. Instead all her guards snaked forward in an uneven, mixed-gender line, with her palanquin at its center.

She felt the palanquin jolt again, and this time she did swear. She hurriedly gripped the edge of a panel again as her retinue came to a stop, voices beyond the curtain rising and mingling in a wave of indecipherable noise. Someone's voice rose higher, and then suddenly she could hear the crunch of booted footsteps against stone, growing louder and then fading away.

Her palanquin was lowered to the ground. The path was so uneven that it tipped slightly to one side as it touched soil—enough to make the curtain flutter, and Arwa's weight fall naturally against one wall.

Arwa wondered, briefly, if bandits had fallen upon them after all. But she could hear no weapons and no more shouting, only silence.

Perhaps the guards had simply abandoned her. It was not unheard of. She knew very well how easily a soldier's loyalty could falter, how much coin and wine and bread it took to keep a soldier loyal, when danger and hardship presented themselves. Steeling herself for the worst, she drew the curtain the barest sliver wider. She saw Nuri's silhouette in the darkness, saw her carefully adjust her own shawl around her head, lantern light flickering around her, as she kneeled down to Arwa's level.

"My lady," Nuri said, voice painstakingly deferential. "The palanquin can go no farther. We will need to walk the final steps together. The men have gone back down the path, and will not see you, if you come out now."

When Arwa did not respond, Nuri said gently, "It is not far, my lady. I've been told it's an easy walk."

An easy walk. Of course it was. Most of the women who took the final steps of this journey were not as young or as healthy as Arwa. She adjusted her shawl and her veil. Last of all, she touched the sash of her tunic, hidden beneath the weight of her furs and her shawl and her long brocade jacket. Within her sash, she felt the shape of her dagger, swaddled in protective leather. It lay near her skin where it rightly belonged.

She pushed back the curtain of the palanquin. Her muscles were stiff from the journey, but Nuri and one of the guards-women were quick to help her to her feet.

As soon as Arwa was standing, with the cold night air all around her, she felt indescribably better. There was a staircase at the side of the path, carved into rock and rimmed in pale flow-ers, leading up to a building barely visible through the darkness.

She could have walked alone and unaided up those steps, but Nuri had already taken her arm, so Arwa allowed herself to be guided. The steps were blessedly even beneath her feet. She heard the whisper of Nuri's footsteps, the gentle clang of the guardswomen before her and behind her, their lanterns bright moons in the dark. She raised her head, gazing up through the gauze of her veil at the night sky. The sky was a blanket scattered with stars, vast and unclouded. She saw no birds in flight. No strange, ephemeral shadows. Just the mist of her own breath, as its warmth uncoiled in the air.

Good.

"Careful, my lady," said Nuri. "You'll stumble."

Arwa lowered her head and looked obediently forward. At the top of the staircase, she caught her first proper glimpse of her new home. She stopped, ignoring Nuri's insistent hand on her arm, and took a moment to gaze at it.

The hermitage of widows was a beautiful building, built of a stone so luminescent it seemed to softly reflect back the starlight. Its three floors rested on pale columns carved to resemble trees, rootless and ethereal, arching their canopies over white verandas and latticed windows bright with lantern light. Within it, the widows of the nobility prayed and mourned, and lived in peaceful isolation.

Arwa had thought, somewhat foolishly, that it would look more like the squalid grief-houses of the common people, where widows with no husband to support them and with family lacking in the means or compassion to keep them were discarded and left to rely on charity. But of course, the nobility would never allow their women to suffer so in shame and discomfort. The hermitage was a sign of the nobility's generosity, and of the Emperor's merciful kindness.

Finally, she allowed Nuri to guide her forward again, and entered the hermitage. Three women, hair cut short in the style worn by widows, were waiting for her in the foyer. One sat on a chair, a cane before her. Another stood with her hands clasped at her back, and a third still stood ahead of the rest, twisting the ends of her long shawl nervously between her fingers. Behind them, leaning over balconies and standing in corridors were… all the other women in the hermitage, Arwa thought wildly. By the Emperor's grace, had they *all* truly come to greet her?

She shook off Nuri's grip and stepped forward, removing her veil as the third, nervous woman approached her. Arwa forced herself to make a gesture of welcome—forced herself not to flinch as the woman's eyes grew teary, and she reached for Arwa's hands.

The woman was old—they were all old to her weary eyes— and the hands that took Arwa's own and held them firm were soft as wrinkled silk.

"My dear," said the woman. "Lady Arwa. Welcome. I am Lady Roshana, and I must say I am very glad to see you here safe. My companions are Asima, who is seated, and Gulshera. If you need anything, you must come to us, understand?"

"Thank you," Arwa whispered. She looked at the woman's face. The shawl she wore over her short hair was plain, as one would expect of a widow, but it was made of a rare knot-worked silk only common in one village of Chand, and accordingly eye-wateringly expensive. She wore no jewels but a gem in her nose, a diamond of pale, minute brilliance. This woman, then, was the most senior noblewoman of the hermitage, by dint of her wealth and no doubt her lineage, and the two others were the closest to her in stature. "It's a great honor to be here, Aunt," Arwa said, using a term of respect for an elder woman.

"You are so young!" exclaimed Roshana, staring at Arwa's face. "How old are you, my dear?"

"Twenty-one," said Arwa, voice subdued.

A noise rippled through the crowd, hushed and sad. Noble-women could not remarry; to be young and widowed was a tragedy.

Arwa's skin itched beneath so many eyes.

"Shame, shame," said Asima from her chair, overloud.

"I truly hadn't expected you to be so young," Roshana breathed, still damp-eyed. "I thought you would be—older. Why, you are near a child. When I heard the widow of the famed commander of Darez Fort was coming to us—"

Arwa flinched. She could not help it. Even the name of the place burned, still. It was just her luck that Roshana did not see it. Instead, Roshana was still staring at her damply, still chattering on.

"...have you no family, my dear, who could have taken care of you? After what you've been through!"

Arwa wanted to wrench her hand free of Roshana's grip, but instead she swallowed, struggling to find words that weren't cutting sharp, words that would not flay this fool of a woman open.

How dare you ask me about Darez Fort.

How dare you ask me about my family, as if your own have not left you here to rot.

How dare—

"I chose to come here, Aunt," Arwa said, her voice a careful, soft thing.

She could have told the older widow that her mother had offered to take her home. She'd offered it even as she'd cut Arwa's hair after the formal funeral, the one that took place a full month after the real bodies from Darez Fort had been buried. Maryam had cut Arwa's hair herself, smoothing its shorn edges flat with her fingers, tender with terrible disappointment. As Arwa's hair had fallen to the ground, Arwa had felt all Maryam's great dreams fall with it. Dreams of renewed glory. Dreams of second chances. Dreams of their family rising from disgrace.

Arwa's marriage should have saved them all.

You could come back to Hara, Maryam had said. *Your father has asked for you.* A pause. The snip of shears. Maryam's fingers, thin and cold, on her scalp. *He asked me to remind you that as long as he lives, you have a place in our home.*

But Roshana had no right to that knowledge, so Arwa only added, "My family understand I wish to mourn my husband in peace."

Roshana gave a sniffle and released Arwa's hands. She placed her fingertips gently against Arwa's cheek. "You must still love him very much," she said.

I should weep, Arwa thought. *They expect me to weep.* But Arwa didn't have the strength for it, so she simply lowered her eyes and drew her shawl over her face instead, as if overcome. There was a flurry of noise from the crowd. She felt Roshana's hand on her head.

"There, there now," said Roshana. "All is well. We will take care of you, my dear. I promise."

"She should sleep," Asima quavered from her seat. "We should all sleep. How late is the hour?"

It was not a subtle hint.

"Rabia," said a voice. Arwa looked up. Gulshera was speaking, gesturing to one of the women in the crowd. "Show her where her room is."

Rabia hurried over and took Arwa's hand in her own, ushering her forward. Arwa had almost forgotten that Nuri was present, so she startled a little, when she heard Nuri's soft voice whisper her name, and felt her hand at her back.

Roshana's outpouring of emotion had both embarrassed Arwa and left her uneasy. She'd treated Arwa the way a woman might treat a daughter or a longed-for grandchild. She wondered if Roshana had either daughter or grandchild, somewhere beyond the hermitage. She wondered what sort of family would discard a woman here to gather dust. She wondered what sort of family a woman would, perhaps, come here to hide from, choosing solitude and prayer over the bonds and duties of family.

She thought of her mother's hands running through her own shorn hair. She thought of the way her mother had wept, as

Arwa hadn't: full-throated, as if her heart had utterly broken and couldn't be mended.

I had such hopes for you, Arwa. Her voice breaking. *Such hopes. And now they're all gone. As dead as your fool husband.*

She followed Rabia through the crowd into the silence of a dark, curving corridor.

The widow Rabia was dying—nearly literally, it seemed, from the way she kept spasmodically pursing and loosening her lips— to ask Arwa questions that were no doubt completely inappropriate to put to a freshly grieving widow. Accordingly, Arwa kept dabbing her eyes and sniffling as they shuffled forward, mimicking tears. If the woman was going to ask her about her husband—or worse still, about what happened at Darez Fort— then by the Emperor's grace, Arwa was damn well going to make her feel bad about it.

"You mustn't think badly of them all coming to look at you," said Rabia. "They only wanted to see you are—normal. And you are. And *so* young." A pause. "You must not mourn too greatly," Rabia continued, apparently deciding to put her questions aside for now, and provide a stream of unsolicited advice instead. "Your husband died in service to the Empire. That is glorious, don't you think?"

"Oh yes," Arwa said, patting furiously at her eyes. "He was a brave, brave man." She let her voice fade to a whisper. "But I can't speak of him yet. It's far too painful."

"Of course," Rabia said hurriedly, guilt finally overcoming her. They fell into silence.

Arwa's patience—limited, at the best of times—was sorely tested when Rabia piped up again a moment later.

"I know some people say the Empire is cursed and that—the fort, you know—that it's proof. But *I* don't think that. This is your room," she added, pushing the door open. Nuri slipped inside, leaving Arwa to deal with Rabia alone. "I think we're being tested."

"You think Darez Fort was a test," Arwa said. She spoke slowly, tasting the words. They were metal on her tongue, bitter as blood.

"Oh yes," Rabia said eagerly. She leaned forward. "All of it is intended to test us—the unnatural madness, the sickness, the blight on Irinah's desert. One day the Maha is going to return, if we prove our worth against evil forces, if we show we are strong and pious. And what happened to your husband, his bravery when the madness came, and your survival, it's *proof*—"

"Thank you," Arwa said, cutting in. Her voice was sharp. She couldn't soften the edge on it and had no desire to. Instead she bared her teeth at Rabia, smiling hard enough to make her face hurt.

Rabia flinched back.

"You've been *very* kind," added Arwa.

Rabia gave a weak smile in response and fled with a mumbled apology. Arwa didn't think she'd be bothered by her again.

It was a nice enough room, once Rabia had been encouraged to leave it. It had its own latticed window, and a bed covered in an embroidered blanket. There was a low writing desk, already equipped with paper, and a lit oil lantern ready for Arwa's own use. One of the guardswomen must have brought in Arwa's luggage via a servants' entrance, because her trunk was on the floor.

Nuri kneeled before it, quickly sorting through tunics and shawls and trousers, all in pale colors with light embellishment, suitable for Arwa's new role as a widow. The ones that had grown dirty from use would be washed and aired to remove the musk from their long journey, then refolded and stored away again, packed with herbs to preserve their freshness.

Arwa sat on the bed and watched Nuri work.

Nuri was the perfect servant. Mild, discreet, attentive. Arwa had no idea what Nuri really thought or felt. It was no surprise, really: Nuri had been trained in her father's household from childhood, under the keen eye of Arwa's mother, who demanded only the best from her household staff, a clean veneer of loyal obedience, without flaw. She'd been sent by Arwa's mother to accompany her on the journey from Chand to Numriha, as Arwa had not had a maidservant of her own any longer.

"The guards," said Arwa, "are they camping overnight?"

"The hermitage provides accommodation not far from here," Nuri said. "They'll leave in the morning, I expect."

"Does the hermitage have servants' quarters?"

Nuri was momentarily silent. Arwa watched her smooth the creases from the tunic on her lap. "I thought I would sleep here," Nuri said finally. "I have a bedroll. I would be able to care for you then, my lady."

"I don't want you to stay," said Arwa. "Not here in my room tonight, or in the hermitage at all. You can accompany the guards back tomorrow. I'll pay for your passage back to Hara."

"My lady," Nuri said quietly. "Your mother bid me to stay with you."

"You can tell her I made you leave," Arwa said. "Tell her I refuse to have a maidservant." *Blame my grief*, Arwa thought. But Nuri would surely do that without being told. "Tell her I raged at you, that I wouldn't be reasoned with. She'll believe it."

"Lady Arwa," Nuri said. There was a thread of fear in her voice. "You...you need someone to take care of you. To protect you. Lady Maryam, she..." Voice low. "I am not to speak of it. But I know."

Ah.

Arwa swallowed, throat dry.

"I will be safe here," she said finally. "You've seen the hermitage now. You can tell her so. It's nothing but broken roads and old women. There couldn't be anywhere safer in the world for someone who is..." Arwa paused. She could not say it. "Someone who is—afflicted. As I am. No one will discover me here. I'll make sure of it."

"Lady Arwa. Your mother—Lady Maryam—*she insisted*—"

"I can keep my own secrets safe," Arwa cut in tiredly, ignoring Nuri's words. "She'll know it was my choice. She won't cast you out for it. I expect she'll be glad of your help with Father anyway."

Arwa reached into her sash and removed a purse. She held it out.

"Take it," she said. "Enough for your journey to Hara, and more for your kindness."

If her mother had trusted Nuri with the truth of Arwa's nature, then Nuri had no doubt been paid handsomely to accompany Arwa. But more coin would not hurt her, and would perhaps soften her to Arwa's will.

At first, Nuri did not move.

"Please," said Arwa. Voice soft, now. Cajoling. "Is it so strange for me to want to be alone to mourn? To have no more eyes on me? Nuri, I am begging you—return to my mother. Allow me the dignity of a private grief."

Hesitantly, Nuri held out her hand. Arwa placed the purse on her palm, and watched Nuri's fingers curl over it.

"I should finish sorting your clothes," said Nuri.

"There's no need," said Arwa. "You should go and rest. You have a long journey tomorrow."

Nuri nodded and stood. "Please take care, Lady Arwa," she said. Then she left.

Arwa kneeled and sorted through her own clothes. She would have to arrange for one of the hermitage's servants to have them washed in the morning. When the job of sorting through her clothing was done, Arwa latched the trunk shut and closed the door.

She placed the oil lantern on the window ledge, sucked in a fortifying breath, and took her dagger from her sash.

She held the blade over the heat of the oil lantern's flame. Her hand rested comfortably on the hilt of the blade, where the great teary opal embedded within it fitted the shape of her palm in a manner that brought her undeniable comfort. She counted the seconds, waiting for the blade to warm, and stared out the window. The dark stared back at her, velvet, oppressively lightless. She couldn't even see the stars.

She lifted the blade up and waited for it to cool again.

She'd been too afraid to use the dagger on the journey, with Nuri always near, with her guards ever vigilant. Her dagger was far too obviously not of Ambhan design. Where the finest Ambhan daggers were richly embossed, etched with graceful birds and flowers and flecks of jewels, her own was austere and wickedly sharp, the opal in its hilt a glaring milky eye. It was an Amrithi blade, unlovely and uncivilized, and any soldier of the Empire—trained to seek and erase the presence of Amrithi barbarians, to banish them to the edges of the civilized world where they rightly belonged—would have recognized it on sight.

She recalled the guardsman's comment on blood-worshipping heathens with bitter humor.

If only you knew, she thought, *that you carried one on your shoulders all along. Oh, you would have tossed me over the cliff edge then, and you would have been proud of it.*

Once in her palanquin, despite the risks, she'd made a small cut to her thumb, and daubed blood behind her ear, in the manner mothers daubed kohl behind children's ears to keep the evil eye at bay. She'd hoped it would be enough, and perhaps it had been. She'd seen no shadows. Felt no evil descend, winged and silent. But every night she had lain awake, listening and waiting like a prey animal braced for the flash of a predator's wings in the dark. She had imagined in great, lurid detail all the things that would happen if her meager scrape of spilled blood was not enough: Nuri's body cut open from neck to groin, her insides splayed out around her body; the guards turning on one another, their scimitars red and silver and white as bone in the bloody dark.

Darez Fort, all over again.

And all that time, Nuri had known what Arwa was. All that time. If Arwa had only known—if she had been able to employ Nuri to distract the guards, so that she could reach her blade . . .

Well. No matter now. The journey was done, and soon Nuri would be gone. Useful though Nuri perhaps would have been, Arwa was grateful for that. She did not want someone to fuss over her with worried eyes. She wanted no spy from her mother, sent to ensure that she was suitably quiet and secretive and *safe*. The thought of Nuri remaining here made her feel suffocated.

Her mother—Emperor's grace upon her—could not shield her. Nuri could not shield her.

Only Arwa could do that.

Once the blade had cooled, she placed its sharp edge to a finger, and watched the blood well up. The cut was shallow, the pain negligible. She placed her finger against the window ledge and drew a line across its surface.

The lantern flame flickered, caught by a faint breeze. Arwa watched it move. She thought of her husband. Of Kamran. Of a circle of blood, and a hand on her sleeve, and eyes that gleamed like gold. Her stomach felt uneasy again, roiling inside her. Her mouth was full of the taste of old iron.

Curious, how even when the heart was silent and the mind declined to recall suffering, the body still remembered.

She wiped the dagger clean on an old cloth and pressed the material to her finger finally to stem the last of the bleeding. She looked at the window. The blood was still there, illuminated by her lantern, a firm line demarcating the dark and the light, the safety of the room, and what lay beyond it.

She sat on the bed, curling up her knees. She placed the dagger by her feet, and watched the flame move. Waiting.

The night remained silent.

Nuri's voice rose up in her. *You . . . you need someone to take care of you. To protect you.*

And who, Arwa thought, not for the first time, as sleep began to creep over her, *will protect everyone from me?*

If there was an answer to that question, she had not found it yet. But she would. She had to.

CHAPTER TWO

A noise woke her in the night, hours before dawn. She opened her eyes. Held her breath. Her heart was a pulsing fist in her chest. There was a call, hollow and cold, beyond the window. The flutter of wings.

It was just birdsong. There was nothing here. She could smell no incense in the air. See no eyes in the dark.

Feel nothing burrowing into her skull, cold-fingered and deathless.

Still, she rose to her feet. Her legs felt like water. She stared through the light of the candle. On the walls and beneath her feet the shadows flickered like beasts, unfurling with the bristle of blades and broken limbs.

It was not here. It was not here.

By the Emperor's grace, let it not be here.

It cannot cross the blood. You're safe, she told herself. *Safe.*

The air was ice around her, as she knelt on the ground, beneath the pooled light of the lantern.

"It is not here," she whispered to herself. Out loud this time, as if her voice would cut through her own terror. It did, a little. "Not here. Not here. And it—*you* cannot hurt me." She raised her head to the light. "If you are here, you cannot cross my blood. I know what you are."

She held on to the words—and the dagger—until the sky bled pale rose with dawn.

The walls of the hermitage were thinner than they first appeared. She could hear women chattering as they headed to breakfast. The widows, it seemed, were early risers. Once the corridors were quiet again, Arwa dressed and left her room. The night's bitter chill had softened, and now the indoor air of the hermitage felt no more than pleasantly cool on her skin. She drew her shawl loosely around her head and her shoulders, her bare feet moving soundless across the stone floor.

She found the prayer room much more quickly than she'd expected to. It was set farther down the corridor from where she'd slept, the scent of incense wafting from its open doors inviting her in. She had hoped it would be quiet, now that many of the women were breaking their fast, and it was. Two very elderly ladies were asleep against one wall, leaning against each other with their shawls tucked up to their chins. Apart from them—and their gentle snores—the room was empty and silent.

Arwa did not know if the women had come to pray at dawn as the most pious did and fallen asleep shortly after, or if they'd come here to surreptitiously share the carafe of wine she could see tucked between them. Although her guess was firmly on the latter, Arwa was just grateful they were not awake to speak to her, to question her or pity her with soft eyes.

Quietly, so as not to disturb the widows, she crossed the room. Behind a curtain, in a nook, lay a small library. Widows were dedicated to prayer and solitude, and were accordingly scholars of a kind. She had hoped there would be books. Books on faith and prayer; books by the Maha's greatest mystics and the Emperor's advisers, on the nature of the Empire's strength and glory. Books that would show a wayward, cursed noblewoman a path out of the darkness she'd found herself in.

But there was nothing. Not in the first book, or the second, or the third. They were nothing but staid religious tracts, the kind Arwa had learned by rote as a small girl, so old that they still spoke of the Maha as living and the Empire as timelessly glorious. Arwa did not curse, but she did bite down on her tongue and press her head to the spines, tears threatening sharply at her eyes. She would not weep. Not over something so trivial. But ah, she was so tired of her own secrets and her fear. She was tired of bracing for the return of the dangers of Darez Fort, with nothing to hold them at bay but the shaky defense of her own cursed blood. If faith could not help her, what could?

She returned to the prayer room, looking around herself slowly as she breathed deep and slow to ease the furious beating of her own heart. One of the walls was a latticed screen, carved to resemble tree roots and great sprouting leaves. The light poured through it in honeycomb shadows. Before the screen stood a statue as tall as Arwa herself. She drew her shawl tighter around her and approached it.

The statue was of a male figure, garbed in a turban and robes. Its upraised palm held the world inside it.

It was a statue of the Emperor—of all Emperors, past and future—and their blessed bloodline. It was a statue of the Maha, the Great One and first Emperor, who built the Ambhan Empire and then raised a temple upon the sands of Irinah province, where his power and piety had ensured the blessings of the Gods would shower for centuries down upon the Empire and grant him a life span far beyond mortal reckoning.

The sight of the effigy's blank face—of the eternity of its varnished, bare surface—brought Arwa an immense sense of comfort that she couldn't fully explain. Perhaps it reminded her of kinder times during her childhood, when she'd prayed at her mother's side, for the sake of the Empire and for its future glory. Perhaps it merely helped her believe that all suffering was finite, and even the anger and grief coiled within her now would one day fade to the void.

There was no one to see her, or to scold her. So Arwa took another step forward and placed her hands against the smooth face. The feel of it reminded her of the opal in her dagger hilt: smooth and somehow achingly familiar against her palms. It was absurd to find as much comfort in her heathen blade as in the Maha's holy effigy, but that was the way of it, for Arwa. She could not change her nature. And ah, she had tried.

She let out a slow breath. Some of that awful tension in her uncoiled. She stepped back and kneeled down before the altar.

The ground was cold. She sang a prayer, soft under her breath so as not to disturb the sleepers behind her. At the feet of the effigy was incense, and a cluster of flowers, freshly picked. Tucked discreetly at the base of the statute were tiny baskets, woven of leaves and grass and filled with soil. Arwa paused in her prayer, thoughtful, and touched one with her fingertips.

She knew what they were. She had seen them on dozens of roadside altars, on the journey through Chand to the hermitage.

Grave-tokens.

Tokens of grief. Symbolic burials, for the Maha, who had died when Arwa was only a girl. Four hundred years, he'd lived, some claimed. And then he had died, and the Empire had been falling to curse and ruin ever since.

Since his death, mourning had been its own kind of prayer. Widows grieved him like a husband, for grieving was their holiest task. Pilgrims traveled across the provinces to the desert where he had died. The nobility wept for him. But all the while, they whispered too, planting the seeds of almost-heresies, unsanctioned by the Emperor, and dangerous for it.

Perhaps, they whispered, he would one day return. Perhaps he had never died at all. Perhaps an heir would rise to take his

place, a new Maha to lead the faith of the Empire and lift the
Empire from the curse that his death had laid upon it. Politics
and faith, tangled together as they were, were never far from the
minds—or tongues—of the nobility.

She wondered sorely if she was going to be privy to heated
exchanges of faith here too. No doubt a hermitage of widows
was rich soil for questions of death and mourning. Rabia was
clearly one of that hopeful number who believed the Maha was
not truly gone, and she was equally clearly stupid enough to
announce her views to strangers like Arwa. Fool.

To speak of the Maha was to court danger. Arwa's husband
had always been careful only to air his views with his closest
compatriots, men he could trust not to mark his many fears of
a world without the Maha as a kind of heresy. Arwa had been
more careful still, and not spoken of faith at all. Were the widows truly so safe from the world, here, that they had no need to
fear the danger their own voices could bring down on them?

A noise dragged her abruptly out of her reverie. Someone had
rapped their knuckles deliberately against the doorframe, startling one of the elderly women mid-snore into wakefulness.

"Wh–what is it?"

"Nothing, Aunt," said Gulshera. Her eyes met Arwa's. "I've
come for the girl. Rest."

The woman mumbled and subsided back into sleep. Arwa
stood.

"Please come with me," Gulshera said.

Arwa followed her out.

In the morning light, Gulshera's hair was as pale as snow, her
skin the lightest shade of brown. As a young woman, she must
have been considered the epitome of Ambhan beauty, despite
the severe shape of her mouth and the way she held herself, with
a ramrod-straight posture reminiscent of a military-trained
nobleman's.

"You ate nothing this morning," Gulshera said, gesturing for Arwa to walk with her down the corridor. Arwa obeyed. "Roshana worried."

Arwa did not think it would take a great deal of effort to worry Roshana.

"I'm sorry. I didn't mean to worry anyone. I only wanted to pray."

"You'll have plenty of time for prayer here," said Gulshera. "Right now, we need to get you some food. The tables have been cleared, so we'll see what the cooks have left."

"If you direct me to the kitchens, I can go on my own," Arwa said with studied politeness.

"Ah, I see." Gulshera's voice was terribly matter-of-fact. "You want me to leave you alone."

Yes, thought Arwa.

"Not at all," she said. "I simply don't want to trouble you."

"Indeed. Well, perhaps I want to be troubled."

She took Arwa's arm imperiously.

"Come," she said. "A servant always brings hot tea to my room in the morning. You'll share it with me."

There was no way to refuse her now, so Arwa didn't try to. She allowed herself to be led.

Gulshera's room was a cluttered, lived-in space, with a low dining table by the lattice window, and large sheaves of paper stacked neatly on her writing desk. Arwa saw silk-bound parchments, marked with the unfamiliar seal of a noble Ambhan family, balanced precariously on the edge of the bed. Letters. So, the widows weren't so remote from the world after all.

A set of bows hung on the opposing wall. The largest of them caught Arwa's attention and held it, drawing her focus away from the letters upon the bed. The bow was taller than her—tall as a grown man—its surface gilded with mother-of-pearl. Arwa had never used a bow, but she itched to hold it. It was astonishingly beautiful. Its ends were shaped like the mouths of tigers, with serrated teeth stretched into an open snarl.

"It's a relic," Gulshera said, startling Arwa back to reality. "It takes a full-grown man all his strength to string and shoot an arrow from it. My husband was full proud of it. But of course, it's only good for display now."

Gulshera was already seated by the window. There was a tray set before her.

"Sit," she said. "You can pour the tea."

There were herbs steeped in water, a small bowl of honey, and a shallow tray of attar-scented water. Next to the tea were vegetables fried golden in gram flour. Arwa poured the tea and heaped in honey for both her and Gulshera, then took a quick sip from her own cup that was burning sweet.

"You didn't sleep," said Gulshera.

It wasn't a question. "I slept a little," Arwa said anyway.

"No food, and no sleep." Gulshera sipped her own drink; steam rose up around her face in coils. "I see."

Arwa picked up a fritter and bit into it pointedly, resisting the urge to bristle. No doubt Gulshera thought she was a fragile creature, a young and witless thing fueled by love and religious fervor, shattered by what she had seen that day and night at the fort a mere handful of months ago.

Let her think it. It was better than the truth.

She waited for Gulshera to begin lecturing her. She stared down at her oil-stained fingers in silence, as Gulshera sipped her tea and took one of the fritters for herself.

Instead, Gulshera said, "Eat. Drink your tea. Then go, when you like."

"Go?"

"When you like," Gulshera repeated. She soaked her fingers in the attar-water, then stood, leaving Arwa alone with her tea and the cooling fritters, under a pale slant of sunlight pouring in through the window. She heard Gulshera settle at the writing desk. The sound of rustling paper followed.

Arwa hesitated.

A memory came to her, unbidden, of the feral cat she'd found in the gardens of her first home in the province Hara, where she had lived as a girl of ten. She'd been determined to make a friend of that cat, with its one bad eye and fanged teeth, but it ran and hid in the foliage whenever Arwa approached it. She'd gained a number of scratches before she'd learned that if she left slivers of meat on the ground near her, it would come and eat by her warily, as long as she studiously ignored its presence. In the end, it had grown warm with her, following her around the gardens, sleeping on her lap if she sat in the right patch of sun. Indifference and food had won it better than any straightforward affection could ever have.

Arwa had the discomforting sense that Gulshera was treating her with the same studied, indifferent regard Arwa had once shown that cat.

She wants something from me, Arwa thought.

She ate another fritter anyway, and drank her tea, before she murmured a suitably gracious thank-you and moved to leave.

"Come back whenever you like," Gulshera said, not raising her head as Arwa left the room. "I always have enough for two."

Arwa had liked the brusqueness of Gulshera's care, somewhat despite herself. But as time went on—as she walked from Gulshera's room across the hermitage, passing rooms and other widows—the memory of Gulshera's words began to feed her disquiet.

You didn't sleep, Gulshera had said. It hadn't sounded like a guess. Perhaps Arwa was simply that transparent, but she went to her room anyway, checking the undisturbed line of blood on her window ledge, hidden carefully beneath her own miniature effigy of the Emperor. No one had searched her room. And her dagger was in her sash, hidden where no one would find it, and recognize it for what it was.

Arwa looked out of the lattice window. Without the press of night beyond it, she could see that the hermitage stood above a deep valley studded with rich swathes of flowers. The hermitage curved like a crescent moon, following the shape of the valley below it. Arwa's window faced another, far at the other edge of the building.

Gulshera's room lay at the other end of the hermitage. She'd walked the journey between their bedrooms, and knew that now. No doubt she must have looked out of her own window in the night and seen Arwa's oil lantern burning. Perhaps she'd looked for a moment only, then gone back to bed. Perhaps she'd watched for a long time, marking the constant flicker of light in Arwa's window, wondering what dark thoughts kept Arwa far from rest.

Either way, she knew the exact location of Arwa's room. She'd stared through the press of the dark at Arwa's lantern light, deliberately, thoughtfully. It disturbed Arwa to be so watched. She stepped back from the lattice and sat on her bed, hands clenched, searching for calm. She had told Nuri she would protect herself. She'd been sure she would be able to keep her secrets hidden. And yet, Gulshera had watched her. Gulshera had marked her strangeness, even if she did not truly know its cause. Arwa thought of how she'd listened to Gulshera's words without discerning their full import, and stared about the older woman's room wide-eyed without using any of the thought and cunning a noblewoman should sensibly employ. Fool. She was a fool.

What else, she thought, *did I miss?*

After the midday rest—which Arwa spent pacing her room back and forth, fear and fury building up within her like a steady poison—Roshana dragged her out to join a small group of widows on their daily walk. Roshana spoke to Arwa anxiously, asking how well she was settling in, and how she liked it here in Numriha, so far from her old home. Arwa clamped down on the instinct to snap at her, struggling to be gracious in response to Roshana's steady stream of questions. She had already raised the suspicions of one widow with her night-long candle burning. She did not need to disturb another with her rage. Still, she was glad when Asima commandeered her, demanding that Arwa walk by her side instead. Asima demanded nothing of her but a steady arm and occasional murmur of understanding. That, Arwa could provide.

She felt as if her insides were coiled tight.

There was a gentle avenue that followed the edge of the hermitage, not quite dipping into the steeper territory of the valley. It was a smooth enough path for the widows of varying levels of health to walk it comfortably. From here, Arwa could see the valley, and also glimpse the guardswomen who walked the roof of the hermitage, on the lookout for bandits who'd normally consider a house of noblewomen a ripe target.

"You should dress more warmly," muttered Asima. "A thicker shawl at least, girl. There's a bitter chill in the air this season. Even the Emperor caught a chill, I hear."

"Did he?"

"Don't listen to gossip, do you?" Arwa did not have the chance to interject that her recent bereavement had rather stood in the way of her gathering gossip, before Asima continued. "Good. You're better than these other prattling owls, then. Pick some of that for me now."

Asima pointed to some gnarled vegetation.

"Not the flowers?" Arwa asked, leaning down.

"No, no. Not flowers. What do I need them for?"

Arwa picked Asima green vegetation, and long grass.

"Can you weave them together?" Asima asked.

When Arwa shook her head, Asima clucked in response.

"Oh dear, oh dear," she said, shaking her head. "A noble girl who can't weave a simple basket! The Empire has truly fallen to shit, Gods save us."

Her words drew a startled laugh from Arwa, quickly quelled by Asima's gimlet-eyed stare. "As you say, Aunt," Arwa said quickly.

"Can you embroider?" Asima demanded.

"Yes, Aunt."

"But you can't *weave?*"

What followed was a demonstration of how to make a grave-token. It was a simple enough lesson, and one Arwa could follow without paying it all her attention. As she followed Asima's directions, taking green roots into her hands and winding them into a miniature braid, she worried over the thought of Gulshera watching her lantern-bright window. She worried over the thought as one worries over a sore tooth, incessantly, unable to soothe the irritation away.

She knows, a chill voice said in Arwa's head. *The widow knows what you are. She can see it. Your ill blood. The curse in your bones.*

She'll have you thrown from the hermitage. She'll set the guards on you, to hunt you like an animal.

You know how they punish people like you.

Gulshera couldn't know. She couldn't. But if she did—if she had even *guessed...*

Arwa shuddered. The air suddenly felt very cold indeed.

Gulshera was not in her room. The door was locked. Arwa waited outside it for the woman to return. Eventually, Gulshera appeared, striding along the corridor. She hadn't been attending to prayer or to mourning, or ambling gently along a well-trodden path, as the other widows had. Her bow was at her back, her face flushed with the heat of the day.

"Arwa," Gulshera acknowledged, tipping her head.

"You watched my room last night," said Arwa, without preamble. "Why?"

She saw Gulshera's forehead furrow into a frown.

"Did your mother not teach you subtlety?" Gulshera asked incredulously. "They would eat you alive in Jah Ambha, by the Emperor's grace! Come inside."

Arwa followed Gulshera into her room, shutting the door behind her as the older woman swiftly divested herself of her boots and her bow, and the long jacket she wore over her tunic. Finally, when Gulshera was done, she sat by the window, and gestured for Arwa to join her.

"I looked out of my window and saw the light in yours. For a *moment*," Gulshera stressed. "No longer. I had no darker motive. I only cared about your welfare. Are you satisfied?"

No, Arwa was not satisfied. Far from it.

"In my experience," Arwa said steadily, "people don't just simply care about one another's welfare. All actions have a purpose. I may be a child to you, Aunt, but I've lived long enough to know what people are."

"Then you've lived a terribly sad life," Gulshera said, not mincing her words. "You'll learn that we have to look after one another here. We're not like the noblewomen you left behind, we have no need to play political games and tread on one another for the sake of our husbands or children or even ourselves. Our time of power and glory is finished.

"Perhaps you don't understand yet," she continued, "that when your husband died, the part of you that shared in his world died with him. We all came here, by choice or by necessity, because we Ambhans hold our marriages more sacred than the lesser peoples of the world, and we respect our vows beyond death. We are the ghosts of who we once were, and accordingly we must take care of one another. No one else will." Gulshera's gaze was fixed on Arwa's, her voice unrelenting. "You'll think me dramatic, Arwa, but I assure you I am a realist. You must be one too. For your own sake."

Fine words. Strong words. But Arwa could not let the bare-fisted blow of them mislead her.

"I know what I know," she said. She raised her head higher, jaw firm.

Her mother had tried to teach her subtlety. But the art of folding secrets inside words and smiles, and hiding the knife of her anger until it was already in someone's gut, too late to be escaped—those things had never been Arwa's strength. *Flighty*, she'd been called as a child, and *mercurial*. She wore her heart, fierce and changeable as it was, right on her skin.

Sometimes, her mother had called her worse things. Out of love, and out of fear. *Tainted. Cursed.*

You must be better than your blood, Arwa. For all our sakes.

Her parents had needed her to make a good marriage, to wed a nobleman of immaculate reputation and stable wealth. They'd needed her to save them. Not from poverty. Not from death. But from the insidious, destructive suffering that disgrace had brought upon their family.

They'd had no son. A man could strive to save his family, could serve valiantly in the military or ascend through the rungs of governmental service. A daughter could only hope to wed well enough to raise her position in society, and raise her family up with her.

So Arwa had done what was necessary. For a handful of liminal years, she had learned to weave a veneer of placidity, for the sake of making herself an attractive prospect as a bride, a worthy noblewoman, better than what lay in her blood. She'd learned to smile and to be soft, to say gentle words when sharp ones came far more easily to her tongue, and in the end her hard-won calm—and her youth—had granted her the older, powerful husband her mother had hoped for her. For a time, she had been better than her true, barbed self. She'd been a commander's wife. She'd been a noblewoman worthy of respect. Her parents had been able to hold their heads high.

But that was before the circle of blood, and eyes like gold. Before Kamran's death. Before she realized there was no running from the curse that lived in her own body: that no matter what she did, no matter how she had tried to obey her stepmother's entreaty, she could not rise beyond what she was.

"I know," Arwa said, "that you have scrolls that were sent to you by an Ambhan noble family. I was a commander's wife, Aunt. I know the seals of the great families. But I didn't recognize the seal upon them, which suggests to me that the seal is not real. Someone of noble blood communicates with you but seeks to hide their true identity. I know you own a man's bow more expensive than anything I have possessed in my lifetime, embellished in a manner intended to please the eyes at court. Your husband, then, was a politician and a courtier. You wear no jewels but I suspect it is not Roshana who is truly of highest standing in this hermitage. You are."

Arwa leaned forward, not allowing her gaze to falter.

"You're not a ghost of a woman, cut off from the world," said Arwa. "You serve someone. You answer to someone powerful. And you seek to take care of me, of all people. Forgive me, if I do not think your motives are entirely benevolent."

"Well," Gulshera said finally. "If we're talking bluntly..." She leaned forward, intent, mirroring Arwa. "I am under no obligation to tell you anything. You have no power here. No standing. I know a little of you, Lady Arwa. You may have been a great commander's wife once, but your father was disgraced—"

"Don't speak of my father," Arwa said abruptly. She curled her fingers in her lap. She saw Gulshera's gaze flicker to her fists, then up again. Reading her.

"You are no woman of a great noble house," Gulshera continued calmly. "Only a woman lucky to wed well. And if you truly believe I am of such high stature and influence, then you shouldn't have spoken to me like that."

"I meant no disrespect."

"Now that is a lie," Gulshera said.

"Then I apologize," said Arwa. "I know you don't have to tell me anything. I know I have no power. I could have been patient. I could have waited for you to reveal what you truly require, in the fullness of time. But I am tired of games, Lady Gulshera. If you do truly care for my welfare, then do me a kindness: Tell me what you want, then leave me alone to mourn."

"If you have a choice between being blunt or being patient in the future, then choose patient," Gulshera said. But there was a thoughtful light in her eyes. "Come back here tomorrow morning, after breakfast. We'll take a walk together."

Arwa let out a slow exhale. *This*, after she'd asked for no more games...

"We'll go down to the valley," Gulshera said. "Just the two of us, where we can't be overheard. And there, you can tell me about Darez Fort."

CHAPTER THREE

The widows ate their evening meal together. Asima had called them prattling owls, and she hadn't been entirely wrong. Gossip flowed between them ceaselessly, its rhythm broken only by the clatter of plates as they passed dishes of sweet melon and lentil broth and large, soft flatbreads between them. The widows spoke largely of their distant families: of sons struggling to hold tenuous command in their posts, as unrest swelled in famine-stricken provinces, and sharp bouts of unnatural terror flared to life in scattered villages and outposts; of granddaughters primping for court, in the hope of earning a powerful husband or a place in the household of one of the imperial women; of friends or siblings who complained of the tedious duties of household management in provinces where food and fuel were in short supply, as the trade routes crumbled and crops rotted in distant fields.

The widows were not as remote from the politics of the Empire as Arwa had first suspected. Far, far from it. They were noblewomen, after all. She should have known their personal concerns would be rich with veins of political significance, that if they maintained any link with their families, however tenuous, they would know something of how the world continued to fracture far beyond the hermitage's walls.

From the sound of their gossip, the Empire's suffering was growing worse with greater speed. Arwa knew she should listen with care, search within their words for seeds of knowledge of use to her. But she could not. She could think only of Darez Fort, and the interrogation that awaited her. She tried not to think of tomorrow, tried not to think of the questions Gulshera was going to ask her. She tried not to *feel*.

She failed miserably.

She was tired of questions about Darez Fort. Even before the bodies had been buried, when she'd still been raw with shock and weeping, a high-ranking noblewoman had sat with her and cajoled answers out of her with cold-blooded patience. *What did you see, Lady Arwa? How did the men die? And your husband—were you there when he passed? Did he fight the terror bravely? Cry, my dear. Cry, if you must. Just answer me. Good girl.*

A male courtier, sent by the Governor of Chand, had spoken to Arwa the evening after the formal funeral. Her mother had been with her then, holding her wrists with firm hands. The man had sat on the other side of a partition wall, clearly uncomfortable with the task he'd been set. Arwa had answered all his question in whispers, as her mother had stared into the middle distance with burning eyes, hot with shame and fury. Another nobleman had come immediately after him—this time a courtier from Ambha itself, sent by the imperial record keepers—and asked nearly the same questions. It was only then that Arwa had finally felt her own outrage spark to life.

Gods curse the lot of them. Couldn't they have left her to mourn, even that day, of all days? Why had they insisted on interrogating her over and over again, when she clearly had nothing she was willing to offer them? Wasn't her grief—the terrible, trembling weight of it—enough?

She had hoped the hermitage would offer her safety from the curiosity of the world, a place where her secrets would lie undisturbed. She'd been a fool, of course. Her first moments in the hermitage, when the widows had come to stare at her en masse, had shattered that particular delusion. And Gulshera...

Gulshera had letters from a noble family and a priceless bow lacquered in mother-of-pearl hung on her wall. Gulshera wanted answers from Arwa. *You can tell me about Darez Fort*, she'd said, as if Arwa would not tell her the same thing she'd told all the people who had interrogated her in the past: The same truths. The same necessary handful of lies.

She'd asked for this, she reminded herself. She'd asked Gulshera not to play games. It was better like this, to speak to her now, to not wait for the inevitable interrogation. She would speak to Gulshera tomorrow, and then she would refuse to answer anyone else. Let the women like Rabia look at her and wonder what had happened to her. Let them pity her. She'd earned the right to silence.

After the meal ended, and the women began to disperse, Arwa returned to her room. She lit her lantern and refreshed the blood on her window. Despite the worry gnawing at her, despite the fact she curled up on the bed with her dagger beside her in her usual vigil, she fell swiftly into sleep, and woke the next morning with a sore neck and her lantern guttered.

She'd had a nightmare. The details had already left her—all she had was the dull echo of terror thrumming in her blood—but it didn't matter. She knew what she'd dreamed.

Today Gulshera was going to ask her about Darez Fort.

Instead of joining the other women for breakfast, Arwa bathed. She dressed. She touched the ends of her hair. It was growing long enough to curl faintly at the ends. Soon it would need to be cut again.

She headed to Gulshera's room and found the older woman waiting for her, a light bow on her shoulder, a quiver at her back, and another bow on the ground at her side.

"You didn't eat again," said Gulshera.

"I wasn't hungry."

This time, Gulshera did not ply her with fritters and tea. Instead she nodded and handed her one of the bows. It was light and elegant, lacquered in a dark varnish. The wood was perfectly smooth beneath her hands; it near gleamed in the light. Although it was not covered in mother-of-pearl, Arwa was sure it was costly.

"I thought we were going for a walk," said Arwa.

"We are," Gulshera replied. "But I'm also going to teach you how to shoot."

They left the hermitage together and walked out toward the valley. They were still near the perimeter of the hermitage, still within earshot of other widows who were sitting comfortably under the cover of the hermitage's veranda, when Gulshera spoke.

"Have you ever used a bow before?"

"No, Aunt."

Gulshera shook her head, world weary.

"If I had my way," said Gulshera, "all noblewomen would learn to use a bow and arrow. It's our birthright, though most seem determined not to recall our Empire's history. Hunting was once a noblewoman's art. Empress Suheila was even famed for killing a dozen deer and a tiger in one single hunt with arrows she fired from within the cover of her palanquin. Did you know that?" When Arwa shook her head, Gulshera gave an exasperated huff. "Of course you didn't. Women don't teach their daughters anything important anymore."

She sounded so much like Asima had when she'd learned Arwa couldn't weave that Arwa almost smiled. Almost. She didn't have the strength for it. Her stomach was in knots. *Stop lecturing and just ask your questions*, she wanted to demand.

"It's a fine story," said Arwa.

Gulshera gave her a thoughtful, sidelong look.

"Go on," said Gulshera. "Speak honestly."

"I have nothing more to say, Aunt."

"Somehow I find I don't believe you, Arwa."

Arwa lowered her head. The walk down the valley was steep, and the grass crunched softly beneath her feet. She thought about how sensible it would be to say nothing, or offer Gulshera only soft words. She thought about how important it had always seemed to smooth away her sharp edges, how long her mother had worked to shape her into something worthy of being loved. But Arwa did not care if Gulshera liked her, never mind loved her. She'd had enough of being mothered and molded. She opened her mouth.

"The story of Empress Suheila—it doesn't sound like a true tale. And what does it matter to me, if it is? I'm no empress, to hunt tigers and be praised for it. I don't care about bows and arrows and archery. I am just a widow."

"Just a widow," repeated Gulshera.

"You said so yourself, Aunt. I'm no better than a ghost now." If the words came out of her barbed, well. She had a right to her bitterness. "Stories of the distant past aren't my business. Mourning is."

"Ah," said Gulshera, eyebrow raised. "And yet you stared at my husband's court bow with such yearning. I don't think my eyes fooled me. Your hands hunger for a weapon, just as much as your heart hungers for a chance to mourn."

"Ask me about Darez Fort," Arwa said sharply. "And leave my hunger alone."

"Archery lesson first," Gulshera said, unperturbed.

They had reached a place deep in the valley, where the sun and wind alike felt distant. Arwa could see white-peaked mountains in the distance. Before them were a group of targets, set at intervals. The targets all looked rather worse for wear: Gulshera clearly dedicated a great deal of time to testing her skill with her bow and arrow.

"We'll start with the grip," Gulshera said. She took her bow from her shoulder, an arrow from the quiver at her back, and demonstrated the proper way to nock the arrow. Arwa copied her. She showed Arwa how to hold the bow and how to steady the arrow with a grip that balanced the arrow shaft on her thumb, so that it would remain steady even if Arwa were in motion, on horseback like a soldier or veiled within her palanquin like Empress Suheila on her mythical hunt. Both options were laughably unlikely.

"I wish," Arwa said, "that you would just ask me your questions and be done with this farce."

"What farce?" Gulshera tapped Arwa's back. "Straighten up. You'll get nowhere slumping. I genuinely want to teach you."

"Why?" Arwa asked, frustrated.

"Because I can't teach you how to use a sword, or fight barehanded," said Gulshera. "Because you're angry, and your anger is going to gut you if no one gets it out of you. You need a way to set it free, and this will do well enough." A beat. "But ah, I forgot. You asked me not to mention your hunger."

Arwa closed her eyes tight. She could feel the terrible, tense strength of the bow in her hands. The arrow shaft, steady in her grip, against her thumb. One beat of her heart. Another.

"I told you," Arwa whispered. "I don't want to play games."

"This is no game, Arwa. You frightened Rabia." Gulshera's voice filled up the darkness. "She came to me, after you scared her. I can't have fear in this hermitage. I won't allow it."

Your Rabia is as easily frightened as Roshana is worried. The spiteful words bloomed to life easily in her throat, ready to be spoken. Arwa swallowed them back and opened her eyes, meeting Gulshera's own. So many poisons lived in her. She would pick the one that burned most sharply on her tongue, and leave the rest be.

"Did she think me tainted by Darez Fort?" Arwa asked bitterly. "Did she claim that I had unnatural madness in me—something strange in my eyes, an evil pressed into me by the curse upon the Empire? I know people fear it's within me. Rabia told me herself. She told me the widows all came to greet me to see if I was normal. *Normal.* Do she and her ilk fear I'll suddenly turn and rip their throats out with my teeth? Or—no." Arwa shook her head. "Perhaps she thinks I will infect you all and let you destroy each other. That is the way of the unnatural madness, after all."

"You have a normal enough anger in you," Gulshera said evenly, which was no answer at all.

"You thought giving an angry woman a weapon was the best thing to do?"

"I thought teaching you how to direct your anger was the best thing to do," said Gulshera. "Besides, you won't have the skill to put that weapon to any good use for a long time yet. Perhaps by then you'll be calmer and less likely to murder us all in a fit of unnatural rage."

"Funny," Arwa said through gritted teeth.

"I thought so," said Gulshera. She gave Arwa a perfunctory smile. "Now," she said. "I'll demonstrate how to shoot. We'll aim for the nearest target."

Gulshera had no trouble setting the arrow against its nocking point, or maintaining its position with the placement of her thumb and fingers. She drew the bowstring in one elegant motion and let the arrow fly. Her hand darted to her quiver; she nocked another arrow and sent it after its sibling.

Both arrows hit their target.

"Now," Gulshera said. "It's your turn."

Gulshera adjusted Arwa's posture again, and also the angle of her arm and her grip on the bow. She guided Arwa on how to draw the bow, how to pinch the string with only her thumb and aim carefully for the target. After a few torturous minutes of adjustment, Arwa let her own arrow fly.

There was some joy in seeing the arrow soar. There would have been more, if it had even remotely touched its target.

"There," said Arwa, staring at the arrow, where it had pitched itself into the grass. "I've done it."

"Try again," Gulshera said, handing Arwa another arrow from her quiver. "This time try to put some of that anger into it."

Arwa could have done the bare minimum Gulshera had asked of her, and simply shot the arrow at a target, as she had before. But there was iron on her tongue, and a knot of feeling in her stomach. She thought of Darez Fort. She drew the string taut, feeling its coiled strength in the lacquered wood of the bow. Her own arms trembled. She fired.

"Once more."

"No." Arwa lowered the bow, then lowered herself. She bent forward, strangely hot and breathless, as if all the feeling inside her had risen to the surface of her skin, drawn up by the feel of the arrow flying from her grip. She felt raw, tender as meat. "No more. I've had enough of a lesson. Now tell me what you want to know."

Gulshera was silent for a long moment. She took the bow from Arwa's unresisting grip and kneeled down at Arwa's side.

"I already know, as everyone else does, that there was a massacre," Gulshera said. Her voice was low, steady. "That the gates of the fort closed, and when they opened again, all of its inhabitants were dead. All, but you. They'd turned on one another. Hadn't they?"

Arwa swallowed, throat too dry for words. She nodded.

Unnatural madness, unnatural rage, the Empire's greatest and most feared curse. Yes. Yes, they had.

"I know," Gulshera continued, "that the woman who survived the massacre—*you*—claimed a dark spirit forced them to it. *It crept into all our skulls*, you said. *It filled us with unnatural rage and turned us against one another.* Your claim should have been laughable." Gulshera smiled grimly. "But it was not. We all know what has become of the Empire, child. The strange horrors that roam it."

Arwa nodded again, wordlessly. Still, Gulshera continued.

"People have begun to claim to see daiva across the Empire. By the Haran coast. In the forests of Durevi. And now, even in Ambha itself. There have been...instances. Of terror, unnatural and strange, consuming villages and travelers. Only briefly. Only rarely. Until now, of course," Gulshera said, tilting her head toward Arwa in acknowledgment of the horrors of Darez Fort. "I know pilgrims who go to Irinah's desert to mourn over the Maha's resting place return with tales of gold-eyed demons, and palaces spun of glass and sand that vanish in the blink of an eye. I know not all pilgrims return. Arwa...You and I both know a curse sits on our Empire. But the curse is growing worse with terrible swiftness. Someone must find a way to put an end to it."

For a widow cloistered away in a hermitage deep in the Numrihan mountains, Gulshera knew a great deal about the darkness racing its way across the Empire, fracturing it better than any war of men and metal ever could. Arwa thought of Gulshera's letters. The family she communicated with had to be strong and old, with eyes and ears in every part of the Empire. Arwa thought of each of the old families in turn—even her mother's own—and wondered which one Gulshera was loyal to, and what she had learned from the gossip of the widows, the secrets of their blood kin that they so carelessly shared between them, a currency between them that hardened to diamond, priceless in Gulshera's knowing grip.

"If you know so much," Arwa said, "what do you want to learn from me now?"

"Only what happened to you," Gulshera said, as if that were not a great deal to ask for. "No more."

"I can only repeat what I have already told others before you," said Arwa. "I don't see what good that will do you."

"Knowledge gained secondhand, through gossip and whispers, is never entirely complete. No tale I have heard explains how you survived, when all others died. You were found surrounded by blood, in an unlocked room, but entirely unharmed. How did that come to pass, Arwa?"

Arwa sucked in a sharp breath.

"Luck," Arwa lied. "It was luck. What else could it have been?"

"Nonetheless, I'd like to hear what happened in your own words. Perhaps then I will come to understand how you survived."

Arwa hadn't been unharmed, no matter what the older woman had heard. She'd made a cut to her arm, that day in Darez Fort—made it too long in her panic. It had bled hard, but it had been shallow and had healed to nothing but a faint silver scar in days. She could only see it now when she held her bare arm up to the candlelight just so.

She didn't tell that to Gulshera. For a long moment she said nothing at all.

She thought of Kamran.

"The family I am loyal to," Gulshera said into the silence, "seek a cure to the curse upon the Empire. Your story may help them."

The hand on her sleeve. Those eyes—

"I wish I knew why I survived," she whispered.

She scrubbed her eyes with her sleeve. She realized she was crying.

"It started," she said, "when a patrol returned from a nearby village."

Darez Fort had been a new military fort, built hastily like so many others to manage unrest in villages and towns distant from the imperial control of the great provincial cities. But it had been better equipped than most, properly fortified, with an experienced nobleman as its commander. Kamran had served in Durevi in his early youth—later, he'd fought the unrest brought on by the Maha's death at the Haran border with Irinah, the blighted desert land where the Maha had met his end. He'd known how to manage a subdistrict boiling over with unrest: good pay for the soldiers to encourage obedience, and the instillation of regular patrols through all local villages.

"The patrol returned late," said Arwa. "Hours late. My husband was less than pleased. He valued discipline in his men. And when they arrived..." She paused. Swallowed. "They had *it* with them."

"The daiva?"

"Yes."

Arwa hadn't known it was a daiva at first. She'd been on the upper floor of the fort, in the women's quarters. It had been deep midday, sweltering hot, and she'd been standing in the shade by the window lattice, watching the fort's great doors as they opened to let the patrol enter. The men entered on horseback. One of them had been carrying a large bundle on the saddle in front of him.

She'd been relieved to see the patrol return. Kamran's mood had grown blacker as each hour had passed, and she hadn't been looking forward to trying to cajole him into a better one. She'd already sent a message to the kitchen asking for his favorite dish to be made for the evening meal, and advised one of the maids to bring up a tray of wine and sweets swiftly, should her husband choose to visit her quarters. It was tiring to be a good wife. When her husband was in an ill mood, the job became much harder. Arwa had learned it was best to be prepared.

She'd seen her husband stride out to meet the patrol, flanked by two of his best men. She could remember the grim line of his shoulders, the way they'd announced his displeasure far more loudly than words. She remembered how one of the patrollers had jumped down from his horse, and gestured frantically back at the bundle, as the doors clanged shut behind them.

Arwa remembered seeing the bundle move.

The cloth had slid back.

She'd seen a head. A neck curled forward. Skin like black smoke.

The smell of incense, sudden and overpowering, had filled her nose, her throat. She'd known, then, what it was.

She'd seen such flesh before, smelled that unnatural sweetness, sacred and strange. Some things were impossible to forget.

"I had seen a daiva before," Arwa said. Her voice came out of her thin. "Before his—disgrace—my father was Governor of Irinah." Arwa did not like to dwell on what her father had been before disgrace, but it was important. Irinah's holy desert was the place where daiva lived, and the place where the Maha had died. "I thought they'd captured a child. For what reason, I couldn't imagine. The cloth slid back, and I saw—a face. I think I saw a face. But it...its face *moved*, as if I were looking at a reflection on water. And its eyes..."

It had looked around the dusty yard, still swaddled in the soldier's arms, and cocked its head to the side with the animal inquisitiveness of a bird or some loping, sleek-furred predator. It had looked human enough, with two eyes and two ears, a neat mouth and two dark hands bound before it, not quite concealed by cloth. But its eyes had reflected the light of the midday sun back, flecks of shattered glass in its wavering mirage of a face. As Kamran had taken a step back—as the soldier who had jumped down from his horse began to speak, swift and panicked—the daiva had looked about, for all the world like a feral thing caged. It had struggled. Twisted.

Its face had cracked, the jaw parted to reveal a thing that was all bone and howling teeth, brilliant and pointed as blades. An utter nightmare.

There had been horrified yells, down in the courtyard. Someone had drawn a blade.

"I don't know why they brought it to the fort," Arwa whispered. "Fool men. I think they thought it was harmless—a child of its kind. I think they sought my husband's advice. They'd wrapped it up and chained its wrists, but it broke the chains as easily as paper. I saw it do so. And I remember...My husband, he looked up at the window where I stood, right before..."

Arwa stopped again, swallowing hard. She didn't want to remember the way Kamran had turned, the tilt of his head, the sun turning his face to shadow, as the daiva had flung off its shackles and stretched itself free from its human form. She didn't want to remember the screaming that had followed, or how she had turned from the window, running. How she had chosen not to watch him die.

She'd learned later that Kamran had died a hero, protecting the doors of the fort. He'd died trying to stop any of his men from leaving and taking their unnatural, nightmare-driven bloodlust with them. But Arwa had not seen it. She'd chosen not to.

"Go on," prompted Gulshera.

"It only looked human for a short time," Arwa managed to say, remembering the way its whole body had yawned, cracking open its child-form like a shell, or a closed jaw, peeling free to show the serrated teeth beneath. "When it changed—when it grew—something happened to me. Something happened to all of us."

"Tell me what happened," Gulshera prompted, soft now. "Tell me what you felt."

"It took something from us. It…it changed us." How to explain the feel of it—like cold claws had been set inside the base of her skull, ripping a seam in her soul, letting the dark within her spill out? "It was a nightmare. It felt like being trapped in a nightmare. I remember nothing but fear after that."

"And then?"

"Nothing but fear," Arwa repeated. "I can't tell you anything more."

"So you don't know why you survived," Gulshera said slowly.

The truth hovered on the tip of Arwa's tongue. She ached to tell it.

She thought of the guardsman's offhand comment about blood-worshipping heathens. She thought of the time one of her husband's patrols had found an Amrithi family, hiding in a local village, and what had been done to them. She thought of the consequences of truth: for her disgraced family, her sick father, her heartbroken mother. For herself.

It was my fault. My fault.

"I told you so at the start," snapped Arwa. She rubbed her hand across her face, angry with Gulshera, angry with herself. "I can tell you I saw a man run through by another man's sword. I can tell you my husband was murdered by his own men. I can tell you what it sounds like when a man howls in agony as his arm is sawed through by his *friend*. I heard the maids—my maids—screaming and screaming and screaming. I can tell you what blood smells like, if you wish. But what I *can't* tell you is why I lived, when so many others died. Now, are you satisfied, Lady Gulshera? May I go and mourn my horrors in peace?"

"Ah," Gulshera breathed. It was a soft, sad sound.

Arwa was trembling, sickened. She was light-headed with a grief that felt more like fury than weakness. She felt like her skin was a size too small.

She saw Gulshera press a palm flat to the earth. The older woman's hand was firm, her breathing steady and sure. Arwa found herself matching the pace of Gulshera's breath instinctively, as if Gulshera were tethering them both to soil, and stopping the great red weight of Darez Fort from drawing them both under.

"Come with me again tomorrow," Gulshera said.

"Haven't I said enough?"

"Oh, you've said more than enough," Gulshera said grimly. "I'll keep to our agreement. There will be no more questions about Darez Fort."

"Good." Arwa let out a breath. "That's good."

"Arwa." Gulshera's voice was careful. "I won't tell you I'm sorry for what you've suffered. My pity won't help you. But discipline might. What you feel..." Gulshera trailed off, shaking her head. "I've seen soldiers who return from battle and forget how to live beyond the blood. Their souls stay trapped within one dark moment and can't escape from it. I see the look of that in your eyes. Come back here again and let me teach you discipline of a kind."

Arwa laughed harshly.

"You think archery will fix me? No."

"I think it will be better than nothing," Gulshera said levelly. "Better than weeping in your room alone. Better than allowing your nightmares to eat you. But you are no longer a man's wife, and you have no father here to guide you. I am not your mother. There is no one left to compel your obedience, Arwa. It's your choice."

Arwa shook her head, wordless now.

"Well, if you change your mind, I'll be waiting."

Gulshera stood abruptly.

"Wait here," she said. "I need to collect the arrows."

Arwa stood too. "I'll help you," she said.

They collected the arrows together, cool wind catching the grass and the ends of their robes. Then they walked back toward the hermitage in silence.

CHAPTER FOUR

Arwa wished she hadn't cried. But that was the way of grief, it seemed. She could never find it in herself to weep when she wanted to weep—when her tears could do her some good in garnering sympathy or banishing uneasy officials with too many questions to ask. She could only cry when it was most inconvenient to her, and when she desperately wanted to appear strong.

Her face was dry from the wind, the sun, the salt of her own ugly tears. When she returned to her room she washed her face clean. Her hands were shaking. She clasped them together, breathing deep and slow, and thought of the effigy of the Emperor. Timeless, its blank face the promise of eternity. There was comfort in that thought.

She wondered what Gulshera was doing right now. No doubt she was writing a message to the family she served, telling them all that she had learned from Arwa. There would be couriers passing the hermitage at some point, carrying messages from distant points across the Empire for the widows or for the guardswomen who protected them. One of those couriers would be able to carry Gulshera's message to her masters swiftly, on horseback, unencumbered by the plodding weight of a retinue, or the necessity of a palanquin. After her long days of travel, Arwa could only envy their ease.

She wondered what Gulshera had written, wondered what message some old, venerable lord would be reading in the weeks to come.

Lady Arwa's experience in Darez Fort was as expected.

Or perhaps: *Lady Arwa has a secret. And I intend to uncover it.*

She shuddered anew, and hoped she'd hidden the absences in her story, the lies, well enough to fool Gulshera, just like she'd fooled all her other interrogators. She'd spoken to Gulshera to win herself some peace, not to draw herself back into the tangled world of men and politics once more.

It hadn't escaped Arwa's notice that Gulshera had kept the noble family's identity secret. Canny woman. She'd peeled Arwa's tale and her tears out of her, all the while keeping her own confidences. Who Gulshera served, and *why* she served— tucked away within the hermitage as she was, far from the political heartbeat of the Empire—all remained a mystery. Oh, Arwa knew Gulshera had access to a wealth of knowledge here, spilled from the mouths of the widows. But information was never gathered without purpose. What was the goal of the family she served? What did they intend to use the knowledge of the widows *for*?

Without answers, Arwa would have to remain watchful and wary. She had given Gulshera her tale of Darez Fort, but no doubt there were other things that Gulshera wanted from her— or would take and offer up to her patrons, if Arwa allowed her defenses to fall and said something foolish, all unwitting and unwary.

Gulshera had claimed to want to help her. But a woman could have many wants at once. And Arwa...

Well. Arwa had complex wants too.

She wanted to avoid Gulshera and hide like a wounded animal. She wanted to adhere close to Gulshera's side, where she could watch her in return and eviscerate her secrets and learn exactly how much of a risk the older woman was to her safety. She wanted the weight of the bow in her hands again, a channel for her rage, and she wanted to feel nothing at all.

Gulshera had claimed that Arwa reminded her of soldiers who remained trapped in one dark moment of suffering, long after their bodies had escaped it. The truth was that Gulshera was not wrong. Part of Arwa was still trapped in Darez Fort. Part of her always would be.

No wonder she hungered for a weapon. She turned her hands over—her faintly scarred fingers, her right thumb scraped raw from contact with the bowstring—and felt the itch in them. The need. She didn't want to be frightened ever again.

Oh, that want was the strongest of all.

Arwa squeezed her eyes shut. She clenched her hands together. Ah, pride be damned. She knew what she wanted to do. Worse, she knew what she *needed* to do.

She didn't go that evening or on the day that followed. But the day after that, when her heart felt less raw and her pride less bruised, she made her way over to Gulshera's room and waited for the older woman to return from breakfast.

Gulshera had the grace to look surprised to see Arwa, which was kind of her. Her expression smoothed quickly.

"Lady Arwa," she said. "I'm glad to see you here."

Arwa nodded, once, in return. Then she said, carefully, "I've decided I would like to learn archery after all. That is . . . I assume you'll still have me."

Gulshera nodded, unsmiling.

"I have a bow for you," she said. "And your own quiver of arrows. But this time you'll eat before we go."

"As you say, Aunt," said Arwa.

There was no time for rest. The widows gossiped and whispered, and Arwa listened and learned how the world had changed since grief had swallowed her. There was a fresh famine in Durevi, a new sickness in a cluster of villages in Hara. Although shadow spirits roamed the Empire, and people spoke of unnatural terror and walking nightmares with faces of bone, there had been no repeat of Darez Fort. That was a blessing, at least.

When the widows slept, Arwa sat with her dagger and her blood and learned how long she could go without rest. Once, she thought she heard it again: a beat of noise like wings beyond the window. Her candle flickered like a baleful eye, and she stumbled to the lattice, her heart racing, terror a knife in her ribs, and saw—nothing. The night dark. The candle's smoke.

She forced herself to sleep after that.

From Gulshera, she learned nothing but the bow and arrow. Gulshera was frustratingly good at keeping her own secrets close to her chest, but she did not ask about Darez Fort again, and for that at least Arwa was grateful. Instead, Gulshera showed Arwa how to string the bow—a job far better suited to two people working in tandem than one alone, as bending the bow against its natural inclination was a treacherous task—and tried to teach her how to shoot and actually hit her target.

"It's lucky no one is relying on me to hunt for dinner," Arwa grumbled, when she failed yet again to hit the easiest target. "We'd all starve."

"You'll manage it eventually," Gulshera said, unruffled. "You just need time."

Time. Everyone claimed that what Arwa needed was time. She was not so sure. Time was eroding her strength. Time was leading her further and further away from hope, as the dead haunted her sleep, as she bloodied her window and waited for the inevitable. There were no answers in the hermitage's library, or the gossip of the widows, or the sharp barb of an arrow through the air.

She found Rabia alone, once, in the prayer room. She stood

in the doorway, holding herself still until Rabia raised her head. Rabia froze at the sight of her.

"Arwa," she said. Swallowed.

"Please," said Arwa. "May I sit with you?"

Hesitantly, Rabia gestured for her to join her. Arwa kneeled down. Apart from the two of them, the prayer room was empty.

"I hadn't expected anyone else to be here," Rabia said quietly, into the silence.

"I'm sorry to disturb you, Aunt."

"Oh no, you're not disturbing me at all," Rabia said, even though that was clearly a lie. "This is your place too."

Rabia sat very still and alert, as if she were a child who feared being scolded. Arwa lowered her head as if in prayer. She looked at the flicker of shadows upon the floor in the lantern light.

"I am sorry for being unkind to you," Arwa said. "You're my elder. It was wrong."

"Oh." A beat. "Thank you."

"But I won't talk about my husband's death," Arwa said, still staring at the shadows upon the floor. Refusing to raise her head. "Not with you. Not with anyone. I can't."

She kept her eyes lowered, hoping it would hide the fire in them. She kept her hands soft and loose in her lap, so she would appear soft herself, and not like a bow strung so tight that its body was all trembling fury turned upon itself, ready to be unleashed. She had no veil, no long curtain of hair, so she was glad her shawl hung loose enough around her face to hide her features, which she feared were like a mirror for her heart.

Being sharp to Rabia had been an error. She'd exposed too much of herself—worn her nature too lightly. She had to put that right.

See, she tried to say—with her lowered eyes and the tilt of her head, her unfurled hands—*you need not fear me. I am soft and meek and gentle. There is no taint upon me at all.*

I have nothing to hide from you.

She heard Rabia huff, rising up from her knees. She flinched when Rabia inched closer to her.

"I lost my husband eleven years ago," Rabia said. "Last week was the anniversary of his death. Do you know, I quite forgot, until today? I only remembered a few hours ago. Foolish of me." Rabia went silent. She reached out and took one of Arwa's hands in her own. Her touch was tentative. "Don't believe I fail to understand your suffering, my dear."

Arwa looked at Rabia's hand. She wanted to pull away. She remained exactly where she was.

"Your husband was a brave man," Rabia said. "I meant it, when I told you that. A good Ambhan soldier. You must hold on to that."

Arwa felt something like despair. It was easier to feel anger than whatever she felt now. She closed her eyes.

She thought of what Kamran would have wanted. He would have wanted her to cry genteel tears. He would have wanted a soft widow, a widow who wilted gently beneath the weight of her grief.

He would not have wanted Arwa. He never would have, if he had truly known her.

There was something wrong with her. She knew it. There was something wrong with her nature, that she could not collapse and weep without feeling shame and fury, that she could not allow herself to like these women without wanting to flinch away from them. All her years of trying to mold herself into a gentle creature worth loving had amounted to nothing.

Arwa opened her eyes. Rabia's hand was still holding her own. The shadows were still flickering in their own silent dance. Nothing had changed. Crushing down the feelings rising up in her, the pain in her heart, Arwa spoke.

"He was a brave man," she whispered, in the softest voice she had. Tender as blood. "A very brave man. I miss him very, very much."

Gulshera invited her to breakfast once more. Shaky from lack of sleep, Arwa was grateful for the offer of tea and fritters and rice flecked with onions fried a deep gold. She sat at the table in Gulshera's room, surrounded by letters neatly piled, and ate gratefully.

Gulshera had a ring for her.

"Here," Gulshera said, handing it over. "You wear it on your thumb. It should protect your skin from the bowstring. Try it on."

She wondered if Gulshera had noticed the wound on her thumb, where she'd drawn blood with her dagger. She resolved to use her upper arm next time. That would be far easier to hide.

The ring was bone, white and worn smooth from past usage. She slipped it on her thumb and flexed her fingers a little. It was thicker than any glittering ornament made of gold or silver that she'd ever worn before.

"It fits perfectly," she said. "Thank you."

"I have a dozen," said Gulshera with a dismissive shrug. "We'll see later if it helps your aim."

Perhaps it would. Arwa had none of Gulshera's grace of fluidity, but she was improving in slow, undeniable increments. She'd managed to hit the easiest targets, and Gulshera was now encouraging her to improve her accuracy.

"I know you spoke to Rabia," Gulshera said, watching Arwa admire the ring. "I'm glad to see you recovering, Arwa."

Recovering. As if Arwa's grief were a spell of illness she would rise out of, with careful enough tending. Forcing herself not to speak, she raised her tea to her lips.

She had her mouth on the rim of the cup when she heard a sudden shriek. The cup jumped from her hands; hot liquid spilled over the table and the hem of her robe as she scrabbled back, cursing sharply. Gulshera rose to her feet.

"What on *earth*," she began.

There was another yell. A rush of footsteps. Without another word, Gulshera turned and strode sharply from the room, turning toward the source of the noise.

Arwa kneeled, wringing liquid from her hem. One of Gulshera's letters had fallen to the floor in the chaos, and was sodden. She lifted it up. Paused.

The seal was already broken, neatly parted.

Without pausing to think—this, after all, was the kind of opportunity she'd been waiting for—Arwa opened the letter.

Dear Aunt,

If your widows mention unrest in the southern provinces, write to me immediately. Matters between Parviz and Akhtar are not proceeding as I hoped—

Parviz. Akhtar.

She knew those names.

She turned the letter over again, pressing the seal back into place. Her fingers were steady. They should not have been.

Footsteps thudded outside the door. Arwa dropped the letter, back to the floor where she had found it, and left the room.

Other widows were also following the sound of shrieking and yelling. They walked toward the prayer hall. Its entrance was already stoppered up by a crowd of other curious women. Arwa tried to peer over their heads.

"Step back, step back!" Roshana yelled, striding forward. For once, her voice was not soft with feeling. Her habitual worry had alchemized into an air of authority that made the crowd part unthinking around her, allowing her access into the prayer room. Through the gap, Arwa saw Gulshera already standing there, and the source of the noise.

One of the two women who regularly drank and slumbered at the back of the prayer room was crying out hysterically. She was gabbling, fierce words tumbling from her mouth as she pointed at the lattice wall with one shaking hand.

"It was there," she was saying. "There, right there! Behind the lattice. Right *there*."

"You didn't see anything," another woman said to her, cutting through her words. "By the Emperor's grace, if you insist in drinking as you do, of course you'll imagine things—"

"*I know what I saw!*"

"Dina," Gulshera said, placing a hand on the hysterical woman's shoulder. "Tell me what happened."

"Please, dear," Roshana added gently.

Dina sucked in a shuddering breath. She dabbed the edge of her shawl hastily against her eyes. "It was just like the stories my mother told me when I was a little girl," she said. "Just like that."

Arwa's stomach clenched. Her face felt strangely numb.

"It had black wings," Dina was saying. "Gold eyes. Exactly how my own mother described it. It was a daiva. I know it."

Arwa took a small step back. She reached for her own shawl and drew it up around her face, as if she could ward off the press of eyes with cloth alone.

"Did you see anything?" Gulshera asked the other elderly lady, who was standing back, bewildered, the bottle clutched in her hands.

"No, I... I don't know," the woman said, nonplussed. "What was I meant to see?"

Roshana focused on the task of calming Dina down, as Dina began to yell again that she was not lying, not drunk, that she knew what she had seen and why wouldn't anyone believe her? The women around Arwa were muttering, their unease palpable.

Arwa was not uneasy. She was not anything. Her mind was a perfect void of sound and light. She turned on instinct alone, easing her way through the crowd, slipping between bodies until she was free of them, alone in the hallway, walking soft-footed toward her room.

She walked. And walked. And then she began to run.

She flung the door to her room open. Nothing had moved. The bed was undisturbed. The lantern was unlit. She went to the window and lifted her own small effigy. The line of blood beneath it was undisturbed.

She breathed in and out, in and out.

The smell hit her a moment later: sweet and cloying, as rich as smoke and perfume on water.

Incense.

She shuddered and bent forward, sucking in great gouts of breath, letting them go. Her ribs ached. Her mouth was full of the scent of incense, the iron of blood.

This was what she'd been waiting for, wasn't it? She'd waited in Chand, when the courtiers had interrogated her and her mother had shorn her hair; waited in her palanquin, with blood daubed behind her ear and nausea roiling in her stomach; waited in the valley with a bow and arrow in her hands.

She'd known, in her heart of hearts, that she could never run far enough. She'd always known.

The daiva had found her again, after all.

Arwa did not go to meet Gulshera. She lay in her bed, shivering, the embroidered blanket drawn up over her. It was easy to convince the maid who came to sweep her room that she was unwell, and to pass her apologies on to Gulshera. The maid returned later with lentil broth and bread for lunch, which Arwa left untouched. Hunger felt very far away from her.

She lay still, as the sun faded from the sky and sunset colored the room in rose hues. She listened to the widows walk outside her room, voices hushed.

She thought of all the secrets she'd carried all her life. She thought of the weight of her own history, always heavy upon her shoulders. She thought of Darez Fort.

Gold eyes. A hand on her sleeve. A circle of blood.

A scar on her arm, silver in the lantern light.

When the darkness finally came, and the hermitage fell silent, Arwa slipped out of bed. She tightened her sash around her dagger. She grabbed her bow and placed her quiver on her back. Last of all, she slipped the bone ring around her thumb. She had never been more armed in her life.

Arwa looked out the window. She saw nothing swoop through the air, saw no flicker of eyes, or wings rustling in the black. But she saw bright points in the dark, and knew she was not the only woman with a lantern lit tonight.

She thought of Rabia's hand on her own, and Roshana's damp worried eyes. She thought of Gulshera. Asima. A dozen grave-tokens, and a dozen more women clustered in the foyer on the night she arrived, staring at her with curious, bright eyes.

She did not love these women. Not a single one. There was no love left in her to be spared. But she would not allow this hermitage to become the next Darez Fort.

She stepped out of her room and closed her eyes. Her blood was pounding in her ears. She sucked in a breath and moved, one foot in front of the other, following the scent of incense, the tug of something beyond sense and flesh. Something in her blood.

CHAPTER FIVE

When Arwa was a small girl, she'd had a sister.

There were many things that Arwa was taught not to speak of, after her family's fall from imperial grace: the loss of her father's governorship; the severity of his illness; the faults in her own nature. But her sister had always been the greatest silence of all.

Her sister, after all, was the reason their fall had begun.

Mehr had been ten years her elder. When their father had still been Governor of Irinah, Mehr had been blessed with all the same comforts Arwa still remembered wistfully from her childhood: grand rooms and gold-armored guardswomen; an army of maidservants and silks and jewels in abundance. But Mehr had never been happy. She'd been a watchful and quiet figure, never quite at home in the walls of the Governor's palace. The maidservants who cared for Arwa whispered about her sometimes, when Arwa's nursemaid was not there to scold them for gossip. *That one has bad blood. She's no good. Even Lady Maryam can't set her right.*

Mehr had never considered Maryam—their father's wife, the woman who had raised Arwa as her own—her mother. Mehr had been old enough to remember their birth mother, the Amrithi mistress their father had banished a year after Arwa was born, and she clung fast to that memory. Clung fast, too, to the Amrithi heritage their birth mother had given her: rites of dance to worship the Gods. Rites of blood and dagger. No matter how Maryam punished her, no matter how she begged or cajoled Mehr to see reason, Mehr stayed firm. She would not give them up.

Arwa had been taught from infancy what it meant to have Amrithi blood. *Cursed*, her mother had called her—out of love, Arwa had known it was out of love. *Tainted*.

Amrithi were heathens. Barbarians. Blood worshippers. To be Amrithi was to be abhorred by good Ambhan people. To be Amrithi was to bring danger down on the family. So Maryam had always told her.

And she had, of course, been proved correct.

When Mehr revealed her heritage in some foolish way, the Maha's mystics had come for her, taken her away to his temple upon the sands. And Maryam had spirited Arwa off to Hara. *To keep you safe*, she'd said. *Until all is well in Irinah once more.*

But things were never well in Irinah again. Months later, her father arrived in Hara, stripped of his governorship, disgraced for having tried—foolishly, desperately—to convince his fellow nobles in supporting him to bring Mehr home. He'd grown sicker and sicker, shattered by his failure and by an illness no physician could cure, a malady that stole his strength and coordination and aged him, it seemed, nearly overnight.

And then the Maha had died.

Rumors began to swirl that the Emperor was executing traitors and heretics. Even mystics—once the loyal acolytes of the Maha himself—were being removed, if they were considered a threat to the Emperor's power. Her mother dismissed all but the most trusted servants, closed the shutters, and remained up all night with only a lantern for light, in a vigil Arwa would repeat many years later for very different reasons.

This is your sister's fault, her mother had told her. Trembling and tired. *If she had only been good, only listened to me . . .*

But there was nothing to be done, now.

Arwa remembered the night she thought the Emperor's men had finally come for her father. She woke to the sound of heavy footsteps in her room and saw the silhouette of a man at the window lattice. She had scrambled up onto her hands, heart in her throat, and seen that it was only her father. He stood on legs that trembled. Stood, and wept.

She remembered—even now—that he held a letter in his hand. A missive crumpled by his fist.

Your sister, he said, *is gone. Gone forever.*

Then: *I am sorry, Arwa.*

She had been angry with her sister for months and months before that—heartsick and furious at the way Mehr had failed to be good enough, and had left Arwa to learn to be a good Ambhan woman all on her own. But that night, she felt nothing but grief like a blow to the gut.

For years after, she wondered how Mehr had died. Had she died alongside the Maha, in the unnatural cataclysm that had begun the Empire's curse, or had he taken her life, as punishment for her heathen nature? She did not know. Her sister was a silence that grew and grew, blotting Arwa's childhood out to a void of fear and loss.

She grew into a woman sure of one thing alone: that revealing her Amrithi nature would be a death sentence to her family. She had to be the daughter her mother had reared her to be. Her mother's voice followed her like a cold shadow.

Amrithi have no respect for laws and vows. You must be obedient. Respectful. Lower your eyes, Arwa.

Amrithi worship through frenzied dances and blood, like the barbarians they are. Distaste in her mother's voice, in the curl of her lip.

You must have faith in the Maha and Emperor above all else. Bow your head and pray.

Be good, Arwa. Above all else, be good.

Arwa had been obedient. Faithful. Good. And if she had yearned as a foolish girl to be the Arwa she was not—the Arwa who was everything she had been taught not to be, free and fierce and faithless and *Amrithi*—she had learned long ago to put that childish want aside.

As Arwa walked through the silent, nighttime corridors of the hermitage, she tried not to think, for once, of the lessons her mother had taught her, about the importance of silence and secrecy, and of shaping herself into something worthy of love. She thought of her sister instead, and of the night she taught Arwa the truth about the daiva.

Her sister had never had the opportunity to teach her much of what it meant to be Amrithi, and Arwa had spent the last decade trying to forget what little she knew. But Mehr had taught her a lesson, on the night a daiva had swept into Arwa's room in Irinah during her early childhood, gold-eyed and shadow-fleshed. That lesson had grown blurred at the edges, softened by time. But Arwa had not forgotten the bones of it.

Her sister had told her Amrithi were descended from daiva. *Their blood lives in us,* she'd told her. Just a speck. Their shared blood drew the daiva to them. But their blood was also their defense. Placed upon a door or a window, it could keep the daiva at bay. For all the daiva were monsters, they were loath to hurt their own kin.

Arwa was cursed, in the blood, in a way she could not deny any longer. Her blood had brought the daiva to Darez Fort. But it had also saved her life.

Arwa had remembered that lesson in Darez Fort. She remembered it now.

She stopped outside the prayer room, breath frozen in her chest. The daiva was back where it had been before. In the silence left by the absence of breath, she could hear the rustle of its wings, whisper-soft. She inhaled then, deliberately, and smelled its daiva scent, sweet as incense, a tangle of water and smoke.

It had been waiting for her.

She entered the room slowly. Through the lattice wall she saw its eyes first, bright and golden in its face of velvet smoke. It had great wings that filled the lattice wall in feathered shadows.

"You're not wanted here," Arwa whispered, voice shaky. "Go."

It didn't move, merely cocked its head, its lambent eyes blinking softly. She realized its wings were not moving, as bird wings moved. It was simply hovering in the air, in defiance of the laws of nature, its vast body stretched elegantly out against the blanket of sky. The sight of it made her stomach roil.

Very, very slowly, she reached into her quiver and drew out an arrow. She pressed the arrowhead to her own skin, just below the elbow. The point drew blood.

Beyond the lattice, the daiva shivered faintly, a great susurration running through its wings.

Arwa placed the bloodied arrow to the bow. In the dark, she had to locate the nocking point with nothing but her fingertips and her memory to guide her.

She raised the bow. The lacquered wood creaked.

She heard an intake of breath from the doorway.

Arwa moved nothing but her eyes, her gaze sliding away from the daiva toward the figure standing in the hallway at the entrance of the prayer room.

Rabia stared back at her, eyes wide. Judging by the sweets clutched in her hand, she'd made an ill-advised late-night visit to the kitchen, heard noise from the prayer room, and turned her head at the wrong moment as she'd made her way down the corridor. Now she was frozen by the sight of Arwa holding a bow and arrow. By the sight of the daiva.

Don't move, Arwa tried to communicate with her eyes. *Don't make a sound.*

The widow's mouth opened. A helpless choked noise came out of her that rose inexorably into a scream.

"Help! Someone help!"

The daiva took flight, swooping toward the valley; the sudden movement of its wings made the wind rise around Arwa. She lowered her bow with a swear on her lips, fury and terror bubbling in her blood.

There was a wave of noise beyond the prayer room. Voices shouting, and bells ringing, as the guards moved into frenzied life on the hermitage roof. Rabia had run, and Arwa was alone. She wouldn't be so for long.

She thought of the daiva she saw at Darez Fort, held in the soldier's lap, its teeth like terrible points of light. Surrounded by the scent of incense, Arwa was terribly sure they were not free of it. Not yet.

This, Arwa knew:

The daiva that came to Darez Fort, the daiva that was here at the hermitage—they were all here for her.

She tightened her jaw, resolute, and ran out of the room.

There were already guards inside the hermitage, and women who'd emerged from their own rooms and gathered in the hallways. Gods, their curiosity would truly be the death of them one day. Someone tried to grab Arwa as she strode forward with her bow still in her grip; she shook them off. She ran faster.

At some point she discarded the bow, and shrugged the quiver from her back. It was easier to move swiftly without them. Every thin slat of a window she passed revealed the daiva in snatches: a wing, an eye, the echo of its presence, that twined scent and sight of incense and smoke. She pushed open the doors of the hermitage, which led across the veranda to the great dip of the valley below.

The daiva was waiting for her.

It had no mortal shape, this daiva, and she was thankful for that. But it was crouched now upon the ground, and instead of claws, it now had great soft-pawed limbs, pressed to soil. She stopped before it, panting hard. She heard the creak of bowstrings behind her, of arrows being drawn. She heard a voice shouting for the guards to stay their hands.

Those sounds felt far, far from her. She reached for her sash, scrabbling for the leather sheath that held her dagger. One of the daiva's pawed limbs stretched out as she did so, changing before her eyes into a delicate mortal hand.

"Don't touch me," she hissed. It stared at her uncomprehending, as she drew the dagger from its sheath. As she cut a line, deeper than she intended, into her opposite palm.

She lunged forward. The shadows of its body surrounded her.

The dagger sank hard and fast into the soil. Around her, over her, the daiva shattered into a dozen smaller birds. Wings battered her face and her hair—even her arms, as she raised them to protect herself. Her hand was still bleeding freely. She was light-headed with pain.

None of it mattered. The daiva was flying away from her, no matter what form it had taken. Most importantly of all, it was flying away from the hermitage.

One of the guards slammed Arwa to the ground. She felt the guardswoman's hands on her arms, tightening and wrenching her back up to her knees. Arwa swore again, panting with exhilaration and something wild, a feeling she couldn't name or suppress.

"Let her go," a voice said. The authority in it was undeniable.

Gulshera had pushed past the other guardswomen. Arwa turned back, craning her neck. Gulshera's eyes were flint.

"But, Lady—"

"Just release her."

The guardswoman released Arwa, who fell back to the ground.

Arwa gave a groan, turning on her side. Gulshera kneeled down, still looming over her, and removed her own shawl. She grabbed Arwa's wounded palm and wound the cloth around it, binding it tight enough to stem the bleeding.

"You're coming with me," Gulshera said. Her voice was savage iron. "Now."

They went to Gulshera's room. A guardswoman came with them, followed by Roshana, who shut the door on the crowd of panicked, curious onlookers in the corridor. The guardswoman was gray with fear, and her hand was altogether too tight on the hilt of her scimitar. Gulshera bade Arwa to sit on the bed, then leaned back against the wall, her arms crossed tight. By the door, Roshana wrung her hands together, eyes darting between them all. The room was far too crowded.

Arwa clutched her own wounded hand. Blood had left the cloth of Gulshera's shawl sodden and red. Beneath the makeshift bandage, Arwa's palm pulsed with a gnawing, throbbing ache. Her head felt light, faintly full of stars.

"I need my dagger," Arwa said.

"Child," Roshana whispered. Then she fell silent.

"It's still out there, stuck in the dirt," Arwa said. "I need it back."

"No one is going to give you a weapon," Gulshera snapped.

"Then at least find it," Arwa said, through gritted teeth, "and put it somewhere safe."

"Go," Gulshera said to the guardswoman. "Get the dagger."

The guardswoman hesitated visibly. She looked between them. "But, my lady…"

Gulshera made an angry sound and leaned forward. She pulled the hilt of a small dagger from her boot. Then she sheathed it once more and straightened. "We're hardly unarmed, and *she* is hardly in a position to snatch up another blade. Go."

The guardswoman went. Roshana made sure the door was firmly shut behind her, keeping the three of them safe from prying eyes.

"Arwa," Roshana said softly. "What happened? Can you explain what we saw?"

Arwa curled and uncurled the fingers of her hurting hand. She stayed silent.

"We don't wish to cause you harm, dear," Roshana continued. "Just speak to us. We can help you."

Still leaning against the wall, Gulshera said nothing. Arwa looked at her. Gulshera's expression was unmoving, her pale eyes blazing and fierce. Even if Roshana had not realized what Arwa had done—what Arwa *was*—Gulshera had.

"I'll speak to you," Arwa said to her. "No one else, Lady Gulshera."

They met each other's eyes, unflinching.

"Roshana," Gulshera said finally. "Please go outside and encourage the others to get some rest. Thank you."

Roshana nodded and left, glancing back at the both of them before shutting the door once more.

Arwa's hand was still throbbing. She tried to ignore the pain, twisting the ends of the shawl tighter.

"You left the bow I gave you flung on the ground in a corridor," Gulshera said. "And my arrows. You don't fret about them."

"The dagger was a gift from family. It has sentimental value."

"More than sentimental value, I think," Gulshera said. Her voice was unreadable. "I know something of the world, Arwa."

"I don't doubt that, Aunt."

"I know the Amrithi people carry such daggers. I know they perform unnatural blood rites. Somewhat akin to what you did this night, Arwa."

"Indeed," Arwa said. Her voice came out of her like snowfall, winter cold, even as her heart crawled.

"Now we come to what I don't understand," said Gulshera. "The Amrithi are a barbaric people. They have no place in the Empire. They exist on the edges of civilization, begging for scraps of our glory. They do not walk on the same land where civilized people walk. They don't marry people of the Empire. I gather in their lawless way, they don't marry at all." Gulshera's voice was unrelenting, her eyes keen fire. "So explain to me: How does a noblewoman, a widow of apparent good blood and standing, despite her father's disgrace, come to have an Amrithi dagger and knowledge of Amrithi heresy?"

"In the usual way," said Arwa. "Irinah was the home of the Amrithi once. When my father was Governor, he had an Amrithi mistress. She gave him two children. I was one of them. But I am not Amrithi, Aunt. My father acknowledged me and raised me like a lawful daughter. My mother—the good noblewoman who married my father—raised me to be better than my blood. And I've always tried to be. Until..."

Arwa swallowed. Her throat was very dry. She was glad the faint, blinding dizziness in her head had faded somewhat. She was very conscious of the throb of her wounded hand, and her thirst, and her fear. She was conscious, too, that the daiva was gone, and that was her own doing. No one else's. She could hold that like a new dagger, should she need to. She could hold it like a shield.

"I wasn't entirely honest about Darez Fort," Arwa said.

Gulshera was silent. She waited, as Arwa sat straight, cradling her hand.

"Almost everything I told you was true. I truly don't remember much, after the daiva arrived at the fort. But I remember reaching for my dagger. I remember—pieces."

She told Gulshera, haltingly, what she could recall.

She remembered running and hiding, after the daiva had shattered to pieces, spreading terror across the fort. She remembered kneeling on the floor, panting in unnatural fear, nightmares swirling through her skull. Her vision had wavered, black around the edges, the ground tipping beneath her.

She'd felt a hand on her sleeve. A hand of smoke. A daiva before her. The hot metal of fear had filled her mouth; she'd flinched, wrenching her wrist back. She could still feel the echo of the smoke of its fingers, a strange brand upon her flesh.

She'd seen her blade on the floor.

"I must have picked it up, when the fear had me," Arwa said. "And thank the Gods I did. It is the only thing I know of the Amrithi blood in me: It can banish daiva away. I reached for my dagger and bled on the ground. A circle of protection. It kept the daiva's hands from me, and it saved my life."

"Your blood," Gulshera said, disbelieving, "saved you from the demon. Your *Amrithi* blood."

"There truly is so much I can't remember anymore, Aunt. I've tried, and I've tried. But I know my blood saved me. That, I have no doubts about."

Arwa pushed Darez Fort away. She focused on the room, on Gulshera, and on her own wounded hand. On the sound of the women still hovering in the corridor, fueled by fear and curiosity. It wouldn't take much for that rage to turn. Only words. Only one muttered mention of blood rites, of Amrithi. She had to make Gulshera *understand*.

"I am Ambhan," said Arwa. "My blood doesn't change that. I worship the Emperor and Maha; I married an Ambhan man, and I mourn him. I know nothing about being Amrithi. I don't *want* to be Amrithi."

"You don't need to justify yourself to me."

Arwa barked out a laugh. "Of course I do. You think I don't know what is done with Amrithi? You think I don't know what you could do to me, if this interrogation ends with me marked a heathen, good only for slaughter?"

"This is not an interrogation," Gulshera said grimly. "This is a very polite conversation. You know nothing of interrogations."

Arwa fixed her eyes on Gulshera again. Gulshera, whose long-dead husband had a mother-of-pearl lacquered court bow; who came from a noble family of high repute; who knew something of Amrithi and interrogations. Gulshera, with her letters.

"I know you serve the Emperor's family," Arwa said.

"And how," Gulshera said, deadly soft, "do you know that?"

"You left me alone in your room when Dina saw the daiva. Akhtar and Parviz. I've heard the names of the Emperor's sons, Aunt." Gulshera was silent. "What I don't understand is why one favored by the imperial family would live within this hermitage," Arwa continued. "You could have so much power. And yet you're—here."

"Power under the heel of court can feel very much like helplessness," Gulshera murmured. She stared at Arwa as if she were a viper that had only just shown her venom. "I asked my mistress to give me leave to have something akin to my own court. Control, as governors and commanders do, while still serving their Empire. She allowed it."

"And you gather information for her," Arwa said. "From the widows. Things they would not reveal if they did not think themselves—safe."

"Yes," Gulshera said shortly. "I do."

"Then there's no need to properly interrogate me. Don't fear.

I am loyal to the Emperor, heart and soul." She curled her pained fingers again. Uncurled. "You told me the family you serve are trying to end the curse on the Empire. Perhaps they will have some use for a loyal Ambhan noblewoman, with strange blood to hold the nightmares at bay."

"They may," Gulshera acknowledged. Then she laughed, a tired and bitter sound. "My mistress asks for many things. Knowledge, information, my return. You would be a worthy gift to take back with me. She has an interest in—magic. In daiva. In the Empire's curse. I knew she would want me to find out what you knew of Darez Fort, of course. But I did not expect..." Gulshera paused. Assessed Arwa once again, coldly, carefully, with the tilt of her head. "You do not have an Amrithi look."

She meant that Arwa was light-skinned and straight-haired and had the sharp features of her father's family. She meant that Arwa dressed and spoke like an Ambhan noblewoman, born and bred.

Arwa thought of her sister. Dark-skinned. The curve of her cheekbones. Her hair always in its long braid, oiled and curling free.

Her wound throbbed.

"I know." Deep breath in. Out. "My blood—my Amrithi blood in this loyal Ambhan body—is part of the curse. But it's also part of the cure. I just don't know how. But the Emperor's family, your mistress...they might. Perhaps they'll find answers in my blood that I can't. You should send me to them, if they'll have me."

A beat. Two. Three.

"No, Arwa." Gulshera shook her head, mouth thin. As if she'd already considered the option and discarded it. "Widow though you may be, you still have a noblewoman's honor. That must be protected. Your place is here, or in your father's care."

"I can't stay here," Arwa said. "I came here for peace, but now the widows know what I am—you think they will allow me to stay?"

"Of course not."

"The daiva follow me. Darez Fort follows me. I can't run any farther from what lies in my blood. Send me to your mistress. Let me offer my cursed blood to her curiosity and her cause. As for my family...You think I wish to carry this darkness home with me, to my mother and father?"

"I imagine not," said Gulshera. "That makes your offer no less foolish."

"I am not being foolish," Arwa said. For once, for *once*, she was not. "I am attempting to be useful. Is that not what we are taught from birth, Aunt? To serve the Empire—to be loyal and dutiful, to offer our service to the Empire's glory—there is no higher purpose, surely?"

Gulshera laughed. A strange, helpless sound, full of bitterness. She looked over Arwa's head, at something in the distance that Arwa could not see—a memory, an image beyond her reach.

"They will eat you alive, and spit out your bones. They will take everything you offer and they will feel nothing for you," Gulshera said. "That is their way. More than that, that is their *right*."

"It is better than being useless," Arwa said softly. She meant it.

To be of no use to the Empire was to be discarded. She had seen what became of her family, when Mehr exposed them to disgrace. She had seen what had become of her father, denied his inherited governorship, his daughter, his health. She had felt her mother's horror as their old friends and old power withered away from them, leaving them utterly alone.

If her father had been well, perhaps in time he would have restored their lost glory. If he had been ill, but still Governor, he would have had the right to retire with honor, respected and feted. But in a world where all his *use* was gone, when the Empire could not benefit from him, he had been erased.

Arwa had no hope of restoring her family's glory, not now that she was widowed. But she could avoid heaping further disgrace upon them. She could take her cursed blood and lay it out before Gulshera as a priceless gift, a weapon and a tool that could be bartered or sold, instead of a reason to destroy what little position and reputation she had left. She could be *useful*.

"This is the first time I've seen a chance for the possibilities in my blood to be put to good use," Arwa said quietly, letting something other than anger infuse her voice for once. "All my life, I've been ashamed of it. I have kept my blood a secret. Even after Darez Fort I knew it would do me no good—do no one any good, only harm—if I shared the truth. But now the truth may serve a use. Now my blood may help the Empire, may be a cure, and..." She released a breath. "That is a relief, Aunt. I can't deny it."

The idea was insidious. She didn't need to hold on to her rage; this awful thing turned both inward and outward, hungry and hurt. She could throw herself to the mercy of larger forces. Instead of being a victim of the Empire's curse, she could be its cure.

"Ah, fool child," Gulshera said. There was despair in her voice. Then she was abruptly silent, passing a hand over her face, as if she could grasp her feelings and draw them away in her palm.

Arwa closed her eyes. The dark behind them felt like it was enfolding her; she was held up by it, distant from her flesh, distant as stars. She could hear something like whispers.

"I think," she said faintly, "that I am going to need a physician very soon."

"Ah," Gulshera said. "Yes."

Arwa heard her footsteps. She took Arwa's wounded hand

and held it gently up, cursing in a short whisper. Then she spoke again, her voice its normal tone and cadence.

"I will write to my mistress," said Gulshera. "If she wants you... well."

"She will," Arwa insisted. "You know she will."

"I expect you're correct," said Gulshera. She placed a hand against Arwa's forehead. Her touch was soft. "I am sorry, child."

"Don't be," Arwa said, not knowing if Gulshera apologized in sympathy for Arwa's pain, or for the fate that lay before her. "This is all my own doing."

CHAPTER SIX

Gulshera wrote a letter to her mistress that night, as Arwa's hand was cleaned and bandaged by one of the servants who refused to meet her eyes. The next morning, Arwa found her dagger by her door, wrapped in cloth and cleaned so that no soil marked it any longer. A terse message lay beside it:

I have sent your offer.

After that, the waiting began.

In this hermitage of widows, Arwa had begun to find a way to survive. She'd found the promise of comfort in her walks with Asima, in the quiet solace of worship and even the gossip that filled the widows' evenings. Most of all, she had found a safe outlet for her anger: a weapon shaped to let her rage fly free. Now all that had to be put away. Her new life had to be folded up, peeled away from her skin. It did not belong here any longer.

Now she had only this: Her clean blade. Her wounded, aching, healing hand. The promise of purpose worth dying for.

Arwa avoided meals whenever possible. There were no more walks, no more visits to the prayer hall where she could seek comfort in the presence of the effigy of the Emperor and the Maha. She did not go to the valley and practice archery again. Gulshera had never returned the bow or the quiver of arrows to Arwa's keeping, after she had so carelessly discarded them.

Instead Arwa took food from the kitchens, which the servants handed over warily, begrudgingly. She sat in her own room, waiting for her hand to heal, struggling to ignore the itch of flesh weaving itself whole, and wrote letter after discarded letter to her mother.

In the end she settled on penning her mother a simple letter, sparse in detail and in feeling. She told her mother she liked the hermitage, that she appreciated the silence, and the time to reflect without disturbance. *Being alone*, she wrote, *suits me well*.

Arwa had never been one for writing letters, after her marriage. She doubted her mother or father would expect that to change, now she was a widow, cloistered away in the isolated keeping of a hermitage.

Besides, she had seen—*felt*—her mother's raw disappointment, the heat of her shame in Arwa. She did not think her mother would be eager to reach out to Arwa now. All her work to make Arwa whole and better, and what had come of it, in the end? Nothing.

Give Father my love, she finished. *I hope you are both well*.

She was likely to be long gone from the hermitage before her mother's response arrived. She had no doubts that Gulshera's mistress would want her. Arwa knew how strange it was, the thing her blood had done. Her blood had drawn the daiva to her. Her blood had saved her. There was cure and curse tangled inside her. That was worth a great deal, in these harrowing times of blight. Especially to the Emperor's line, who had brought the Empire all its glory, and must have felt keenly the Empire's pain.

One evening, Gulshera came to Arwa's room. Arwa had been sitting on her bed, reading a book of poetry—a tangle of beautiful, lyrical verses—when Gulshera rapped on the door and entered. Arwa snapped her book shut. She moved to stand, a question hovering on her lips. Gulshera shook her head. She knew what Arwa had intended to ask.

"No reply yet," said Gulshera. "I'm here to cut your hair."

Arwa reflexively reached a hand up and touched the ends of her hair. Her hair had always grown fast. When it had been long it had been her pride, and had lain in thick black waves to the small of her back. At its current length—not long, but not quite as short as was seemly for a widow—it curled faintly where it touched her jaw.

"With your hand as it is," Gulshera said, "you can't cut it yourself. And you need to make yourself presentable."

"I could ask a servant," Arwa offered cautiously, wary of Gulshera, who was expressionless, arms crossed.

"I doubt they would help you," Gulshera said.

"Do they say I'm an Amrithi barbarian? Do they *fear* me now?" Arwa knew she should not have asked, should not have let the bitter, hurt words pass her lips, even before Gulshera shook her head, just one weary turn, as if Arwa's words and Arwa's very presence exhausted her.

"It's natural for them to fear," Gulshera said. "Do not worry about them, Arwa. Worry about your future. Sit at your desk and let me begin to make you fit for it."

Gulshera had brought shears with her. She smoothed the curls of Arwa's hair with her fingers, then began to cut them away neatly. Arwa felt the strands fall away from her. She sat very still, conscious of the sharpness of the shears, and the cool regard of Gulshera's eyes on her.

"Apart from the dagger and the blood, you really don't seem very Amrithi at all," Gulshera said, voice approving but detached, as if Arwa were a piece of flawed livestock, a thing to be weighed up for its quality. The snip of the shears was glittering sharp in Arwa's ears. "I would not have guessed, if you hadn't betrayed yourself."

"I told you. It's just an aberration in my blood," Arwa murmured, wrapping her memories of her early childhood away,

away. "That's all. As for the dagger..." She curled and uncurled her fingers, testing the flexibility of her healing skin. "It's a necessity. That's all."

Gulshera gave a low hum of acknowledgment. Then she said, "It shows, at least, that you can learn how to behave appropriately, when you need to. Beneath your rage is a mind that can think." Snip. Snip. "I need to teach you about the protocol a widow must adhere to."

"I know that," Arwa said.

She heard the huff of Gulshera's breath. It almost resembled a laugh.

"You learned how to behave in your family's own women's quarters, or in a hermitage made up solely of widows. The behavior of a widow in another household must be different. It must be beyond reproach." She brushed the cut strands of hair from Arwa's shoulders. "I served at court after my husband's death. In the very household where you will soon go, in fact. I learned the standards of behavior expected of women like us."

Ghost women. Shadow women. Women who had lost their purpose.

Arwa resisted the urge to nod, her body itching with restlessness. She waited and listened.

"You must be demure. Limit your laughter. Limit your smiles. Do not engage in dance or celebrations. Focus on prayer."

"I know all of that," Arwa said.

"You know, but you falter. Here you have the luxury of forgetting what is expected of you. That is the benefit of life in a hermitage, or among loving family willing to turn a blind eye to transgressions. The imperial palace..." Gulshera paused. In the silence, Arwa heard a dozen things that Gulshera discarded, unsaid. The tension in her coiled at that. "You cannot forget," Gulshera continued, finally. "You'll be watched constantly for many, many reasons beyond your widowhood. Do not allow anyone a reason to smear your name."

Arwa could feel cold air on her bare neck. She shivered, and unable to resist the urge, she touched her fingertips to the surprisingly neat ends of her newly shorn hair.

"Have you heard anything?" Arwa asked tentatively. "From your mistress?"

"No," said Gulshera. "Not yet."

But she would. And Arwa did not think she would receive a simple letter in response.

Four days later Arwa was woken by sharp rapping on her door. She shot awake, and wrenched open the door. Gulshera was waiting for her. She was dressed for travel, her veil thrown back, her expression firm.

"They're here," she said.

"Who?" Arwa asked.

"The guards who are going to accompany us to Ambha."

"*Us?*"

"You have a great number of inane questions," Gulshera said. "Dress. I assume you've already packed your possessions."

Arwa veiled herself appropriately, dressing in a white robe that covered her body from head to toe. A servant arrived to take her possessions; she assumed Gulshera had arranged it and was thankful. She could barely think over the tense joy and fear running simultaneously through her.

There was a void ahead of her. Unknowable. It brought her far more pleasure than it should have.

There was no great crowd of women, waiting to send Arwa off with tearful farewells, although they watched from their rooms through cracked doors, or hovered guiltily at the edges of the corridors, eyes shadowed, shawls drawn protectively around their faces. Only Roshana and Asima met them at the foyer, Asima leaning heavily on Roshana's arm.

"You've been avoiding us all," Asima said, overloud. Arwa winced, offering a soft murmur of apology, which Asima discarded with a pointed wave of her hand. "You should have come," Asima continued. "I would have defended you. I like you better than those other silly owls, ill blood or no."

She gestured for Arwa to come closer, which Arwa did. She glanced at Roshana's face, which was downturned, and realized the older woman was crying.

"Take this with you," Asima said gruffly, shoving something into Arwa's hands.

"Thank you, Aunt," Arwa murmured, reflexively. "I'll miss you. Both of you."

"Good of you to say," Asima grumbled, even as Roshana softly murmured, "Take care, Arwa. Please."

"They're waiting," said Gulshera.

Asima and Roshana watched them go.

"I didn't think you would come with me," Arwa said, tentative, not yet quite willing to frame a full question, as Gulshera walked ahead of her, and adjusted her veil carefully into place.

"I knew I would have to return to my mistress eventually," Gulshera said. Her voice was grim. "You are my gift to her. I offered you up. Of course I intend to accompany you."

That was not correct, of course. Arwa had offered herself up. Her history, her blood. But she made a noise of agreement, lowering her own veil into place.

It was only when she and Gulshera had exited the hermitage, unfamiliar guardswomen waiting to greet them and lead them down the mountainside, that Arwa looked at what Asima had pushed into her hand. It was a grave-token, empty but expertly woven, the grass that had formed it still warm from Asima's palm. She thought of the way it curved around soil, the way the world cupped the bodies of the dead. Arwa curled her own fingertips over it gently. It would not do to crush it.

The palanquin the soldiers had brought with them was no more comfortable than the one Arwa had traveled to the hermitage in. It was larger, at least. Large enough to accommodate both Arwa and Gulshera comfortably, protecting them from the eyes of the male soldiers who guided the palanquin. Their female retinue was sparse, but the guardswomen were heavily armed and alert, light on their feet around the palanquin's curtained sides. They'd made no complaints the first—or second, or third—time Arwa had asked for the retinue to pause and allow her to throw up her guts at the roadside.

"They come from my mistress's own household, I expect," Gulshera said, speaking to Arwa softly, as Arwa lay on the palanquin's cushions, trying to regain her composure once again.

It was impossible not to converse, confined as they were with no other entertainment, on their interminable, lurching journey through the mountains. Gulshera had remained pointedly silent for a good day after Arwa first removed her dagger and made a small cut, daubing a crook of the palanquin wood with blood. But in the course of time, she had thawed to Arwa again. Perhaps she was even grateful.

"Tell me about your mistress," Arwa requested, not particularly expecting a response. She was not surprised when Gulshera merely huffed, reclining back and closing her eyes.

Arwa was already lying on her side, her shawl drawn tight around her, as if the shell of it could keep the full weight of her nausea at bay.

"You will need to trust me eventually," Arwa pointed out. "I am your gift to her, after all."

"I suppose," Gulshera said slowly, "you need to be prepared."

That would be nice, Arwa thought, with instinctual acidity. She wisely maintained her own silence.

"My mistress," said Gulshera, "is Princess Jihan, the Emperor's only legitimate daughter. When I left for the hermitage, she had just risen to the head of her brother Prince Akhtar's household. She is . . . *was*, very much like her mother once was. A clever woman. I have no doubt she has only grown in strength."

There was something akin to affection in Gulshera's voice.

"Were you a friend to the Empress?" Arwa asked, speaking of this Princess Jihan's mother.

A real smile graced Gulshera's face. She shook her head.

"Arwa," she said. "The imperial family do not have friends. But I was one of her women, and Princess Jihan's wet nurse. A great honor." Gulshera leaned forward, palanquin jolting around them, and pressed her hands flat to the palanquin's floor. "When you meet her, Arwa, remember: Show her the same respect you would show your father. Your departed husband. She is no green girl. She is the Emperor's blood, his legitimate child. Do not forget that. She has more power than you can comprehend."

Arwa shivered, not sure if Gulshera's words or her own nausea had set her insides roiling.

"You keep warning me about my behavior."

"Because I have to. You're too blunt," Gulshera told her. "You speak without thinking. You're too direct. Your survival will rely on your behavior now, Arwa. You must not forget it. Think on that for a while. *Prepare* yourself."

"What else," Arwa said, "should I know about Princess Jihan?"

"I have told you all you need to know for now," Gulshera said, clearly weighing up kindness against her iron-clad loyalty for her distant mistress.

"The more I know, Aunt, the more likely I am to survive," Arwa argued.

Gulshera shook her head. She would not relent today. "Remember your status. Remember what is expected of you. That should be enough. I will be there to guide you anyway."

Arwa was often a fool. She didn't deny that, even to herself. She drew her knees up to her stomach, tucking her wounded hand protectively into the crook of her own body, and closed her eyes. She felt too ill to argue further. Perhaps when their retinue stopped to rest for the night, she would pepper Gulshera with questions again, and attempt to erode some of that reserve. But not now.

Gulshera had not been wrong to ask Arwa to think on her behavior. She could not be a flighty, mercurial, grief-stricken creature any longer. In her hermitage she had sloughed away her strongest defenses. Now she needed a new carapace. She had worn the armor of a wife: attentive to her husband, charming and soft, beautiful and ephemeral with it. Now she needed to wear the flesh and garb of a widow. Not yielding, but barely visible. A ghost. A shadow.

Numriha and Ambha were divided by a great swathe of mountains, jagged and near impassable. But in the years since the Empire was first formed, one great road had been carved into the mountainside, clearing a winding path between the Emperor's own province, birthplace of the Empire, and Numriha, land of mines and artisans, and source of all the pale, flawless marble that now filled the imperial city of Jah Ambha. There was good reason for Numriha to be accessible.

Whenever Arwa peered through the curtain surrounding the palanquin—properly tied in place, because Gulshera had carefully impressed on her the importance of adhering to protocol—she sometimes caught sight of the outposts lining the road. Some were set high in the mountains; others were near the road itself. She saw small, distant figures move—the reflection of torchlight.

Ambha was well-protected. The closer they came to it, the greater the number of guards became, and the less Arwa was able to leave the security of the palanquin when sickness hit her. There were too many eyes.

Gulshera did her best to distract Arwa instead. She told her the road had not always been so forcefully protected. But the time since the Maha's death had been one of a steadily swift descent into watchfulness, earned paranoia. Daiva had been seen, and bandits had roamed with greater and greater ease, even so close to the heart of the Empire. Somehow luck always seemed to be against the soldiers in their outposts. A man would fall asleep on watch at an inopportune moment; supplies sent to them would go missing, or be stolen, leaving soldiers hungry and inclined to desertion. The only solution had been to expand the number of outposts and increase their provisions at the expense of the local populace, who bore the brunt of the taxes necessary to put food in the soldiers' mouths.

It was a familiar story. Arwa had heard similar things from her husband, on the evenings when he had returned to his chambers and asked for her presence. She'd listened to him attentively, making soothing noises when appropriate, softening the knots in the bruised muscle of his ego with gentle, tender words. It was novel to hear stories of strategy and taxation and hunger for her own benefit, for someone to attempt to soothe *her*.

There was nothing to mark the moment when Numriha became Ambha, but Gulshera knew. Like Arwa, she had begun peering through the gap between the curtain and the resinous palanquin wood. She turned to Arwa sharply.

"We're almost at the palace," she said, sudden urgency in her voice as she unknotted the curtain and gestured at one of the guardswomen with her arm.

This time, despite all her emphasis on protocol, it was Gulshera who demanded the palanquin be stopped and the men move to a respectable distance up the path. Veiled, she and Arwa left the palanquin and stood on the road, great gouts of dust staining the ends of their robes as they stepped out of the shadow of the palanquin.

"Follow me," she said to Arwa, leading her to the curve of the road. Below it was a sheer drop. And below that—

"Ah," Arwa breathed. She had no words. The sight before her had stolen her voice.

There was a great swathe of space between the arms of the mountains. At their heart lay a lake—a great sheet of silver, rich with the glittering reflection of sunlight. And upon it stood the Emperor's palace.

The palace was not one single building, as the Governor's palace in Irinah had been. Instead it was a complex of multiple constellation palaces, bound by bridges to the great palace at the center of the lake, its surface a clever, complex heart of sandstone and gemstones, a brilliance of white marble and gold. It burned as bright as the bloodied heart of the sun overhead. Around it, connected by bridges, stood four smaller palaces, each one a closed flower, rich in color and beauty. She barely noticed the surrounding, white-marbled city. The palace—the *Emperor's* palace—had swallowed her attention whole.

"Ambha," Gulshera murmured. In that word, Arwa heard *home* as clear as if Gulshera had said it aloud instead.

"We're going there?" Arwa said helplessly.

"There," Gulshera said. She pointed a finger at one of the smaller palaces set on the water. "The Palace of Dusk. That is where Princess Jihan lives, and where we will live now too."

CHAPTER SEVEN

It took time for the soldiers and guardswomen to negotiate entry, and all the while, Gulshera sat in silence, her tension palpable. At the edge of the lake, at a great gate that guarded the crossing bridge to the Palace of Dusk, all of Arwa's and Gulshera's luggage was opened and searched by women robed in livery of imperial green. The guardswomen spoke to the women of the imperial household; the palanquin was raised; it was taken to the shadowed entrance of a gatehouse.

One of the guardswomen untied the curtain. When she gestured for Arwa to exit the palanquin, Gulshera said, "Is our entry barred?"

"No, my lady," said an imperial maidservant, standing just beyond the guardswoman's shoulder. The maidservant stood in the entrance of the gatehouse with a companion. Their heads were deferentially lowered, but their backs were iron straight, and the voice of the one who spoke was firm. "Prince Akhtar commands that all new visitors to the palace are cleansed. Please, follow me."

Gulshera remained still only for a moment. Then she gave Arwa's hand a squeeze—of warning and comfort—and stepped free of the palanquin. Arwa followed her.

They kept their veils lowered until they entered the sanctuary of the walls. Then they were separated, one maidservant leading

Arwa to a small room, where a covered bowl waited, and a mirror. The maidservant gestured for Arwa to sit.

She checked Arwa's eyes, opening them wide and gazing at the whites. She held Arwa's wrists and felt her pulse. She asked Arwa questions: about her health, about her journey.

"What is the purpose of this cleansing?" Arwa asked in return, when the maidservant finally released her.

"To keep ill forces at bay, my lady. Sickness and…" Here she hesitated. "Other sicknesses, my lady. That are not of the flesh."

Arwa thought of Darez Fort and said nothing.

The maidservant lifted a cloth away from the bowl, revealing clear water.

"The water was touched by the Emperor's own hands," said the woman, placing a pitcher into the bowl of water. The bowl, Arwa saw, was marked in flowing script: long lines of mantras praising the Maha and Emperor both. "Please, my lady, hold your hands over the bowl."

The maidservant poured the water over Arwa's outstretched hands.

This will accomplish nothing, Arwa thought, as she watched the water pour over her fingers. But she made no complaint when the maidservant bid her wash her face also, and offered her a cloth to dry herself clean.

"We are done, my lady," said the maidservant.

Arwa's hands trembled a little, as she clasped them in her lap. The maidservant offered her a smile, as if to comfort her.

"You need not fear," said the maidservant, her voice knowing, as if she understood why Arwa shivered in her seat. "You have not drawn our prince's ire. All who come to the palace are tested so. Soon our prince's wisdom will ensure cleansings are performed across the Empire, and they will keep us safe, by the Emperor's grace."

"By the Emperor's grace," Arwa murmured in return.

The maidservant nodded. She covered the bowl once more.

"Now," the maidservant said. "If you will rise, my lady, and return to your palanquin, you will be taken to the prince's household."

Finally, they entered the Palace of Dusk.

"Good," said Gulshera, some of her tension visibly unfurling from her limbs as they were led farther through corridors of ivory. Her hands, which had been clasped so tight in front of her that the knuckles had whitened, eased their grip just enough for the skin to flush again with blood. "We are not being provided a formal audience. She has chosen to treat us as women of her household."

Arwa had not known that Gulshera was so nervous. But Gulshera had not seen the princess in years. Gulshera did not know what—if anything—had changed at court in her absence. And the cleansing had shaken her. Neither of them had expected it.

Arwa raised her head and looked around. They were, indeed, being led away from the grand hall to the left of the hallway, which Arwa caught glimpses of between a string of half-opened doors: a room large enough to encompass the hermitage whole in its palm, its floors covered in sumptuous rugs of a red richer than blood; a raised dais set high above the floor, surrounded by a corona of gems. Arwa was keenly grateful not to have been guided to that room and compelled to bow before that dais. Formal audiences were intended to intimidate, and Arwa knew she would have been appropriately overawed.

Facing a woman of the Emperor's holy blood was a daunting enough prospect on its own. Even now, as she walked down the corridor with Gulshera's steady presence at her side, Arwa's skin felt far too tight, her nervousness a sharp knife in her lungs. She could barely breathe around it. Instead she lowered her eyes, and fixed them once more on the shape of Gulshera's clasped hands.

Arwa heard music and faint laughter long before the guards-woman guided them across a threshold that led to a veranda overlooking the gardens. There was a musician by the door plucking lightly at the strings of a sitar. Beyond her were a dozen noblewomen reclining on bolster cushions, sherbet and wine set on low tables between them.

Gulshera bowed, and Arwa followed her lead. As they straightened, one of the women also rose to her feet. The room quelled to silence around her.

The woman was unusually tall, with great dark eyes and her hair bound back in an impossibly long braid, unconcealed by a shawl. When she took a step forward, moving from shadow into bare sunlight, Arwa saw that her braid was laced with diamonds. They glimmered in the light, giving her black hair the iridescence of a snake's flesh.

"Dear Gulshera," said the princess. She smiled and crossed the room, clasping Gulshera's hands in her own. Her voice was rich with feeling, sweeter than wine. "Oh, I am so glad you are returned to me!"

"Princess Jihan," Gulshera said. "You look well."

"How was your time in Numriha?"

"Cold and quiet, my lady. Very different from your fine household."

"Come," the princess said, amused. "You must have found some sort of entertainment."

"The solace of prayer," said Gulshera. "No more than that."

Arwa thought of archery and gossip and wine, and kept her mouth carefully shut.

"I have brought a companion with me," said Gulshera. She gestured at Arwa. "Lady Arwa. The young widow I told you of, my lady."

"Princess," said Arwa. She bowed her head, lowering her eyes. "I am honored by your kindness."

"Oh, she is young," Jihan said softly. She touched a cool hand to Arwa's chin, raising her head. "Where is your family, my dear?"

Arwa hesitated. "My husband had no living kin, my lady."

"Your father, then?"

"My father is in Hara, my lady."

"What is his name? His status?"

"Suren, my lady. Son of Karan." Her father's name was a simple enough answer. As for status...

She swallowed, then said: "My father was Governor of Irinah—once."

"Ah." Jihan's voice was an alto, rich and soft. She was the Emperor's daughter. No doubt she knew the history of the Governor of Irinah's fall from imperial favor. Her expression was gentle, her gaze shrewd. "And now?"

"My father has been unwell," said Arwa. "Very unwell, my lady. By the Emperor's grace, he survives. But he has been unable to restore the family's fortunes, or regain imperial favor, although he ardently desires it."

"And your mother?"

A beat. The knife in Arwa's lungs turned, slow and inexorable, bleeding the breath from her.

What could she say here—before a room of watchful noblewomen, before imperial guards and a musician, before a deferential serving girl pouring fresh wine—about her mother?

Jihan knew the truth of Arwa's blood. She had received all of Gulshera's careful letters; she had summoned Arwa on the basis of that blood alone. She knew Arwa's mother was some long-gone Amrithi woman, a barbarian who consorted with spirits and made no vows or contracts, a woman with no place in the Ambhan Empire. She knew the wife of Arwa's father was not

Arwa's birth mother, for all that she had raised her and molded her and taught her how to survive, tainted blood or no.

But Arwa could not bring herself to speak of her Amrithi mother before the women of court. She touched a finger to her lip. Lowered it. Said, "Lady Maryam. She has raised me with… great generosity and kindness."

"You have a good lineage, my dear," said Jihan. "A shame about your husband. Gulshera told me he passed away at Darez Fort. You have my most sincere sympathies."

A rustle of unease ran through the reclining noblewomen. One of them drew her shawl over her face, as if she could not bear to look at Arwa a moment longer. Jihan gazed at Arwa unwavering. Then she smiled.

"I have a mind to go for a walk, while the day is still pleasant and cool," said Jihan. "Gulshera, you may accompany me. I have missed our talks."

"Princess," Gulshera acknowledged.

"Bring your young friend," said Jihan.

A guardswoman trailed after them as they walked along the corridor. Jihan's skirt whispered against the floor as she walked, gossamer and beads trailing gently against marble.

"Walk next to me, Gulshera," said Jihan. "Let me lean on you."

Gulshera moved closer to the princess, who clasped her arm with great tenderness. Arwa trailed after them awkwardly. Her palms were damp with sweat. She felt foolishly, thrillingly anxious.

She was in the imperial palace. She was following the Emperor's daughter. She had thrown herself headlong into the service of an imperial scion without thought, without cleverness or reason, but for all her fear—for all that her skin felt tight and her lungs too small—she regretted none of it.

"A tour for you, Arwa," said Jihan. "My brother Akhtar trusts me to care for his household, and I have done my best to make it a pleasurable home. This palace does not compare to my father's, of course, but humble though it is, it is my pride."

Humble was not a word Arwa would have applied to the opulence around her, but she murmured an acknowledgment regardless. Jihan described the changes she had made in the years of Gulshera's absence: the swathes of silk to soften the austere marble of the walls; new mosaics set in the floor, deep green and turquoise. She spoke of the artisans she'd cultivated, the musicians one of her women, a niece of the Governor of Hara, had brought into her household as a gift.

She was no longer the woman new to her position and power that Gulshera had described during their journey from Numriha. Now Jihan was the established head of her brother's household, with her own retinue of noblewomen and a sharp elegance to her carriage that reminded Arwa—as if she could forget—that Jihan was the Emperor's own blood.

Her words were clearly calculated to make Arwa and Gulshera both aware of that reality. *This is my household now,* her tales said. *And here, everything is under my control.*

"He is generous, my brother, and he has improved his palace extensively at my request," Jihan finished. She looked at Gulshera. "You remember my mother's passion for pigeon breeding?"

"Yes," Gulshera said slowly. When Jihan stared at her, Gulshera shook her head. "Oh, my lady, no. They're vermin."

"Your hermitage would have benefited from its own dovecote, Aunt," Jihan said. "I know how you hate my birds, but think how much more easily we could have exchanged our letters by carrier."

"Hawking is a much more respectable hobby," said Gulshera.

Jihan laughed. "Oh, Aunt," she said fondly. "Perhaps, but it is far less useful. Come. Let me show you my brother's gift to me."

A set of winding steps led them up to the highest point of a tower. Pale-bricked, open to the sky and air, the tower was covered in miniature structures of tessellated bricks, small dovecotes with nooks for pigeons to roost in.

Arwa resisted the urge to bring her shawl to her nose. Everything smelled faintly of bird shit.

Jihan did not seem to have noticed the smell. She led Gulshera around the dovecote tower with genuine pleasure, cooing over the pigeons, expanding volubly on Akhtar's efforts to build a dovecote tower befitting his sister. She seemed to have forgotten Arwa, so Arwa took the chance to move to the tower's edge. Even the walls had nooks for the birds. One, plump and raisin-eyed, with feathers a mixture of brilliant green and ash gray, rested serenely on the edge of the wall. It didn't even rustle its feathers when Arwa leaned on the wall beside it and stared over the tower's edge.

Set on the edge of Prince Akhtar's minor palace as it was, the dovecote tower gave Arwa an unimpeded view of both the vast imperial gardens of the women's quarters and the world beyond the palace's walls. It was that great world that drew Arwa's attention. She gazed down at the fortified walls of the imperial palace and the water that lay beyond them. She stared at the city of Jah Ambha. Arwa could only stare at it in astonishment. She had never seen a city so large or so strange.

"... unrest again," Jihan was murmuring. "You were right about your Lady Roshana's nephew. His mistress claims he's too deep in his cups to collect tax revenue from Demet, no matter how well he's hoodwinked the Governor into trusting his word. I'll speak to Akhtar, and see what can be done."

Gulshera's gaze slid to Arwa, and in response Jihan went silent. Then she smiled once more.

"Ah, Arwa," she said. "We're talking of the Empire's ills—there are so many of them, my dear, too many to enumerate now." She walked toward Arwa, a kernel of pity in her voice when she next spoke. "But you will be familiar with such things."

Jihan placed a hand on Arwa's shoulder.

"I was so pleased when Gulshera offered you to me," she said, voice gentle. "The offer felt like a piece of good fortune, a change in the Empire's ill fate. You are something we can use, Arwa. I am glad to have you."

A piece of good fortune. Ah, thank the Gods.

"You and Gulshera will stay," said Jihan. It was not a request.

"Thank you, my lady," Arwa said, lowering her eyes.

"It is natural for a royal woman to care for noblewomen who do not share her blessings," murmured Jihan. "The elderly, the widowed—you will see many of them in my household, Lady Arwa. And in return for my benevolence, I am fortunate to have the wisdom of my elders, to receive their advice and guidance. Your presence here will not seem strange, I assure you. But your true purpose—well. It will not be guiding me."

There was a beat of silence. Arwa heard the soft coo of birds, the rustle of wings, as the pigeon at her side took flight.

"What will be my true purpose, my lady?" Arwa asked, still staring at the ground. "How may I serve?"

"You will assist my brother in his work," said Jihan.

"Prince Akhtar, my—?"

"His name is Zahir," Jihan cut in, voice suddenly as smooth as a blade. "And he is no prince, my dear. But you will honor and respect him regardless."

"My lady," Arwa agreed, uncomprehending.

"A guardswoman will show you the way tonight. You must be obedient, Lady Arwa. Whatever he may ask of you—think of yourself as a tool that may save the Empire, a tool my brother must utilize, and act accordingly."

Arwa murmured her agreement once more.

She felt Jihan's eyes trace her face, slow and assessing.

"You do not look very Amrithi," Jihan said finally. "Lucky girl. I think you'll do well enough."

The wing of the women's quarters set aside for elders and widows was beautifully appointed. A maidservant showed Arwa and Gulshera to a seating hall that was shared by the household elders. It opened to a small garden of fruit trees, with a fountain at its center. Gulshera and Arwa walked out into the garden. The air was full of the wafting scent of citrus and water.

"You gave this up for the hermitage," Arwa murmured, gazing around in awe.

"You think this is paradise, I suppose?"

There was a sharpness in Gulshera's voice that made Arwa bite her own tongue, holding back her reflexive retort. She waited in silence.

Eventually Gulshera sighed and rubbed her knuckles between her eyes, as if forcing a headache away.

"Court has teeth, Arwa," she said. "Teeth and claws both. Don't forget it. Allow it to do so, and court will hurt you terribly."

"You served court even from Numriha," Arwa pointed out. "You returned here willingly."

"I expect you have a point to make," said Gulshera flatly.

"Princess Jihan could have ordered you to return, and you would have done it for duty and political gain. But I don't believe you returned for that alone."

Gulshera gave her a look of exasperated pity. "Despite your widowhood, you remain a child," she said. "I returned for love, yes. Love has a longer reach than politics. It can hold you fast across any distance. But when it comes to the imperial family…

Arwa, they cannot be disentangled. Love and politics are one and the same. I returned with you for political gain, and for Jihan's affection both, because one cannot be earned without the other."

Arwa remained silent for a moment, until she could stand it no longer. She was clamoring with questions.

"The brother the princess spoke of," Arwa began tentatively. "Is he...?"

"He is a blessed," said Gulshera. "Entirely unacknowledged, of course."

A blessed. Any other child would have been called a bastard. Arwa had been, many a time. *Behave, Arwa, or people will realize you are a bastard. Please, dear one. I want better for you than your blood.*

The Emperor did not acknowledge illegitimate children. It was rare for anyone to do so. Only the Maha had ever honored them, drawing the fatherless and abandoned into his service, naming them his mystics, his closest servants. But men were not as generous as the Maha, who had forged his people an Empire. Oh, Arwa's father had acknowledged her and her sister both, loved them and honored them, but his actions had been unusual. The fate of other illegitimate children had been held over her as a warning often enough for her to know that many ended up discarded, with no father to shelter them, no mother to rear them.

Society had no place for aberrant blood.

But the Emperor's blood had greater value than any mere mortal's: To be an illegitimate Emperor's child was to have the makings of greatness. Illegitimate imperial sons had become great governors and generals. Illegitimate imperial daughters had served in the households of their legitimate sisters, or made great marriages, bringing the bright stroke of their lucky blood into many a noble family's lineage.

Still…*my brother.* Those words should not have been spoken. They were a claim Jihan had no right to make on an unacknowledged son of her father. Yet she had.

"Can you tell me anything at all about him?" Arwa asked.

"I knew him, when he was a small boy," Gulshera said. "He and his mother…" A pause. "The Empress was fond of them both. But Jihan loved the boy especially. When his mother was—removed—she claimed him and protected him."

"Removed," Arwa repeated.

"Many people were, after the Maha's death," said Gulshera. "Arwa—I do not know what the boy's work involves. I do not wish to know." Her tone brooked no argument. "Whatever he asks—obey him. That is all you can do."

Night came. Arwa could not sleep. She stayed dressed and placed her veil over her hair, readying herself to face the princess's blessed brother, a man and a stranger to her. Then she sat, cross-legged, on the edge of her divan and waited for a guardswoman to collect her, as Jihan had promised.

The room she had been provided with was in the wing for elders, but was far removed from the gentle peace of the fruit garden. Arwa understood the need for that. If she was to leave her room in secrecy and silence on a regular basis, she could not be close to the other widows, where her comings and goings would be noticed.

A guardswoman rapped lightly on the door, then entered.

"Lady Arwa," she said, bowing her head. "Follow me."

Arwa stood and followed the guardswoman from the room.

"What is your name?" Arwa asked.

"Eshara, my lady," the guardswoman said, as she led Arwa along a winding corridor, barely lit by silver lanterns upon the walls. "If you need me, I am on watch in this wing on most nights. If not me, then Reya will be here. No doubt you'll meet her tomorrow night."

The guardswoman stopped. On the wall beside her was a large tapestry. She moved it to one side, revealing a hidden door. She drew it open, and gestured for Arwa to enter. Arwa did.

CHAPTER EIGHT

The hidden door led to the gardens. Not the small, private space allotted to the widows, but the vast gardens of the women's quarters. They were laid out in the typical Ambhan style, with a long avenue of water lined on each side with lush, symmetrical diamonds of green.

Eshara did not lead Arwa near the canal. Instead she guided her to a path at the edge of the gardens, cleverly concealed beneath a canopy of trees. Dappled moonlight broke through the leaves, lighting their way.

"In the future you will walk on your own," said Eshara. "My priority is to protect the women of the house. Not to guide you in—this."

Arwa did not know what *this* was yet. So she remained silent, and did not argue.

"There," said Eshara, pointing. "You'll find him waiting."

Ahead of them stood a small building, barely visible between creeping vines. It was pale, pearly marble, with lattice walls and an arched doorway that opened on darkness. Above the door was an alcove, with a faceless effigy of the Maha and Emperor at its center. Arwa swallowed.

"That," she said, "is a tomb enclosure."

"It no longer contains a tomb," said Eshara, which did not

exactly put Arwa at her ease. "But I will leave you now, my lady," said Eshara, turning to go.

"Wait," Arwa said sharply. "He isn't—that is. He is no family to me."

Eshara continued to stare at her uncomprehending.

"I should not be alone with a man who is not my family," Arwa said slowly. "It is a matter of my honor."

"I have other duties, my lady," said Eshara. "I can't remain here with you." The guardswoman hesitated then. Her eyes darted to the enclosure, then back again. "Be careful of the steps. They are not well lit."

And with that comment, Eshara bowed her head, turned once more, and left.

Arwa stared at the darkness before her. It stared back.

Her honor did not matter—not to the guardswoman, and not to the princess. But she would not be meeting this blessed brother of Jihan's, in the dark of the night and in utter secrecy, if *someone's* honor were not at stake.

There were dangerous secrets here. Work that Arwa was required for—Arwa with her Amrithi blood. Work Gulshera did not want to think of, that Eshara did not want to witness.

Work that could, perhaps, save the Empire.

For the Empire's sake, Arwa reminded herself. She felt a familiar thrill at that thought, a fire that eased the dark weight of grief and fear pressing on her skull.

She lowered her veil and crossed the threshold.

The stairs were dark, just as Eshara had warned her they would be. But darkness soon gave way to soft light, as Arwa entered a room set low in the earth, with lanterns burning bright on the walls. The lattices, far above her head, let in the moonlight.

Arwa walked farther into the room. Much to her relief there was no sign of a tomb—the outer appearance of the building had only been an illusion, an artifice. Instead of bodies, there were only shelves upon the walls, neatly crammed with books and scrolls. If Arwa had not been able to smell green and soil, she would have believed herself to be in a scholar's library.

One quiet step farther. At the far end of the room, beneath a lattice and close to one fierce burning lantern, sat the man Arwa had been sent to meet.

He was seated at a low table with a book before him, his head rested on his knuckles as he stared down at the pages. Absorbed as he was, he hadn't yet seen her.

She savored that moment of power, standing utterly still. Assessing him.

Zahir—bastard and blessed—was thin and fine-boned. In the spill of moonlight and lantern light, gold and silver-milk, she could see the narrow bones of his wrists, revealed by the too-short cuffs of his tunic. The nape of his neck, between the sweep of his turban and the collar of his tunic was a warm ivory, pale from a lack of sunlight. She stared at it, strangely transfixed.

She had not known what to expect from Jihan's brother. But vulnerability...no, she had not expected that.

"My lord," she said. His head rose sharply, eyes wide and colorless in the dark. "I was told you were expecting me."

"Lady Arwa," he said slowly. He closed his book. "I thought Eshara would introduce you."

"She said she was busy, my lord."

"Did she." He frowned and stood. He bowed his head respectfully to her, and took a step closer through the lantern light. Knowing that her face was hidden from him beneath her veil, Arwa allowed herself to stare straight at him.

He did not look very like Jihan, this brother. Jihan was tall and dark-eyed and imposing. In contrast, Zahir was a man of insignificant height, with a face that—for all that his nose was slightly crooked, and his bones too sharp—verged on *pretty*.

When he frowned at her, she felt a tug in her chest, an attraction she was appalled and fascinated by in equal measure.

"I hear you are to be my assistant, Lady Arwa," he said.

"I gather, my lord," she replied. "Though I am not yet sure how I am intended to serve."

"What has Jihan told you?"

"Nothing, my lord. Only that I must assist you."

"Jihan likes her secrets," said Zahir. "Here is proof that she has not been especially unkind to you in particular, Lady Arwa: I know very little about you. Only that you are a widow, and that you have Amrithi blood."

"Yes, my lord."

"How did that come about?"

"The widowhood, my lord, or the Amrithi blood?"

"Both," he said. "Or either. Whichever you think more telling."

"My apologies," Arwa said in a low, deferential voice. *Be soft, Arwa, soft. Do not show him the sharp edge of your tongue. No man likes a woman who speaks in the language of knives.* "I am sorry if I have offended you, but I do not understand what you require of me."

"I am not being very clear," Zahir agreed. "It is only that I am curious about you, Lady Arwa. I am curious what sort of woman would throw herself into danger, knowing nothing of the service she has elected for herself. I wonder: Are you a faithful zealot, or simply desperate to break yourself on a cause?"

Ah. That stung.

So Arwa was not the only one with a sharp edge to her tongue, then.

Arwa had to bite her lip to hold back the words she wanted to rain down upon him. She reminded herself that it was better to apologize than to argue, better to sweeten than to sour, when faced with a man's ire. Better to let him see her wilt. Better to let him believe he had won. She had been good at such things, once.

"I think, my lord, that you mean to hurt me. I am sorry if I have done you any wrong."

"Wrong? No." He shook his head. "No, it is not the nature of what you do, but the why of it that makes me curious. Why you have made the choices you have—*that* is the source of my confusion."

"Do my answers change whether I am of use to you, my lord?"

"A fool won't suit this task," he replied. "So yes. Your answers have weight."

"I am not a fool," Arwa said, faster and more sharply than she should have.

"Fools rarely know they are fools," Zahir said levelly.

She owed him no answers. She owed him nothing of herself at all. But she had offered herself up for this task, as he had said, without knowing its dangers or its costs. If it required her honesty, her heart—

Well then.

"Do you know, my lord, of Darez Fort?"

"Somewhat," he said guardedly.

"Then I may tell you of my widowhood and Amrithi blood both," she said. "I am Ambhan raised, my lord. But my father had a concubine, once. And I was the result. My father's wife raised me as her own. She raised me to be a true noblewoman, and that is what I have been. By her training and the Emperor's grace, I married well. My husband was commander of Darez Fort, serving under the Governor of Chand. As I am sure you know, Chand was and remains rife with unrest, and my husband was famed for his success in quelling its strife."

I was proud of him, Arwa should have said. Or: *I admired him.* But neither would have been a true statement, and she did not have it in her to claim such things. So instead she said, "He died in Darez Fort. At the hands of a daiva, or something akin to it. He died as everyone in the fort died. Everyone but me."

Here, she paused to breathe. It felt appropriate. Zahir had his head tilted to her, intent on her voice. He said nothing to fill the silence, merely waited, as Arwa found her words once more.

"It is a strange grief, Lord Zahir, to live when others die, for no reason but your blood, a thing quite beyond your control. Strange and...difficult. If I were a man, I would give my grief a purpose, and to the sword. I would fight for the sake of my Empire. But I am only a widow, and I have nothing to offer beyond my blood." She held out her hand, scarred palm upraised. She wondered if he could see the new silver of her scar. "My blood is the only tool I have. Make use of it, my lord. I entreat you."

He looked at her hand. She wondered if he was noting the pale scars on her fingertips; her calluses from archery; the faint curl of her fingers toward her wounded palm. She could almost see the thoughts flickering through his eyes, swift as birds.

"I see," he said. "Thank you, Lady Arwa."

"Perhaps you still think me a fool, my lord."

"I don't know what I think of you," he said softly, slowly. His gaze was intent. He watched her lower her hand with all the focus of a hawk. "But I find I am not...averse to introducing you to my work." The frown marring his forehead eased. "You should not have offered yourself up for this task, Lady Arwa, and I should not accept your help. But I am glad you are willing and here. I believe the help of someone of your blood will be invaluable to me. Now I have the opportunity to discover whether I am correct."

"I will help you, my lord," said Arwa. "You will see."

"By the Emperor's grace." The smile that shaped his mouth was so lovely against his sharp bones.

"What will you have me do?" Arwa asked.

"Read."

He turned from her abruptly and walked over to the shelves. Tracing the spines of his books with a finger, he paused, and plucked down a slim volume. He handed it to her.

"Before you are introduced to the practical work, you need to learn. You need to understand the shape of the world and the arts we will meddle with."

"Arts?"

A pause.

"Occult arts," said Zahir. "Forbidden arts."

Arwa looked down at the book in her hands. Occult arts. Of course. She should have guessed, should have known, that any efforts to save the Empire that involved her birth mother's blood would be forbidden art. No wonder Eshara refused to enter the tomb. No wonder Zahir had hesitated before he spoke, his gaze wary and sharp.

"You speak of heresy," she whispered.

She could not imagine that any act sanctioned by the Emperor's daughter would be heresy. But she remembered her suspicion that someone's honor was at stake here, and felt a thrill of fear spill through her.

Heretics and Amrithi shared the same fate.

"Lady Arwa," he said, after another pause that had stretched long and awkward between them. "What I do—what we will do—is a necessary evil. It is necessary in order to save the Empire from its unnatural ill luck. We must seek the only knowledge that can save us. The Maha's knowledge."

Arwa clutched the book tighter.

"Does this book contain his knowledge?" she asked in a small voice.

He shook his head. "No. The book is the foundations of our work. I have made notes that may help you within."

"Notes," she repeated.

"Guidance," he added, as if that made anything clearer to her. "Consider this the start of your apprenticeship, Lady Arwa. When you have your bearings we are going to make use of your blood—and mine—together."

CHAPTER NINE

She returned to her new room long before dawn. She did not see Eshara again, but she heard her tread on the corridor floor, her armored boots producing an unmistakable clang.

The book was small, almost ephemeral in Arwa's hands. She felt as if it could easily fade to dust in her grip, as if it were barely real at all. But nothing about the night felt entirely real: the tomb that was no tomb; the not-prince reading in the shimmering lantern light; the tug of want in her, a thing that—if she were a proper noblewoman, a widow worth her salt, as she had so tried to be—should have died in her at Darez Fort.

Forbidden. That was what Zahir had called the arts she was to learn. Nothing about this path she had been set upon seemed right or proper. Any want in Arwa, even unspoken, and never acted upon, was a transgression—that, at least, was a simple truth. But Zahir's mission—his occult arts—were true heresy. In a world where the Maha and Emperor were worshipped, where their lineage were glory and solace...

No wonder Zahir's presence—and his work—were secret.

Arwa opened the book. To her surprise, it was full of poetry.

hollow are the eyes when ash is untasted / oh, beloved, my pyre knows / the shape of light born of flame—

Each poem was signed by the same author, in the same hand.

The Hidden One. A false name, certainly. But between the careful, elegant script used for poetry were neat notes in another hand. Zahir's hand.

Do not eat the ash.

She turned page after page, searching for his guidance.

Do not let go of your roots. This was heavily underlined.

Travel where the worlds break.

The answer is in—blood. (Lineage?)

His words were as cryptic as the poetry, she thought sourly. She read one final poem—*the blazing eye sees the lamp of truth / the lamp of truth reveals the world*—in a frustrated attempt to understand what on earth he wanted her to learn.

She snapped the book shut, and snuffed out her lantern.

She was already on the edge of sleep when she thought of bloodying her window. She rose from the bed and fumbled through her luggage. To her relief, her dagger was safe, still wrapped in its leather sheath. She used it to carefully mark the single latticed window to her room, before lying down once more.

She did not have the energy to keep her vigil, but she also found that her fear was curiously distant. She had fought and defeated a daiva. She had survived the journey through Numriha with nothing but a trace of blood on the palanquin wall. She could hold the daiva at bay, and no longer needed to fear discovery. That was a great weight lifted from her shoulders.

She was not safe, but this was the closest she had come since her widowhood. For now, while she was useful, a *piece of good fortune*, she could rest.

When she next opened her eyes it was hours later, but the dark was only beginning to fade from beyond her window. Her sleep had been deep, blissful, and empty of dreams. Waking left her disoriented, her mind still clouded with exhaustion. She would not have woken if she had not heard her name.

"Arwa," a voice said again. "Time to get up."

Gulshera was sitting on the edge of the bed, a cup of mint tea clasped between her hands.

"Take it," Gulshera said. "I had to ask a girl to bring me tea three times this morning." She shook her head. "They wouldn't allow me to visit the kitchens."

"Well, I'm very grateful," Arwa said honestly, and took it from her. She tried not to yawn.

The tea was lukewarm, but not unpleasant. Still, Arwa couldn't help but think of breakfast in Gulshera's room: blisteringly hot tea and warm, spiced fritters. For all the opulence of the palace, she felt as if Gulshera had lost a precious measure of freedom she would not be able to regain.

"You're well," Gulshera said shortly.

It took a moment for Arwa to realize that Gulshera's words had been a question, not a statement. She lowered her cup.

"Yes," she said. Hesitated. "Lord Zahir was—"

"Best if you don't tell me," Gulshera cut in. Her gaze was distant, firm hands clasped in her lap. "I spoke to Princess Jihan. I was...concerned. The princess informed me I should not question or interfere. So I will not."

"Questions are not exactly interference," murmured Arwa.

"Perhaps." Gulshera's mouth thinned. "But Jihan tests the people she trusts. She has asked me not to pry. So I will not. But I am...very glad that you are well, Arwa."

Arwa understood. Jihan had so clearly wanted Gulshera to know the influence she'd gained, in her absence: the changes she'd made to the Palace of Dusk, the tower her brother had built for her, in a reflection of his regard for her. Controlling what Gulshera knew was a further demonstration of her strength. It was a form of showing off, like a child demonstrating a newly learned poem or song. But Jihan was no child, and her newly honed skill lay in the hoarding of information, and with it, the hoarding of power.

What would she do to you, if you betrayed her? Failed her?

Judging by the tension in Gulshera's shoulders, Arwa did not want to know the answer, and Gulshera would not provide it anyway. So Arwa took one more sip of cooling tea, then said, "I am glad you are well too, Aunt."

Gulshera gave Arwa an unreadable look. Then she stood.

"Get dressed," she said. "We must attend on the princess. The Emperor is holding audience." She hesitated. "Jihan told me he has missed a number of audiences lately. She feels it is important her household attend his return to court in full force."

"Asima told me the Emperor had been unwell," Arwa said carefully.

"I've been assured his fever has passed." Gulshera did not sound convinced. "Asima told you, did she?"

"She did."

"Gossip travels very fast," muttered Gulshera. "Let's have no more of it now. Get dressed. The audience begins soon after dawn."

Society was held together, warp and weft, by rituals and duties. Arwa understood the nature of duty. But she had never experienced imperial ritual before, in all its grand weight, immense and heart-stopping. The rituals of her life were a mere shadow by comparison.

Once every seven days, at dawn in the imperial palace, before his audience with his nobles, the Emperor stepped on the Balcony of Beholding and showed his face to the public. An endless crowd of pilgrims—city-dwellers from Jah Ambha, travelers from the Empire's wide-flung provinces of Chand and Numriha, Hara and Irinah, even Durevi—bowed low to the ground before him. To gaze upon the Emperor's face, mortal and endlessly glorious, was a blessing beyond compare. Arwa had heard poetry about that moment: the halo of rose-gold dawn illuminating the turn of his head; the way the sun shone through the pure, unveined marble of the balcony, filling it with light.

Although he had maintained the tradition of Beholding, the Emperor's missed audiences had not gone unnoticed. The charity women of Jihan's household—the widows and elders that Arwa now belonged among—spoke about it in low, anxious whispers as they dressed. *He's well now, of course. Entirely well.* But it was his one missed Beholding, at the height of his illness, that had caused the most distress, and sent ripples of unease across the Empire.

But today, the Emperor walked to his balcony. As he was beheld, the members of his disparate satellite households assembled. The women of Prince Akhtar's palace gathered together in the audience hall Arwa had seen only yesterday, through half-opened doors. Jihan awaited them upon her dais, surrounded by her closest noblewomen. She wore a shawl over her hair; a veil was swept back from her face, ready to be lowered.

Her eyes were fierce and bright.

"Are we prepared?" she asked, gaze sweeping over her women—over noblewomen young and old. There was a murmur of assent, a lowering of eyes. Jihan smiled in response and stood. She lowered her veil, concealing her face entirely beneath a length of soft gauze.

Her retinue mirrored her and lowered their own veils with a rustle of cloth. Jihan looked down upon them for a long moment, shrouded and utterly in control.

"We go," she said.

Great doors opened before them, one by one, as they made their way from the women's quarters of Prince Akhtar's palace to one of the great bridges that joined the princely palaces to the World Palace, grand seat of the Emperor.

The dawn air was crisp and cold. Light reflected on the water beneath the bridge. Guardswomen lined their way. Ahead of them, a set of gates embellished in gold and obsidian were drawn open.

They entered the Hall of the World.

The Hall of the World was the Emperor's audience hall, and Arwa—who had spent her early years in the opulence of the Governor of Irinah's own court—had never seen a place of greater beauty. Through the intricate lattice screen that concealed everything but silhouettes of the women from the male court, Arwa could see pillars of marble, covered in bursts of inlay: flowers of emerald and carnelian, birds of lapis lazuli. The domed ceiling was lacquered in pure gold, with a sun whittled from mirrored glass in its center.

Upon the floor of the hall stood courtiers and nobles, organized in discrete clusters, intended to mimic the order of the universe: stars and planets alike, the most powerful courtiers set closest to the Emperor's seat. Hall of the World, indeed.

"Follow me," whispered Gulshera. It was an unnecessary order. Arwa would hardly have done anything else. She could barely think through her awe, only follow Gulshera as they kneeled down far behind Jihan, who sat to the left of the dais visible through the lattice. Golden, inlaid with gems carved to resemble constellations of stars, it was the Emperor's throne.

To the right, another woman kneeled, mirroring Jihan's posture. She wore an archaic style of dress: a high coned silk cap, and a voluminous robe, with a heavy sash of velvet at the waist. Her veil was long enough to pool at her waist. Her hands, lined with age, were demurely clasped and weighed down by jeweled rings.

"Princess Masuma," murmured Gulshera. "The Emperor's sister. She has been the highest lady in his household since the Empress's death."

Gulshera touched a hand to Arwa's wrist. Arwa wondered if she could feel the rush of Arwa's pulse, the sheer intensity of it.

"Be quiet and calm," Gulshera counseled. "I will direct you. Do not fear."

A conch was sounded, twice in succession. The courtiers bowed their heads as two men entered. One was slight, barely out of boyhood; the other tall and elegant, in a green embroidered jacket and a turban of silver cloth. They kneeled facing the throne.

The princes.

One, she realized, had to be Prince Akhtar. Strange to think that she belonged to his household, and yet knew nothing of him at all.

Another conch sounded. Distantly, she heard the thrum of drums. This time the courtiers did not simply bow their heads. They lowered themselves to the floor.

"He arrives," whispered one woman.

They did not bow low as the men did. Barely visible behind the lattice, their bodies blurred to soft shadow, they were free to watch the Emperor's approach.

The Emperor entered the room on foot, walking beneath a canopy of silver and gold held above his head by attendants. He had walked from the Balcony of Beholding across one of the great bridges of the imperial palace. He walked now across the Hall of the World, walked between his sons and made his way up the steps to his throne. For a single moment, his face was visible to the women who sat concealed behind him. Arwa saw a severe face, wrinkled with age. Light hazel eyes and thick brows; a thin, puckered mouth.

He is frail, thought Arwa. Even though she knew he had been, it surprised her, somehow. He had always seemed greater than flesh. Greater than time. And yet, here he was, a mere man. *Frail, and old.*

The Emperor turned and sat. At the sounding of a second conch, his courtiers rose back to their feet.

The petitions began almost immediately. This, after all, was the purpose of an audience with the Emperor: an opportunity for the nobles of the Empire to bring him their grievances and beg his favor, to argue for greater supplies or men or resources for their province, to enter into the business of politics and war that occupied all men of high stature.

The women of the imperial household were not uninvolved. Sister to the right, daughter to the left, the imperial women were carefully positioned to allow them the ability to advise the Emperor. Occasionally, Princess Masuma would consult one of the women seated around her, then lean forward and place her veiled face close to the lattice, so she could whisper in her brother's ear. Whenever she did so, the Emperor would raise a hand, instantly quelling the rest of the court to utter silence. Then, after a moment, he would speak once more.

Although Jihan's closest attendants—noblewomen of pure, powerful blood, every single one of them—whispered advice or information in her ears, she did not speak. Instead she remained still and silent. Watchful.

One minor noble, clearly nervous, petitioned for more men and funds for what he called his land's sanitation, though he did not speak of drainage or irrigation as Arwa would have expected. He spoke for some time before she understood he meant the cleansing Arwa had experienced on her arrival at the palace, on a greater scale. The Emperor directed him to consult Prince Akhtar privately for funds. Another nobleman requested an opportunity for his son in the service of the Numrihan Governor. After a protracted discussion, the next noble stepped forward to make his petition and bowed low to the floor.

"Lord of lords," he said. "King of kings. My Emperor. I beg the generosity of your household for my youngest daughter."

One of Jihan's women whispered to her once more. Arwa heard a name, a brief scrap of words. *Influential* and *fiscal*, of all things. Jihan listened for a moment, then leaned forward, her fingertips pressed lightly to the lattice.

"Father," she said. "I will accept Lord Ulegh's daughter, if Akhtar allows it."

"My daughter has kindly offered your daughter a position among her women," the Emperor stated. His voice was low and rich as velvet. Unlike his body, his voice and his mind clearly remained undimmed by time. "Akhtar, my eldest, will you allow it?"

Akhtar bowed his head.

"Emperor. Of course."

"I pray she will prove herself worthy, Most High," said the nobleman, eager and grateful.

"I am sure she will be an honor to your name," the Emperor said.

The nobleman bowed and withdrew.

The Emperor raised his hand once again, silencing the room. He made a gesture to the edge of the hall. There, a group of scribes sat, discreetly recording each of the Emperor's proclamations. One scribe stood. Bowed his head.

"Emperor."

"May special note be made," said the Emperor, "a proclamation to be shared across the city: our son Parviz returns imminently from Durevi. He has quelled all rebellion, and returns victorious, a credit to his lineage."

There was a roar of approval from the crowd. The women behind the lattice were silent; Arwa did not know if they smiled or not. Behind the quiet of her own veil, Arwa watched the way Jihan's shoulders grew tense, visible even beneath the gauzy cover of her shawl.

"His actions deserve our especial gratitude," the Emperor

continued. "And we will honor him accordingly. Feasts shall be held for both the women and men of court. Gifts and coin shall be arranged for the poor."

The Emperor continued his litany of celebration. Arwa noticed—as no doubt, did all the women—that Masuma was nodding, head close to the lattice, her fingertips gently pressed to the marble. The tension had eased from Jihan's shoulders. Now she sat still and serene, as if entirely unmoved. But Arwa had seen her control slip. She knew something tumultuous lay beneath that veneer of calm.

The thought of feasting and gifts had cheered the crowd, who were effusive in their response, a roar of approval filling the chamber. Prince Nasir cheered with them, but Prince Akhtar sat still and tall and merely smiled—a strange, formal smile that did not suggest any real joy.

It was only when the Emperor rose once more to his feet that silence fell. Every noise and every man in the hall moved to his whims like the tide beneath the moon.

Arwa's own breath had caught in her throat. The tide controlled her too.

As the Emperor departed the Hall of the World, the men bowed. The women lowered their veiled heads. One heartbeat. Two.

A conch sounded.

The women stood as one and exited the hall. Princess Masuma's entourage crossed to another door. Jihan and Masuma did not speak—did not even look at one another.

They crossed the bridge. Arwa touched her hand to Gulshera's sleeve. She realized she was trembling, faintly.

Ah, Gods. She had seen the *Emperor*.

"It has been some time since I have belonged to the world," Arwa murmured, forcing the words from numb lips. "But I believe open rebellion in Durevi was quashed in the first year of my marriage. Certainly, my husband was pleased to receive greater funds for provisions, as a result of the spoils."

"It was," said Gulshera.

"Prince Parviz has chosen an interesting time to return." In her head, she calculated how long it would have taken for the news of his father's illness to reach him, and his own journey across the Empire to progress. The timing was clear enough.

"Indeed he has." Gulshera's voice was grim.

Jihan had not been happy. Of course she had not. She was the head of her brother Akhtar's household, as her aunt Masuma was the head of the Emperor's. A woman's fortunes rose and fell with the fate of the man she served. And for all that Prince Akhtar held a clear position of power at court, the Emperor had not yet named him heir. *That*, Arwa would have heard.

If Prince Parviz believed the Emperor's health failed, if he returned in the hope of being named heir himself . . .

A woman like Jihan, who reveled in her power, would rightly fear to lose it.

Jihan's tension was only one of the events that had filled Arwa with disquiet, since she had arrived at the palace. The rift between aunt and niece; the blessed not-prince hidden like the dead; the distant son quelling rebellions, as the two close at hand kneeled at their father's feet, all of them waiting for the Emperor to anoint them as heir. The loyalties that ran like blood, holding the imperial household asunder and yet intertwined. These things hung in the air, unspoken, knife-edged. Arwa had known the Empire suffered, but she had thought—believed, with the constancy of a woman who had prayed her whole life to the Emperor's effigy—that court would be a bastion of stability within the Empire's chaos. Instead, she was strangely afraid a misplaced word would tip it all into chaos. She drew back her veil, as Gulshera drew back her own. Gulshera's jaw was tight.

"Arwa—"

"Lady Gulshera." One of Jihan's favored noblewomen approached, veil thrown back. "The princess requires you. Please."

"Of course," said Gulshera. She squeezed Arwa's arm—in comfort or warning, Arwa did not know—and vanished, leaving Arwa alone in a crowd of elders, her mind full of questions without answers.

CHAPTER TEN

A different guardswoman walked the corridors that night, when Arwa left her room, book of poetry in hand, and headed toward the gardens. Arwa remembered that Eshara had told her a guardswoman named Reya would be on duty that night, and bowed her head in acknowledgment.

Reya bowed her head in return.

"My lady," she said, voice soft. "Do you need me to accompany you?"

Arwa shook her head, murmured her thanks, and continued walking. Behind her was a brief silence, followed by the renewed stride of booted feet.

Arwa walked through the night to the tomb enclosure; she lowered her veil and walked in. Zahir was waiting for her.

"Did you enjoy the book?" he asked.

"Somewhat," she said guardedly. "I had very little time to read. There was an audience at dawn."

"Ah," he said. "Of course."

She wondered when he slept. Certainly not at night. Did he live here, within the women's quarters, hidden away within the walls of the tomb enclosure? She was filled again with the sense of unreality she'd felt when she'd read the book of poetry in her own room by lantern light. He should not have been here. He should not have been staring at her, eyebrows raised, waiting for her to speak—as if he were a real man, and not some strange mirage enclosed in what should have been a grave. He should not have been in the women's quarters—even their grounds— at all.

"Prince Parviz is returning from Durevi," Arwa continued.

"Indeed," Zahir said neutrally. "What did you think of what you *did* read, Lady Arwa?"

Arwa considered the not-prince carefully through the soft haze of her veil. There was no irritation on his face, no fear or tension or anger. His expression was utterly calm.

"The poems were—beautiful," she said haltingly. "But I don't believe I fully understood them, or your words, my lord."

"Well then. Let me provide you more context. Sit, please," he said, gesturing at the low table where she had first seen him reading, only the night before.

She sat. There was a tray on the table, something brewing in a small samovar. Tea had already been poured into small ceramic cups, curls of steam rising from the liquid's surface.

As she waited for him to join her, she opened the book of poetry once more. The words wavered before her, softened by the gauze of her veil and the fragile shimmer of lantern light. She gave up on the book. Instead she watched him trace the edge of his shelves with searching fingertips, his eyes narrowed against the flickering dark. Eventually she could not suppress her impatience; she shifted uneasily in her seat. Spoke.

"It would be easier, perhaps, to work by daylight." A beat. "My lord."

"Yes," said Zahir, which was no response at all. He looked at her then, fingers paused upon the shelf. "But I doubt your veil helps your vision."

"I will not remove it," Arwa said swiftly. "I will not compromise my honor."

"I have not asked you to," he said, just as swiftly.

He crossed the room and placed a new book in front of her. This one was far larger than the thin book of poetry still in her hands. She placed her poetry carefully to the side. She opened the new tome. The pages were heavy in her hands.

"The next page," said Zahir. "Please, Lady Arwa."

Arwa turned the page. Her breath stopped.

In front of her was a lustrous image, so heavy with color and detail that it near breathed with its own life: a world carved into fragments by a great chariot wheel, spoked and lacquered in gold. Between the first set of spokes sat a familiar world, of lush forests and white-blue mountains and pale gold desert. Between the next set of spokes, tangled with the edges of the desert...

"It is—"

"A storm," whispered Arwa. "Dreamfire."

She propped the book against the table. She traced the pages with her eyes, hungry, her heart wild and seething in her chest. Flames burnished across a desert sky. Flames of rose and indigo and umber.

"I saw dreamfire in Irinah," she murmured. "When I was a small girl."

He looked startled for a moment. Then his expression smoothed.

"Of course. You grew up in Irinah."

"Yes."

She had watched the dreamfire from her bedroom window, once, as a girl of only nine. Not long before her mother had spirited her away to Hara.

But ah, she'd been so *young*. Her heart had turned so easily then, liquid, easily biddable. At first she'd been afraid of the dreamfire—terrified, in fact. But then she had stared at it, night long, through her window lattice. And those flames...

Well, to claim she had become less afraid would have been false. But the terror had alchemized with time: sharpened to a joy all the sweeter and deeper for the fear. She had felt something akin to it, when she had chased a daiva and embedded a bloodied dagger into its flesh. When she had offered herself up for this task, unknowing and uncaring about her unknowingness, the bitterness of blood on her tongue.

"I cannot describe it," said Arwa. *You would think me mad. Monstrous.* "I am no poet, my lord. It was a sight that marked me, but I did not understand what it was. I still do not." She stared, longer, at the image before her. "I have long considered it a part of the cursed nature of Irinah's desert."

"Cursed?"

She looked at him. His head was slightly tilted, his eyes intent.

Ah. It was a real question.

"Where else," she said slowly, "has daiva and Amrithi both, and storms of fire—and is the site of the Maha's death?"

"The Maha could only die in one place. But as to the rest..."

She had no time to consider whether he was calling her a fool—*the Maha could only die in one place?* Ah, Gods, how barbed this boy was—before he leaned forward, across the cups of steaming tea, and touched one long finger to the turn of the wheel.

"This wheel is a representation—one theory alone—of the shape of reality." He touched a fingertip lightly to the forests and deserts, nestled between the spokes, emerald green and dusty gold. "Here lies the world in which we live. A world of flesh and blood." His finger moved from the green and gold of the forest to the deep blue and rose of the storm. "And here, where you see the dreamfire, lies the realm of where the Gods sleep, dreaming our world into being.

"Dreamfire is a sign of Irinah's nature, but not a sign that the desert is cursed, Lady Arwa. Instead, it reveals that Irinah is a threshold, a bridge where our two worlds touch. The world of their sleep and the world of our waking. The Gods dream..." He touched the spoke of the wheel that held their world and the one of the Gods apart. "And in Irinah, mortals have the honor of beholding it."

"I did not know," Arwa whispered. "Any of it."

"You had no reason to know heresy."

The illustration contained within the next spokes of the wheel was drab, a spill of gray-black ink. But...

Arwa looked at it more closely. Between clouds of gray and black were figures of whittled bone. She felt suddenly quite cold.

"And this?" she asked. She touched her own fingers lightly to the darkness, then drew them back. "What place is this?"

"The realm of ash," he said. "And the locus of our study."

He traced the place upon the page where the dreamfire and desert merged with a fingertip once more, voice soft and liquid with reverence. "Just as the Gods dream in another realm, so do mortals. We enter it naturally, in sleep. It is a shadow place. It lives in our dreams. In the quiet of our minds. It is a place both of flesh and beyond flesh."

"And what lies in this place, this realm of ash?" Arwa asked.

"The dead," he said.

She thought of her sister. She thought of Darez Fort. She thought of Kamran, her husband, and the taste of iron rose in her mouth.

"Ah," she whispered. She could not say anything else.

"I'm sorry," he said, voice softer now, in a mimicry of her own. "I should be more precise. It is not the dead that lie in the realm, but echoes of their dreams, their memories, their knowledge. Their ash." He tapped the spoke of the wheel where the mortal world met darkness. "Sleep is a bridge of a kind. Just as the dreams of the Gods touch the world in Irinah, molding it, in sleep the dreams of our ancestors shape us.

"There were ancient mystical orders—orders that existed long before mystics joined the service of the Maha—who carefully studied what could be found in the realm, and through their study, they discovered that if one can enter the realm conscious, in a waking dream...a mortal can access the knowledge of their ancestors, the accumulated knowledge of all their dead." A beat. "You must see, my lady, the great value of that."

In that moment she could not. Her thoughts were a hum like a hive of insects in her skull.

"How can you know this?" she asked faintly.

"I am a scholar," he said. "I have many, many books."

"Please," said Arwa. "My lord, do not mock me."

"I don't," he said with a frown. "I really do have many books. Few are so lucky. You cannot gain knowledge of a thing without sources of information to shape your study."

For a man who had seen through her like paper on their first meeting and focused his occult studies upon the nature of reality and the soul, he was distressingly literal. There was an exactness to him that made his whole nature an indiscriminate blade that cut deep through the surface to the bone truth of things: be it to the truth of a widow's furious heart seeking martyrdom, or the dull necessities of scholarship.

There was a pulse beating fiercely in her jaw. She ground down her teeth hard, then forced the tension to loosen so that she could pry her own words from her lips.

"Your books—they have truly led you to believe that we are no more than soil shaped by the dead? You have placed your faith in a great heresy, my lord. Our souls are in the keeping of the Maha and Emperor. Their nature is not our concern beyond that. We must have faith, and think no further on that matter."

"I know," he said. His voice low, soft. A liquid thing. "I know, Lady Arwa. I do not forget it. But I take comfort in knowing my faith remains with the Maha and my Emperor father still. It is not faith that guides me in this. Dozens—thousands—of mystics before me studied the realm and theorized upon it, and tested their theories, then tested them again for good measure, until they could say with some assurance that this is the truth: We are shaped in part by the dreams of the dead, molded by an echo of their griefs and joys and pain. Whatever I may believe, Lady Arwa, whatever the shape of my faith, I *know* this. As far as anyone may know a thing. And if my knowing is at odds with my faith—well. I accept that burden."

His voice was lilting, compelling. Given enough time, he could perhaps convince her this knowledge was no evil thing, but a force entirely separate from the powerful strictures of faith.

Arwa wanted to be convinced. More fool her.

Instead she shook her head. Leaned back from the table, and clasped her hands before her.

"Even the smallest application of reason would shatter the distinction you have made, my lord, between faith and knowing. But it was kind of you to seek to assuage the fears of this humble widow. Although I abhor it, I will face heresy with you, my lord. For the Empire's sake, as I told you when we first met."

"Perhaps it is not your fears I seek to ease," murmured Zahir. He smiled to himself—a small, curiously bitter curl of his lips. Then he said, "I am the Emperor's blood and through him, the Maha's also. His knowledge was fathomless, his power endless. His death was our ruin."

Arwa nodded. She did not doubt it. The Maha had founded the Empire. The Maha lived for centuries and brought the Empire its glory, its fortune, its God-touched blessed status. Everything had been lost, upon his death.

"If I can walk the realm of ash," Zahir continued. "If I can sift through countless generations of my blood and find the Maha's ash, I can access the Maha's centuries of memories. Perhaps I can find the knowledge to save us all. I can only hope, Lady Arwa."

Arwa closed her eyes. The effigy of the Maha and the Emperor loomed beneath the closed lids of her eyes, a spill of faceless white against ink dark.

"When you walk upon the path of ash, child of my blood, you walk upon your ghosts / Do not look where you tread / My dreams will feed you grief as honey."

Zahir looked startled.

"You read the book after all."

"I may have little knowledge of heresy, my lord, but I am not uneducated. I often assisted my husband in his work; a good memory was a necessary tool for me to cultivate."

"Tell me what you remember of my notes."

"Do not eat the ash. Something of roots."

"Do not let go of your roots," he corrected.

There was so much she could *not* do, it seemed, and very little instruction as to what she could.

"You also wrote of blood carrying answers," Arwa said. "I understand that now, I think."

"I learned my first lessons of the realm from that book," he said. "The poetry was intended to capture the feel, the sensation of the realm, by those who had walked it. My notes were intended as clarification."

"I did not understand them, my lord." She had intended her words to sound like an apology. Instead, they came out hard, as a kind of challenge. His gaze fixed upon her clasped hands, as if he could read something of her feelings in them; then, once more, he raised his head to her veiled face.

"You will when we enter the realm," he promised. "But you must remember those lessons, when we proceed. And you must obey my instructions, as any apprentice would, for the safety of both of us."

"Why do you need me at all, my lord? You have the knowledge of mystics. You have your own blood. What need have you of mine?"

"The bridge of sleep is a fragile one. With it, we can only travel so far into the realm of our dead. To reach the Maha's ash I need a greater bridge. And your blood..." He hesitated. "I have a theory, concerning your blood, and its power. But I require your willing assistance within the realm to test it."

She thought of worlds—realms—bound together. She thought of daiva, and of her own nightmares—of the dangers that haunted her nights and her blood both.

She thought of being useful.

"You know you have it," she said. "Anything for the Empire."

He nodded in acknowledgment.

"Enough for tonight," he said. "You cannot take this book with you, but I have one which contains a fair copy of the wheel. Let me retrieve it for you, and you may leave."

He stood, and lifted the book from the table, closing it gently and returning it to the shelves.

It would have been sensible to leave, as he had offered. Sensible to feel more than foreboding. Zahir had upended her understanding of the world, and made ghosts rise within her heart. She should have abhorred the heresy of the evening, and approached the task he offered her with dutiful reluctance. She should have been afraid.

And she was afraid. She was.

"Show me," she whispered. There was a thrill running through her blood. It felt like holding a bow. Like piercing a daiva's skin. Fear and joy both, tangled together as wholly as soul and flesh. "Show me this realm. Show me how I can help you, Lord Zahir."

He gave her a sidelong look.

"I thought you would want time to consider what I have told you."

"No, my lord. I do not."

There was a pause. His face was in shadow.

"I suppose that isn't your way," he said finally. "But it isn't a simple task, Lady Arwa. I have tried to enter the realm of ash before. On my own, and with a tutor, when I was a boy. It was a fraught experience. It is not... entirely safe. I cannot promise this will be pleasant for you."

"I understand," said Arwa. "Still, I am prepared."

"You are not prepared. It is impossible to be truly prepared."

"Nonetheless, my lord, I am ready." She filled her voice with certainty, iron and sure. "I promise you. Please."

She thought he would dismiss her plea outright. Despite the hungry beat of her heart, she expected it. But he did not. He was silent. He stepped toward her once more, lantern light on his face. His eyes were narrowed. He was looking, she realized, at her hands once again, which were pressed flat to the table, fingers fanned out and pressed hard into the grooves within the wood.

"Well then," he said. "What can I say? Follow me, Lady Arwa. Please, bring the tea."

She balanced the tray carefully in her hands, as she followed him from his ill-lit library to the second room of the enclosure.

Tomb enclosures were often multichambered, built to accommodate entire departed families beneath the press of the earth. This room was smaller than the first, and equally empty of the dead. Arwa counted that as a blessing. Its ceiling was partially open at its center, perforated by a circular grate that was visibly stained with soot. Beneath it sat a fire vessel: a deep high-walled container of blackened copper, used for holding flame.

On one side of the grate was bedding. There was a pile of

books by its side. They were not scattered on the floor—that would have been utterly disrespectful—but were neatly set on a wooden book rest, its two feet holding the books safely away from the earth. Arwa spied ink also, and a scrap of paper, covered in words she could not read from a distance in the weak light.

That answered the question, at least, of where Zahir slept.

As Arwa watched, Zahir lifted a blanket—thin, soft cotton— from the bedding and took it to the opposite end of the room. He laid it out upon the ground. Then he kneeled by the vessel at the center of the room and began preparing a fire.

"Place the tea wherever you like," he said. "And sit. Please."

Arwa placed the tray upon the floor and—after a moment of hesitation—sat on the blanket cross-legged. Closer now, she could see that the vessel was marked with symbols so old and faded that they were nearly unreadable.

Zahir filled the vessel with fuel: wood and clarified butter and resinous, sweet perfume.

"To enter the realm of ash consciously, scholars realized that they need a bridge akin to Irinah. In order to widen the bridge of sleep, we use these." He gestured at the wood, the resin, the perfume, then began to set it alight. "All of this has been sourced from Irinah because it is—hopefully—imbued with some of Irinah's nature."

"And the fire?" Arwa asked. "What is its purpose?"

"Why do we have prayer flames?" Zahir asked. "Fire is power. It is a light in the dark. It is alchemy, turning one thing to another, a bridge between states. The old orders utilized it. *My pyre knows / the shape of light born from flame / the lamp in the dark / the lamp of truth.*"

"The Hidden One was a mystic, then?"

"It was a shared moniker. But of course." Hint of a smile around his mouth. "A very fine one."

He murmured a soft prayer as the flames grew.

He was still tending to the flames. Adding wood to the fire. Arwa could feel the heat of those flames. Beneath her veil, her face was warm.

"The bridge that this ritual offers is still narrow," he added, eventually. "And I've long considered what other theories to put to the test. Some books speak of the power of graveyards and how consumption of the bodies of the dead can build a bridge. Others speak of intense meditation, of fasting until the body is near death. And some speak of the Amrithi: of blood that is shaped by the Gods, by Irinah and by the mortal world. A natural—and powerful—bridge. I would have tested any theory. But there you were, in my sister's grasp. And now you are here." A beat. "Though I must say I am relieved to avoid cannibalism."

"I imagine you are," Arwa said, pushing away an all too familiar nausea.

Her Amrithi blood. She had taught herself not to be Amrithi in any way beyond her blood, which could not be altered. She had assured Gulshera that she was not. And yet she had yearned as a foolish girl to be the Amrithi woman she was not allowed to be. She knew exactly the shape of that shadow Arwa who had never been allowed to live: knew her fierceness, her hunger, her magic. And she carried a tangle of memories too, sharp within her as a shard of glass: a memory of her sister dancing an Amrithi rite, her feet whispering against marble; a memory of a gold-eyed daiva, sitting upon Arwa's windowsill; a fresher nightmare, of a daiva taking her trembling hand. Just...

"What must I do with my blood?"

He drew a blade from his sash and offered it to her, hilt first.

"Your blood must enter the fire. A drop will do."

"Is the blade clean?"

"Yes."

She took the blade from him.

"Blood is a sacrifice I am familiar with providing." She made a swift cut. With great care, she held her thumb over the fire vessel and allowed a bead of blood to fall.

Zahir looked at her briefly. Said nothing. She handed him the dagger, and he added his own sacrifice to the fire vessel, making a shallow cut to the turn of his wrist and holding it close to the flame.

"By combining our blood, we enter the realm together," he explained, in response to her questioning look.

"And now?"

"The tea contains opium," he told her. "It will help you sleep, if you require it. I am sorry you do not have a more comfortable place to rest."

"It's no trouble," she said swiftly. She was glad he had not offered his own bed, and did not want him to consider doing so. It felt far too intimate.

Tired as she was, Arwa knew she and sleep were not always on the best of terms. She adjusted her veil and drank the tea. Then she lowered the cup back to the tray. Zahir did the same.

They both lay down at opposite ends of the room. It took a long moment for the haze of the opium to settle over her. Arwa curled and uncurled her fingers. She had never tried to sleep with her veil on, and its weight—combined with the smoke of the fire—was distinctly uncomfortable.

"What was it like," she asked Zahir, attempting to distract herself, "when you last attempted to enter the realm?"

"Beyond words," he said softly. There was a slur to his speech that had not been there before. He was lying flat, staring at the ceiling. "I am glad you are here, Lady Arwa. The realm shouldn't be entered alone."

She turned away from him. She could not say she was glad in return. It was death that had brought her here, after all.

"Promise me something, Lady Arwa."

His voice came out of the smoke and dark. She breathed in the sound of it.

"Yes."

She felt strange. The moon was black. The fire burning.

"Please. If you forget all the rest: Do not let go of your roots."

CHAPTER ELEVEN

Arwa closed her eyes. Opened them.

A strange sensation came over her: a sense of being split in two halves, when she had previously been one whole creature. In the place where her body slept, wreathed in perfumed smoke beneath moonlight, her eyes remained stubbornly closed, weighed down by laced tea and sleep.

In the realm of ash her eyes opened. Her soul—a thing she had never been conscious of—gazed out at the realm of ash with eyes it should not have had. Sucked in a breath with the mirage of lungs. And yet her soul's eyes, its skin, felt *real*, and the sense of doubleness, of being two instead of one, was disorienting beyond belief.

It took her a moment to see through her internal turmoil to the world around her. Around her there was no sign of the tomb enclosure where her flesh slept. There was no ornate garden. No sky above her. There was only a storm. It was no storm of dreamfire, but a whirl of gray and white, ash and the bitterest snow. Carefully, she rose up on her elbows.

Ah. Her elbows.

With fascination and dread both, she stared down at her own arms. Her skin, here, was not a sand-warm brown. Instead it had no color at all. Clear as glass, faceted by the curl of her fingers and the jut of her elbows and wrists, it gleamed. She thought absurdly of the marble of the palace, so pure that light could pour through it nearly unhindered.

When she pressed her hand to the ground in an effort to raise herself up, something moved beneath her. A sudden burst of flowering red. It coiled around her wrist. When dread overtook fascination, when she tried to wrench herself free, she felt the strangest sensation: a sharp racing of her body's heart. An intake of breath from her body's lungs.

Ah. This is terrible, Arwa thought, squeezing her eyes shut. Opening them again. She was still split in two, no more awake or unconscious than she had been moments before.

"Lady Arwa." Zahir's voice. An echo through the storm. She turned to the sound of him. Saw him: a blurred figure, like a shadow distorted by water, kneeling upon the ground a fair distance from her. "Please. Be calm. Sit up slowly. Don't stand yet."

She had told him she would obey him. She did so, clambering up onto her knees. The red, wisps as fine as a string of rubies, or a weft of lace, followed the rise of her hands and her arms. Like an infant prone to mouth anything, poison or sweet alike, she touched the back of her wrist to her mouth, and tasted bitterness and grief. The blood of memory.

"The red," his voice said urgently, "is your roots. The bond between you and your flesh. Don't try to remove yourself from it."

Arwa shuddered and lowered her arm.

"What would happen," she replied, "if I did?"

"Nothing positive, my lady."

"You should have warned me," she said. "Of the roots, and— my skin, it—"

"I warned you not to let go of them."

"More context would have been helpful," she gritted out.

"I'll remember that in the future."

She saw his shadow stand, and mimicked him, drawing herself to her feet. The roots spun about her fingers and her ankles, gossamer but unyielding. She did not think she would have been able to pull free from them, even if she had tried.

"I am sorry." Zahir's voice once more. It had the sound of real regret in it—and awe, also. "In truth, I didn't expect this. I did not think we would have so much time. You must understand, when I entered briefly in the past I was aware for mere minutes at most. It was...vaguer. Hazier. You have made this place *whole*, Lady Arwa. Your blood has accomplished a miracle."

She looked about her, at the howling lightless wind surrounding her, shapeless and ragged. *Whole* and *miracle* did not entirely seem to apply.

"And what of the storm?" asked Arwa. "I am not sure I can move through it."

"Ah," said Zahir. There was a moment of silence. Then he said, "I assume you can see no forest?"

"What?"

"One moment," he replied.

Arwa watched his shadow grow closer. As he drew near her, the liquid blur of him solidified. There was a moment when the air seemed to—rip—and then Zahir was through the storm, holding a hand out to her, his gaze clear in a face of hewn glass. He was unworldly and strange, roots wound about his arms, and yet the most familiar thing she had seen so far. She took his hand without complaint, and if she gripped him far too tight, he was kind enough not to say so.

"Thank you," he said, exhaling as her grip tightened. Perhaps he, too, was grateful for the familiar.

He looked around, the facets of his face—sharp as mirrorglass—narrowing with consideration.

"If you enter the realm naturally, you can only walk your own path. Mystical orders used to enter the realm together in order to allow exploration of a richer landscape than offered by their own blood. This storm is part of your path. Your realm of ash, shaped by your own dreams and those of your ancestors. My path is—rather different."

"If you must seek the Maha, then I imagine you need to return to it," said Arwa.

She did not say, *Please don't leave me here.* She was no green girl, to be afraid of the howling of her own heart. But when he said, "Come with me," she was relieved regardless.

"Tell me what to be aware of," she said. "My lord, now would be an ideal time to give your guidance context."

"We will be moving farther and farther from the mortal realm," he said promptly. "Losing your grip upon your roots means you may lose yourself here. But—you're familiar with grave-tokens? The weaving of them?"

"Yes."

"When you wind the green together, you gain a stronger material. When you wind blood roots together, mine to yours, they hold you faster to your flesh."

Her distant lungs inhaled. Exhaled.

"Show me," she said.

His hand moved around her own.

As she watched, their roots coiled together about their joined hands. Winding into a whole, like coils of rope or strands of vegetation lashed together to make a stronger whole. Just as he'd told her.

She did not ask him what greater numbers provided protection from. Howling, strange, laden with the dead—a better question would have been to ask what *was* safe within this realm. Instead she said, "Show me the way, my lord. I am your obedient apprentice."

They walked. She felt a moment of dizziness, as if her roots were trying to hold her fast. She felt the tug of another time and place: of lungs rising and falling, of a heart racing. Her body. That was her body.

Abruptly the storm faded. They were beyond the barrier that had previously separated their paths. Here, trees rose around the both of them. Great leaves the color of bird wings; ashen roots and trees, tangling with the ruby gleam of his own roots.

Arwa looked back. Her roots formed an equally tangled path behind her. Body and soul still bound together. She shuddered again, and looked away.

He was looking at her.

"I would like to continue, Lady Arwa." There was hesitation in his voice, in the clouded marble of his eyes. "But if you wish to turn back, try again on another occasion..."

Arwa shook her head. She did not allow herself to think of an alternative. To consider fear, when adventure lay before her.

"Although I wish you had *warned* me, my lord, I want to continue."

He nodded.

"Don't let go," he said. "Please."

"I won't," she told him.

They walked farther. There was no sound but their own voices. Not even breath. Where her—*path*, he had called it—had been all wildness and fury, his was a deathly place, thick with its own growth and silence. In slivers, she saw more trees hidden by the skeletons of the closest: great old banyans, peepal and ashoka, all of them ink dark, incongruously entwined. And between them...

People, she thought. *Those are people.*

She stumbled, and felt her heart again, a dreamlike flutter. He gripped her hand tighter.

"What happened?" he asked, eyes wide.

It was only then—curse it—that she realized he was meeting her eyes. That he was looking at her bare of any veil—bare of even the protective carapace of her own body. If she looked anything like he did, she resembled herself, but was more glass than woman, more shadow and marble than skin. Still, it was not to be borne.

"Do not look at my face," she snapped.

He lowered his eyes sharply.

"I—"

"Please," she said. "No apologies. Explain the people. Among the trees."

He hesitated. Thinking of his books, no doubt. Searching for answers experience could not give him.

"Most likely my dead," he said. "On your path, you have your own."

"Will you look for the Maha among them?"

"He will be far deeper in the realm," he said. "Not here. Not so close."

As they walked, the path and the forest around them began to change. The trees grew lush, then withered once more. Shadowy figures moved closer, fingers curled around branches, eyes lambent—and then vanished entirely, behind a mist so thick that it burnished the air a blinding white.

They finally stopped when their path—Zahir's path—was barred. The trees had formed together before them into an arch. Beyond it lay no forest. Instead the ground beyond the arch was covered in a sumptuous carpet, heavily embellished with birds and flowers, but curiously devoid of the rich colors Arwa would have expected of such an artful masterpiece. But there was barely any color here, and the floor was as much a mirage of ash as everything else that surrounded them.

Zahir stared ahead. He did not move.

"Tests," he said slowly. "Everything must be tested. The Maha is not here, not in this place, but I believe another ancestor's memory lies beyond the bough." There was a pause.

"Somewhere my heart is beating very quickly. Do you feel the same, Lady Arwa?"

"Of course," she whispered. "How could I not?"

"Of course," he echoed. He looked at their joined hands. "Two ropes twined together are harder to break than one," he said. She had the sense he was repeating the claim for confidence. "Together, we are less likely to lose ourselves to the path. Lady Arwa, no matter what you see, do not let go of me."

"What will I see?"

He frowned, the expression forming a luminous crescent on the glass of his brow.

"I don't know."

"Ah. Well then, my lord. I suppose we learn together."

Without allowing herself another thought, she stepped over the threshold, drawing Zahir with her.

They were in a room surrounded by lattice and silk, shawl discarded in a heap of silver embroidery upon the floor cushions. A large divan stood at the room's center, strewn with pillows. Flowers sat in bowls of water, to sweeten the air.

"This is not a man's room, I think, my lord," said Arwa.

"No." Zahir was looking up, a waver in his voice. Arwa followed his eyes.

The ceiling was covered in stars, tessellated silver-gold. Cloth, she realized, had been pinned to the domed roof, giving the large chamber unusual warmth and intimacy. As Arwa watched, the stars wavered. Moved.

"Are they—?"

"An aspect of dreaming," said Zahir. "Nothing remains exactly as it should. We do not dream perfectly, as Gods do."

He stepped forward. Once. Twice.

"She is by the window," he said softly. "Come."

Across the room stood the silhouette of a woman. Arwa could

not think of her as a woman whole. Even from here, the absences were apparent: no fully formed legs, to shape the hollow curl of her skirt; no face upon that turned head. Her skin was nothing but ash. She was a barely real thing, a scrap of memory carved into limbs and the turn of a head, a soft fall of ash-white hair, bound into a thin braid.

Zahir moved closer to her first—held a hand out toward her, his roots strange and bright, his eyes hollows of feeling.

She heard him whisper a prayer, a mantra spoken at funerals, with grief and love for the dead. Then he curled his fingers, touched a hand to the woman's ash—and shattered her.

No more woman. Just ash—great gouts of it, swirling about Zahir, about the both of them. Arwa yelped and gripped Zahir tighter. Somewhere, distantly, her jaw was grinding, her hands balling into fists as she slept. But here she only held on to him as the ash surrounded his head in a corona, as ash seeped into his eyes and his ears, as it filled his mouth, consuming him.

Do not eat the ash.

So he had written and yet he was consuming it now, before her eyes. Suddenly, his soul's skin was burnished with the luster of embers still hot from the fire, of ashes cooling to chalk and amber. Suddenly Arwa's own head was full of facets of memory, as fragmented as her own unnatural skin. Her hand (*not her hand*) holding a needle, fine muslin upon her lap; her grandson (*not her, not her*) pressing his cheek to her knee.

Arwa cursed, revolted, but did not let go, even as the smoke of strange memories coiled around her own head. She felt the distant shudder of her own body, turning upon the ground; smoke in her true lungs, as the fire in its vessel began to gutter and die.

In the realm of ash, Zahir turned his gaze upon her face once more. Holding her hand, he turned to the roots tangled between them, turned and *wrenched*—

Arwa woke. She scrambled onto her elbows, back bowed, turned her head to the side, pushing her veil askew so she could breathe, simply breathe, great gouts of true air, barely tainted by fire. Her eyes were wet.

She could hear Zahir retching.

"What was that?" she asked him. "What did you do?"

His hands on stone. The sound of his palms sliding. She drew her veil back into place. Turned her head to look at him. His head was pressed to the ground, the back of his tunic damp with sweat.

"I remember." His voice a gasp. "Cold grapes in a silver bowl, and learning to taste citrus and salt. I remember—the fine bone needle, my favorite—*her* favorite—I remember—I am not myself. I...who am I?"

She did not choose to stand up. It was simply a thing that happened. The same was true of the way her hand found its way to his jaw, drawing his face up to the moonlight seeping through the grate.

"Lord Zahir. What do you need?"

He blinked hard. Some semblance of awareness returned to his eyes. "Water," he forced out. "There is a carafe. By the second shelf. Other room."

Thank the Emperor's grace that the room was orderly. She found the carafe and returned to his side. Kneeling by him, she offered him the water, which he took with trembling hands. He drank it fast, gratefully, then lowered the carafe to the ground.

"I apologize. That was a great deal...*more*. Than I expected."

"I gathered," Arwa said. "As your apprentice, I am going to require access to your other books. I don't enjoy being so surprised, my lord."

"Anything," said Zahir. He sat up carefully, with a wince.

"You wrote that the ash should not be eaten, my lord."

"You should not consume it certainly. Gods be thanked, you

have no cause to do so. To access an ancestor's knowledge, to eat their ash...it is not an act without price. It's a dangerous thing, Lady Arwa. It can consume you whole, if you are not tethered to the strength of your roots." A faint smile. "Or so I have gathered."

"From your books."

"Partly. And also from our experiment today. Sometimes books have curious gaps. Theories are flawed. I have not been able to consume ash before, Lady Arwa. Not when I entered with a tutor. Not when I entered alone. But with your help..." His voice faded. Faraway eyes. "We accomplished so much. I believe we can seek the Maha's ash after all. My hope finally has flesh."

Arwa closed her eyes. In the dark she saw it again: a place entirely strange. A place where she felt as if her very nature had been flayed open, exposing more than her heart or her skin to the light.

She thought of the Empire. Of the Maha and Emperor. Of a long tradition of order and faith and adherence of standards of civilization. Standards that defined who had earned the right to call themselves human—and who had discarded it.

Arwa had spent her entire life training to be adequately human: to be pretty and obedient and honorable. To be *not* Amrithi. She knew what it meant, to stray from the path. She knew what heresy was. The realm of ash, in all its wildness and inhumanity, its death and hollowness, was heresy personified.

"That place is wrong," she said finally, bluntly. "I accepted that we would meddle with heresy, and I will do so again. But it is—terribly wrong."

A beat.

"Yes." His voice was shaky, his expression incongruously calm. "It is somewhat. But is it any more wrong than the dirt and guts and spillage of war and needless death? I think not."

He winced again. Blinked once, twice, slowly. His eyes, she thought, had a strange sheen. Silver-gray, liquid shadow.

"Next time we can try to move farther along the path. Seek the Maha. But no longer tonight. Go back to your room and rest, Lady Arwa. You have done enough."

CHAPTER TWELVE

Arwa did not bother attempting to sleep the night before the Emperor's next dawn audience. She had never been one for falling easily into slumber, and had always woken at the slightest sound, even as a small girl. After Darez Fort, nighttime rest had become even more difficult for her to achieve. Now she had even more reason to stay awake through the dark hours. She had the not-prince and his library tomb; she had an apprenticeship.

She had Zahir's books.

Zahir had interrogated her about her experience in the realm of ash, pried every bare scrap of knowledge she'd gained. He'd been fascinated by the fragments of memory she'd gained from him. He'd muttered something of unexpected consequences and roots and shared dreaming, staining his fingertips with ink as he scrawled notes into the margin of a book, and had not spoken of it since. But she knew it mattered to him. The book had remained on his table since, the page creased from overuse, as he turned to it over and over again and stared at the words with furrowed brow.

He had not asked her to enter the realm of ash since. Instead he had begun teaching her in earnest, leading her away from slim tracts of poetry to dense texts of study. Mystical orders from the distant past—long before the Maha had made the Empire whole and powerful, and given the mystics the blessing of service to him—had cobbled together vast tomes about the nature of the soul and the body, the nature of death—the nature of the realm of ash, and how to walk its paths, aware and unharmed.

Together she and Zahir sifted through their theories, their claims, weighing them against their own experience of the realm for their worth. Theories on the manner in which a person's own history could shape the realm over time were carefully studied. Even more focus was given to the texts that discussed the blood roots: their strength, their nature, the relationship between flesh and soul.

Not all books were useful, of course. A bloated text that claimed souls and paths could be melded together via the conduit of shared roots was swiftly dismissed as untestable nonsense, and one discussing the anatomy of the soul's manifested body in the realm was put aside by Zahir with a muttered claim that it was *a headache in the guise of paper.*

Together, they were piecing together a picture of reality. A map, to lead them into the Maha's waiting ash.

She often returned to her own room with a large book hefted up in her arms, so that she could read in privacy until daybreak. After a handful of nights bent over her burning lantern, reading until the dawn chorus, Arwa had asked Eshara for more light.

"Another lantern, if you can provide it," Arwa had said. "But I would be grateful for more fuel. My lantern burns too quickly."

The guardswoman had frowned and ignored Arwa entirely.

"I want no part of it, my lady," she'd said, when Arwa had persisted.

Thank the Gods, then, for Reya, who had turned up the next night with fresh oil and wick, and the promise of more in the future.

"I don't care what you do, Lady Arwa," she'd said, a faint

frown marring her forehead. It was a much gentler expression on her face than on Eshara's. "Only—perhaps you should consider working by sunlight. Your eyes will thank you."

Arwa had agreed—and how could she not?—but in truth the study of the realm of ash felt like Zahir's business, his possession, and Zahir was entirely a creature of night. She could no more study the realm by daylight than she could imagine Zahir strolling along the central path through the garden at midday. It was an unnatural thing.

Arwa sat in the Hall of the World, her sleepless mind full of ash and poetry, as the Emperor announced edicts and dispensed justice, as the court scribes inked his words, as Akhtar offered his input on imperial administration, as Princess Masuma whispered through the lattice, speaking for the women of his household. When the Emperor once again announced Prince Parviz's imminent return, declaring that his son would be greeted that evening with appropriate pomp and ceremony, a whispered message passed from Masuma's retinue through the women: the feast in his honor would also be tonight. Although most women murmured in pleasure, at least one of Jihan's confidantes was not happy about the lack of notice.

"She wants to make our lady look foolish. Oh, you know what she's like—"

"Hush before one of *her* favorites hears you," another hissed.

Arwa blamed the high spirits of the women around her and her own exhaustion, but it was only when the audience ended and they returned to their own household that Arwa's addled mind realized that she had not seen Gulshera all morning.

In fact she had barely seen Gulshera at all since the first audience. Gulshera rarely ate with the other charity women of the princess's household. She did not join them when they spent the mornings and afternoons embroidering or writing letters, or discussing news from the larger Empire. She had seen Gulshera only briefly, once or twice, walking at the princess's side, among her circle of close companions.

Arwa went to the fruit garden and sat in the shade, arms curled about her knees. As the other widows and elders entered their shared hall, gossiping, removing their veils, she closed her eyes and sought some brief ease from her tiredness and her own thoughts.

She did not want to miss Gulshera, or require her counsel, but here she was regardless, mulling over the imperial household, wishing for Gulshera's blunt, even-handed guidance.

The princess informed me I should not question or interfere. So I will not. That was what Gulshera had told her. Did that extend to all aspects of Arwa's role in this household? Was Gulshera required to leave Arwa be, or did she simply have a much grander purpose, as one of Jihan's favorites?

"Lady Arwa," said a voice. It was not Gulshera, but another widow, still veiled. Arwa recognized her by the rings upon her hands, each embellished with rough-cut blue gems. An unseemly display for a widow, but Lady Bega was cousin to the departed Empress, distantly imperial by ancient blessed blood, and no one dared treat her with anything but respect.

"Lady Bega," Arwa said deferentially, rising to her feet.

Bega drew back her own veil, wrinkled eyes focused on Arwa's face. Considering.

"You are too young by far," she said, shaking her head mildly. "Wear your veil tonight, at the feast. Trust an old woman's advice. The princes are good men, young one, but they are still men. You understand?"

"We are dining with the princes?" Arwa said, feeling herself become pale. She had expected a celebration—something to honor the prince appropriately—but she had not expected to see him face-to-face, or any of them. The worlds of women and

men who were not kin, not bound by blood or marriage, were
not meant to cross. That was the way of any noble household.
"Aunt, my honor—"

"Ah, ah!" Bega tutted. "My dear, there's no shame in it. This
is the imperial household. You think the Emperor's kin obey the
same rules as the rest of us?"

"I—"

"You're a woman of the household, aren't you? No different from any widowed aunt in her brother's or her nephew's
care. Regardless, do be careful. *We* know there is no difference
between you and I, age or no age . . . But men, even the very finest of them, they are . . . easily misled by a young and pretty face."
She tapped Arwa's cheek lightly.

Her touch made Arwa look toward the other widows, seated
around their fountain. They were watching her and Bega both.
Had the widows been discussing who would speak with her, this
painfully young and tragic widow thrust into their lives? Arwa
swallowed and bowed her head deferentially. She knew a warning when she heard one.

"Thank you, Aunt," Arwa said. "I appreciate your wisdom."

Arwa wore her veil.

Jihan led the retinue as always, with Gulshera once again at
her side, where Arwa had no opportunity to speak with her.

They crossed the great bridges of the silver lake to the imperial
palace proper once more, but this time they did not go to the
Hall of the World. Instead they entered the women's quarters of
the Emperor's own great palace. Arwa stared about, wide-eyed.
Arwa had near laughed, when Jihan had called her household
humble. But she had not been lying. In comparison to the central
women's quarters, they *were*. The ceilings were gold, the walls
mirrored with gems and silver alike.

They were led to a grand hall. Musicians were playing in the corner of the room. A courtesan was dancing, dressed in a long skirt of deep blue and imperial green. Large tables, arranged to reflect the importance of their occupants, were set around the room to hold lesser members of each imperial household.

The table of the imperial family was unmistakable. At the center of the room, small but wrought of ivory carved to resembled roses, it was surrounded by a corona of cushions of brocade and velvet where the family's closest companions knelt in attendance. At the table itself, an older woman with henna-red hair drawn back beneath a high coned cap was already seated. Princess Masuma, surely. Next to her sat the boy Prince Nasir. He was smiling, chattering volubly to his aunt beside him.

On the other side of the table, expression set and grim, sat Prince Akhtar. He turned as Jihan and her women entered. His expression thawed a little at the sight of her. He quirked an eyebrow, still unsmiling.

"Have you come to save me from this farce?" he asked.

"Of course not." She glided forward and performed a graceful bow to her brothers and her aunt. Then she rose. "I see you began without me. A shame. I do so love our family gatherings."

"I told Akhtar he should ask you to hurry," said Nasir, practically squirming in his seat. He had a great deal of energy, this one, when propriety did not force him to be still. "Parviz will be here soon."

"And I told Akhtar not to rush you," Masuma said, smiling sweetly. Her eyes were flat. "I know how young girls are."

"Thank you, Aunt," Jihan said, with equal poison. "How kind."

"This is a celebration for your brother, Jihan," Masuma said. "Do try to sound less—difficult."

"I will do my best, Aunt."

"What does it matter? He won't appreciate it," Akhtar said

to Masuma, drumming his fingers idly against the table. "Oh, don't look at me like that, Aunt; he may be your favorite, but you know him. He'll make sour faces and revile you for wasting your coin on frivolity. He doesn't understand the value of making people happy."

Masuma's lips thinned.

"Sit, Jihan," she said sharply. "Let your retinue go and enjoy themselves."

She spoke to Jihan as if she were a child, and Jihan kneeled at the table with a sweep of her skirt and a tilt of her chin that was all defiance. Her smile was sharp enough to cut, and Masuma's expression soured all the more at the sight of it.

As Arwa moved to her own distant table, slowed by the press of women around her, she heard Nasir begin to describe Parviz's arrival to the city with anxious enthusiasm. There were flowers, he told them, roses and carnations and marigolds, thrown in abundance so that Parviz's chariot crushed them as he moved and released perfume into the air. And he threw gold coins to the people watching too—

"I'm surprised no one was harmed," muttered Akhtar. "But he does like to make a spectacle of himself."

Masuma gave him a sharp look.

"More drink for you, I think," she announced, gesturing a servant over. "Perhaps it will soften your tongue."

Nasir wilted into silence.

Oh, child, Arwa thought, as she walked. She felt suddenly rather old. *You will never soften that family of yours, though you may break yourself trying.*

Food was served. Great platters of fruit, fish and meat charred to sweetness and rich with spices, bread so thin it flaked in her fingers, and rice dotted with raisins and pomegranate seeds that burst sharp and sweet against her tongue. The courtesans danced; the musicians played; the women gossiped and laughed and ate. Parviz arrived in the midst of all the revelry without fanfare. Only the lull of silence that fell over the feasters made Arwa aware that he had entered.

His tunic was plain gray, his turban unadorned. She would not have known him for who he was if he had not crossed the room to face his family, if he had not had a military man's posture, straight and tall. He walked with a soft, weighty tread. He bowed his head to each of his siblings and his aunt in turn, without speech, without meeting their eyes. Then he sat, made a curt gesture to a trembling maidservant, and took the carafe of wine from her hands. And drank.

Arwa watched him. They all watched him, celebration tilting ever so slightly into unease. Even seated, even silent with wine in his hands, he had a terrible, compelling gravity to his presence. He belonged somewhere more severe, more dangerous, a world of steel and war. Beneath his gaze the feast felt...frivolous. Small.

Masuma tried to make conversation, her smile painfully fixed. Nasir looked between all of them, eyes darting to and fro.

Akhtar said nothing. His mouth was thin.

Jihan raised her own glass.

"To family," she said, in a loud voice, clear as a bell.

"Jihan," Masuma said sharply.

Jihan only smiled and drank deep.

The merriment—for what it was worth—continued despite Parviz's presence, the unease giving the laughter around Arwa a frenzied edge. There would be no visit to Zahir's workroom tonight. Arwa bore it for as long as she could. Eventually, when other widows had begun to leave and she could see no sign of Gulshera in the throng seated at Jihan's back, she decided to depart.

She entered the corridor leading away from the dining hall,

not far behind a small group of other women, when she felt a soft hand on her arm, spinning her on her feet. Her heart rattled in her chest.

Jihan.

"Arwa," said Jihan. "You're leaving so soon?"

"I am, my lady," said Arwa.

"Why are you veiled?" Her mouth was a play of amusement, lips upturned.

It was oddly absurd to be alone with Jihan, who was constantly in the company of others, surrounded by maidservants and guardswomen and her small coterie of favorites. Arwa was almost sure that Jihan had cornered her only because she had drunk far too much wine.

"Come," said Jihan. "You may tell me."

"My lady, forgive me, but your brothers are not family."

"What reputation do you need to protect, with no husband left to care if you reflect well on him now?"

"My father's," Arwa offered, unsure what Jihan sought from her.

"Did he give you leave to come here? No." Jihan shook her head. "I think you placed the defense of his reputation aside a long time ago. Or he did, when he fell into disgrace, and won my father's ire."

"My reputation, then," Arwa said, some sharpness bleeding into her voice. Jihan blinked at her, as if struck.

"Does your reputation matter so much?" She touched a hand to the end of Arwa's veil, making the soft gauze flutter. "You are a widow, Arwa. A ghost."

Arwa remembered Gulshera's warnings. *Jihan likes to test people*, she'd told her. *Court has teeth and claws*, she'd claimed. Arwa felt the weight of Jihan's regard, and knew all Gulshera's warnings had been true.

"What else do I have?" Arwa asked.

Jihan laughed at that, a soft laugh. Arwa could hear distant music from the hall. A man's yell, and more laughter.

"How do you like my brother?" she whispered.

"Which one, my lady?"

"You know which one, ghost. The one I am relying on to save us all, as my true brothers play foolish games while their Empire burns." She shrugged, all grace. "Akhtar is good enough. For all his pride, he listens. He understands the hard, dull work that builds an Empire. But Parviz…" Sharp turn of her mouth. "Well."

A breeze entered through the lattice. The nape of Arwa's neck felt cold.

"I like Lord Zahir well enough," she said guardedly. "He is a good teacher."

"Good. That is good. You will do whatever it takes to help him, won't you?"

"Of course, my lady."

"Try to make him happy," said Jihan. She sighed and touched a hand to her own cheek, which was rose-tinged with warmth. "Zahir is so very alone. When my mother lived, we protected him together. We assured him a place in her household. *This* household." She touched a proprietary hand to the bejeweled wall as if to say, *This is by rights mine.*

"But my mother is no more," she continued, "and politics are…complex. One day, Gods willing, this will be my palace again. But, Arwa, if you wish to please me, think a little less of your reputation. Think of the gift Zahir has, and focus on proving your faithfulness to me, and to a cause far greater than you, in all ways."

Try to make him happy.

The words burned. Arwa's skin crawled.

"Princess," Arwa murmured. Deferential.

Jihan looked back at the hall, a smile still playing upon her mouth.

"Go, then," she said. "Rest well, Lady Arwa. I have a celebration to return to."

Then she was gone, back into the light and pomp, leaving Arwa alone to clutch at the lattice, her mind whirling, stomach knotted with fear and with fury.

CHAPTER THIRTEEN

She walked across the bridge, over water black as the night sky above it, and through the doors and gates that enclosed the women's quarters of Akhtar's palace. Guardswomen opened the doors, unbarring the way. Arwa did not look at them. She focused on simply striding forward.

Rage and feeling. That was all she was, and all she could think of. Her skin, her bones, ached with it.

Instead of returning to her own room, she made her way out to the gardens, not caring if she was seen. And who was here to see her anyway? Only a handful of elders, too infirm to attend the celebration; only guards and maidservants who saw and knew everything regardless.

She should not have been there. She should have calmed herself, collected herself, remembered the training her mother had given her. She'd known the trick of locking away her feelings once. She should have gone directly to her own room and remained there until morning, breathing through the fury until she could not feel it any longer.

But Arwa had offered herself to service, body and soul. She had held out her palm and asked Zahir to make a tool of her. Her cheeks burned at the memory. Her insides knotted. Foolish. Foolish.

It was the shame that compelled her to keep on walking and make her way down the dark staircase into Zahir's workroom. He was there as he always was, seated at his table with his studies laid out in front of him. He was making a clean duplicate of the book, the original placed to his left, the fresh copy to the right, where he could ink in line after line with neat strokes of his hand.

"Lord Zahir," she said.

He lifted his head.

"Lady Arwa. I was not expecting you tonight." He lowered his pen and rose to his feet. "I heard that Parviz had returned."

Who had told him? Were there maidservants who swept his room and cleaned his clothes, who also imparted gossip? Did he ever emerge from this place to eat or sleep or simply experience life beyond the confines of the tomb enclosure's walls? Did he have a place in Prince Akhtar's household of men, as an impoverished relative, as Arwa and the other elders and widows did in the part of the household under Jihan's purview?

None of it mattered. In truth, he should not have been here at all. He was a blessed. He should have been given a position as a military general serving under a governor, a commander of a garrison fort, even a governor of a far-flung province. He had the talent to be a scholar. He could have served as a scribe or in the imperial court. Anything but this strange half life, hidden away in darkness and secrecy.

The thought of his incongruity, his strangeness, only made her angrier.

"Princess Jihan spoke to me alone," said Arwa. "She wanted to impress upon me the importance of making you happy. She asked me whether I would be willing to discard my reputation for the sake of service. To you."

"Did she." Zahir's voice was carefully neutral.

"I believed I was serving you in order to save the Empire. That was what I offered. And, my lord, that is *all* I offer."

He closed his eyes, head tilting back. Exhaled.

"I suppose I should be grateful," Arwa said shakily. "I suppose I should *want* to make you happy, of my own volition. I am only a widow, after all. Only the illegitimate, Amrithi-blooded child of a nobleman in disgrace. What do I matter, compared to you?"

His eyes snapped open. He lowered his head.

"Lady Arwa," he said. "No."

His eyes were fixed on her hands now, which were fists before her. She uncurled them, and he raised his head, gazing at her veiled face.

"I want nothing from you," he said. "I promise you."

Liar.

She knew he was drawn to the movement of her hands, that something about her fascinated him. Perhaps he did not even know it. *Lonely,* Jihan had called him. But Arwa could only look at him and think of his vulnerable neck, his wrists, the moon-light on him and think, *Starving, he is starving.*

It only made her more furious to think it. She was starving too.

"So, then," she said. "Is this what you want, freely offered, my lord?" She lifted her veil, her mother's voice winter in her ears. *Fool girl. Fool.* "What do you think? Will I suit?"

He looked upon her face. Of course he did.

He had seen it before, in the realm of ash. But there she had not been flesh. She was flesh now, skin chilled by the air, her shorn hair curling faintly around her ears, lantern light flickering on her skin, just as it did on his.

Abruptly, he blinked. Sucked in a breath and looked away.

"Put your veil back in place. Please."

She didn't. She was in no mood to obey him.

"I am waiting for an answer, my lord."

"You do not understand. I only seek an apprentice, Lady Arwa."

"That was not what Jihan said."

"My sister's will is not my own," he snapped. There was color in his face, creeping up his neck. "I am loyal to Jihan, I love her, but I also know what she is. Surely you recognize that she is not—as we are."

"As we are, my lord?" She took a step closer to him, their shadows melding upon the floor. Her voice felt viperous in her own throat, sweet. "Please, explain that to me."

"We know the necessity of being useful, do we not, Lady Arwa? We know the weight of it. The danger of not being what we must be." He looked over her shoulder, at a fixed point in the distance; even the way he consciously avoided her face was like a brand upon her. "When my mother fell into the Emperor's disfavor, Jihan was the one who begged for my life to be spared. She will say, perhaps, that I was saved for love or for pity. But I know her mother saw the use of me—I had the knowledge of such arts even then—and as a result I was spared and given a place in the imperial household. I had tutors. I was given a home and a purpose, by her grace and favor. But I do not forget that I live for my worth alone. And Jihan is..."

Zahir trailed off. Gestured helplessly. "She is clever in the ways of court. She knows the value of knowledge, and of power. She knows how to play the games the court play. She could have remained in her father's court and cultivated his ear as Masuma does, but she chose to become the head of Akhtar's household instead because she has a measure of freedom here that she would not have under Masuma's thumb. She has the right, among other rights, to keep—me." Zahir shook his head, a bitter and fleeting smile on his face. "She knows how to spin people to her whims, my sister. And she does so whenever she deems it necessary."

"And she thinks she will gain some benefit from giving my honor to you?"

"She cannot give what you don't offer."

Arwa laughed harshly. She could not help it.

"Of course she can."

"She cannot give what I won't take, then," snapped Zahir. "You came here of your own free will, Lady Arwa, came to this service out of loyalty and love for the Empire, and I am grateful. But I know how free will can bend to necessity and survival. I *know*. And I do not ask for more."

There was silence. Arwa touched a hand to her own throat. She felt her pulse, a harsh rhythm beneath her fingertips. She breathed.

"Whatever Jihan may attempt," he said finally, "whatever she may believe, I have told her and I tell you now: I called you my apprentice, my assistant, and that is all I want, and all I need from you."

Need and want.

"She called you lonely," said Arwa. "And I am..."

She trailed off. She would not tell him what she was. She could not even tell herself.

He raised his head as she lowered her veil. This slight man, with a disarmingly lovely face and cool, clever eyes. She looked at him through gauze and felt her stomach knot.

Starving, she thought again. *Starving*.

He looked at her as if he knew, as if he had always known what Jihan had hoped. There was pity in the turn of his mouth, but something sharp too.

"My sister's will is not my will," he said. "Now, Lady Arwa, I have work I need to do. You don't need to stay."

She went to Zahir the next night. She did not know what to expect from him. She prepared herself for barbed tension, for awkwardness, even to be banished away. But Zahir had placed new books on the table for her: slim, simple volumes of poetry and essays. He had placed cups of tea, poured fresh from the samovar, upon the table too.

"Don't fear," he said. "This is the normal kind of tea."

Arwa recognized a peace offering when she saw one. She sat down and took a cup. Adjusted her veil and drank.

Zahir sat down across from her and took up his own cup.

"We should discuss the terms of our arrangement." His voice was tentative. Gaze fixed on the tea.

"There's no need."

"I think there is. Your apprenticeship would benefit from clearer rules. Clearer boundaries."

"I am sorry if—"

"Please don't apologize. You believed I erred. That I broke the boundaries that define your honor. I understand the significance of such a thing. My mother..." His mouth thinned. His voice was careful. "My mother was a successful courtesan. But when she tried to be more, to use her scholarly knowledge to help the Empire... Well. It was not her place, in my father's eyes. And she paid a high price for her transgression."

He lowered his cup to the table.

"Lady Arwa. I am familiar with the fear a relationship without rules engenders. I am a blessed. I am a man. And yet here I am, in the imperial palace, in the women's quarters, in this— *place*. There are no rules for what I am, and that means I have no guidance on how best to ensure my own survival. You have, perhaps, realized that I am a person who appreciates guidance."

She looked at the books behind him and said nothing. Yes. She'd understood that about him some time ago.

"For your sake and mine, we should establish rules between us. A contract of a kind."

"I cannot make contracts," Arwa said, strangely numb. "Beyond the choice of whom I marry—that is a boundary of my honor as a noblewoman, also."

Noblewomen were the treasures of their husbands and their fathers. Their care—their futures—lay in the hands of their men. Zahir knew this as Arwa did, but he kindly did not point out all the ways Arwa had vowed herself to him and Jihan both, in ways that she had no right to.

"Of a kind," he repeated. "A discussion, then. An act of trust. Is that more agreeable to you?"

She nodded wordlessly. She kept her tea clasped between her hands, taking comfort in its warmth.

He began.

"I will not ask anything of you—*anything*—beyond what is required to reach the Maha's ash. I cannot promise you will not be harmed in this endeavor. As you know, I am not aware of all the risks."

"I am not afraid of harm."

"No," said Zahir. His gaze flickered to her hands, and back to his own cup. "I know."

She clasped her fingers an increment tighter. Heat against her scarred palm.

"Beyond that, Lady Arwa, your honor is your own. The terms of your reputation are your own. How you maintain it— the behaviors you choose, the actions you take—are in your hands. And I will respect the parameters you choose."

"You have no boundaries of your own? No rules I must abide by?"

He paused.

"I have never considered it," he said. Then: "No, Lady Arwa. But if you're willing, I would like to enter the realm of ash again. Will you join me?"

"Of course," she told him. It was what she was here for, after all.

She removed her veil when he lit the fire. He did not comment on it. He carefully avoided staring at her face as he brought the flames to a gentle smolder, as he poured laced tea, and gave her the dagger so she could add her own blood to the glow of the flames.

If he had asked, she would have explained that the smoke made her feel as if she were choking, that combined with the weight of her veil it made her feel trapped, that she could not sleep covered as she had been. But he did not ask. Arwa drank the tea and fell into a swift, unnatural sleep.

Zahir was there instantly. The storm surrounded her, and then his hand was on her own, their blood roots binding fast. She followed him, stumbling through the feel of her body's quick heartbeat, into the forest of his path of ash.

"Are we going to seek the Maha's ash?" she asked.

Zahir was silent for a long moment.

"Consuming ash was—not a comfortable experience."

Arwa felt no more at ease in the realm of ash than she had the first time they had entered it. The feel of being cleaved into two halves was still distinctly terrifying. Dizzying. But she had enough familiarity with it to now marvel at the smaller elements of its overall strangeness: the pulse of the blood roots, shifting across and beneath the facets of her dreamed skin. The refracted strangeness of her own limbs, and Zahir's, as they rippled and changed, glittering beasts of glass.

Zahir was entirely still. As he pondered, the ground shifted beneath them, pale-leaved.

"Are you prepared?" she asked him.

"Yes," he said finally. "We must try. It's our purpose, after all."

Our purpose.

"Together, then," Arwa said softly. "Lead the way, my lord."

They walked along his path, deeper and deeper into the realm of ash. As before, the trees loomed and changed. Arwa saw figures moving in the gloom. It became harder and harder to move through the ash. She could feel the tightening grip of the blood roots, and far away, the beat of her own heart, the rattle of her own breath in her lungs.

The air was closing around her.

"That's it," he said, when Arwa's grip tightened. "Hold on tightly."

They had moved far. Far. It felt like centuries had slipped away beneath their dreamed feet, trampled bloody and soft. Around them the world narrowed. Arwa felt strangely crushed. Every step was growing harder.

Beneath them the haze of the ground had altered.

They were standing upon sand. Pale, white sand.

"This reminds me of Irinah's desert," she told him. Her distant heart speeding, jaw tight. "We must be close to him. The Maha. Surely we are?"

"I think I can feel him." She felt more than heard the trembling hope in Zahir's voice. Around them the branches of the trees twisted, becoming sharp knifepoints that speared the ivory sky.

She felt the sand rising around her ankles. Her distant breath felt shallow, far too shallow. Her ears strangely ached, full somehow of the howl of a storm, wailing—

"I don't think I can go farther," she told him. "My flesh. My head—"

"I know," he said. "The pain is—"

"Too much," Arwa wrenched out. "My soul hurts. I did not know a soul could hurt."

Zahir paused, silent. An unreal wind blew the sand around their feet.

"The bridge is not strong enough after all," he said finally. "Despite your blood. We'll have to rethink."

He took a step back, leaning into the tug of those roots. Arwa felt the moment soul and flesh joined, like a piecing together of two halves, roots fusing her whole—

She woke. Gasping.

Her limbs ached strangely. They felt like ill-fitting clothes; they felt as if she had outgrown them. A moment, and the feeling passed. But still, she didn't move, her face pressed to the blanket beneath her, her breath and tears damp on the cloth.

"Lady Arwa." Zahir's voice. "I have water."

She took it and drank gratefully, straight from the carafe.

"How do you feel?" he asked.

"Fine."

"I will do some study," he said. "We cannot go farther, if the realm affects us so. Can you stand?"

"I think so."

He stood and stepped back, allowing Arwa to rise to her own feet. She followed him then back into his library. She steadied herself with a hand on the shelf, making a show of staring at each book in turn to hide her weakness, and following the titles with the brush of her fingers, as she had seen Zahir do many times before.

"You have a number of books by the Hidden One," she noted.

"The poems are important to me," he said.

"I'm not surprised, Lord Zahir. They are rather beautiful." There was an intimacy to them that appealed to her, resonated in her mouth, when she followed the words.

"Take one of the books with you, if you like," he said. A pause. Then, careful: "Or read here, if you prefer."

Her finger paused upon the shelf. She hesitated.

Arwa thought of Jihan, telling her to make Zahir happy. The memory was utterly bitter.

My honor is my own, Arwa told herself. *My boundaries my own.* So she and Zahir had agreed.

Oh, she knew what a paper-thin fiction that was. Reputation and honor were the business of society, and Arwa's only responsibility was to adhere to the laws the world laid out for her. But here, within these strange walls, she could almost convince herself of the sweet lie Zahir had offered her, that the pact of trust they had concocted together protected her from dishonor. She wanted to believe *she* had such power—that she defined her worth and her status.

So in that moment, she allowed the fiction to stand.

"The company would be pleasant," she told him.

They both sat at the table. He began his copy work once more, and Arwa read the poetry, the crackle of the lantern and the hum of the breeze the only noise between them.

Eventually Arwa lifted her head. She saw then that Zahir had fallen asleep, head against the wall, chin tucked against his chest. A strand of dark hair had somehow escaped his turban, and lay across his forehead. He looked younger, in sleep.

The night was cold, and he wore no jacket, just a long-sleeved tunic and trousers. In a fit of sudden compassion, Arwa removed her shawl and draped it around him. He didn't even stir.

She snuffed out the lantern upon the table, then stood and left him. She walked through the garden, beneath the rustling trees, as rock doves flew free from their tower over her head, black shadows against the star-flecked night.

CHAPTER FOURTEEN

She and Zahir returned to their quiet work. On her next visit, he handed over her shawl without comment. When she returned to her room, she found small stars sewn along the edges, discreet in white thread. It took her a few days longer to realize that their order accurately reflected the arrangement of constellations above Irinah at midsummer—one of the very maps they had perused together many nights past, when they began piecing together the veracity of scholarship on the realm of ash.

She said nothing to him, and he said nothing to her. But she wore the shawl often, and sometimes when they studied the problem of the bridge between worlds—the *damnable bridge*, as Arwa would often refer to it viciously, in the safety of her own head—she would trace the constellations with her fingertips in quiet comfort.

The pain—the result of that damnable, weak bridge—had stopped them from progressing any farther along the path of his soul. Arwa read his books on her own, selecting volumes that drew her interest. When she had questions—which was often—Zahir always answered her, no matter how preoccupied he was with his own research.

"There must be an alternative to incorporating cannibalism

or starvation," Arwa muttered, flicking swiftly through a thick tome.

Zahir laughed. When she looked up, he was smiling.

"If there is, I'm sure you'll find it," he said.

She paused. Finger upon the page.

"I expect," she said, "that you cannot go to Irinah."

"Ah. I wondered if you would question that." He shut his own book. "It would be ideal. It has long been my preferred avenue of inquiry. But no. I cannot. Jihan has her spies, her women, but her power is constrained by her position."

A daughter, no matter her power, was infinitely more constrained than a son. Arwa nodded in understanding.

"And Prince Akhtar...?"

"He understands the need for resources," Zahir said. "For courtiers loyal to him. For administrators in his pocket. For a sister with political acumen and spies. But I have not yet proven myself useful, in his eyes, and heresy makes him uneasy. And it hurts his pride to need someone like me. A bastard, and a traitor's son." Bitter twist of Zahir's mouth. "He tolerates me for Jihan's sake, but he will not send me to Irinah."

"Do you ever go beyond the palace walls?" Arwa asked.

"No, Lady Arwa." He said it gently enough, but she thought she heard the pain of it, beneath the softness of his voice. "Jihan has not arranged me that privilege. But then, I have not asked for many years."

There was a lump in her throat.

She lowered her head, breathing through it until it cleared, and she could find her words once more.

"If we can find no other answers in these books, then we'll make our own theories," said Arwa. "We will test them and we will break them, and then we will draw new theories from the breaking, and test those too. And we will continue, Lord Zahir, until we find a theory that does not break, and the bridge is strong enough to carry us directly into the Maha's arms."

Zahir stared at her for a long moment. Then his face broke into the warmest, sweetest smile she had ever seen. It stole her breath a little, to look upon it.

"Lady Arwa, that is by far the nicest thing you have ever said to me."

"Well." She touched one finger to the shorn ends of her hair. "I can be a scholar too when I try, my lord."

"You are always a scholar," Zahir said softly. "If I ever have suggested otherwise to you—well. I am often a fool. And cruel. But I will endeavor to learn to be better."

"Thank you, my lord." She began flicking through pages once more, gazing unseeing at the words. "I will be sure to evaluate your efforts honestly and fairly."

"I can ask for no more."

She grew used to her new routine. Sat with the widows and ate and prayed with them, just as she had done when she had lived in the hermitage. She slept in snatches often during the day. And at night, she worked with Zahir, continuing her apprenticeship.

She saw Gulshera only rarely. Gulshera was always in Jihan's presence, at her salons for her favorites, or at her meetings with Prince Akhtar. Only once that week did Arwa find Gulshera alone. The older woman was seated in the front garden, her own eyes closed, face tilted up to the sun.

"Aunt," Arwa said in greeting.

"Don't ask me anything," Gulshera said tiredly. "Only sit with me, if you like. *Quietly.*"

And that had been that.

It was the Emperor's next public audience that shattered the order of Arwa's new life.

The princes sat before their father, as always, in close proximity to his greatness. Petitions began. Another request for assistance for a scheme of cleansing was proposed, by an old nobleman serving in Haran governance. He was directed to seek assistance from Akhtar. As the next petitioner approached, Parviz stood, and raised his hand in a gesture that demanded stillness. A ripple—of fear and unease—ran through the surrounding nobles.

"I must speak," he said.

Through the lattice and gauze, Parviz was a bulky, intimidating figure, carved from shadow and steel, his tunic and jacket an austere gray, his turban unadorned even by a jewel to mark his status. His voice was a signal of strength, booming and vast. His very presence seemed to draw the air from the room, just as it had on the night of the feast celebrating his return.

"I beg my gracious father's indulgence," Prince Parviz announced. "Father, your humble servant pleads for the right to plead before you."

"My sons have the right to private audience," the Emperor said, voice silken. Arwa could not tell if he was angry or simply curious. Either way, her heart was beating fast, her palms damp with sweat. The women around her were utterly, terribly silent. "What need have you to speak before these good assembled men?"

"This lowly servant does not deserve the comfort of private audience, to soften the weight of his crimes." Arwa saw Parviz raise his head, his jaw all firm, noble angles. "Father, I will speak honestly before all these men: I have failed you."

"There is no need for false humility. We have amply rewarded you for your service in Durevi. I have judged you. You have not been found wanting."

"I served you loyally in Durevi," Parviz agreed. "I quelled rebellion from barbarians and fools, who do not recognize the strength and glory of the Empire. Years of absence, Father, and

I return to discover...whispers. Of heretics. Of people who do not respect your absolute right to master the law and faith of the Empire. Whispers of people who worship superstition and occult arts over your holy self." He held his arms out before him, for all his booming voice, his straight-back stance, as if he were a supplicant before the Emperor. "Your sons are your hands, Father. We circle your light. We serve you and our line above all else. But we have not destroyed heresy." There was real anguish in his voice. "Your sons have betrayed you, Father. We deserve any punishment you see fit to provide."

A beat. The vast hall was utterly silent.

The Emperor said nothing. It was no invitation to continue. Nor was it a command to stop. To Parviz's left, Nasir was wide-eyed; Akhtar, thin-lipped, sat still in his seat.

"Heretic mystics speak against you, Father," Parviz continued. "They speak of a new Maha. They speak of evil arts, worship of demons, spells and sorcery that the Maha banished long ago, for the good of your Empire. We cannot focus our attentions on petty matters of *sanitation*, when such a threat faces you."

"Brother," said Akhtar. "Stop this."

Parviz—to no one's surprise—ignored him.

"I know my duty, Father. I know our duties. We are your tools. We preserve the Empire's greatness and its future. But in allowing heresy to continue, we fail you.

"I have tried to remedy my failures," continued Parviz. "My men—loyal soldiers who served me in Durevi—have apprehended a group of mystics who claim the Maha has been reborn among their number. I hold them now in my own palace. Most High, I captured them for you. Order what you will of me: My hands are your hands. My will your will."

Silence. How could a hall full of so many people be so silent? How could even the thunder of Arwa's heartbeat go numb and still in her ears, as if she hung suspended out of time by her own fear?

Prince Parviz castigated himself by tone and deed—hands before him, face lowering in contrition—but his words were truly a condemnation of his brothers. He had, after all, been in Durevi. It was Akhtar and Nasir who had not weeded out heresy.

It was Akhtar who harbored Zahir—Zahir with his books and his poetry, his fire vessel, his realm of ash—within his own palace.

"You were always the most emotional of my children," the Emperor said. "You think I do not know what happens in my own Empire? What heresy occurs? Step forward, Parviz."

Parviz did. He stood directly before the dais, as many a noble and criminal had before him. He stared at the Emperor. From behind the lattice, blurred to shadows of gauze and bright clothing, the women stared back as one.

"If one of my nobles had brought news of heretics before me in such a manner, I would have had them stripped of their titles and wealth. I would have cast them from court for their sheer gall."

"If I have overstepped, Father, then I accept any punishment I have earned. I humbly—"

"Enough."

The Emperor sounded angry—and suddenly, undeniably, exhausted. Arwa heard the tremor of the Emperor's voice, and felt something twist in her chest, clutch painfully at her heart. The Emperor was frail. An old man. No more than mortal. She thought of the statue of the Maha and Emperor both, timeless and strong; she thought of ash, crumbling. She twisted her hands together tight.

"My sons have no need for humility. You are a descendant of the Maha, Prince Parviz. You carry within you greatness beyond compare. I recognize your zeal." Soft. His voice carried, but oh it was soft. "After our great ancestor passed, I dealt with many heretics. I meted out death for the sake of the Empire. I had hoped such ill belief had been snuffed out entirely. But I am an old man. I do not have the fire of the young."

The Emperor leaned forward, just slightly, upon his golden dais. He stared down at Parviz. The women could not see his expression. All that was visible to Arwa was the curve of his spine, his wrinkled hand forming a fist, and then relaxing.

"Mark in the records," he said to the court scribes. "The heretics in Prince Parviz's possession will be put to death, their heads displayed upon the city's walls."

Arwa saw Jihan stand, then crouch by her aunt's side, whispering furiously to Masuma. Despite her veil, none of Jihan's feelings were concealed. Fury and urgency radiated off her skin. Masuma placed a hand upon Jihan's own. With her free hand she touched the lattice with trembling fingers. For once, the imperial women were united.

Arwa did not know what Masuma whispered to her brother. Only that he sagged back; only that he shook, a little, as if her words had thrown him.

"So many voices," the Emperor. His voice creaked like old wood, its silken edge frayed. "And I find I no longer have the will to heed them. This audience is done. Go."

A ripple ran through the hall. This was no ordinary end to an audience. The Emperor had not risen to his feet and departed. The business of the court was not yet complete.

"Leave me," the Emperor said. "*Now.*"

Belatedly, a conch sounded. The courtiers began to uneasily depart.

Before his father, Prince Parviz stood straight and tall. There was something triumphant about his stillness. Something watchful.

Arwa thought of Zahir and his occult arts. The arts Jihan,

and by extension Akhtar, had invested in to save the Empire. She thought of the Emperor's words, his age and frailty, and the flame of Parviz's eyes, as he stared up at his father's throne.

Her mouth was full of the taste of iron.

Nothing good will come of this.

CHAPTER FIFTEEN

The walk back to Akhtar's palace was tense.

"Come with us," one widow said gently. She steered Arwa toward the wing for elders, and away from Jihan's closest women, who were whispering to one another urgently.

The elders settled on the floor. To Arwa's surprise, she saw Gulshera standing by the lattice, her back to all of them. Every line of her body screamed her desire to be left alone. Arwa, for all her propensity toward foolishness, knew better than to disturb her. Instead, Arwa sat on the floor cushions with the other women. From here, she could see Gulshera's profile. Gulshera's jaw was tight, her pale eyes flint.

She looked like a soldier preparing for battle.

A maidservant brought in refreshments. The cups and pastries went notably untouched. Lady Bega drummed her fingers against her knee, the clink of her jeweled rings the only noise to break the weight of silence.

"Heads staked upon walls," she said finally. "It's been years."

"Oh, don't speak of it," said another. She drew her shawl around her face.

"And what shall we speak of, then?" Bega rolled her eyes and cursed under her breath. "Soft woman, you are. If Parviz pours more honeyed apologies into his father's ears, there may be many more heads upon walls, you mark me."

"Bega."

"The commoners will love it at least," said Bega, clearly relishing the drama. "They love a spectacle."

"Some of them found solace in charlatans, Lady Bega." Gulshera's voice was leaden. "I would be surprised if the people of Jah Ambha are entirely celebratory."

There was knowing in Gulshera's voice.

Arwa thought of the days Gulshera had spent at Jihan's side. Jihan, who saw and heard everything, who had far-flung eyes, who received regular missives from across the Empire and consumed knowledge with the same ease and intensity that Zahir sought to consume ash.

Oh, Gulshera knew something of the fractures in the Empire's faith. Of that, Arwa was certain. Even Arwa, tucked in the shell of her own grief and circumstance, knew the people sought to fill the void left by the Maha's death in any way they could. Executing mystics and heretics would not heal the wound in the Empire. The rift left in the Empire's faith, in its *hope*, was not one that could be healed by force of arms alone.

A guardswoman entered. Heads turned as she crossed the room, as she kneeled down by Arwa's side, and in a soft voice said, "Lady, you are wanted. The princess has called for you."

Gulshera had turned. Gaze sharp. But there was no opportunity to speak to her now, if indeed she wanted to speak. The elders were staring at Arwa. The guardswoman was waiting. All she could do was swallow, and straighten, and nod in acknowledgment.

The guardswoman led her out into the corridor, then said, "Lady, you will need to lower your veil."

"What need is there for that?"

"We are attending the prince," the guardswoman said. Her gaze flickered to Arwa, then back again.

No more needed to be said. Arwa hastily lowered her veil, as instructed.

They walked through the pale corridors of the women's quarters, to doors Arwa had never acknowledged, and had never seen unbarred. The doors were drawn open. Arwa walked through them, and entered the halls of Akhtar's palace that lay beyond the women's quarters. The world of men.

It was the past that haunted Arwa, as she walked toward Prince Akhtar's study, hands clasped demurely in front of her, face veiled, hair shorn, a widow in all the ways she could muster. Beneath the mask of her widowhood, though, the memory of her marriage rose up. Haunting her.

Kamran's study. She thought of it, even as the guardswoman announced her, even as she crossed the threshold into a space where she did not belong. The inescapable, sticky heat of Chand; how his ledgers and his maps, the tools of his command, grew mold when the rains came, a fact that had driven him mad. He'd had officials to help him manage his papers, but often when he'd worked through the midday heat, Arwa had sat with him as he worked, and sifted carefully through his letters, adding to his ledgers, listening when he paced and worked his way through one thorny knot of imperial administration after another. She remembered the feel of his eyes on her. The sound of his soldiers in the courtyard below.

"You are a great help to me," he'd told her, once. And Arwa had felt relieved. She was a thing that was useful after all. A thing she had worked very hard to be. She had not failed her family after all.

She bowed low as she entered the study. Jihan stood before her, her veil thrown back. Prince Akhtar was facing his sister, his head tilted down to meet her eyes. His mouth was thin.

And there, standing by the far wall, arms clasped behind him, was Zahir.

It was a cold-water shock, seeing him here. She had never seen Zahir in daylight before. He was still oddly unreal, still sharp-boned and pale from lack of sunlight. But he also looked... different. Somehow, in the light of day, he loomed larger. His sharp bones were somehow more severe, his gaze more cutting. Although his hands were clasped behind his back, there was something unnerving about him—something that drew the eye and held it, pinned like a moth by lantern light.

In that moment, he reminded her of Parviz. His presence drew the air from the room, molded the world to his will. Then he looked at her, one flicker of his gaze, a darkening of his eyes, and he was only Zahir again.

Arwa felt a shiver of dread run through her. Why had they both been brought here?

Jihan and Akhtar did not seem to have yet noticed Arwa's arrival.

"He's met with Father's favorite courtiers," Akhtar was saying to Jihan, face mottled tight with fury and feeling. "After all my years of slowly winning their favor and hoarding their secrets, they're going to fall for his propaganda. The military already love him. They like his brute idiocy—*strength* they call it, as if hacking off heads is a virtue he's cultivated—"

"He's impetuous." Jihan's voice was soft, soothing. "He's always been one for grand gestures. But you are better than that, brother. Better than his base actions."

"His base actions are *working*."

"Parviz has always been able to sway Father," Jihan responded levelly. "But court? No. I think not. Court requires different tools than war, and more subtlety than that demanded by a loving parent. Father's favorites will see through him."

"He mocked my efforts to protect the Empire in front of them. They will remember that," Akhtar said tersely. "And believe me, he says a great deal more when he's not under Father's eye. He's been claiming there is no curse on the Empire at all, and nothing *to* be cleansed. No curse. The bald idiocy of it, Jihan!"

"I'm aware," Jihan said, with exaggerated patience. "He hasn't yet managed to explain away the shadow spirits, though. Or the massacres—"

"He does not have to. He believes order and iron rule will save us all, that Father is just too weak to maintain our true glory, and he is not alone in that belief. And he quelled Durevi, Jihan—people think that's proof enough."

Jihan snorted.

"Killing the local populace isn't quelling. It's a famine for the future; when we have none of Durevi's fruits and crops, after the lack of rainfall in Chand—"

Akhtar waved her off with a look of vibrant irritation on his face.

"Logistics don't matter to the people of this court, and the views of court are the ones we must consider right now. What if the nobility sway our father's choice of heir, Jihan? What then?"

"The logistics of food production are all that matter," Jihan snapped. *You fool* seemed to be heavily implied. "The court need full bellies and loyal citizens, and they know it. If we can't ensure that our trade routes function as they should…"

"Be that as it may, sister, that is not what is in question right now," Akhtar said sharply. "Your experiment is. Playing into your schemes is beginning to actively hinder me. Parviz is taking a clear stand against heresy, and when he reveals Zahir's presence in my household, he will damage my reputation at court. I *cannot* afford to lose any of my reputation. It's the only true weapon I have."

"He knows how I love Zahir," Jihan said calmly. "He won't want to hurt me."

"Love won't hold him forever, Jihan. Or me." Bite to his voice. "Have you accomplished anything you hoped for? At all?

Has your pet bastard managed to find the Maha yet? Solve all our problems with a sweep of magic?"

Jihan turned then, gaze sweeping over Arwa, before settling on Zahir. A look passed between the two of them.

"Prince Akhtar." Zahir's voice was soft. Cool. "When you were a small boy your grandmother doted upon you. She would let you sit with her when she entertained visitors. She fed you grapes from a silver bowl."

Spasmodic twist of Akhtar's mouth.

"Anyone could have told you that, boy."

"They can't tell you what she taught you," Zahir said, voice silken and cold and eerily reminiscent of the Emperor's own. "She taught you how to recognize poisons. Salt, bitter, sweet. The women of the imperial family have always known such things. But learning about death made you afraid. You couldn't sleep. You had nightmares, brother, you—"

Akhtar took Zahir by the throat.

"You don't call me brother. And you certainly don't demean my grandmother, when you're no more than a whore's son. Don't try to anger me, *bastard*. I'll be sorry later when Jihan cries over you—but not that sorry."

He held Zahir for one beat, two. Jihan did not cry out. Did not defend him. She was very still, staring into the distance, her expression remote.

Arwa trembled. Hands in fists.

Do something, she wanted to cry out. *Jihan, have you brought me here simply to watch Zahir suffer? What test is this?*

Very carefully, Jihan tilted her head toward Arwa. She looked at her, dark eyes fixed and intent.

Finally, Arwa understood why she had been summoned here. Not simply to witness an argument between siblings, a political tussle in which she had no place—but for this.

She stepped forward.

"Stars," she blurted out.

Akhtar turned. Blinked at her, as if he had not even thought of her, until that moment. She had faded into the background, as all guards and maidservants faded, as all insignificant women faded, to people of his stature.

Stars. Arwa breathed deep. Spoke once more.

"You did not like the dark as a child. And your gracious grandmother told you she could arrange for the stars to remain with you always. She stitched them in gold thread on gauze, and placed them upon the ceiling of your chambers. Sometimes she would watch you sleep, and she would see you clutching for them with your hand, as if in a dream..."

Arwa felt the ash like a physical thing: a memory coiling up from the base of her skull, unfurling across her mind's eye. For a moment something of the Emperor's own mother lived within her, breathed within her, then faded to sudden dust. Lost.

She had no more. Paused. Glad for her veil, she squeezed her eyes shut for a moment and breathed, and breathed.

"And who," said Akhtar, face gray, "is this witch you have dredged up?"

"This honorable widow," Jihan said coolly, "studies with Zahir. She has been here a mere handful of weeks. And no one told her about your childhood bedroom, I can assure you. I had hoped to have her demonstrate for you how far my experiment has come, brother. But not like this. I thought you would be more—civilized."

Akhtar released Zahir with a curse. Zahir doubled over, coughing, heaving for breath.

"We found—all. Memory of her soul," Zahir forced out, voice raw. "In the realm of ash." He coughed again, massaging his throat a little. "I will learn what the Maha knew. I will give you his knowledge, so that you may save us from the curse, when you are Emperor."

Akhtar's eyes narrowed. Calculating.

"He can do this," Jihan said, "because I procured him Lady Arwa's assistance."

"Is she a witch, then, sister?" Akhtar asked. "A heretic in widow's clothing?"

"She has Amrithi blood," said Jihan. "It makes her useful. And she dearly wants to be of use. Don't you, Lady Arwa?"

"Yes, my lady," said Arwa. "Anything for the sake of the Empire."

"Barbarian blood. Wonderful. My brother spills it, and I bring it into my household." For all the harshness of his words, Akhtar's tone had finally softened. "You think you can find the Maha's knowledge, Zahir? Truly?"

"Yes."

"Yes, *my lord.*"

Zahir raised his head. His eyes were red, his skin flushed, but he looked at Akhtar with a stare that was quietly, clinically eviscerating. It was a look that could flay a man's soul from his skin and *study* it, with terrible, dispassionate care.

"Yes," he said. "My lord."

Akhtar's hand made a fist.

"You are still a dog that should have been drowned with its mother," he said softly. "You know that, don't you?"

"Yes, my lord," said Zahir. "I know."

"No matter what Parviz believes, the spirits, the unnatural ill luck—they remain a threat to all we have," Jihan said, forcibly drawing Akhtar's attention back to her. "One Zahir's work can put right."

"I know," Akhtar said. An exhalation. "I know. So get on with it. Fix it."

"As my brother wills." She bowed her head. Turned to go. "Come, Arwa."

Arwa turned and followed her, looking back once at Zahir.

His own hand was still around his reddened throat, as if he held his own death and life both in the palm of his hand.

She had thought, once, that he had a nature like a keen blade. She had not considered that he lived his entire life on a knife edge. It would take so little to see him dead: a shift in the familial balance of power; failure in his work; an expression on his face that foolishly revealed the glittering sharpness of his mind.

She touched her own fingers to her throat. Her pulse was river-fast; she could not hold it.

His eyes met her own.

Go, his gaze said. *Go now.*

She did not want to leave him.

But she turned away from him regardless, doing as she had been bid, the image of him imprinted on her eyelids.

CHAPTER SIXTEEN

She sought out Gulshera.

The widows often rested at midday, and perhaps as a result of the tense, subdued mood of the women's quarters, not a single one of the elders was present in the communal spaces of their wing. Arwa went directly to her own chamber.

Arwa entered her room and found Gulshera there waiting for her. She was not even sitting on the bed, but standing at attention, coiled with energy, head tilted forward, pale eyes hooded.

"Tell me everything," she said.

Arwa shook her head.

"You told me that we can't discuss him. Lord Zahir." There was an edge of malice to her words. She knew it. Gulshera had avoided her, denied her company and a confidante, for the sake of keeping a promise to the princess. And Arwa could not blame her for that—she knew an imperial daughter had infinitely more power and value than either of them possessed—and yet the viciousness bubbled in her regardless.

"True," Gulshera acknowledged. "I did. And yet I am asking: Tell me as much as you can. As much as is safe for both of us."

Arwa nodded. As much as was safe.

She did not know what was safe anymore.

"I was taken to Prince Akhtar's study. I remained veiled. Princess Jihan and Lord Zahir were both present. Prince Akhtar was angry about Prince Parviz's actions in the Hall of the World. He feared Prince Parviz would supersede him. Then he and Princess Jihan spoke of..." Arwa paused. Said: "Of Lord Zahir."

"Go on," prompted Gulshera. "Leave that tale in silence. Tell me what happened next."

"Prince Akhtar tried to strangle Zahir." She said it entirely without feeling. Her insides were burning with a fury she could not feel. Not about a prince. Not about a blessed. "He put his hands around Zahir's throat. Princess Jihan did...didn't stop him. He only stopped when I—interfered. I think she wanted me to."

Arwa had not told Gulshera of Jihan's barely veiled message, of the princess's desire for Arwa to make Zahir happy, to give him...more than simply her apprenticeship. The thought of speaking of such a thing made her throat burn, stoppered.

It was, after all, not a safe thing to tell Gulshera of.

"Damn Jihan and her games." Gulshera touched her fingertips to her forehead, pressing at an invisible pain. "I am tired of being so constrained. Ah, what I could do if she *allowed* it."

"Aunt?"

"You tell me nothing, as ordered," Gulshera said grimly. "But Jihan said nothing about what I could tell you, Arwa. Sit."

Arwa sat. Gulshera paced before her, back and forth, with the same fierce tread she'd had upon the grass outside the hermitage. There, it had given her an air of confidence. Here, she simply looked caged.

"Do you know when the Emperor usually chooses his heir?"

"In his old age," said Arwa. "Often upon his deathbed."

Gulshera nodded.

"It has never been a difficult task, Arwa. One son is always superior to the others. They say our current Emperor was born with a halo of light about his brow. But now…well." A shrug. "The Empire is changed, is it not? We all know it. Many men of court have long believed his eldest son would inherit. Akhtar is fit for it. Well-educated, versed in the nature of court politics, surrounded by able advisers…" Gulshera's lips thinned. "But he is also—as you have seen."

As you have seen. She thought of his hand around Zahir's throat, his words to Jihan. She remembered how Jihan had spoken of Akhtar's temper, the night of the feast. Arwa needed no further clarity than that.

"Parviz has a military bent," said Gulshera. "And a level of— zeal—that many consider a strength. He believes in the Emperor's might and that crushing heresy will return the world to its proper order. But the world has changed since the Maha's death, in ways that cannot be easily undone without great bloodshed."

"What ways?"

A narrow look.

"You think he will be gentle with pilgrims and mourners, who collect relics of the Maha and pray for his soul? Or those who place folk charms outside their windows to keep the daiva away? I think not."

"And Prince Nasir?"

"He is no danger to anyone," said Gulshera dismissively. "No more than a boy. But two princes at war is enough, in these terrible times. No. Prince Akhtar must ascend the throne. He must become Emperor, when his father passes." A pause. "There is little time."

The Emperor's visible frailty. She had wondered. Her heart clenched.

"Must it be Prince Akhtar who rules us?" Arwa asked, soft, knowing the danger of her words.

"It is what Jihan wants," said Gulshera. "And her, I trust above all others. So Arwa: Be careful. Consider your role. Consider what must be done, in the time left to us all."

When she entered Zahir's workroom that night, raising her veil, he was lighting his candles, wick to oil, shadows flickering on his hands. His face was turned away from her.

"Lord Zahir," she said.

"Lady Arwa," he responded. He didn't turn.

"Look at me," she ordered, soft, and felt a thrill when he turned to the sound of her voice.

The thrill soured when she saw the bruises mottling his throat.

"We can enter the realm of ash directly, if you like," he said.

"How can your family treat you so?"

"I am not family, to Akhtar," Zahir said. "I had no right to call him brother. In fact"—a rueful smile—"perhaps I wanted to anger him."

"I hate it," Arwa burst out. "He should not have done it. It is so—so very wrong. You have worked so hard to help them, you have done everything in your power, placed yourself in terrible danger to save the Empire, *their* Empire, and yet they scorn and hurt you like this? No."

She took a step closer. No veil, nothing to hide the sheer way she felt everything—too deep, too fierce. "You are a person, you are their blood. You deserve their respect."

She felt like an animal, wild with feeling. She thought of the dreamed tenderness of Zahir's grandmother, her sewn golden stars, his grandmother who had never treated him with the same kindness she'd shown her legitimate grandson. She thought of the stars upon her shawl. She knotted her own fingers in her embroidered shawl, with its strange sparse constellations—and froze.

Zahir's fingers were pressed to her knuckles. Feather light.

"Please," he said. "You'll damage the cloth."

Gently, he untangled the shawl from her hands. Then their hands were simply touching. Skin to skin.

"I don't require your fury, Lady Arwa. I am in truth very lucky."

"And who," she said shakily, "convinced you of that?"

"I did. I should be dead, Lady Arwa. I should have died with my mother."

He drew his hand back. Touched it to the mottled skin of his neck.

"I don't often have the opportunity to tell the tale. In many ways it is not mine to tell. But my mother was from—a long heretical Ambhan mystical tradition. An order of women scholars, courtesans by trade, who worked in secret, who sought a world where even those who were not men of noble blood could rise in service to the Empire. A world where choice and merit were prized, where all could serve and rise beneath the Emperor and Maha's benevolent eyes. In honor of their own secrecy, they named themselves the Hidden Ones. You will, of course, recognize that name."

Arwa inclined her head in silence. Her mind was racing. Mystics. Courtesans. Poetry. A history of women seeking a stake in the Empire's games of power and knowledge from the realm of the dead itself.

And Zahir, here, alone. A man and a blessed, bound to them by a thread of scholarship and blood.

"My mother and the Empress were—friendly." Voice halting. "A courtesan must be entertaining. My mother not only danced and—did as courtesans do. She also sang. Recited poetry. Performed at salons of women, at feasts and celebrations. The Empress took a liking to her. She would invite my mother to sing to her, and when my mother shared a little of her esoteric interests, the Empress saw the potential benefit of them." Ghost of a smile. "Jihan is very like her."

"So I have been told."

"When the Maha died, my mother believed she could help the Empire. She offered her knowledge to the Emperor, and recognizing it as heresy, well..." Eyes closed. Opened. "Perhaps she thought the Emperor's fondness for her would protect her. Or the Empress's. But of course—not.

"When the Maha died, and the Empire fell into the first chaos of grief, my mother believed she could help the Emperor raise a new world from the ashes of the Maha's dead: an Empire like a lamp of truth, a beacon saved and shaped by many hands. She pleaded with him to seek the support of the people. *Alchemize their grief into service*, she told him. *Let your people serve you, and they will build you a stronger Empire from their love.*"

"No," Arwa whispered. She knew her horror was written upon her face.

Zahir inclined his head, acknowledging the look.

"The Emperor had to secure his power. He could not allow his position to be weakened by her heresy. Respect for noble blood and hierarchy and order had to be maintained. I understand this." He said it matter-of-factly. Confidently. As if it were a thing he had told himself, until the words had worn a groove into his soul, until they had the bone-deep quality of truth. "If not for Jihan's intercession—if not for the skills my tutors gave me, that my mother gave me—I would have died long ago. I have the opportunity to serve the Empire. I have the opportunity to show Jihan my gratitude."

Arwa said nothing. Her voice seemed to have left her.

"I am a pragmatist," Zahir continued. "The world owes me nothing. Prince Akhtar owes me nothing. And yet, I have been given the opportunity—the possibility—to save the Empire. I cannot estimate how many will die if a miracle does not save the Empire. I like precision, Lady Arwa, but the numbers are—impossible, too terrible to calculate. That is what I focus on. The aspect of my life I can control. The deaths I can, perhaps, avert. The work I can do, that I have chosen. And all of this is—not insignificant. I have tried to mold myself into someone worthy of the task."

"I don't think you are a pragmatist," said Arwa.

"No?"

No.

I think you are a furious idealist, so passionate you'll splinter yourself on your idealism, so hungry for your purpose you would die for it.

I think you understand love is finite, and you strive for the small scraps you receive.

As I have. As I do.

"No," Arwa said, unable to shape the words. Her voice shook like a reed. "No, you are not."

He stared into her eyes. She stared back.

"Who have you molded yourself for, Lady Arwa?" he asked softly. "If I may be so bold."

She was struck, again, by the way he could look through a person, the way her nature felt like a bare wound before him.

She swallowed.

"Everyone, of course. What else could I do? But I am afraid, since my husband died, I've lost the talent for it." She didn't know how to express to him how she felt: the anger in her, and the desire for a war worthy of her fury; the grief in her, and the way it swallowed all her learned goodness whole. She was not sure she wanted to offer him such knowledge about her—such power over her. And yet...

He had told her about his mother. She could offer him a truth in return. Besides, the words were burning in her throat, hot as coals. She couldn't contain them.

"I am not like you, my lord," Arwa said. "I am a widow and

illegitimate and my blood is— my blood. I deserve little. I should
be grateful for what I have. But whatever I deserve—I do not
want it."

She did not say, *I want more*. He understood.

"The wanting will not help you accomplish anything," he
said. Guarded. Reading her with his eyes.

"I know, my lord. Nonetheless, I still want, and grieve, and
rage. I cannot stop myself, it seems." *Want*. She should not have
said *want*. There was a flush of color to his face, and she was sure
her own burned also.

"Now," she said. "I would like to begin our work, my lord.
May we?"

"Of course," he said. Cleared his throat. "Follow me."

They entered the realm of ash as always: by blood and flame and
drug-laced sleep.

Arwa had theorized that further exposure to the realm of ash
would give their souls the strength and stamina to travel deeper
into the realm.

"I watched soldiers train often enough to understand the
logic of building the body's strength for a task," she'd explained.
"Some of the green boys who joined my husband's service could
not even hold the weight of their armor at first. But Kamran
would make them wear it, and in time the body would find a
way to carry its burden. The same may work for the soul."

"Except that the soul has no bones, no musculature," Zahir
pointed out.

"Do you want to discuss the way our souls mimic our bodies
and the possible implications of that?" Arwa asked, cocking her
head, allowing a challenge to flicker in her voice.

"I don't want a headache tonight," Zahir had said, shaking his
head with a smile. "We'll test your theory and see what becomes
of it."

Luck had been with them. They had begun, in small increments, to move farther and farther from flesh, farther along Zahir's path of ghostly, inherited dreams. They held their roots tight and entwined, the shimmer glass of their hands jointly clasped.

They moved through strange gossamer rooms of ash. Forests of bodies that hung suspended, caught frozen between laughter or tears, memories preserved in amber. Arwa saw figures upon thrones, worlds in hands and mouths. Bodies caught mid-dance, hands outstretched, skirts whirling. She saw women and men. Caught in his history was an imperial line, ancient and powerful, a bloodline that awed her. And another bloodline—of scholars and mystics and courtesans. His mother's blood.

His mother who had died for the Empire, for the sake of knowledge, and all the dangers it brought.

They were on the sand again. Pain tugged at Arwa's insides, soul and flesh both. She looked at his glasslike face. There was no feeling in it; nonetheless, she knew he felt as she felt.

"Just a little farther," he said.

She nodded. There was too much at stake for either of them to hold back.

They walked one step farther. Two. Suddenly Arwa felt— strange. The sand sharpened, jagged around her. The grains were moving, whirling softly around her ankles. As if...

As if they were on the edges of a storm.

There were not trees, not any longer; no canopy, no shadows of leaves, not even bare sky. Instead there was a whirling, white-edged storm. It took her a moment to recognize the storm for what it was. It was the storm Arwa always woke to, when she entered the realm of ash. It was a memory of dreamfire.

Arwa gazed at it, her attention drawn as if by cold fingers. White, gray, ash, and smoke. Within it, she saw shadows of figures, no different from the ones she had seen in Zahir's forest of ink-dark trees.

One of the figures moved. And for the barest moment—a heartbeat, at most—the ash parted. And Arwa saw her.

Turn of a skirt. Long braid of curling hair. Skin, brown as rain-drenched soil, a face of high cheekbones and a soft mouth and a blue shawl at the throat, of flesh and not ash, and Arwa *knew that face—*

Mehr.

"What is it?" asked Zahir.

She squeezed her dreamed eyes shut, felt her distant body move a little upon the ground where it slept. When she looked again, her sister's too-mortal figure was gone. Somewhere her heart raced and raced, and her skin flushed with grief so sharp it was a knife in her belly, but she could only feel it distantly here, and she was thankful for that.

"Lady Arwa," Zahir prompted. His voice was low with concern. "Speak to me."

My sister, she thought. *I saw my sister.*

She could not say it. If she did, she would shatter entirely. And what good would she be then? Instead she said, "Something is different here. I feel as if...I'm on my own path of ash, and not yours." She spoke carefully, glad her voice was steady, glad her racing heart could not shape her voice here. "I think our paths have—crossed, somehow. Joined. Or bled into one another."

"That would be—an interesting development," he said tightly.

"When you last ate ash, you know I saw a little of what you saw," she said. "Perhaps when people travel the realm of ash together, their paths begins to...connect."

"I think we may need to research this further, before we continue."

"As if you haven't read every book in your library."

"Ah, you forget the key quality of books," he responded. "They have a far greater capacity than a man's memory, and doubtless contain answers I can't recall." His grip tightened. "If we let the roots draw us back—"

"No."

She thought of Akhtar's hand around Zahir's throat, of the Emperor, old and trembling. She thought of Mehr.

And she thought—as she always thought, every moment—of Darez Fort.

"Lord Zahir. You are running out of time. The Empire is running out of time. Besides, what better way is there to test the limits of what we can accomplish, than to try?"

He said nothing. But when Arwa stepped forward, he did not argue. He followed her.

Another step. Another.

On the storm-burnt sand that was their joined paths, they stopped once more. Horror rose in Arwa's throat.

They were surrounded by bodies.

This was not a scene of war: a dream she could understand being left behind in this realm of mortal dreaming and ghosts. This was...children. Women. Men, young and old, their ash figures too sharp in her vision, broken into segments of limbs, half buried, as if a storm had lifted the sand and revealed their remains.

Their presence should have repulsed her, sent her stumbling back to her own skin. She should have felt the tremor of her own heart, a sharp cold breath in her lungs.

Instead she felt a terrible longing. A *knowing*.

These bodies lay upon both their paths. But they were as much hers as the dancing figures, the throned ones, that existed under the shadow of Zahir's great trees. Her sister had been a sign of them, somehow: a portend, a bright beacon. A blazing lantern in the dark, guiding Arwa to the truth.

"Arwa," Zahir said, voice urgent.

"Step forward with me," she insisted. He spoke again. She did not hear him.

She kneeled down despite Zahir's distant protests, drawing him down with her. She felt the call of the limbs before her like a song. She saw a shadow memory of a hand, broken from a body, a dagger clutched desperately in its fist.

The dagger. It looked like—

The dagger her sister had given her.

Mehr's dagger.

Distant breath tight in her chest. She reached for the hand, feeling the ash shatter at her touch, sweeping over her glass-boned fingers, gray clouding it from within. If she remained where she was, it would fill her.

"Arwa!"

Zahir wrenched her to her feet. The storm drew the ash away.

"We need to leave here," he told her.

"These are Amrithi dead," gasped Arwa. "I know it. I recognize the blade. I can feel them drawing me to them."

"Lady Arwa, you need to be careful."

"I know who they are. I can feel it. And I saw—"

"You know there are dangers here," he cut in, desperate. "Please—"

He was reaching for their roots, ready to allow the tethers to draw them both back to their flesh. But Arwa could not leave. Not yet.

She wrenched free from his grip. Roots wrenching, unfurling. She was suddenly only one soul, alone. She felt the thud of her heart, lungs seizing. But her path of ash had a terrible magnetism.

There was no sign of her sister. No bright beacon to guide her. But there was a figure lying between the rest, its edges somehow clearer and sharper than all those that surrounded it. A torso, a face turned against the sand, a single arm flung out, knife in its throat. The eye opened. A jumble of parts. A jumble of bodies.

Arwa leaned over it, terrified. She thought again of her sister in the storm, a cruel mirage, too bright and alive.

She had to know. Had to know.

She parted her mouth. Pressed her hand down. The ash rose to meet her.

She was not Arwa anymore.

She was a woman named Nazrin. She knew what it meant to be an Amrithi woman: to live in Irinah's vast desert, to travel with her clan and children, to avoid the Ambhan authorities, who had no love for her people. She knew how to barter with local villagers, offering them her blood as defense against the daiva in return for food and resources. She knew how to dance rites of worship.

She knew what it meant to have been born both gifted and cursed. As a child, she had watched a storm of dreamfire with her clan. Reached for it . . . and felt the dreamfire reach back.

She'd known then that she possessed the gift of *amata*.

Some Amrithi women and men had too much daiva blood still in their veins. Some, like their daiva ancestors, could not make vows without the weight of those vows being burned into their skin and souls. Some could move the dreams of the Gods to their will, if they knew the way, if they were willing to indulge in a terrible world-breaking heresy.

How her mother had wept, when it was discovered that Nazrin was one such Amrithi. *You are something the Maha will steal from me*, she'd said. *He will make you vow yourself to him and use you to crush the ill dreams of the Gods and make them dream unnatural glory for his Empire. I know it.*

Nazrin had insisted he would not. He would not steal her like he had other Amrithi with her gift. She would hide her power. She would be clever and canny and quiet. She would not show her face in villages too closely allied with Ambhan officials in search for her kind. She would survive. She told her mother so, but her mother only shook her head and wept all the more.

The monster will destroy you, one way or another.

Nazrin knelt upon the sand, weeping. Remembering her mother. Her nose was clogged. She could not move her arm to wipe it. She needed her left arm to hold herself up from the ground. She needed her right to hold her blade, which was at her own throat. Closer, and she would cut herself; farther away, and one of the figures surrounding her would take it from her, and then she would be lost.

"Woman," said the mystic. His face was wrapped in blue cloth. His eyes were terrible, compassionate and unyielding. "The power in you belongs to the Empire and our Maha. Lower your blade."

Nazrin thought of her children. She was grateful beyond measure that neither of them possessed the *amata*. She had taken them into a dreamfire storm, watched, heart in her throat, for any sign they shared her burden. There had been nothing. Although they would face the same dangers all Amrithi did, the same persecution, they would never kneel, as she did. They would never be forced to make the inevitable choice: slavery, or death by their own blades.

I am Amrithi, she reminded herself. *Amrithi, and my freedom is my right.* And yet her heart quailed; she wished for something—someone, anyone—to save her.

But there was no one, and as the mystic drew toward her, she drew the blade firmly across her own throat.

Flicker. Ash, sweet as wine.

Arwa was not Nazrin anymore.

She felt new ash unfurl beneath her skin.

His name was Ushan.

His mother had lain with a daiva in the heart of a dreamfire storm, and Ushan had been the result. He'd been born more or less human. His mother had told him so. She had counted all his fingers at his birth; peeled back his lips to see the unformed gums, the tongue, the wailing cry of mortal lungs. And yet he dreamed strange dreams, and sometimes his shadow changed, transforming into inhuman shapes: a bird, a snake, a panther; a thing hooded, a thing naked and all bones.

He met his daiva parent once. Tall, they had been so tall, with hair like a dark flame and eyes of gold; lush mouth and bones like blades. Ushan had offered his parent blood, and they had tasted it, and wrapped him up in a shroud of shadow, lifting him with great wings carved from shadow. This, Ushan had recognized as love.

The memory slipped away.

Arwa. She was Arwa. For a moment.

Then the storm descended once more.

A knife lay in a man named Tahir's hand. He held it to his throat, trembling, biting his tongue. He thought of his little girl; his girl who would be Tara and lead her clan. At least she was not here. At least she would not have to know what had become of him.

Then Arwa was Ushan again. Stretching his arms wide. Bitter fury bubbling in his blood. Body changing. Grief stretching its wings within him.

His arms were feathered and sharp. Her arms were feathered and sharp. Her mouth opened.

His mouth—

"Girl," he said. His voice rumbled out of him. "Return to your flesh, before it's too late."

She felt something grip her arm. Fingers strong, firm. Something dragging her back, back—

She heard screaming. Her throat hurt. It took her a moment to realize she was the one crying out, that Zahir was holding her and whispering her name, firm against her hair, as he held her pinned.

"Arwa, Lady Arwa, Arwa, please, speak to me. Speak to me. Can you hear me?"

Arwa. She was Arwa. She was not Ushan, daiva-blooded. She was not Nazrin. Not Tahir. She was not an Amrithi with a knife to their own throat. She scrabbled wildly, gasping for words, until finally he understood and released her.

"Do you know yourself?" he asked. "Are you well? Are you safe?"

"Yes," she forced out. "I know who I am." *No, no, no.*

"You let go of our shared roots," he said. "You consumed ash. You could have—anything could have happened to you, Arwa." Through her own screaming trauma, she realized he was honestly shaken. His face was gray with fear. "You saw how I nearly forgot myself, when I consumed my grandmother's ash, and that I did with *you* bound to me, to ground me. You could have lost yourself. Arwa, you should not have done it. What possessed you to risk your soul and mine?"

But his words were distant. A buzz in her ears.

She could still feel the blade at an Amrithi throat.

When she remained silent, he swore to himself. Then he shook his head, and stood.

"I'll get you some water," he said.

She rose to her feet.

"I need to go," she told him.

He reached for her once more. She shook him off, and walked up the steps of the enclosure, unveiled. The air pinched her skin.

"Lady Arwa," he called, his voice all mingled rage and worry.

"Don't follow me," she said. "Please, my lord."

She left despite his protests. Walked for a while, then kneeled down among the plants and retched and wept, blocking her own voice out with a hand between her teeth.

Amrithi. Dead Amrithi. Ah, Gods.

CHAPTER SEVENTEEN

Her sister. Her sister.

It was as if the loss of Mehr were a book, a great tome, like the ones in Zahir's library. But half the pages had been ripped out brutally, pointedly. The rest were in a state of ruin: water-damaged, mold creeping up their edges, the words smudged to indecipherability. Arwa could only read a sentence here or there, piecing together a patchwork grief.

She knew Mehr had revealed her Amrithi-ness. She knew the Maha's mystics had taken Mehr. She knew Mehr had died.

Now here she was, the damaged fragments of a dozen other tales strewn in her lap. Tales of persecution and death; tales of Amrithi with a gift called *amata*, a gift that allowed them to control the dreams of the Gods, stolen by the Maha for their power. Stolen by the Maha, in order to shape the Empire's glory.

Just as she and Zahir had worked to piece together an image of the realm of ash, so too was she forming a picture of Mehr's true fate, and true death.

Arwa had witnessed a dreamfire storm, and soon after her sister had been taken. Had her sister called the dreamfire to her—revealed a seed of *amata* in her blood?

Her sister had told her she was getting married. She had given Arwa her Amrithi blade, and told Arwa not to fear, and told her she would see her again. And then Mehr had gone to the Maha, and died. But she had not simply died. She had been used and enslaved and forgotten. Her gift—her Amrithi gift of *amata*—had been used to manipulate the dreams of the Gods, suppressing dreams that would bring ill fortune, raising up dreams that would continue to burnish the Empire's glory.

After the night her father wept by her bed, Arwa had heard no more of her sister. Once, she had asked her mother Maryam about her, tentatively questioned where Mehr had been buried. Her mother had gone quiet, and cold, and told her not to ask again. *Some things*, she'd said, *will only hurt you. Let it be, Arwa.*

Arwa had grieved for Mehr, but she had blamed her too, for the fall of their family into disgrace. For being so Amrithi, when she could have made the choice Arwa had made, to mold herself into a quiet Ambhan daughter and wife. She had blamed Mehr because she had been ignorant. Because she'd known nothing.

But now Arwa knew. And she was hurt—yes, as her mother had told her she would be hurt. But she was also furious she'd been denied the right to that pain. To the truth.

You were stolen, Arwa thought. *You were stolen, and no one told me. I did not know. Oh, Mehr.*

Mehr had died because of the Maha. Her father had tried to bring Mehr home, and in return the Maha—his Empire, his nobility, the world he had carved—had flung her family into disgrace. The blame for that lay at the Maha's feet too. Not Mehr's.

And Amrithi—generations of them, beyond Arwa's graceless understanding—had been enslaved or died by their own knives. Over and over again. The Maha had used them. Taken their magic. Built the Empire's glory upon their bones.

Her sister. Her poor sister. Arwa retched again, a visceral reaction.

Her head was full of ash, full of flashes of preserved memory, sharp as splinters. She was Arwa. She was Arwa.

Nazrin. Ushan. Tahir.

Arwa made it back to her room somehow. She was glad not to see Eshara or Reya patrolling the halls. She reached, fumbling, through her own trunk of possessions, between pale folded tunics and sashes, trousers and scarves until she found her own dagger and held it in her hands. Trembling, she unfolded it from the protective casing of fabric that surrounded it.

She thought of her sister, again: of being raised to put aside her Amrithi-ness; of carrying the shadow of it inside her nonetheless, the ghosts of all the people who had come before her, buried and lost, in a desert of the Maha's dead. She thought of the history and the people she had never known, the culture of her birth mother that had been stolen from her, cleaved straight from her body. She thought of the Arwa she was not: the shadow Arwa fashioned from all the Amrithi things she had taught herself not to be. The Arwa she had yearned to be, once.

She barely slept.

In the morning she washed herself, and then took her own shears to her hair. Looked at herself in her mirror: her sand-brown skin, her deep brown eyes, large in her fine-boned face. She looked like an Ambhan woman. She knew it. It seemed almost cruel, after all, that she could see nothing of her sister in her own face.

We have the same blood, her sister had told her once. Arwa had no vows burned into her skin, had said her marriage vows without ancient magic binding them to her soul and flesh. She had no *amata*.

And yet she couldn't help but think of the Amrithi families that military commanders like her husband had driven out of villages. She thought of the warnings her mother had pressed into her of the suffering of faceless Amrithi, and how Arwa had thought: *That could be me.*

I cannot allow that to be me.

She remembered Mehr's smile. The sound of her singing a lullaby. The feel of her arms, as she held Arwa close.

The same blood. They all had the same blood.

The heretic mystics were put to death. The women of the imperial household were not expected to attend, for which Arwa was grateful. But Jihan, as Emperor's daughter, was expected to witness. Gulshera accompanied her, as did Jihan's closest noblewomen.

Arwa waited for their return for a time. She thought of death. Of Amrithi. Of Darez Fort. Of soldiers, and their fears. She searched through her belongings and left her room.

She found Gulshera in her own chamber.

The room was sparsely furnished. There were no piles of letters, no tray of tea, no pen and ink. Her husband's lacquered court bow was not even upon the wall. Gulshera was lying on her divan, eyes closed. Arwa sat on the edge of the divan, thumped a carafe on the floor beside her.

Gulshera cracked open an eye.

"I don't want wine."

"It isn't wine," said Arwa. "It is—was—a drink my husband liked. Liquor made from soured milk."

"You want to make me ill?"

"It will ease your pains," said Arwa. "Kamran would give it to his men, sometimes, when they were afraid. *A drink like this,* he told them, *will make you strong.* I kept a bottle in my trunk. For memory's sake."

Arwa nudged the carafe toward Gulshera.

Gulshera gave her a look. Rising to a seated position, she took the carafe. Opened it and drank it. Grimaced.

"You are trying to poison me."

"Some poisons are good for you," Arwa said. She took the carafe from Gulshera, and drank herself. The arrack was viciously sour, a sweet burn down her throat. She grimaced.

"There," she said. "I feel better already. Don't you?"

Gulshera gave her a faint scowl.

"I'm certainly distracted. My mouth feels foul."

Arwa took another swig and Gulshera said, "Ah, Gods, put that swill down."

Arwa resisted the urge to roll her eyes, and obeyed.

They sat in silence for a moment, before Gulshera spoke.

"The Emperor was merciful. Their deaths were quick."

"Good," Arwa said tightly.

"There will be a celebration tonight," said Gulshera.

"A celebration?"

"Parviz's suggestion," Gulshera said tiredly. "More merrymaking to lift the spirits of an uneasy nobility."

"Prince Parviz doesn't care for merrymaking."

"He's learning the ways of court quickly. Murder a few men, lavish favors on a few others—soon you'll have followers driven by greed and fear aplenty."

Arwa frowned and lowered her head. *They can merrymake all they want*, she thought. *It will not change anything.* Child daiva with bone faces. Winged daiva. Famine and rebellions, and a dying Emperor.

"Does it matter if the courtiers like him?" Arwa asked.

"If those courtiers have influence over the Emperor, of course," Gulshera said dryly. "But no one truly knows the Emperor's mind."

"I think," Arwa said slowly, "I understand why you chose to leave here. It is like being caught in a net, isn't it? The longer you are here, the less you remember what it means to move freely. To know the cool air on your face. The shape and heft of a bow."

"We serve the Empire," said Gulshera, after a moment. "That, at least, is a good thing."

It was not disagreement.

Arwa wondered, somewhat helplessly, what difference there was, if any, between serving the interests of the imperial family and serving the Empire.

"Yes," Arwa said softly. "I'm glad of that."

Gulshera placed a hand on Arwa's back. Through her touch, Arwa felt the sharpness of her own bones, the fragility of her spine, her lungs as she breathed in and out, in and out, as birds sang beyond the window lattice.

Arwa didn't remain long at the feast. The thought of doing so was unbearable. She could not eat. Could not think. She left, but didn't go to Zahir, and didn't go to her own room. Instead she found herself walking to the dovecote tower.

Here, she was high—high enough to feel as if she could reach the stars. The pigeons cooed, some rustling around her. She leaned against the wall and placed her face in her hands.

For so long she had run from the true shape of her grief. She had sought to grieve as was expected of her, at the hermitage. Here at the imperial palace, she had tried to alchemize her grief into a purpose, a mission. But in the end all her efforts had failed her. Her grief was a beast without a leash. Now it hung about her close, and sharp. It was not simply a product of Darez Fort. It was ingrained in her bones—her very soul. She felt overwhelmed by the scope of the suffering that had shaped her, as she strove to be the good Ambhan daughter, all unknowing.

She could not be a good soldier or sacrifice to overcome it; worse still, sacrificing herself on the basis of her Amrithi blood filled her mouth with metal. It felt like a betrayal of the dead. Of the culture and people who she had always known were part of her.

Of her sister.

Face pressed into her arms, she finally raised her head. And smelled incense.

She whirled around.

The pigeons cooed faintly around her. They rustled gently in their nooks. There were no daiva.

No daiva, until she looked up.

At the peak of the tower were a dozen birds in shadow. But they were not, she realized, in shadow after all. They *were* shadow. They stared down at her with eyes like blazing lights, burnished gold.

Bird-spirits.

At the hermitage, when she had stabbed the daiva, it had broken into dozens of smaller birds. They watched her now, those same birds, not rustling or cooing, only utterly still, barely visible against the velvet dark of the night.

Arwa swallowed. Her throat was clogged—with terror and with wonder both.

She remembered Ushan, lifted off his feet by a winged daiva progenitor that had loved him.

She remembered the daiva at Darez Fort. Inhuman hands on her own. The dagger at her feet, that she could remember fumbling for in her rooms, that she could not remember laying beside her, as unnatural fear fell over the fort.

All her life, by everyone but her sister, Arwa had been told the daiva were monsters. But to her Amrithi dead, they were family. The daiva had loved their Amrithi children. Loved them enough to make a binding vow to protect them.

A vow made on blood.

"I am sorry I harmed you." Her voice sounded small. Felt small. The night seemed to swallow it. "I should never have turned my knife on you, at the hermitage. You tried to save me from the—*thing*—at the fort, didn't you? It was no daiva, that creature of bones. You brought me a knife, you gave me the chance to use my blood, to seek your protection from that—nightmare. And this is how I have repaid you." She sucked in a breath, shallow, her heart racing. "I am sorry for trying to keep you at bay. For using my blood as a barrier against you. I didn't understand that we are kin."

The daiva birds were silent. Watchful.

She was a fool, speaking a mortal tongue to immortals. She did not know their language.

The taste of salt and ash rose in her throat. She did not. But Ushan had. Nazrin had. They all had.

She lifted her hands. Feet solid against the ground.

The Amrithi danced rites. Rites of worship. Rites to communicate with the daiva in their own language. Sigils were their language; stances were feeling. She knew this in snatches, vaguely, secondhand knowledge coming to her. She shaped a sigil for *debt*, another for *grief*.

Her hands faltered.

"I am sorry," she said again. She had no sigils for that.

The birds flew down, drawing together swift as an arrow; she saw the semblance of a human figure, felt it clasp her hands with very human hands, the beginning of a face...

Then Arwa flinched, instinctual terror, and the daiva flinched with her.

"Wait!" she shouted, but it was too late.

It broke apart again and flew away, leaving her on the tower, hands outstretched to nothing.

When she next went to Zahir he was waiting for her, bruised and cross-legged and grim.

They did not greet each other. Only stared, unwavering.

"I deserve answers, Arwa."

"Do you," she said.

"You risked both our lives, when you ripped away from me,"
he said. "I expected better."

"I am sorry for disappointing you, my lord."

Zahir laughed. A bitter thing.

"No, you're not," he said. Arwa did not answer him.

"What did you see," he said, "in the realm of ash to make you
act so rashly?"

"Exactly what you saw. Bodies."

"Yes," he said. "But that did not surprise me, and surely did
not surprise you. You are a noblewoman and a commander's
widow. You know the Maha fought many wars to establish the
Empire."

"There were children," Arwa said. "Women."

"He was ruthless, Lady Arwa," he said softly. "We know
that."

"Zahir. Lord Zahir. They lay upon my path of ash. You know
those were *my* dead. People of my blood. Amrithi. I recognized
a blade. Like my own."

He closed his eyes.

"We both know the Empire has murdered Amrithi."

"And that does not concern you? Upset you?" she challenged.

"I do not allow myself to feel pain for things I cannot alter.
You know this, Lady Arwa."

"Do you know he has done worse?" Her voice wavered.
"Worse than murder?"

He was silent. Then: "It would not surprise me."

"Don't you care?"

"I have told you, Arwa. I can't." A sudden fierceness honed his
voice to a blade. His eyes snapped open, fierce. Fixed upon her. "I
have one use. One task. If I waver from that, what will it accomplish? Who will I save, if I crumble? And you, Lady Arwa—you
live in the Empire also. You were raised a noblewoman. Do you
spend your days pondering the suffering the Empire has inflicted

on those who are not part of it, or do you choose to sweep their pain aside and focus on your own survival?"

"I made no choice," snapped Arwa.

"Did you not?"

"I have merely lived my life, Lord Zahir. As best as I can."

"Living is a choice, Lady Arwa." Zahir was leaning forward, eyes bright and fierce. "Believe me. I know."

Arwa looked away from him. Ah, his eyes burned.

"You make it sound so simple," she said.

"It truly is that simple."

"No." She shook her head. "No, it isn't."

She thought of the life she had lived. She had tried to be a good and dutiful daughter, a pleasing and gentle wife. She had been exactly what was expected of her.

Until the daiva in the hermitage. Until the surface of her world had splintered. Until she had offered herself up for this task, and opened a new door onto—light.

"It is like...your lamp. Your Hidden One's lamp of truth." She spoke slowly, weighing her words. "We know monsters with teeth live in the darkness; we know ill things live in the warp and weft of our world, but they are...no more than children's tales to us. They are hidden in deep shadow. We cannot see or feel them. To us, they barely exist. We need not acknowledge them at all. But the *lamp*, Lord Zahir."

She looked at him, and at the glow of lantern light on his skin. The hollows of his face, carved by shadow, illuminated.

"*The lamp of truth reveals the world.* But when we lift the lamp we see—knowledge that cannot be unknown or undone. That is what your poems do not say, my lord. What do you do when you find the truth at the end of the path?"

She met his eyes.

"I cannot unsee what I've seen. I can't unfeel what I felt in the realm. I know what was done to the Amrithi. More than death,

more than exile from the Empire's grace. I know what my sister…"
She stopped. The words threatened to choke her.

"I had a sister," she continued, finally. "A sister who was more
Amrithi than me. Who kept our—her—birth mother's traditions. She entered the Maha's service, married, I was told, and
then she died. And now I know what became of her. Of what
became of so many like her. And I can't look away," Arwa said
helplessly. "I can't possibly look away."

"Lady Arwa," he said softly. His eyes were wide. He said
nothing more.

And oh, that infuriated her. She took a step toward him,
hands in helpless fists.

"You are so curious, Lord Zahir. You question everything
with such care, but you surround yourself in such—such *darkness*. And I know it must be a choice. Your mother offered
her knowledge to the Emperor and was executed. Your Hidden Ones work in secrecy because exposure would see them
destroyed for heresy. You gut yourself for the Empire and the
heir apparent names you a *dog*." She spat the words. "You say
saving the Empire will save countless lives, but how can you
bring yourself to do it, when the Empire eats its own people,
when it gorges on the living and the dead alike? How can you
bring yourself to sacrifice yourself for this Empire, which will
only accept you when you are useful in the way it commands,
when you crush your true self in order to survive? *How*, Zahir?"

She was not talking of Zahir anymore. Or not simply Zahir.
She was talking of herself.

He knew it, just as she did. She could read it in every line of
his face. His gaze was shattering soft, his face an open carapace.

"What did you see in the ash?" he asked, urgent. "What did it
show you, beyond death?"

He did not deserve to know. He did not.

But perhaps *deserve* was a pointless measure of the right to know. Did Arwa deserve the truth? She had been nothing, done nothing, saved no one. Not even herself. The truth needed to be known. That was enough.

In the night the bruises around his neck were deep and dark.

"We can go back into the realm of ash," she told him. "If we had still had our roots twined together, you would have seen some of it. As I saw what you saw, the first time we entered the realm. We can go into the realm, and I can show you. Come with me again. Let me show you what the Maha did. Follow the lamp of truth, my lord."

He exhaled, a low, shaky breath.

"I'll begin the fire," he said, and turned on his heel into the next room. Arwa sagged.

Their blood had barely touched the flame when Arwa felt the pull of it. As if she already slept, a void had opened in her mind. A door. She shivered.

But she didn't tell Zahir. Only drank the tea. Only slept.

They entered the realm of ash fast. Arwa knew it better now. The red roots unfurling around her gossamer body; the new ash that clung to her dream skin. She turned to Zahir and reached her hands out to him. Stopped.

"Are you sure you're prepared to see?" she asked him.

"Yes," he said. "Show me the way."

They crossed the realm, through familiar shadowy trees, to the white sand, to the dead.

Arwa raised her hands before her. The roots rose with her. Ash gathered between her fingertips. Ash from her own path. Ash from within her own soul.

"I can show you," she said. "But the choice is yours."

He looked at her hands. He always looked at her hands.

"For good or ill, then," he said. "I promised you a bond of trust."

She did not know what compelled him—curiosity, thirst for knowledge, trust, or guilt—but he placed his head in the space between her hands. The ash rose from her skin to meet him. Her mind filled all the memories her soul had consumed: Nazrin, Tahir, Ushan. The blades. The mystics. The Maha. Great wings; a parent's love.

She saw gray creep through Zahir's blood roots. His skin. He closed his eyes. The storm around them, on Arwa's path, rose wilder and wilder. Closed upon them, neat as a lock.

When Arwa next opened her eyes—her true eyes—she was lying on the workroom floor. The fire had guttered. Dawn was beginning to brighten the sky.

Zahir was slumped against the other wall.

"Lord Zahir," she said, and clambered to her feet.

"Well," he said hoarsely. "You have lit the lamp, Lady Arwa. If I could have...?"

"Yes," she said. She brought him water from the library. Placed it next to him.

"I see now," he said. "I saw."

"What did you see?"

"I saw people forced into unbreakable vows. I saw those people—those Amrithi—forced to use their magic to manipulate the dreams of the Gods. I saw them used to death. I saw a people and civilization decimated. I see. I saw..."

He stopped.

"I saw what he did, Lady Arwa. I saw it all," he said finally. He sounded raw, broken. He turned his face away.

She didn't comfort him.

"The Empire's strength," he murmured, "was built on Amrithi magic."

"Yes," she said.

"That brings us a little closer to the truth. To...the nature of the curse upon the Empire." He spoke slowly, as if piecing the truth together through a numb veil of horror. "Our mortal world is shaped by the dreams of the Gods—multitudes of dreams, woven into the fabric of everything. Dreams of life and death, light and dark, growth and decay. He used Amrithi magic—"

"*Amata*," Arwa put in quietly.

"Yes. He used—*amata*—to crush the ill dreams, that would have brought the Empire ill fortune of any kind. He forced them into the dark. And brought only good fortune up to the light. To our world." She heard him exhale, slow, shaken. "It was not his innate glory or the worship of his loyal mystics that made us strong, after all. It was the Amrithi."

"He built the Empire on their blood," said Arwa. "On their dead. *My* dead."

"The knowledge he must have had." Zahir's voice was cold, a whisper. "The knowledge he must have had. Of reality. Of all things."

She flinched from that. Her body drew back, back. There was a wall behind her, holding her steady.

"Do you *admire* him for it? For this—monstrousness?"

"No," he said, shaking his head. "No. To know so much, as he must have done, to know the world is shaped by the dreams of the Gods and to then consciously, *arrogantly*, pervert the laws that govern reality, without thought or care or ethics—to commit a genocide..." He stopped sharply.

Then, after a moment, the fire dying between them, he said, "The Maha is gone. He cannot use the Amrithi any longer, and it is clear he has left the world...wounded. The unnatural terror, the sicknesses sweeping the Empire, the floods and the failed crops, the strange ill-starred luck our Empire suffers—Arwa, I think they are all the Empire's dark dreams, long suppressed, finally coming for us. And every day, they grow ever worse."

She saw him raise a hand, hold it before him, watching his

own fingers tremble. "He broke the world, Lady Arwa. The curse is growing worse. Growing swift and strong. I have never read a book that could put to rights his work. There is no theory that can encompass the damage he may have wrought, because the act was...untested, unmeasured. The consequences—we see them all around us. Thousands of people will die. The Empire will be a husk, empty of the living. I do not know how to fix his ill work." His hand lowered, still trembling, trembling. "I do not know how to fix it. But he still might."

He must have sensed her horror, seen it written upon her face. His eyes were reddened; his cheeks tracked with tears.

"No," she said. "No. You cannot still mean to seek his ash. You can't, can you?"

"To fix a broken tool, you must understand the intent of its maker," said Zahir. "The Empire is broken, Lady Arwa, but it is a terrible weapon, built of the living and the dead alike. If it falls, all the people within it..." His voice cracked like kindling wood. "He is a monster. I do not deny it. I saw what you saw. And yet I cannot see—cannot imagine—what else to do but seek what he knew."

She made a sound—almost a howl, that rose out of her unbidden. He looked at her with those eyes, those eyes that saw too much, and yet he didn't see at all, she was at the center of her own storm and he *did not see her*.

"You would not speak this way if he'd murdered your people," she forced out. "If your Hidden Ones were strung up upon the city walls. If everything your mother loved and learned was stolen from you—you would not *dare*. You have your history, Lord Zahir, in all these books around you. Your father's history *is* the Empire. But I have a void where half my history should be. My sister is dead. And all my life I have thought myself cursed. Tainted. You can't possibly understand how that feels."

"Lady Arwa," he said softly.

"Do not ask me not to be angry," she snapped. "Do not. And do not be kind to me. You don't have the right, I do not *give* you the right."

He pressed back against the wall, as if she had pinned him fast, as if her hands held him and choked the life from him, as Akhtar had done. He tilted his head back, his throat a dark bruise, his skin ivory-cold.

"You're right," he said. "I can't. But can you see another way? What is there but the Empire and the Maha's path for all of us? Can you even dream another world, Lady Arwa?"

Arwa swallowed hard. Stood in frozen, wordless feeling, her limbs seized with it.

She could not.

Zahir drank the water. His hands shook.

"You should go. It is almost light."

CHAPTER EIGHTEEN

Arwa did not go to Zahir the next night, or the night after that.

When she thought of returning to his side—to books and the realm and his face by firelight—she couldn't bear it.

He had seen the history of her blood. And it had...hurt him. She was sure it had. She'd seen his face etched with tears, heard the roughness of his voice, as if horror had broken its edges and left it ragged.

But it had not hurt him as it had hurt her.

He would not stop searching for the Maha's ash. He would not stop looking for answers within the faded memories of a man who had murdered the Amrithi and used them, blood and soul, to build the very Empire crumbling around them. *To fix a broken tool, you must understand the intent of its maker.*

She wanted to hate him. Hate would have been easy. Anger, too, would have been acceptable.

But instead, all she felt was despair.

Can you even dream another world, Lady Arwa?

She had not answered him.

The truth was that she couldn't. The Ambhan Empire was all she had ever known. She had been born in it, raised within it. She had watched the edges of its glory peel and fade, revealing monsters and massacres. Oh, she'd yearned as a girl for an Amrithi life, but she knew nothing in truth of how to live in a world unshaped by the Empire. Its end was not a thing to be desired. What lay beyond its death could only be chaos. An Empire empty of the living.

And yet its faded glory sat upon broken backs. On broken limbs spread across a desert of ash, a desert of trauma and of memory.

Ah, but it was part of the insidious power of the great tool the Maha and Emperors then and now had built, was it not? A world where only their voices defined heresy and rightness, where there were no other ways of being, of *living*, than the one they offered.

There was nothing but this, because they had made it so.

She wanted to run from that knowledge. She wanted the hermitage, the valley, the bow and arrow in her hands. Sweat on her skin, tensile strength of the bow trembling in her grip. She wanted anything but the ugly weight of her own thoughts, and of knowing the vast shape of the horrors that had formed this very moment: her head in her hands, her mind turning over the same words constantly, soft as a noose.

I don't know what to do.

She did not want the Empire to fall. She did not want it to survive either.

She did not want to help Zahir. But she did not want Akhtar's hands upon his throat ever again. She did not want the people of the Empire dead.

The Hidden One claimed walking the path of one's ash would lead a person to truth, to something *good*. They believed knowledge found and shared could be used to build a better world. But Arwa had only found another path, cloaked in utter darkness. And Zahir...Zahir had chosen to walk the same path he had walked all along. The Maha's path.

She did not know where to go next.

* * *

She knew someone would demand she return to her work eventually. Of course Zahir did not seek her out. She had not expected him to, truly. He seemed to consider the exit of the tomb enclosure the limits of his world and acted accordingly. Besides, the women's quarters were forbidden territory, and Arwa made a point of not walking in the gardens anywhere near his hidden home.

She was not ready yet to make a choice.

One day after the evening meal, she found Gulshera waiting for her in her room.

"If you're going to tell me to return to him," said Arwa haltingly, "I can only assure you that I will. When I am—ready."

Gulshera shook her head. She did not remind Arwa that the topic of Zahir was a forbidden one. She only said, "Arwa."

Her voice...the hairs rose on the back of Arwa's neck.

"Aunt. What is it?"

"The Emperor is dying," said Gulshera. Her voice was leaden. "He has days, perhaps. Hours."

"He—no. He can't be dying," Arwa said.

"Of course he can," said Gulshera. "You saw him. It is amazing how swiftly old age can become illness, and illness can become death. You are young, and perhaps will not be familiar with that reality."

"You always think me a fool," whispered Arwa. She did not have the energy to be hurt. She closed her eyes. Touched her fingertips to her eyelids. The soft pressure grounded her.

"Tomorrow at dawn he should hold his Beholding and audience," said Gulshera. "He will not. Then everyone will know."

"Jihan? Does she...?"

"Of course she knows. As do I. And now you."

"Why have you told me?" Arwa whispered.

In the close-eyed dark, Gulshera said, "Because I want you to accompany me to his deathbed, Arwa. Jihan has asked for me, and I ask for you."

Arwa stopped for a moment, stopped entirely, breath and body both. She swallowed. Spoke.

"I have no place there."

"You do, because I have asked you."

"Why?"

"Do not choose to remain in ignorance, Arwa." Sharp words. "Come with me. The world is about to change; the battle you have chosen will alter. You told me you chose this path. Do not give me all the guilt of ensuring you survive it."

"Do not pretend my fate concerns you that much, Aunt."

"I accompanied you here," said Gulshera levelly. "I have advised you as best as I can, despite the duties Jihan demands of me. Of course I care." She shook her head. "I have grown somewhat fond of you, Arwa," she said, in a voice that was softer than it had the right to be. They were no family to one another. No family. "Trust me or don't, Arwa. But come with me now."

Gulshera stared at her. Waiting.

In silence, Arwa nodded.

The Emperor, dying.

Ah, Gods.

The room where the Emperor lay dying was not a private space of sanctuary or intimacy. But then, an Emperor did not have the luxury of dying a private death. In a pale mimicry of the Hall of the World, scribes sat upon bolster cushions at the edge of the room. The council of his favorites kneeled. The Emperor's closest advisers kneeled also. Men on all sides kneeled in silence, and watched, waiting for the Emperor to die.

They were separated from the sight of the Emperor's dying form by a circle of gauze: great curtains unfurled from the

ceiling, forming a perimeter vast enough to both encompass his
bed and allow his women to hold vigil.

The women knelt around his divan in a circle. When they
entered, Jihan threw back her veil and kneeled at his side.

Physicians had cared for the Emperor. He wore poultices, to
stimulate his blood. Someone had placed a cloth on his forehead,
scented with attar and herbs, to soothe his head and cool his
fever.

Medicine had done all it could for him. It was the women
who comforted him now. A jug of wine laced with opium sat at
his bedside.

A guardswoman came to the door.

"The princes come," she said.

"Veil yourselves," Masuma said woodenly, and her women
covered their faces. Only Jihan and Masuma, and a scattering of
blood cousins, remained bare-faced. The princes were, after all,
their kin. The lax propriety of feasting had no place here.

Arwa lowered her own veil, and stared through the cloth at
the princes as they entered the wall of gauze and bowed low.

Nasir had obviously been weeping, but Akhtar and Parviz
both wore equally strange expressions—part grief and part hope.

No woman bowed. Their heads were turned to the Emperor.

When Parviz moved to speak, Masuma raised a hand to
silence him.

"We must wait," she said, "until your father wishes to speak,
as is right. He is still Emperor, Parviz."

She tilted her head. Raised her voice.

"Forgive this woman for speaking before you, lords," Masuma
said impassively.

A ripple of uneasy acquiescence ran through the courtiers
beyond the curtain.

The doors opened. A guardswoman walked forward. Hesitated.

"I have brought him," she said awkwardly. "As requested by the Emperor." She bowed her head, and quickly departed.

Zahir entered.

The ripple, this time, among the courtiers, was far more pronounced.

He entered tentatively, calm-eyed but pale. Arwa looked at him, heart in her throat. She felt Gulshera's fingers tighten, subtly, over her forearm.

"Enter, Zahir," the Emperor said. His voice creaked like old wood.

Parviz made a noise of disgust. Akhtar's jaw was tight enough to grind rocks.

"Father," said Nasir, the youngest and the most doted on, eyes wide. "Why?"

"He is part of my household, is he not? My daughter has acknowledged him as brother, though I have not named him as son. Bow now, Bahar's son."

Zahir bowed, deeply, face to the floor. Then he stood to the side. His gaze was steady. He said nothing. He did not even tremble, which was astonishing. Arwa supposed she was trembling enough for the both of them.

Arwa thought of his order. His analytical nature. How he disliked situations without rules, situations that could end in hurt.

And yet he was here, unacknowledged, his sister's hidden tool, before the dying Emperor.

How this could end well, she didn't know.

"My sons," the Emperor said. "I suppose it's time to name one of you my heir. And for the rest of you to vow your loyalty."

He coughed. Hacking. Laughed, showing strong white teeth, eyes crinkling in a way that revealed lost handsomeness.

"A difficult task, no? It was simpler in my youth. I had only one brother, and he was not my equal. We both knew it. I was born to be Emperor. I blazed. And I proved my worth. I conquered

Durevi, crushed it beneath my boot. My Empire was vast and beautiful. But you...my sons." He shook his head. "You inherit an Empire blighted by the Maha's death. I will not prevaricate: His death has wounded our Empire. It will need strong hands to steer it. It will need you to be loyal to one another. You are all strong in different ways, my sons, and I have asked myself what the Empire requires from its new Emperor. I have asked myself what will preserve our glory. And I have made my choice."

He looked at them with real affection. And real, clear-eyed knowledge.

"Akhtar," he said.

"Father."

"You will do, as Emperor. Keep good advisers around you, hm?"

"Father." Akhtar was desperately trying to look solemn, even as joy blazed on his face. "Father. I will."

"Parviz. Nasir."

"Father," said Parviz.

"You will respect my decision."

"Of course, Father," said Parviz. If anything, Nasir looked relieved.

"Let it be recorded, then," the Emperor said. "When I pass, my son Prince Akhtar shall become Emperor, his old name struck from him, his body crowned to an everlasting throne."

Ritual words. Strong words.

Jihan must be glad, thought Arwa. She had bound her loyalties to him, after all.

But Arwa could not yet be glad.

"Bahar's son. Come here."

Zahir came forward and bowed once more.

"Stand," said the Emperor. He gave Zahir an assessing look, cold, clinical. "You look very like your mother. She was a beautiful woman. A shame you were not born a girl. You would have been easy to marry off, simpler to deal with."

Zahir said nothing.

"She was a clever whore, your mother. Too clever. If she had invested less energy in heresy and more in being pleasing to me—well. I would not have had to put her to death, for one."

The Emperor gestured, and a maidservant hurried over, offering him wine. He drank. Lowered the cup, which clattered in the tray.

"A shame that you are not simply like your mother in looks. In truth, Zahir, you are a problem," the Emperor said bluntly, "that must be solved."

He is going to die, Arwa thought. Her stomach was in knots.

"When your mother proved herself a heathen, you were spared by the soft-heartedness of women. But the imperial family do not acknowledge or keep bastard sons for a reason. I have enough sons. Strong sons. With good blood. And you make the case for your continued survival... difficult. You may speak," the Emperor said, into the silence that swelled in response to his words.

"Everything I do, Emperor, I do for the sake of the Empire," Zahir said.

"Yes. Bahar claimed something similar. But no one named her the Maha's heir, for her work."

Zahir's head shot up. Eyes wide.

"Ah." The Emperor's voice was silken once more. "You did not know. I am relieved you did not encourage it."

"I would never, Emperor. I know what I am."

"And yet the rumors swell," the Emperor said. "I am not the old fool my sons believe me to be, boy. Even now. When you were still young, your tutors boasted of your perception, your talent. Then one idiot claims you'd be fit for the next Maha. I dealt with him. But somehow the whispers spread. Servants have loose lips. Soon the common people are whispering about a Maha's heir hidden away in my own palace. And my dear Parviz guts a fine throng of mystics who babble tales of a blessed boy who died with his whore mother and rose from the grave, the Maha's spirit in him. Tale after tale, and *you* at the heart of all of them."

That could not be true. Arwa *knew* it was not true. She had heard so many tales after the Maha's death—tales claiming he still lived, or would return from the grave; tales hoping for a new Maha to be named from the royal sons, or to rise haloed from the masses. None had named Zahir.

But ah—she looked at Zahir's blanched face, at the courtiers and guardsmen and servants listening intently beyond the gossamer walls surrounding the Emperor's deathbed, and thought of the power of the Emperor's words. All tales spoken from this moment onward would name Zahir. The Emperor had ensured it would be so.

Whether they named him a true heir or a false claimant awaited to be seen.

"Emperor," said Zahir. "I am no heir to our illustrious Maha. I am sorry for this falsehood. It was not my doing."

His voice was even, calm. His expression was resolute. Arwa saw the acceptance of death in it, the utter terror, and clenched her fingers so hard against her knees that her nails stung like dull blades.

The Emperor looked at him. "Bahar's son. I find old age makes me soft. My daughter loves you. My wife thought fondly of you, in her time. You are a pretty thing. You inspire soft hearts. Therefore: Maha's heir," he said softly. "That is what I name you. Prove yourself fit for that title. Or my sons will do what I should have done many years ago, when my soft-hearted daughter begged for your life. Let it be recorded: Bahar's son lives, and wears a new title. For now."

A tide of noise moved through the room. Jihan made a choked sound, quickly cut off.

Parviz's face was stone, his eyes murderous. A look of revulsion flickered across Akhtar's face, for only a moment. Nasir merely looked between his brothers and Zahir in confusion. He had, perhaps, not known that Zahir existed at all.

The Emperor began coughing again and Masuma began speaking to him in the softest, most urgent voice. It was Akhtar who touched his hand to the end of his father's bed, reverent, who then said, "Let us allow the Emperor to rest now. Father, with your leave..."

"Enough pronouncements," the Emperor said tiredly. "I will rest now. No more."

CHAPTER NINETEEN

Time passed interminably. For an endless stretch of hours Arwa sat behind Jihan and Gulshera as the women wept over the Emperor, as crying gave way to soft-whispered words of comfort, as Masuma gently fed him a tincture of poppies to lull him into an uneasy rest. Finally, the Emperor slept.

Slowly the men beyond the gauze began to drift away, until only the most stubborn courtiers remained. The guardsmen, not having the luxury of choice, continued to maintain their vigil, their gold-armored figures lining the walls.

Masuma rose to her feet, wincing with pain from having too long sat by her brother's side. Jihan rose as well. With a respectful sweep of her head, Jihan veiled her face and turned to leave. Her women followed her, the briefly formed grand court of women cleaved in two once more.

It was deep night. As they entered Akhtar's palace, Gulshera touched a hand to Arwa's shoulder. Arwa drew away from her. She did not want to be comforted.

"I am sorry, Aunt," said Arwa. "I want to be alone, to . . . to think."

She began to walk away.

Arwa heard the rasp of embroidered silk behind her and felt a new hand on her arm, cold-fingered. Not Gulshera's hand.

"Arwa," said Jihan. "Come with me. You want to see him, don't you?"

Jihan's expression was utterly calm, but her eyes were red, her cheeks drawn. She wondered if Jihan had cried for her father or for Zahir, or for the both of them.

"Princess," Arwa murmured. She followed in Jihan's footsteps.

Jihan's chambers were vast, lushly decorated with the scent of fresh flowers in the air. Usually Arwa would have stared about herself in awe at the beauty of the place, but she could not.

Zahir was standing in a stance Arwa recognized as the one he'd taken in Akhtar's study: hands together, head slightly lowered and tilted.

He looked at Arwa. Looked at Jihan.

"She was searching for you," Jihan said, nudging Arwa slightly forward, before sweeping farther into the room herself. "Worrying for you, Zahir."

His mouth thinned. No doubt he was thinking of the last night they had entered the realm of ash together, just as Arwa was.

"Perhaps," he said.

"Leave us," Jihan said to the maidservants tidying the room, the guardswoman at the door. "*All* of you. Quickly now."

The servants were gone in a flash.

Jihan's eyes narrowed. Her voice came out of her suddenly furious, lashing out like a whip.

"Tonight, Zahir. Find the Maha's ash tonight. Do you understand me?"

"Is my execution so close?" Zahir asked.

"Don't be so dramatic."

"I am never dramatic," said Zahir, with that cutting edge of feeling to his voice that Arwa knew so well. "I am being factual."

"Factual, factual," Jihan repeated bitterly. "If you spent less time thinking and more time doing, perhaps we would not be in this position."

"I have done nothing but study, try—"

"Enough." Her voice quelled him to silence. "Zahir, don't you see? I have protected you, often at the cost of my own reputation. I have done it for love of you, as the brother I have acknowledged, *chosen* no matter what others may say. And I have done it because I believe that what you can do—what your mother studied and sought to do—has the power to restore the Empire's glory."

Jihan crossed the room. She stood near him; her voice was no longer furious, only fierce, almost pleading.

"I have tried to make Akhtar believe it too. I succeeded for a time. But I can't make Akhtar protect you now. He no longer thinks you are of use. You are a hindrance. So you *must* act quickly, Zahir. You must prove yourself the Maha's heir."

"Maha's heir?" Zahir laughed tiredly. "I can't prove myself to be a thing that I am not."

"But, Zahir, you *could* be. Father has named you such."

"As a death sentence, Jihan."

"As a test, Zahir. And one at which you can succeed, I'm sure of it. You are no Maha now, but if you find his truth, his secrets, a part of him will live in you, won't it? A part of you will *be* him."

His gaze slid to Arwa. She held it and returned it.

She did not know what he saw in her face. But when he turned back to his sister he said, "We have discovered—something."

"Tell me."

"The Maha used the Amrithi to build our Empire," Zahir said. "He enslaved those with a special form of magic. He used their gifts to compel the Gods. To dream the Empire's strength and glory." A beat. "Did you know this, sister?"

Jihan said nothing.

"Ah," Zahir said finally. "I see. Did you not think that information would be useful in my task?"

"Once you discovered the Maha's ash, you would know anyway," Jihan said. The fire was gone from her voice, which was suddenly, terribly cool. "So I thought. But you haven't found the Maha's ash yet, I take it?"

"Do not claim you were testing me," Zahir shot back. "That is an excuse, and worse, a lie. It makes no sense, Jihan. You have trusted me with so much. Why not this?"

"Because you have a soft heart," snapped Jihan. "You wept for weeks after your mother's death."

"I was a *child*."

"You still feel far too much. You have no idea what it is like here at court, Zahir, the dangers I face, the spite my brothers hurl at one another and the world. You crumble when Akhtar shows you the smallest cruelty—you lack the skills to defend yourself. Lady Arwa had to save you last time."

Arwa bit her tongue hard enough that she tasted iron. *That is not what happened, not at all.* She must have moved, must have flinched, because Zahir was turning toward her, mouth parted, a furrow between his brows—then Jihan touched his face, and held him still.

"Zahir. Look at me, dear one." Her voice softened. She clasped his face, ever so gentle. "Ever since your mother passed, I have tried to protect you. I always have, have I not?"

"You have."

"I have only ever wanted to protect you: from our father, from court, from yourself. In truth, I have kept secrets from you because I am soft too," she confessed. "I couldn't bear to see you—hurt. Or burdened. As I am burdened. I wanted to protect you from this as I have always protected you from all things."

Arwa looked at Jihan's glistening eyes, the softness of her face.

Oh, the princess was a politician in truth. She lied so very beautifully.

Zahir nodded, once. It was enough. Jihan lowered her hands.

"Besides," she said. "The knowledge of how the Amrithi were utilized—that secret belongs to select people. The imperial family. The mystics. Our Maha. No one else."

Zahir did not flinch.

"Not to the Maha's heir, Jihan?"

"Find his ash, and then you'll be his heir. I'll lay all the knowledge you like in your hands, then."

"I am curious," Zahir said. Voice smooth as stone. "What if I find the Maha's ash and discover he had nothing to preserve our Empire but Amrithi magic? What then, Jihan?"

"He knew everything," she said. "He created the Empire from nothing. The Gods gave him the Amrithi. He was blessed. He will have answers for us, Zahir, you know it must be true. After all, who else is there, who can possibly save us?"

"That, I don't know," said Zahir.

"Please just find answers from him in the place beyond. Please."

"Of course, Jihan. It has always been my goal." He lowered his head, avoiding her gaze. His brow was still furrowed, jaw tight.

"Will you give your all to save the Empire, Lady Arwa?" Jihan asked.

Ah, you remember me, thought Arwa. But she did not allow herself to be viperous. She lowered her own eyes demurely.

"Princess, I will give everything."

"Good."

Jihan did not touch Arwa, but her voice was cold-fingered regardless, and made Arwa shiver as if a chill, proprietary hand had passed over her soul. "You should give everything, Lady Arwa. Your fate and Zahir's are intertwined now, after all. Whatever befalls him, befalls you."

It was a threat. And a promise.

*   *   *

Your fates are intertwined.

She should have realized the significance of the easy way Jihan had allowed her to see Akhtar's furious ugliness, the cracks in his nature; her own drunken mirth; Zahir's vulnerable throat.

She had never planned for Arwa to leave.

Arwa had not known. She had not considered it, in truth, only thrown herself headlong into her own destruction. Even now she could find nothing inside herself that called her to fear for herself. Instead she felt strangely hysterical, as if grief and horror had carved away what little good sense she had.

"All this time," murmured Zahir. "All my study, and yet Jihan hid the truth from me. How did she expect me to save the Empire, when I worked with nothing but a shadow of knowledge?"

Arwa laughed. She couldn't help but laugh.

This, at least, she could answer.

"Because you are a tool, Lord Zahir. A tool does not need to know why it does what it does. It need only—be used."

Oh, Arwa knew all about being fashioned into a thing that had utility. A good noblewoman had to be useful, or so she had been taught, all her life. And she had embraced her utility, after the hermitage—embraced a soldier's purpose, one that provided her direction without demanding thought from her.

"Too much knowledge gives a person power," she added. "Too much knowledge forces people to think. And choose."

"A tool," he murmured. There was a long silence. She listened to his breath, the tread of his footsteps, as they walked across the gardens. "I suppose that is the price of a—home."

Arwa laughed again. Soft, almost drunkenly. She felt dizzy with strangeness.

"You live in a tomb. That is not a home."

"Don't," he said. "Please."

Arwa fell silent. She could not say she was sorry. She wasn't. She was still uneasy with him, after their last night in the realm of ash. But she had seen the way his father had treated him. She had seen how Jihan loved him. Used him.

You deserve more than this, she wanted to say. But she already knew he would not agree, and there was something brittle about his face and the turn of his head that kept the words from passing her lips.

"Jihan likes to use my tears as evidence of my softness," said Zahir. "She doesn't understand that I wept when my mother died not out of grief alone, but because I wanted the Empress to pity me. I needed her to consider me valuable, but I could not make the mistake of my mother and be too strong, you understand? I had to be weak enough to keep. And to love."

"I understand that very well," Arwa said.

"Jihan thinks I am soft-natured. Akhtar thinks I am a stain upon his name. My father thinks I am a pretty, troublesome trinket, like my mother was to him. But they do not know my nature as I do." His voice was low now, almost contemplative. "I am nearly certain I could have found the Maha's ash long ago, if I had allowed myself to take the logical steps that lay before me. All it would have taken was a handful of unwilling Amrithi. Jihan could have smuggled them in as servants. The bodies of the dead, to be consumed or burned, to build a bridge. Experiment after experiment, until the Maha's ash was found. It would have been a swifter way, albeit bloodier. But I would have told myself it was for the Empire's good, and I would have slept well enough in time."

He looked up at the sky. The dark of it reflected back in his eyes.

"But I kept my theories to myself. I only told Jihan that I would try starvation. She pressed for more. I told her an Amrithi-blooded apprentice, a person trustworthy and clever, would perhaps be of help to me. I told her, if you cannot trust my soul to them, they will not do. And I thought she would find nothing."

But here I am, thought Arwa. She could not speak. Horror had stoppered her throat.

"You have shown me what the Maha is, Lady Arwa. All my life I have worshipped him, revered him. I thought he was greater than all of us—infinitely wiser in all ways. And now I know better. I fear..." He paused, holding his breath for a moment, as if he did not want to let the words go. "I fear how like him I am, in the precise and cruel part of me that I revile. I fear that in my nature, he and I are the same."

"You are not," Arwa said sharply.

He lowered his head and looked at her with an expression that was entirely vulnerable, entirely flayed open, as if he were the gentle child who had wept on his mother's death, and not the sharp-edged not-prince he was, built for learning the world by paring it down to its bloodied bones.

"You don't know that. You don't know my heart."

"When you indulge in slavery and cannibalism, I'll rethink my assessment. *Evidence*, my lord. You know the value of it."

"Experience of thought and feeling is evidence in its own right."

"Do you want me to provide you forgiveness for your thoughts? Because I will not. You will need to make peace with your own heart, Lord Zahir. It's no business of mine."

Arwa was no stranger to dark thoughts, to fury and vicious-ness and bloodlust. But his confession should nonetheless have made her flinch. But she could not. She had read books at his side, worn a shawl embroidered by his hands. He had taught her and studied with her and held her when she woke screaming, the dead in her skull. And more than that—more than all of it—he had treated her as an equal. Apprentice, he called her, but in the

white-gray expanse of the realm of ash, he had wound his soul's
roots with her own, and in the world of nighttime and lantern
light he had listened to her theories with the respect due to a
fellow scholar.

Zahir inclined his head, a gesture of acknowledgment. Still,
he looked troubled.

"My father has attempted to weave a trap for me," he said
eventually. "He thinks I will fail, that I will prove myself unworthy of the title, and my death will end all rumors surrounding
my name. Akhtar will rule without rumors to hound the stability of his throne. Even if I succeed and find the Maha's ash, it
will not be enough. Akhtar will take my knowledge, and ensure
I die swiftly. I am a threat that cannot be allowed to remain. To
survive, I would need to be—worshipped. Holy. And powerful, drenched in terrible magic, in blood, the leash of faith in
my hands. I would need to be the Maha's heir in truth. Whatever you may say, Lady Arwa, I know what I am capable of. If
I wanted to—if I chose to—I could do it. I could prove myself
to be his scion. And that, Lady Arwa, I cannot do. I *will* not. I
would rather embrace death."

Zahir might have thought his father had set him a trap, but
Arwa could only think of the whispers of the nobility and the
gossip of the widows, the fears the people of the Empire suffered, in the void left by the Maha's death. Their faith needed a
focus. They needed someone to believe in—something to hold
at bay the terrors of the curse that lay upon the Empire.

Zahir did not see it, perhaps. He had not walked the political
realm as Arwa had. Even now, he did not see his own family,
the beating heart of imperial politics, with eyes unclouded by
hunger and love.

The Emperor had named Zahir Maha's heir, and now no
other claimants would be able to rise and seize the faith and

power the Maha had once commanded. Whether Zahir failed or succeeded, they would use him all the same: make a hollow puppet of him, a symbol and a tool to support their power. They would hold the tale—and the flesh—of the Maha's heir in their chains.

Arwa swallowed. Her chest felt very tight.

"Then what," she said, "will you do now?"

They walked into his workroom together.

"Lady Arwa." Zahir's own voice was careful. "Your father. Would you return to him, if you could?"

"What are you suggesting?"

"I am not—entirely without resources," he said. "I could arrange—that is. The possibility of you returning home. Despite appearances, I have not always been enclosed here. When my mother was the Emperor's mistress, I was raised among her own people. Until the Maha's death, and her own, I lived outside the palace."

He turned to her. The lamps were guttered. She could not see his face any longer and that was . . . strange.

"I am admitting something to you that even Jihan does not know," he told her. "From time to time I still communicate with my mother's people. The Hidden Ones. There is a servant who . . ." He shook his head, suddenly guarded once more. "No matter. But if you wish to leave, if you wish to survive—as I hope you do—it can be arranged."

"A kind offer, I think," said Arwa. She tried not to think of her father. Her mother. "But my father has already paid the price, once, for protecting an Amrithi-blooded daughter. I won't ask him to do so again."

"Lady Arwa." A released breath. "If you will not return to your father, I can still arrange for you to leave. You deserve to survive."

Would she die, if she remained? She had no worth in the tale of the Maha's heir. No worth beyond her use as a resource: a vessel of blood. A lever to ensure Zahir's compliance.

Perhaps, then. Perhaps.

"I hope you wish to survive too, Lord Zahir," she said. "If you have the means to leave here, you should."

"I may be no more than a tool, after all," he said, voice soft, "but I am needed here. I have a job to do. I still believe in its worth."

"Still?"

"Still."

"Well. You cannot do the job without me. Unless your family have a secret store of Amrithi blood to utilize?"

"As far as I know, they do not." A faint laugh, sharp at the edges. "But of course, I know very little."

She heard him move away from her. She saw the silhouette of his body in the murky night darkness as he moved to light the lanterns around the room.

"You wish to do this, even believing your brothers will see you dead for it?"

He lit the rest of the lanterns, one by one, without answering her. Then he leaned back against the wall, head bowed, heavy with exhaustion.

"Yes," he said finally. "But it is my choice."

She nodded, although he was not looking at her.

"I keep thinking of the Amrithi," she said. "My ancestors. And I have wondered, since then . . . I've wondered what to do." She curled and uncurled her scarred palm. "I have worshipped the Maha all my life. And yet . . ."

She thought of the Amrithi. The feel of Nazrin's tears clogging her throat. She thought of her own sister, dead. Her own father, poisoned by loss, and her mother poisoned by disappointment, never quite the same again.

She thought of Kamran. Of Darez Fort. Of fear burrowing into her skin, the slick terror of a walking nightmare.

She thought of two worlds, feeding on one another's tragedy.

The Empire was corrupt, but it was home. The bitter knowledge of bloodied foundations and bloodied consequences swam through her skull.

"Then this is my choice, my lord: I will not leave."

His head rose, finally.

"You have given me the opportunity to see the realm of ash," he said. "For that, Lady Arwa, I am grateful. More grateful than I can say. But now, I may have chosen this path but—you. No." He shook his head. "You do not deserve to die, Lady Arwa. You can still live."

"I am not afraid," Arwa said.

"I know," said Zahir, a strange twist of a smile upon his face. "I wish you were."

She could not understand his expression—she only knew that it made her heart flutter in an unwanted fashion. So she clenched her hands to fists and said, "You are not the only one allowed to make terrible choices, Lord Zahir. Do not deny me my right to be a fool."

"You do not need to sacrifice yourself. You could be—you are—so much more."

"So are you, Lord Zahir. And yet here we are."

He closed his eyes, fierce furrow in his brow. Then he looked at her once more. Said, "If you change your mind. If you want to go, if you doubt even for a moment..."

"I will tell you," said Arwa. "I promise."

"Then," he said, "I suppose all we can do is continue to try."

The both of them did the only thing they could, now that they had made the choice to face their fate. They entered the realm of ash.

Again, Arwa felt the tug of the realm—the yawning, breath-stealing deep of it—before the tea was drunk or the fire lit and blooded. The ash in her head loomed large. But she said nothing to Zahir, only followed the parameters of the ritual, and entered sleep.

They moved through the realm of ash, from Arwa's storm to Zahir's forest of great trees and shadows. They moved from forest to desert, over broken bodies, limbs smooth as stone. They moved farther than they ever had before. In the swirling storm, Arwa thought she saw her sister once more, a distant silhouette wreathed in shadow with a familiar braid flung over its shoulder. Brown, living skin. Head turning, as if to the sound of a voice. Arwa's heart twisted with hurt, a terrible knot. She looked away.

She could not indulge her grief. Not now.

Abruptly, Zahir stopped.

"I cannot go farther," he said.

"Can't or won't?" asked Arwa.

"Can't." He held his hand before him. Around the blood roots, his hand had faded; light poured through shattered facets of flesh that barely resembled the shape of fingers, of a wrist, of a palm. "This feels," he said, "like an end."

He stared into the distance.

Then: "Your blood, the fire built from the dust of Irinah—none of it is enough. We cannot do it."

"Pull back with me," she said softly. "Let the roots take you home."

They returned to the waking world. Rose to their feet. Arwa grabbed the water carafe as Zahir rubbed his knuckles over his closed eyes, frowning and thoughtful.

When she offered him the water—after drinking some herself—he said, "We need to go to Irinah. Nothing else will work. Nothing else will be swift enough for our need."

"And you think," Arwa said, all even disbelief, "that anyone is going to allow you or me to visit Irinah? To leave the palace, after what the Emperor said of you?"

"I can ask Jihan," he said.

"She has no more power than she did before, my lord."

"She is now the head of the household of the Emperor's heir," Zahir replied. "And there is no other way to reach the Maha's ash. I can only ask. And hope."

He did not sound convinced. Arwa was not either.

"I will talk to her," he said. "Don't worry, Lady Arwa."

Of course she worried.

She went to the dovecote tower to watch the dawn. She saw no bird-spirits there this time: only pale light rising in the distance, and the city of Jah Ambha spread out before her, beyond the expanse of water surrounding the sprawl of the imperial palace.

When she returned to her own room she thought unceasingly of the realm of ash, of the defeated slump of Zahir's shoulders, of Ushan and Nazrin and all the ghosts within her still, their ash in her skull and soul. She thought of her sister's ghost, a thing so horribly alive that it filled her gut with poisonously false hope.

Zahir had told her the dangers of the realm of ash, of breaking away from the protection of shared blood roots. Well, Arwa was now reaping the consequences of her own foolishness. She had broken away from him, felt the ash of her broken ancestors, and carried it with her now. She could not shake it. Sometimes, in truth, the world of the ash—of Ushan and Nazrin, of her sister smiling and *alive*—felt more real than Arwa's own mortal life.

What the ash had done to her was no different from the way

Zahir could now embroider, could shape familiar stars. And yet it was entirely different. Traumatic. A colder, more difficult burden.

What would it be like holding the Maha in his skin? Worse. To know what it was to be Amrithi was to know family and love, and persecution and fear, rites of worship and magic in the blood. To know what it was to be the Maha...

A shudder ran through her at the thought. The ash rose within her too. She felt its shadow steal through her veins. Her flesh.

She held her hands before her. The one scarred, the other nearly unmarked. She turned them before her. She remembered the shape of a knife in her hand. The shape of sigils her ancestors had used to speak to the daiva in their own language. She reached for that knowledge now, out of curiosity, out of a fear that was half hunger: How much still remained with her?

She felt the ash rise higher within her, felt knowledge bloom, somehow sharp as glass. A rite was a form of worship. A rite communicated with the daiva, worshipped the daiva. Feet firm to the ground, tying one to earth. Hands to the air, to touch sky. The body as the conduit between.

Arwa raised her hands. Widened her stance.

Breathing deep, she moved. Sigils flickered on her fingers, hands drawing into unfamiliar shapes. Muscles unused to the actions took a hairsbreadth of a moment to respond, but respond they did.

It was only when she stopped, panting, that she knew what she had done, cobbled together from a patchwork of ash. The Rite of Shelter. A safe harbor from the storm. A rite Nazrin had performed, to protect her children, foolish as the hope was.

She had prayed for safety with the same foolish hope as her ancestors. She stared down at her hands, then drew them up to her face, holding them to her skin. In the cover of her own palms, she felt shielded from the weight of her own crushing fear.

I don't want to die, she thought. *But I can't leave. I won't.*

I chose this path. I will see it to the end.

CHAPTER TWENTY

The Emperor was not yet dead, but the household was already preparing for mourning. Even Jihan's women—unmarried noblewomen, or wives of senior courtiers—put aside their usual bright silks for pale clothes, unmarked and austere. In the interim, there were no feasts or parties, no wine or dancing girls or soft music for evening entertainment. The men, Arwa gathered from whispers, were equally subdued. The court was holding its breath for the Emperor's death, and for the inevitability of a new Emperor's reign.

Akhtar's reign.

In quieter whispers still, Arwa heard of the naming of the Maha's heir. *A blessed son. Yes, named before the Emperor's own courtiers.* But they did not know this blessed, the widows and charity women, and if Jihan's confidantes knew of Zahir, they were careful to maintain their silence.

Jihan was pale and withdrawn. If she was glad Akhtar would soon rule, erasing himself beneath the title of Emperor, she did not show it. Her warnings sat heavy on Arwa's overfull skull.

Arwa sought out Gulshera, who for once was not at Jihan's side. Instead she was in the prayer room set aside for the elders. She sat on the floor, cross-legged before the faceless effigy of the Maha and the Emperor. Her back was ramrod straight.

"I have something for you, Aunt," said Arwa.

Gulshera turned. There were shadows beneath her eyes.

"Arwa," she said, by way of greeting. She tilted her head, gesturing with the jut of her chin at the small bundle clutched in Arwa's hands. "What is that?"

"Letters," said Arwa. "For my mother and father. I don't care for writing letters usually, but..."

Here, Arwa swallowed. "Aunt, I am not unaware of what lies before me. If the worst should happen, please see these delivered. It would mean a great deal to me. I've said nothing of my task. Only that I'm gone and that—I will miss them, and I am sorry."

Gulshera's expression—hard with exhaustion—did not soften. She rose to her feet and took the bundle from Arwa's hands. Her gaze was steady, without pity or malice.

"Is this what you wanted, Arwa?"

"I wanted a chance to save the Empire."

"So you have one," said Gulshera. "Just as you wished."

"Yes," Arwa said thinly. "I do."

What a bitter fulfillment of her wish. She missed the old blaze of certainty in her blood. It had burned away her grief for a time. What a relief that had been! But she had a new grief to carry now: not just Darez Fort, but a long strand of Amrithi dead.

Two sets of deaths, two griefs, one the cause of the other. It was a terrible balance, and just her luck, she lay at the middle of it, her heart torn neatly in two, at the seams.

"I'll see them delivered," said Gulshera. And finally— finally—Arwa heard pity seep into her voice. "I promise it."

She met with Zahir that night. They moved through the realm of ash and woke no closer to a solution, to neither of their surprise.

"What did Jihan say?" Arwa asked him, once they had properly awakened and the fire was quenched.

"She said going to Irinah is unlikely to be an option."

"Not entirely a no," Arwa said, even though she knew it was.

Zahir only smiled in response, eyes distant. His hand was at the sleeve of his tunic, tracing the cuff.

"She arranged new clothes for me," he said. "Mourning colors."

She looked at his tunic, worn and faded, she knew, from wear. The flash of gold at the cuff.

"Show me your sleeve," she said.

"Why?"

"Humor me."

He gave her his hand. She rolled down the cuff of his tunic.

"You've been distracting yourself," she observed. The interior of the cuff was stitched with another expanse of stars. "You embroider beautifully," she said.

"I have plenty of time to look at the sky above us at night," he said. "Besides, I need to test how long the gift of my grandmother's ash will remain with me."

She stared at the cluster of stars. His wrist.

"The Amrithi I saw in the realm of ash, their dreams that I consumed..." She hesitated. "They're with me still too."

"Arwa—"

"I am fine, my lord," she said, a bite in her voice. "It is no different from when you consumed ash. You embroider. I remember the dead."

"Death and embroidery are hardly equivalent." There was frustration in his voice, but concern too. "Lady Arwa. Please. Are you sure you're well?"

She hesitated. Only for a second.

She hadn't told him of the sigils and stances she remembered. The daiva that had come to her. She had not told him of her sister's bright ash. Some things were not for him. She barely understood them herself.

"Yes. It's only memory, my lord. No more. I only meant—have you considered what consuming the Maha's ash will do to you?"

Zahir looked away from her.

"Having the memories of my ancestors in me has not been without pain," Arwa pressed on. "And the Maha was—what he was. You will remember everything that he did. Everything that he was, everything that he felt. How will you stand it?"

"I try not to think of it." His gaze met hers again. "I cannot know what impact centuries of knowledge will have on me. I can only hope that I will not lose myself. Not forget myself. And that I will be—better than he was."

She knew how fragile that hope was. He had told her so himself.

He stared at her. Reading her face. He let out a breath.

"I need to consume his ash. So I won't think more of it. It would only make me afraid."

"I don't believe you," said Arwa. "I know your mind, my lord. You want to know everything. You *must* think of it."

"Sometimes," he said. "When I sleep, I dream of it."

"You have nightmares," she whispered.

"Nightmares," he repeated. "Yes. That is—accurate. Thank you."

"And you like accuracy."

"I do," he murmured. It was only then, his voice so soft and close, that she realized she was still holding his wrist.

She was hit—not by the ugly hunger she expected, but by something softer. A loneliness without sharp edges.

She wanted to remain here. She wanted to sit at his table and read his books, watch him sleep with his head against the wall. She wanted...well. It did not matter what she wanted. She was a widow, still.

But the want felt like a wound. She looked away from him, walked over to the shelves, and touched her fingers to the spines of the books. There were gilt edges, paper bound in silk cloth to keep its interior pages pristine. Books that smelled of age and mold. Books new and crisp and fresh, pages practically knife-edged, bristling beneath her fingers.

She reached for one and took it down. When she cracked it open she realized the writing was neat and cramped, and undeniably his own.

"You can take it, if you like," he said. "Take any of them. These books are as much yours as mine."

"That is hardly true, my lord. I am only an apprentice to you."

"On the subject of the accuracy of words…" He paused. "You've walked the realm with me. I could not have done it alone. You…" She remembered his gratitude, saw it in the shape of his mouth, the light in his eyes. "Perhaps," he continued haltingly, "*partner* is a more appropriate word."

"Partner," she repeated.

"You have a more appropriate term?"

"We're keepers of a lost art," said Arwa. "We are not Hidden Ones, I think. *I* am not. But I suppose we are…a mystical order."

"Of two?"

"Yes. A mystical order of two. It is *accurate*, don't you agree?"

They were smiling at one another.

On the edge of death, and we're smiling, Arwa marveled. She clutched the book tighter, butter-soft leather yielding in her grip. Its weight was significant, despite the way it fit easily into her hands.

"I should let you rest," she said.

"Yes." The light in his face dimmed a little. "Take the book with you. If you like."

He turned from her then, rolling the cuff back into place, head lowered.

She looked at his lowered head. She thought about how easily her hands would fit to the back of his neck: how warm his skin would be, and how soft.

She turned and left.

Unsure she would sleep, she lay on her bed, lantern precariously close to her, and read.

In small, painstaking writing—so laborious and so terrifyingly neat that it could only be Zahir's—lay a record of his lessons. Images painted on separate scraps of animal skin and paper. Tucked between the pages, perilously likely to come loose, was poetry from the Hidden One, and lesson notes from his own tutors.

She traced his words with her fingertips. Watched the confidence in his script grow. This was no diary of feelings, but a scholarly record. Mantras, too, and scraps of knowledge sewn together. Ever since the Maha's death, Zahir had searched for answers, as much a Hidden One as his mother—or as much as he could manage to be behind the palace's walls. And in her time in the palace, Arwa had done the same. She had come a long way from the widow crying tears of frustration in the library of the hermitage's prayer room, full of questions without any access to answers. She had new questions now.

They truly were a mystical order of two, she and him.

One of the final images was not copied art, but something Arwa knew could only have come from his own hand: a human built of pale lines and the silver of glass, run through by great roots, red and deep as blood. He must have drawn it after Arwa arrived at the palace, after her blood opened the doors to the realm of ash. She looked at it a long moment.

She heard a noise, and looked up from her book. Froze.

At the end of her bed, shadowed by night and candle glow, sat a figure small enough to be a child.

It raised its head. A child's face, carved from shadow, looked at her. Eyes like fractured silver. As she watched, heart in her throat, its face fractured too, skin unfurled, peeling away, to reveal a face beneath it, flat as bone, a nightmare made flesh—

Her lungs filled with rattling fear. She woke up, shooting into heart-pounding awareness. The room was entirely dark.

Even the lantern had guttered.

It took her a moment longer to realize the lantern should not have guttered, that she had grown adept at knowing how to keep a lantern burning all night long, the necessary measure of oil to wick.

It took her a moment longer, still, to realize there were thin facets of light winking in and out of sight. That there was something concealing her lantern with the shadowy bulk of its body.

Daiva.

She rose onto her elbows. The shadowy bird-spirit bristled upon her lantern. When she moved, it lifted its wings and rose, letting the light pour over Arwa's bed and the book beside her once again. She looked around herself, careful.

The walls were covered in shadows. No Darez Fort child-nightmare in sight. But that did not matter. Arwa knew what she had dreamed, and what lay before her now. Hundreds of bird-daiva upon the windows and walls.

Arwa rose to her feet. Carefully, ash whirling through her mind, she shaped a sigil of respect, a hint of a question in her stance. The tilt of her body. The turn of her head.

The daiva broke into wisps. Coalesced into one formless being, that took her arms, shaping them, then curled over her like a black shawl. Heart still hammering, she repeated the gesture it had made for her.

What had it meant? The ash within her answered.

Blood.

Arwa's hands were shaking. She went over to her trunk, searching blindly. Ah. There.

She picked up her dagger and tucked it into her sash, where it was properly hidden. She raised the book too, holding it against her chest, and opened her room, stepping out into the corridor. For a moment she stood still, entirely still, and listened.

Silence. Utter silence. She felt the daiva melt away, slipping into formless shadow. For a moment, Arwa stood alone in the corridor, listening to birdsong as dawn approached. She felt terrified, but also strangely a fool.

Then she heard footsteps. A figure, gold-armored, came around the corner. The guardswoman spotted her and approached.

"My lady," she said. "Why are you awake?"

"I heard a noise," Arwa said. "I was afraid. My apologies."

The guardswoman shook her head with a smile.

"There is nothing to be afraid of, my lady. Go back to your rest."

Arwa turned. Hesitated.

"Where is Eshara?" she asked. "She usually patrols this corridor."

"Sick," the guardswoman said shortly.

"Or Reya? She—"

"Go to sleep," the guardswoman said. "My lady."

And Arwa would have, perhaps, if she had not paused for a moment longer—breath still in her throat, heartbeat no longer a roar in her ears—and heard the slow, steady drip of liquid against marble.

She turned.

Saw blood drip from the sheath of the guardswoman's scimitar to the floor.

The guardswoman saw that she had seen. She looked at Arwa, expression resolute.

"Go into your room," she said softly. "Allow me to bar your door. Sit silently, and you will live. I have not been tasked with killing women tonight."

Not women. Then—

Zahir.

Arwa made a choked noise, suitably small and terrified. Nodded. Shaking, she edged back toward her room. Drip. Drip.

Her fingers tightened on the book.

Using all her strength, she flung it at the guardswoman's head.

The book was heavy, but the guardswoman's helm should have protected her entirely from harm. Arwa was lucky—the shock of the blow stunned the woman for a moment, giving Arwa all the reprieve she needed. Barefoot, unveiled, she ran for the hidden passage that led to the gardens.

She heard a yell and the sound of steel being drawn behind her, but she did not stop, and did not look back. Hesitation would have been certain death.

Familiar path, concealed by high trees. She ran. She ran.

She tripped, but didn't fall. Instead she paused and turned, her breath ragged, and saw what had blocked her path. Curve of a shoulder. Long rope of hair.

Someone had not been averse to killing women this night.

The maid was undeniably dead. The grass around her, the paving stones, were red.

Blood, the daiva had told her.

Arwa held an arm to her face, shaped her teeth around the skin of her forearm, and breathed deep and slow. She had seen death. She knew death. She would be damned if she wept like a widow here, out under the fading night.

She kept on moving.

She moved more slowly now, in the shadows thrown by the trees. Through the leaves, she saw that Zahir's workroom was surrounded by unfamiliar figures. Armed women. Armed men.

Her stomach fell away. She had hoped—somehow—that she would be able to warn Zahir. That he would be well. But how could he be?

A step back, under the cover of trees. Then she began to walk more hurriedly; her vision was almost black with something akin to grief. She stopped—she didn't know where—surrounded by trees, a canopy of leaves concealing the sky above her.

She heard the crack of wood. Her vision snapped into focus.

In the shadows, she saw movement. A man. Watching her.

A guard. He had to be a guard, though he dressed like a soldier, his garb not ceremonial but worn by use, scuffed and stained and bloodied. He looked at her. There was no resolute sympathy in his eyes. Arwa's insides curdled; she looked about herself, wild, a thing caught in a trap.

Under the cover of trees there was nowhere to run to.

There was no softness on his face. Not even particular malice.

"Who are you, then?" he whispered. "Another maid?"

Arwa said nothing.

"No," he said. Still soft. "A widow. So, widow, do you know where the bastard is hiding?"

She took a step back. Another.

The man followed.

Arwa could feel the sweat at the nape of her neck, the fistlike thud of her heart. She felt wood at her back. Her legs numb.

I am going to die, she thought. *After all this time.*

Dappled light fell on his form, concealing his face. But she heard him exhale and saw his hand move for his scimitar.

"Well then," he said. Began to draw his sword.

The shadowed light, coming from the branches above him, moved.

A figure jumped down, arm hooking around the soldier's neck, drawing him brutally down to the earth. They hit the soil hard. A strangled yelp came from the soldier's throat. He scrabbled for his scimitar, fist around the hilt. But the figure at his back was drawing his neck back, back, choking the air out of him with a fierce wrench of their arm.

Arwa should have run. But she could not. She knew that figure, the face half buried in the dirt, flushed and narrow-eyed.

Zahir.

He should have been a comical sight, fighting an armed man much greater in strength and size than himself. But he was using what upper hand he possessed to full effect, pinning the guard's scrabbling arm with his knee, his own arm still around the guard's throat. He fumbled—clumsy, pale with pain—then lifted his own dagger up. Wrenched the guard's head back.

Without finesse, he jammed his blade into the guard's throat.

There was a wet, gargling sound. Zahir jammed the dagger in again. And once more.

Silence.

Arwa felt dizzy. For a moment, she feared she would faint. Then her good sense returned to her, and she stumbled over to Zahir, and heaved the heavy weight of the body off him.

Zahir was breathing unevenly. He looked almost as shocked as she felt. His hands were trembling. The dagger dropped from his hand.

"Is he dead?"

Arwa nodded. She did not need to look at the guard to make sure. She had watched him die, after all.

"Good."

Zahir exhaled, winced. Still trembling, he clambered to his feet. His tunic was ripped. He wore no turban, his black hair bare and bloodstained.

"I thought *you* were dead," Arwa managed to say. She looked him over. He was hunched, one hand hovering over but not quite touching his side. "Are you...did he injure you?"

"I was already wounded." His voice was raw. "Had to run. One almost caught me." He took a step forward. Winced. "I escaped—the fire grate. But they're searching. Still."

They would be milling about the women's gardens then, among the trees and the wide-open paths across the water, under citrus and fruit trees outside the wing for widows. There would be no easy way to run from them.

She took his arm.

"Lean on me," she said. "We're getting away from here."

"And where," he said, "do you suggest we go?"

They could not go back to the women's quarters. Could not reach the palace.

"The dovecote," said Arwa.

There were voices somewhere. Shouting.

"I know the way," said Zahir.

They made it to the entrance, miracle of miracles. Not the door from Jihan's palace, but an entrance for servants, set at the base of the tower. The stairs were narrow and dark.

"If anyone is on the staircase, we will be trapped," Zahir pointed out. There was a sheen of sweat on his face that worried her.

"What a change from our current circumstances that would be," said Arwa. "Come on now."

They climbed.

He leaned his weight on the wall, on her shoulder. She heard his breath, ragged with pain. It was a relief when they reached the dovecote, and she heard the soft flutter of wings, and felt the cold dawn air on her face.

Zahir gave a hollow gasp. Lowered himself carefully down against the wall. His side was dark with blood.

Arwa kneeled on the ground, sucking in gouts of air. Her relief was short-lived. She heard the distant thud of footsteps.

"They're here, I think," said Zahir.

Arwa swore colorfully, and Zahir laughed, a helpless out-of-place laugh.

"How did they find us?" It was a foolish question, but she had been foolish to think they could run. To think they could *live*.

"Ah," said Zahir. "The trail of blood I left behind us probably didn't help. Besides, where else did we have to go?"

She watched the rise and fall of his chest. The dark spread of his blood.

This blessed, this not-prince, had murdered a man. She had not thought he was capable of that. He was more than what he appeared.

Well, so was she.

She took her own dagger from her sash. Zahir followed her with his eyes, as she rose to her feet.

"You can't fight them."

"I could try."

"Arwa." His voice was hoarse. "Why were you in the garden?"

"You're asking me now?"

"You should be safe."

Safe.

She thought of her sister. Her father. Her mother, disappointed and terrified, always terrified. She thought of her husband, dead against the gates of Darez Fort.

"Yes," she said. "But I'm not. I never have been."

She could hear the footsteps drawing closer. The rustle of wings. She stepped over to him, her shadow swallowing him whole.

"I told you to make a tool of me," she said shakily. "And you did, Lord Zahir. But I... I think it's time for me to make a weapon of myself."

She placed the blade to her finger. Made a cut—small, only enough to bring blood to the skin.

She placed her finger against his brow. Left her mark, invisible in the grime and guard's blood marking his face. He looked up at her, his gaze watchful. Waiting.

She touched her own forehead. Turned, ash in her soul, her mouth. With trembling fingers, she began to shape a rite.

She moved through clumsy motions, no magic in her, no faith, no music. Still, it was a rite. It was a rite for beckoning family, a thing Ushan had used dust-blood generations before her, to call his own daiva parent to him, on Irinah's sands.

Before her, darkness. Birds flocked together, their shadows merging into one. The daiva was one creature now and large, impossibly large, with dozens of eyes, disparate lambent stars. It did not seem surprised that she had beckoned it. She felt—in her blood and her bones—that it had been waiting.

She heard the distant yelling of men.

Instinct took over. She reached for it, touching her blood to its shadow-skin. She felt the softness of its flesh, silken as water.

"Please," she said, voice trembling. "You vowed to protect people like me. Your descendants. Your—family. Didn't you?"

The daiva did not respond. How could it? She was not speaking in its language, but oh—her hands, she could not hold them steady for the shape of sigils. She could not. The men were getting closer.

"I am not the kind of kin you hoped for, perhaps. I—do not know what you expect of me, or what it means to be Amrithi. But I am still one of your own, I think. Please. Forgive me for mistrusting you. Save me."

Silence, still.

She kneeled down.

Zahir was looking at the daiva. Wonder and terror mingled on his wan face.

"I am dying," he whispered. "Aren't I? I cannot be seeing what I am seeing."

"You're not dying." *I hope.* "Hold on to me. We need to stand."

He held on to her. She helped him to his feet. The edge of the tower wall was narrow, but Arwa managed to climb on it, balanced precariously. She sat, Zahir leaning against her. She could not help but think of the fall beneath her—the sheer empty drop to black water.

"Arwa," he said hoarsely. "They're nearly here."

"I know."

"If you're planning to jump…" He coughed, a hoarse rattle. "The fall from here will kill us."

"It probably will," she admitted. "But their knives are a certainty. Jumping from here—"

"Is also a certainty."

"I know." The daiva was looking at her, with all its prayer flame eyes, and Arwa…

She closed her eyes. Listened to the shouts of the men, the tremor of her own heartbeat.

"I have been keeping secrets from you," she said. "I survived Darez Fort because a daiva saved me from a creature—a nightmare, with a face like white bone. And I hope—although my hopes may be false, and foolish—that a daiva will save me again. Save us."

He raised his head, staring at the many-eyed daiva watching them.

"So I'm not hallucinating, then," he said shakily. "Ah, that's good."

"I am sorry," said Arwa, apologizing for her lie of omission, although she did not regret it. She regretted only that they were here, that they had so few choices, that they were both so close to dying with nothing they'd hoped for done. No Empire saved. A worthless sacrifice indeed. Her face stung; her lips were wet with the salt of her own tears. She had not realized she was crying. "I can't promise we will survive. But at least we can choose the shape of our death. At least that, Zahir."

He was silent for a moment. Then he turned a little. Touched his forehead to her arm. His lips parted. His released a long, slow breath.

"You have me. I go with you."

The despair of that act—and the trust—was staggering. She pressed her forehead to his hair, one moment of foolishness, one moment of touch. It could not hurt anyone anymore.

"I have marked you," she whispered. "My blood is on you, and I hope—I hope that's enough. The daiva—they. They protect their blood. That's a promise, and they do not break their promises. They will not let us die."

The daiva was watching them both. Waiting.

She held her hands out. Shaped the sigil for *bird*. She had no more time. A man burst up the stairs, blade before him. He stopped at the sight of the daiva, frozen by sudden terror.

Zahir turned and, wincing with pain, kneeled on the edge of the tower with her. They gripped each other tight.

"Are you ready?" she asked.

"No." He shook his head, eyes fever-bright and fierce. "Not at all."

"Neither am I," she told him. Touched her forehead to his own, face-to-face this time. Their breath mingled for a moment, terror-sweet. "Don't let go of me," she said.

"Arwa," he whispered. "I won't."

The man had shaken off his fear. He was running toward them.

Holding her breath, insides a knot of terror, Arwa gripped Zahir tighter.

And jumped.

CHAPTER TWENTY-ONE

They were falling. She could feel her stomach lifting, her limbs abraded by the wind. They were falling...

And then abruptly they were not.

Zahir was still holding on to her, and around him—around both of them—were wings, great and glossy and black, the dawn light burnishing their edges with a sharp gleam like that of honed steel.

Ushan, she thought with relief. She had not been wrong to hope. She could feel the ash rising in her again, blotting her already tear-muddled vision. Ushan with his daiva progenitor. Ushan lifted by great wings. The memory was beating in her ears, pounding like her heart, like blood...

She was dizzy with ash. She closed her eyes, as the wings swept the air, as their bodies continued not to fall and saw—darkness.

"Come," said Ushan. "Take my hand."

Ushan held his hand out. Dark from the sun, lighter at the palms. She took it. Her own hand was small in his, truly a child's hand. She walked on a child's mildly unsteady limbs. She was young. She was, once again, not herself. She was Iria, Ushan's child.

They walked for a time. There was sand beneath their feet,

and a hot sun beating down on them from overhead. They were walking up a dune. Ahead of them, Iria could see figures surrounded by tents. Iria loved those tents. They were large and made of pale cloth, but their surfaces were etched with intricate designs in lush colors, swirling and twisting like the patterns created when wind disturbed sand. The tents were surrounded by a mass of people, all talking to one another, children yelping and running, their shadows shifting in strange shapes behind them. Iria wanted to play too, but her child legs were tired, and she could only stumble. Ushan let go of her hand.

"If you're tired, I can carry you," Ushan said, and Iria held her own arms up. Understanding, he laughed, and lifted her.

She was his child. She knew exactly the best way to rest her chin against the crook of his shoulder, to fist her hand in his tunic, as she stared off into the distance. There, she could see dark figures flitting through the air and beneath the sand, and felt comforted. This was home. And they were family.

Her jaw widened. She yawned.

"Wake up," he whispered, tender against her ear. "Don't be a lazy thing, now."

Iria was not asleep yet, but she was tired, and could only mumble something incomprehensible in response.

"You delved too deep into memories that aren't your own," he said. His voice was gently disapproving. "And it has worn you thin, hasn't it? That does not surprise me. The ash is no place for a mortal, no matter her blood."

Ash.

It was a cold-water shock.

He was not talking to the girl he held in his arms, once, many lifetimes ago.

He was talking to *her*. And she was . . .

She was—

"You need to leave here," he said. "Or soon you will not be able to."

She was not his child. She was not in Irinah, upon its sand, returning to the embrace of her home clan. She was—

She blinked, and she was a child no longer. The realm of ash surrounded her, gray and empty, all twisting storm, and within it a woman slept curled on her side, breathing soft and alive. Arwa made a choked noise, panicked and helpless, and the woman's eyes snapped open. The woman raised her head, and Arwa saw a long braid, an achingly familiar face. Mehr met her eyes and—

"Arwa," a voice called. Thin with pain. "Arwa, wake up, please. I can't carry you any farther."

"Wake up," echoed Ushan. His voice in her ear, a susurration of ash. "Or you die."

The heat of the sun was long gone. The air was gray. She felt cold hands on her shoulders. Flinched.

"Don't shout," he said hurriedly. "It is only me. Zahir."

"Who am I?" she gasped, lungs working, the taste of iron in her throat. "Who—who am I?"

Zahir was looking at her through a haze of falling ash. But he was not glass-skinned, made of dream flesh. He was human and pale with pain, a bruise blossoming on his cheek.

He pressed a hand to her face. He stared at her, gaze steady. She could feel his hand tremble.

"You are Arwa," he said. "Lady Arwa. Scholar. Daughter of Suren. Widow." His lips thinned, holding in his pain. He gripped her under the arms. Lifted her to standing. "But right now," he panted, "you need to think less, and simply walk."

"You're not...strong enough to carry me," she slurred out.

"That's the woman I know," he said. "One foot in front of the other. Come on now."

Trembling, she rose from the wall she had been leaning on.

As she found her footing, the ash began to recede, color returning to the world around her. It was daylight, but they were in a narrow street, walls near closing in on them. She could smell rotting food, animal shit, cooking fires. The window lattices above them had flowers or fabric laced through them, to cover cracks between the frameworks of wood and stone. They were not in the refined corridors of the imperial palace any longer.

"Where . . . ?"

"Jah Ambha," he said. "Your—spirit. Daiva. It lowered us to the ground just beyond the lake. We ran from there."

Arwa could not remember running.

She looked down. Her clothes were caked in soil. Zahir's own tunic was stained and ragged.

"You don't remember," he said. "Do you?"

She shook her head, and instantly regretted the action, as very real flesh-and-bone nausea made the world tilt around her. He grabbed her before she could fall, then swore; holding her up was aggravating his wounds. Biting her cheek, Arwa straightened up again, leaning the barest increment of her weight on him.

"I can walk. I—I think. For a little while."

Not long, though. Not long.

"I'm sorry," he said. "I don't know the city as I once did. But I think this is the way. I *hope*."

She did not ask him where he was taking her. Her vision was fading once again. She was becoming a stranger to herself. The realm of ash had her in its grip, and she was older than flesh. Old as dreaming. She exhaled, one long pained breath, and black wings unfurled darkly around her.

"One foot in front of the other," he said. "That's it."

Somehow, she obeyed.

Something soft beneath her head. The sound of someone humming, a lilting and melodious tune.

Vision returned to Arwa slowly. There was light coming in from a high window, its lattice shaped to resemble a tree with great swirling branches. The wall beneath it was faintly cracked; it made it appear, absurdly, as if roots were burrowing through the plain room. There was a woman at the other end of the room, bent over a steaming pot, head lowered.

Arwa's mouth was dry. Her entire body hurt. It was hard to stay conscious. She blinked. Blinked again. When she opened her mouth, nothing but an embarrassing croak came out.

The woman turned.

She was an older woman, with a sharp nose and full mouth, full-figured in a plain robe bound with a sash covered in bright flowers. She walked over to Arwa cautiously.

"Are you awake?" she asked. Arwa managed to blink—answer enough, it seemed for the woman to continue. "Do you know who you are?"

Arwa had a faint memory of Zahir's voice, sharp with the grit of pain. *She doesn't know herself. I think she's sick. You know what I can offer you in return for your help. Please—*

"Where is Lord Zahir?" Arwa asked. Her own voice hurt.

The woman's face creased with worry. She took a step closer, and Arwa's hands curled into involuntary fists.

The woman stopped.

"Ah, not confusion, then. You just don't trust me. Well, that's fine, dear," the woman said. She held her hands up and open, in a placating manner. "He is well, I promise you."

Arwa said nothing.

For a long moment the woman was silent. Then she crouched down, hands clasped, and said, "He tells me you're a scholar."

"I am," said Arwa.

"Perhaps you know this, then," said the woman. And then she began to recite one of the Hidden One's poems, low and mellifluous, her voice made for music.

"I know it," Arwa admitted, when the woman went silent.

"His mother was a sister in my order," said the woman. "My name is Aliye, and I have known Zahir since...ah, since he was only a small boy. I have not seen his face for many years, but we've exchanged letters for a long, long time."

Zahir had told her he had connections beyond the palace. Arwa swallowed, throat sore, and said, "I know who I am, Lady Aliye."

"I am not a lady, dear. But you may call me aunt, if you wish." She rose back to her feet. "You should rest. I have water. Medicine, too, in the pot."

For all that her throat hurt and her body ached, Arwa did not want water or medicine. She was not so trusting yet, hurt or no, ash or no.

"Zahir," said Arwa. "Is he well? He was—wounded."

"Yes," Aliye said. But there was a waver in her voice, a sound leeched of color.

She urged Arwa to have some water again, but Arwa shook her head, dizzy and sick with it.

"I want to see him. Please."

The woman hesitated, then turned.

"I will bring him to you." A mutter. "Better he sees you're well for himself, anyway."

There was a long wait, and Arwa was not sure she would be able to stay awake. She closed her eyes for a moment, wrung out with exhaustion. In the distance, she could hear singing—a faint, warbling song about lovers and their amorous games. If she'd had the energy, she would have blushed.

Zahir walked in. He wore no turban, and his hair was longer than she had expected, pin straight where it touched his jaw. He was wan, and he walked carefully, his tunic loose enough to accommodate a bandage. But he was whole.

"Lady Arwa," he said. "I'm glad you're awake. And you— remember yourself?"

"Your wound," she murmured. "Is it paining you?"

A faint smile. "We will see if it heals clean. But I hope it will."

She wanted to ask him many things—of the palace, of daiva, of their flight that hung in shards in the storm of her memory. Of the soldiers and his blood and her own. But instead she said, "Can I trust...?"

Could she trust Aliye? Could she trust this place—trust anyone but him?

It was terrifying to realize how much weight she placed upon his answer. She trusted Zahir, at least, implicitly. In the panic of that bloody night, she had not even considered leaving him behind.

"I trust her," said Zahir. "You can also, if you wish."

"You promised her something."

"Nothing I can't afford to give."

Aliye cleared her throat. Zahir looked down and said, "Drink a little. You have a fever." A line of worry knitted his brow.

If he trusted Aliye, it would have to be enough.

Arwa drank, clumsy. Zahir helped her, carefully holding the cup.

Arwa closed her eyes then, resisting the urge to ask him not to go. All well and good. When she next opened her eyes, he was gone.

She fell in and out of slumber and fever over and over again. Sometimes she saw ash before her eyes. Other times she simply dreamed. Sometimes Aliye was there, sometimes not. Once, in something like a dream, Arwa thought she saw a new woman watching her from the doorway, her long shadow reaching across the floor. But that was only once, and fever lied.

Aliye brought her food fit for an invalid, and showed her where to bathe and relieve herself. She was a kind nursemaid, but Arwa had a sense she was consuming time that Aliye did not readily have available. Sometimes the older woman appeared with rouged lips and a brocade gown, hurrying in and out of the room, leaving the scent of perfume behind her. At night, Arwa heard not just singers but distant male voices and women's laughter.

"You say you are a Hidden One," Arwa said tiredly one morning. The noise and ill dreams had left her restless.

She had asked after Zahir—as she often did—to no avail. *He is also recovering*, Aliye would tell her, as if that were answer enough. Better, Arwa had decided in the end, to ask different questions. Perhaps she'd eventually receive some helpful answers.

"I am." Aliye was wetting a cloth for Arwa's forehead. The coolness, she claimed, would fight the weight of the fever. Arwa accepted this, although she had always had fevers sweated out of her as a child, swaddled in blankets, banking the heat until the sickness passed.

"And you are a courtesan, too?"

"Courtesan, dancing girl, brothel madame," said Aliye with a shrug. "Call it what you like. A woman must make a living. Well," she amended. "Most women. I know ladies do not." She gave Arwa a shrewd look. "But perhaps the world would be better if you ladies were allowed to give more to the Empire. And if we were also."

Arwa did not know if the *we* Aliye spoke of were the Hidden Ones or courtesans, but she supposed it made little difference. All people in the Empire had their service. All had boundaries they could not cross, for fear of the punishment that would face them on the other side.

The thought quelled Arwa to silence. She looked past Aliye to the lattice window facing—she assumed—the household's courtyard. Light was pouring through its roots and its leaves, casting winding shadows upon the floor.

"You like the decorations?" asked Aliye, clearly having followed the direction of Arwa's gaze.

"I spent time in a hermitage," Arwa said hoarsely. She needed more water. Her throat burned. "There was a similar lattice there. In the prayer room."

She remembered the daiva rising on wings beyond it.

Tasted ash.

She heard the cool sound of water being wrung from cloth.

"Do you know the tale of the tree and the doe?"

Arwa mutely shook her head. Aliye smiled.

"It isn't a tale commonly told anymore. But once it was a tale mothers granted their daughters." She turned the cloth between her hands once, twice. The pause stretched between them. "I'll tell it to you now," she said eventually. "Perhaps it will entertain you while you recover."

She placed the cool cloth against Arwa's forehead, then returned with a pile of sewing, and sat cross-legged on the floor mat by Arwa's bedding.

"There was a man, long ago," she began. "A boy, but also a prince, who lost his first throne and sought another. He walked with his family and his soldiers across the world: from beyond even Kirat, which lies untouchable beyond the mountains. His family loved him dearly, and followed him uncomplaining, even as their hunger grew, and their old and their young perished. Still, they would have died, had the boy not met the woman."

"You're telling me a love story," murmured Arwa.

"You are listening," Aliye said, pleased. "Good. Well, you're correct. He loved her. He came upon her when he reached a bitter mountain-ringed valley, arid and colorless. But she—ah—was beautiful beyond compare."

They always were, in such tales.

"Skin like the heart of a tree, hair like black smoke," Aliye went on. "Oh, it was clear she was no normal woman. The prince had gone hunting when he stumbled upon her instead of the prey he had hoped for. It was her beauty that felled him instead, struck him just like an arrow to the heart. He fell in love with her instantly, and she with him. They wed. It should have been a happy time, but alas—his family and his soldiers were dying. Hunger and sickness both had them in their grasp."

Aliye drew the needle through cloth. Snapped the end of the thread, deft and neat, with her teeth. Then she continued.

"The woman, of course, was not a normal woman. She was something born from the earth. Not a God, or anything kin to one but—old. We have no names for her kind anymore. But she saw his despair, and she could not allow it. The next time he went hunting, she came to him in the form of a golden doe, so he would not recognize her. She told him if he took her life, her blood would shape the land. *His* land. It would give him trees and fruits and nourishment, for these are the things that build thrones. But she also warned him: 'I am a living creature, ancient and powerful, and my death will have a price.'"

"He killed her, didn't he?"

Aliye hummed noncommittally in response. Then: "He shot her, yes. And from her blood grew flowers and crops, rich vegetation where before the soil was arid. Where her body lay, a tree unfurled, rich with fruit. Then a forest. And the man who would be king of Ambha, long before our Empire was born, had a fertile land now and a future for his people. But he kneeled by his bride, dead in a pool of her own blood at his hand, and wept, knowing the price of power was his heart."

"I can see why this story isn't told," murmured Arwa.

"Oh?"

"No one likes to think their world is—born out of spilled blood. It's too sad. And it makes the Empire seem..."

Although she had no more words, Aliye was nodding, even as she stitched. "Just so," she said. "And yet you widows build grave-tokens, don't you? Where do you think those began?"

Arwa rolled fully onto her side. She looked through the weight of fever and sleep at the lattice once again.

"I've never heard that story," Arwa said. "Not once. I would remember it."

"And yet," Aliye said, "it has not truly been forgotten. Its ghost squats within us. We place it in grief, our walls. We seed it in our women. There is nothing finer, after all, than being a sacrifice. Stories can have great power. Give a story blood, let its roots settle, and any tale can bear fruit. A story of a sacrificial love." She paused, then said lightly, "The story of a Maha's heir."

"You've heard, then," Arwa said, voice thin with exhaustion. "About Zahir."

"Courtesans hear everything," said Aliye.

What bargain did Zahir make with you? Arwa thought.

Aliye lowered her sewing, touching a hand to the cloth on Arwa's forehead.

"You feel a little better," she said, approving. "But you should rest now, dear. I've taxed you enough."

When Arwa next woke, she knew three things: her fever had broken; she was painfully hungry; and Zahir was at her side.

CHAPTER TWENTY-TWO

Aunt Aliye told me you're recovering."

"I feel much better," she said. "But where have *you* been? She wouldn't tell me a thing."

"You're angry."

"Oh no, my lord. Not at *all*."

He was looking down at his hands, moving them restlessly upon something that gleamed silver. He looked suitably ashamed.

"Arwa," he said. "Lady Arwa. I owe you an apology. I am sorry I have not visited. I have been unwell also, and..."

"Your wound," she said. "Has it healed now?"

"Somewhat," he said. "It still hurts. I gather that is to be expected, when you have been stabbed."

Arwa rose up onto her elbows, then into a seated position. She leaned forward, clasping her hands, her head blessedly clear for the first time in...how long had she been here? Days?

"Is this where you grew up?" she asked, attempting to distract herself from her own distress, the moth-eaten gaps in her memory. From the cold pit growing in her stomach at the way he would not meet her eyes, the fragile hunch of his shoulders. "You told me your mother had a home beyond the palace."

"My mother had her own establishment, but she came here

regularly," he replied. "They were good friends, she and Aunt Aliye. After my mother…" He smiled once more, thinly. "After. I found a way to continue to write to Aliye. There was a guardswoman who was kind enough to help me."

"How many years since you last saw her?"

"Since my mother's death. Perhaps before that." A faraway look in his lowered eyes. "I did not know if she would recognize me, but she did."

His hands paused, their restless motion held in check.

"Did you know you had the power to compel spirits? To use them to—save us?"

"It wasn't compulsion," said Arwa. "I only begged. I told you the truth, on the dovecote. Spirits saved my life in Darez Fort. I didn't ask them to. In fact, I wanted them gone. Then I ate the ash of my ancestors, and I understood a little more of what the daiva are. Not monsters. Simply…my blood. They saved us because I asked, in their language and because they…wanted to. I think."

"You think?"

"I don't know," Arwa said, voice sharp with frustration. "I know they vowed to protect the Amrithi. But I have no understanding of why they chose to protect me, when so many Amrithi have not been protected—have been beaten or murdered or driven from the Empire. There is so much I don't know about what it means to be Amrithi. I only know what the ash has given me. I have sigils and stories. I have no *context*."

"I think we need to speak of the ash too," Zahir said. "You forgot yourself again."

"Unusual circumstances, my lord."

"You were not in the realm. You were in your own skin. And you still lost yourself. It has harmed you, no matter what you claim. Done something to you. I should never have…I…"

He exhaled and turned his head away from her, so she could see only his profile.

"I'm fine," she said. "I know who I am now. No harm has been done."

A bitten-off laugh.

"Lady Arwa, you can't possibly believe that."

"I do. In the end, Lord Zahir, whatever it has done to me, we are both alive because of it, and I am grateful for that." Still, he wouldn't look at her. "Now," she said. "Tell me."

"Tell you what?"

"Tell me why you won't look at me. Tell me what has happened."

One heartbeat. One more.

Finally, he turned to face her. The look on his face...

Even before he spoke, she felt dread rising through her limbs.

"Well." His voice shook faintly. "You need to know. Perhaps you guessed. On the night we fled the palace, my father died."

Her breath left her. She had known what the Emperor was—seen it. Frail and mortal and spiteful. But she had also worshipped him her whole life, taken comfort in his faceless, eternal image. Her grief was reflexive and undeniable.

"I am so very sorry," she whispered.

"I do not know if he died peacefully, but you saw him near the end. No doubt Masuma saw to his care. But after he died, it seems Parviz was not willing to let the Emperor's decision stand. He..."

Zahir bowed his head once more.

"Akhtar is dead," said Zahir. "Nasir—I don't know. But it was Parviz who arranged for their deaths, and my own. I'm sure of it. No traitors have been arrested, and only Parviz has loyal soldiers at his beck and call. Lady Arwa, he has proclaimed himself Emperor. He has had new coins struck to honor the dawn of his reign." His restless fingers paused then. She knew now he held the new coin between them. "He has taken the Empire, against the wishes of his father, and claimed it is because the Gods blessed him with the power and might to do so."

He clenched his fist around the coin.

"It is strange, to try to piece the truth of that night together," Zahir said, a sudden bite in his voice. "I am used to mending knowledge, taking fragments and making them whole. But this..." He sucked in a breath. "I do not know Nasir's fate. I do not know Jihan's fate. I know only what Aliye has gleaned from patron gossip and from the Hidden Ones, what has been announced in imperial proclamations, and what I—we—saw on that night. Nothing, Arwa. I know *nothing*."

Gulshera. If she had seen the soldiers walking the corridors, what would she have done? Had Parviz planned to lock Jihan and her women into their rooms, ensuring they would be under his direct control? Had all the women survived—Jihan's attentive noblewomen, her widows?

So much unknown. All she and Zahir had was the knowledge of dead servants, and soldiers with bloody weapons, and the choice they'd made between certain death and a literal leap of faith.

He was right. They had nothing.

"I am not sure how to make my knowledge whole. And I am afraid if I do... Arwa. I am afraid of what I will find."

There were tear tracks on his face. He did not even seem to be aware of them.

"You're crying," said Arwa.

"Ah." He touched the back of his hand to his cheek. "I am."

Arwa did not think. She placed her hand on his arm. Her head on his shoulder.

"I am so sorry," she whispered, as if her apologies had any weight, any power to comfort him. "Weep, if you want."

"I don't want to weep."

"Better to tell yourself it's a choice," she said. "Grief will drag you under whether you like it or not. So weep, Zahir. You have the right."

He was frozen for a long moment, as if he couldn't accept the comfort of her touch, or bring himself to move away from it. Arwa understood. Neither of them was good at the business of being vulnerable, of letting the softest blood of grief rise to the surface.

And yet the softness bloomed within her regardless, more easily than it ever had before, something gentle born from pain that had little place in the hard forge of her nature, when he leaned his chin against her hair, and breathed slow, ragged breaths, wet with grief.

One breath. Two. Three. Four. His breath finally softened.

They remained like that for a long time. How long, she didn't know.

Eventually he lifted his head, and she lifted her own. His eyes were sticking with the salt of tears, his face wan from pain both physical and quite beyond the flesh.

"So," Arwa said finally. "What will you do now?"

"I don't know," he said, and there was something strange in his voice. "I don't know."

CHAPTER TWENTY-THREE

They healed, and hid. Once Arwa regained a measure of her normal strength, she began to learn and explore the small segment of the haveli she and Zahir were limited to: a few small rooms, a collection of carefully tended to books, and a narrow corridor with finely latticed windows that overlooked the central courtyard of the haveli beneath it.

From evening until daybreak the haveli courtyard was full of laughter and music. At night the women of Aliye's house entertained men in the haveli's rooms or danced for their entertainment in the central courtyard. Dancing girls and female musicians—all courtesans by trade—were hardly an unusual sight in typical women's quarters, and certainly not unusual in the imperial palace. But Arwa had never had the opportunity to watch courtesans who were also members of an ancient mystical order perform. So she sat at the window lattice, chin on her knees, and watched the women sing and dance.

Arwa had known how the Hidden Ones afforded to adhere to their scholarship and mysticism, independent and unseen. But it still surprised her to hear a dancer's bells in distant corridors or in the courtyard during the quiet daylight hours, followed by a heated discussion of theories of the afterlife, of new manuscripts traded by Hidden Ones from eastern Chand, of women moving through the finest households of Jah Ambha and collecting knowledge alongside their gold. In the households of the nobility, the Hidden Ones had the positions of influence and invisibility. They were as clever and vicious and charming as any noblewoman Arwa had ever encountered—and they were thriving.

Her mother Maryam had always taught her that fallen women were to be derided—that her own concubine birth mother had been a low, corrupting influence for reasons beyond her Amrithi blood. An influence Arwa had to rise above.

Maryam had been wrong.

There was so much Arwa did not know. The breadth of her ignorance was staggering. Her life was so small and insignificant in comparison to the scope of the world. And yet she had believed if she acted a certain way—reshaped her nature and molded herself into a true Ambhan noblewoman, worthy of an Ambhan marriage—she would matter.

There are so many ways to live, Arwa thought. *And I know only one, and I am no good at it.*

Applause broke her out of her reflection. A woman below had finished dancing, her skirt of mirror-glass whirling to stillness around her. She laughed and bowed her head, black hair a curtain around her.

With the performance over, Arwa slipped away from the window.

Their section of the haveli was small, but had one particular benefit: a ladder that led to the roof. She climbed it and rose into the cool night air.

Zahir was sitting on the edge of the roof, near a bare sleep mat. He was staring out at the flat roofs of Jah Ambha, at the scattered lights of the houses and businesses that made up the city, and beyond them—set upon its inky expanse of water—the imperial palace.

She approached him. He near jumped out of his skin when he heard her footsteps. He reminded her for a moment of the mangy, wary cat she'd found in her garden as a child. Then just as swiftly he calmed, hands unfurling, some of the panic fading from his eyes.

"Arwa," he said. Strained. "You shouldn't have come up here. You need to regain your strength."

"Climbing a ladder is hardly going to exhaust me. Besides, *I* am not the one with the wound in my side."

She sat down on the ground near him.

Zahir spoke.

"I feel more at home here than I did in all my years at the palace." He sounded contemplative. "I thought I had forgotten my childhood. But now I'm here, I remember it very well."

"What do you remember?" Arwa asked.

"My mother had her own establishment. But this place... it reminds me of her own. Of a time when life was—different." His fingers twitched, as if searching for the coin he'd twisted in his hands, when he had told her his brother Akhtar was dead, his brother Parviz crowned. "I remember the meetings the Hidden Ones held. Women from across the city would gather at her salons, and share their knowledge. And argue." A smile. "They loved to argue. Though knowledge was shared, each woman had her own understanding of truth, and feelings often ran high."

"What did they debate on?"

"Theories. The right wording for a poem. Politics. They often discussed the Emperor. His advisers. Strategies to win him—and them—to the Hidden Ones' cause." He shrugged. "I barely remember. I was only a boy. But I always wonder what I would have been, if my mother had not offered up her knowledge to my father. If she had chosen a different way, and I had continued to be my mother's son. In time the Emperor would have ensured I had a suitable post and a suitable wife, I expect. But no more than that. Perhaps that would have been…" He trailed off. Exhaled. "Different," he said finally. "It would have been very different."

"Yes," said Arwa. She could not imagine what Zahir would have been like, raised without tomb walls and the threat of his own death hanging over him. That saddened her. "I expect it would have been."

For a long stretch of time they sat in silence. Finally, in a low, serious voice he said her name.

"Arwa. I need to understand how you saved us."

"I told you what I know."

"My mind isn't at its best," Zahir said, mouth a brief, bitter curl of a smile. "But I would appreciate your patience. I'd like to understand."

Taking a deep breath, she told him what she could of Darez Fort, and the nightmare and daiva she had seen there. She told him of what the ash had taught her of blood and vows, of rites of worship and sigils as language. She told him how she'd used the knowledge of the ash to save them both.

"Before we entered the realm of ash, before I found the Amrithi dead, I believed I was cursed," she admitted. "Cursed with a daiva's presence. It followed me to the hermitage. It followed me to the palace. I thought it was a murderer, that it killed everything I loved. I thought it was my ruinous blood that brought it, and that only my blood could keep it at bay."

"You believed your cursed blood drew the daiva *and* repelled them?"

"I can see the illogic of that *now*, Zahir, but fear is not a beast of reason. But…" She swallowed. "I know the daiva are no curse, now. And neither am I."

Zahir was quiet. Arwa looked at him, his ink-black hair, bare of a turban. His eyes, near colorless in the dark.

"So," she said, "now you know everything about me."

"No," he said softly. "I know only the barest part of you, still. And everything I learn, I marvel at. Have you carried this burden entirely alone? Since your husband passed?"

"Gulshera knew of it. Somewhat." Arwa shrugged. "I did not need a confidante."

"Arwa," he murmured. "Thank you."

Together they stared at the black sky, the glittering city, in companionable silence. For a moment.

"Is there a daiva here now?"

"Gods, Zahir, there's no need for more questions, is there?"

"I can ask tomorrow instead, if you prefer."

"You could not ask me at all."

"That...is an option." His voice sounded a little strained.

Ah, how he hungers, she thought. For knowledge. For hope. She shivered.

"I don't know. I don't think so."

"How can you not know?"

"I am not its master."

"Could you call it to you if you wished, using your sigils?"

"Possibly," said Arwa with a shrug.

"Why does it protect you?"

"I don't *know*, Zahir."

He shook his head, and she glared at him.

"I don't think on it much," she said.

"A spirit follows you and you don't think on it?"

"Of course I have. I do. But I've been preoccupied with finding the Maha's ash, just as you have been, Zahir."

"We can study the question together," he said. "If you'd like to. We can try to find out why this daiva seeks to keep you safe. Aliye has books we can use."

"Maybe," Arwa said, after a time. "Let me think on it."

"If I were you," he said, "I would want to study its relationship to me. My power over it. And its power over me in return. The mechanisms of our relationship. Everything."

"You'd write a book, I expect," said Arwa, not without fondness. "You take a joy in scholarship that I simply do not. In that, we differ."

Oh, she hungered for knowledge. But she hungered for something no amount of study could give her: a history that was not a book with pages ripped out, bare-spined. She wanted to understand the daiva, and rites, and her Amrithi heritage. She wanted knowledge that would lie soft and easy in her bones. A thing that needed no codifying. A thing she had not had to fight for.

Arwa looked behind them at the sleep mat, distracting herself. "You sleep out here, don't you?"

"Foolish though it may be, it allows me to feel as if I'm keeping watch. If Parviz—if the Emperor—knows I live... well."

"You think he knows you've survived?"

"I don't know. Aliye tells me people claim to have seen a dark shadow fly from the palace the night my father died. An ill omen, they call it. So perhaps he does. Perhaps not. All I know is that he is not here, and I hope that does not change." Zahir's voice was grim.

Arwa thought of the guards that had watched her and Zahir drop from the dovecote tower. The expanse of wings that had opened at Zahir's back. She had no words of comfort for him. Only ash in her mouth, and a voice in her ears. Ushan.

"You should rest," she said.

"At dawn, I'll consider it. Perhaps."

"Believe me, I know you're competent with a blade," Arwa said gently. The memory of his blade stabbing through the soldier's neck would stay with her a long time. It absurdly comforted her. *You were right. You are not as soft as your sister thinks you are, Zahir, and I am glad for that.* "I'm sure you could dispatch a dozen of your brother's men, if the need arose. But as we've discussed, I have spirits ensuring my survival. I can keep watch."

"You're mocking me," he said, after a pause. Rubbed his knuckles against his forehead. "Fine. I suppose I can rest."

"Good," she said. "Lie down now."

He muttered something unsavory under his breath, then lay down on the sleep mat. He was unconscious in minutes.

Arwa's own eyes stung with exhaustion, her head full of ash. She did not have the energy to fear that palace soldiers would come crashing through the doors, as Zahir did. But she would remain awake for his sake. She tucked her chin against her knees once more and closed her eyes. She listened to the hum of the city, and didn't open her eyes again until dawn lightened the sky and turned the dark of her closed eyelids red.

Aliye was waiting for them at the bottom of the ladder. Her lips were reddened, her kohl-rimmed eyes slightly smudged from sweat. She had been awake all night, but her gaze was still sharp. Urgent.

"Zahir," she said. "I have a visitor for you."

"A visitor," Arwa repeated. She looked at Zahir askance, but his gaze was fixed on Aliye. He nodded slowly.

"Well." Exhaled breath. "Could you take me to them, Aunt?"

Arwa nudged his arm, trying to draw his attention. He studiously ignored her. Kept walking.

Coward.

Aliye led them along the narrow corridor. At the end was a door; she drew the bar back and guided them through, to a bedroom. There was a woman within, leaning against the wall, her arms crossed. She raised her head.

Arwa knew her.

"Eshara," she whispered.

"Lady Arwa." Something flitted across her face. An expression somewhere between disbelief and hope. "Lord Zahir. You both live."

"You survived," Zahir said. Voice tight. "I wasn't sure. I hoped, of course."

"It wasn't my shift," Eshara said. "I was lucky."

"Reya?" Arwa whispered.

"As I said. I was lucky."

They stared at one another, a long moment in which words were not spoken.

"You know Eshara, I see," Zahir said finally, clearing his throat a little.

"Yes," said Arwa. "She patrolled my corridor in the women's quarters."

"She's a Hidden One born and reared," said Zahir, looking between them like a man attempting to solve a dangerous puzzle. "As a girl, she attended salons at my mother's home, with her own mother. She's carried messages from time to time between Aunt Aliye and me, as a kindness to me."

"That was brave of you," said Arwa.

"I couldn't tell you about me, of course," said Eshara, her expression guarded. "I did not know if you could be trusted."

I still don't know, her gaze seemed to say. And why would she? Arwa had never won her trust. After their first conversation, she had barely spoken to Eshara, wrapped up as she'd been in the realm of ash and the promise of service to a higher purpose.

She'd thought Eshara despised Arwa's own service. She hadn't looked beyond that surface veneer of distaste. No doubt Eshara had never intended her to. That veneer had been its own protective veil.

"I'm here with news," Eshara was saying to Zahir. "Do you have any idea what kind of rumors are sprouting up around your name?"

Zahir looked at Aliye.

"No," he said. "Please, do tell me, Eshara."

"Apparently, no one has seen the body of the Emperor's blessed son, the one he named Maha's heir before his death," Eshara said levelly. "No one has seen him alive, either, of course. But on the night Prince Akhtar and his closest confidantes were murdered, many people claim they saw a man fling himself from the palace walls, grow wings, and *fly*." Eshara shook her head. "Those people babbled, of course, and though many believe the man was Prince Akhtar or Nasir or the dead Emperor himself ascending to the Gods, even more still claim that the Maha's heir survived. They whisper that he must have used his Maha-touched power to save himself from death at the new Emperor's bloodied hands. They say, *The Maha's heir lives, as gifted and Gods-graced as his great ancestor, and he will save us all.*"

Zahir lowered his head and swore.

"I didn't quite believe it," Eshara said. "But here you are. Wings, Zahir?"

"They should have seen a woman and a man," he said tersely. "How far have the rumors spread?"

"Oh, everywhere. I haven't been back to the palace since— Reya's death." Eshara's voice caught, just for a moment. "But you can't find a shop or drinking house where people aren't talking of the deaths of the princes and the survival of the Maha's heir."

Zahir swore again and pressed his knuckles to his forehead.

"Before we lament further," said Aliye, cutting in from where she stood by the door, her arms folded, "have you decided what you will do, Zahir?"

Zahir shook his head. Aliye frowned.

"You told me you wish to go to Irinah."

"*Wished*," corrected Zahir. "Things are different now, Aunt. The Empire is greatly altered. Parviz is more likely to hack off my head than accept my counsel, Maha's ash or no."

"You know it is not only the Emperor who seeks to preserve the Empire, or has the means to do so."

Zahir was silent for a moment. Then he said, "I promised you information. I've given you and your sister scholars my knowledge of the realm of ash. I offered no more than that."

"I don't ask for the Maha's knowledge out of a desire to barter with you further. Giving us the Maha's knowledge would be the right thing to do, Zahir." Aliye's voice was suddenly rich, impassioned. "We do not have armies and thrones, as your brother does, but we are not lacking in influence. We are everywhere, seeking and learning, holding the Empire as it crumbles. You do not know what we have already averted, through carefully chosen lies and truths, through the men we cultivate, through the light of knowledge alone."

"No," he said. "I don't know."

"If you hear nothing of the fall of Atara Fort, it is the work of a group of my sisters, who betrayed one soldier's traitorous pillow talk to his commander. If you *do* hear of a fatherless man of low blood raised to commander or noble adviser, then you see our efforts to ensure the strongest in the Empire rise. And if the royal mortician tells his pretty mistress in confidence that Prince Akhtar was strangled to death, and she spreads the knowledge of it, so that Parviz may not sit easy on his stolen throne..." Aliye made an expansive gesture. "Small gestures can have great power."

"The spread of the story of the Maha's heir," Arwa whispered. "You had a hand in it. Didn't you?"

Aliye said nothing. But she nodded, eyes on Arwa, as if to say, *You have the measure of me.*

"Aliye," Eshara said, in an aggrieved tone. "Tell me you haven't."

"You were not there when we conferred, Eshara," Aliye said. "But the will of the Hidden Ones is united in this. We honor the Emperors who rule by right of the Maha's blood. But Parviz is no true Emperor. He was not his father's chosen heir. He has broken the imperial line of legitimacy, and worse still, he abhors everything we believe in." Her voice lowered. "We know what became of Durevi, under his rule. We will not see the people of the Empire suffer as Durevi has for what he names heresy."

"Spreading tales will only anger him, Aunt," said Zahir.

"He may be angry, indeed," she agreed. "But his court will remember that he strangled the fine, upstanding brother who should have ruled them. They will remember that the Maha's heir has slipped beyond his reach. And when he gives his orders to seek out heretics and see them gutted, his court will hesitate. Perhaps they will even disobey." She shrugged, one elegant lift of her shoulders. "Better for us all, that his throne rests upon such a bed of sand."

Eshara muttered something unsavory under her breath. Then she said, "It paints a target on Zahir."

"It does," Aliye acknowledged. "But, Zahir, you need not be in danger. You can travel invisibly. There are plenty of pilgrims making their way to the Maha's grave. A few more would not be noticed. Eshara has offered herself for the task, and I can provide your provisions. Coin, food, supplies."

"That is all your Hidden Ones can offer?" Arwa asks.

Aliye and Eshara both turned looks upon her.

"Only coin, and no defense but a single guardswoman. It suggests," said Arwa, chin raised, "that your power is limited."

"Not limited," Zahir said, an edge of bitterness to his voice. "Divided. Isn't that so, Aunt?"

"Knowledge is complex, the path to truth shaped by the individual's own nature," Aliye said softly. "But we have one rule, for our sisters. One alone. The Hidden Ones remain secret. Secrecy keeps us alive. Bahar was wise to try to influence the Emperor and Empress to look kindly upon our vision of a better world, one shaped by more than circumstance of birth, but she revealed too much. She broke our trust. For her son to continue her work..." Aliye shook her head. "A traitor's child, and a boy. Many of my scholar sisters will not be willing to provide resources to his work."

"And others are willing," Eshara said. "Like me. Obviously. Zahir, there are scholars enough that may not support you, but will accept the Maha's knowledge. They'll make use of it—build the better world you hope for, as we do—"

"No more."

Zahir said it quietly enough, but his voice was so cold and hard that it silenced the room.

"I find," he said, "that I am growing tired of being a tool in the vast games of others. And the players seem to keep dying. Aunt Aliye, Eshara, it's your division that makes me doubt the worth of placing the Maha's knowledge in your hands. I revere the work of the Hidden Ones, but I won't break myself upon this cause if it will all come to nothing."

Aliye sighed. Her eyes were sad.

"Then what would you do, Zahir? Stay here? Take up your mother's profession perhaps?"

"You think to shame me into going?" He sounded incredulous. "Do you think so little of my regard for you? For my mother?"

"No. I only think to remind you that your skills have been honed to this purpose, and this alone. Pursuit of knowledge. Service to a higher power. So *use* them, dear one. Try to save the Empire. And trust that the Hidden Ones will do all in their power to use your knowledge well, and see it placed in the wisest hands."

"I need time," he bit out.

"Go, then," said Aliye. "You have it."

Zahir left. Without pause, Arwa turned on her heel and followed him.

CHAPTER TWENTY-FOUR

He was on the roof once more. The sunlight was blazing now. It took Arwa a moment to adjust to it—to blink the painful burst of new light from her eyes and fix her gaze on Zahir, sitting on the edge of the roof, his head in his hands.

Arwa sat down beside him.

"Don't," he said.

"I'm not doing anything," she replied. "I'm just sitting here."

She kicked her feet idly back and forth as she stared across the city in daylight. At night, it glimmered. In the day, the bright paint of the buildings of the pleasure district was clearly peeling. The streets were festooned with burnt-out lamps. People milled about, bullocks and carts, food traders; there was the smell of flowers in great baskets, and sweets and fried dough. The air was rich with noise and life.

"Jihan may be dead."

It startled her, when he spoke. Her legs froze mid-kick. She lowered them and turned a little to look at him.

"After my mother's death, she arranged my tutors. My housing. My life. And now she may be gone. Arwa..." Exhale, shaky with feeling. "I know I have a duty to the Empire. To do what's right. And it's time. My wounds are healing. But." Voice a whisper. "My soul feels like a thing splintered. I do not think it is strong enough for the Maha's memories. Grief has undone me."

Arwa swallowed. Her throat, her heart, felt full of grit.

"I know something of grief," Arwa said.

"Yes," Zahir murmured. "Do you miss him, your husband? Mourn him still?"

He'd never asked her about Kamran. But she was a widow, of course. Some things were inviolable.

She thought of Kamran. Of trying to be worthy of love. Of meals carefully arranged, and papers tidied; of his careful eyes on her, seeking to read her, to understand her, always finding the void where their natures could not meet.

It had not hurt, trying to be a good wife. Given the chance she would have done it all her life without considering how carefully she had to fold her true nature away—her fire, her biting tongue, the mercurial sweetness of her own joy—and how the folding erased her, piece by piece. Being a good wife to Kamran had felt like a success in its own right. She had won her family a future: reputation, a measure of honor. Bartered herself, but for an outcome she'd considered worthy of the cost.

"Yes," she said finally, into the silence left by his voice. "I mourn him still. Just not as he deserves to be mourned. I loved him. Just not as he deserved to be loved. We weren't well suited to one another. He was older and . . . he didn't know me. I think in truth I knew little of him. We shared one soul, one duty, but we were strangers to one another."

"Arwa," he whispered. "I am sorry for that."

Arwa shook her head.

"You shouldn't be. It was my fault. I wasn't—right, Zahir. I was too angry. Too mercurial. Too . . . Too much myself," she said. "Kamran thought he was marrying an impoverished noble-woman who would love and obey him and instead he had . . . me.

But he tried to be good to me. He did what he could. It was love of a sort."

She swallowed. Ah, the way grief burned. "In truth, it's my sister I still mourn. Ever since I saw the Amrithi dead in the realm of ash, her death has felt like a fresh wound all over again. Sometimes in the realm of ash, I've seen her," Arwa admitted. "I know she is dead, and yet to me she looked so *alive*, Zahir. I couldn't help but think if I reached out and touched her I'd feel real flesh and she would be right there, alive before me. But I knew she would have just turned to ash in front of me and it would have been like death all over again. So I just—looked at her. And loved her. And missed her. And it—hurt me."

She felt warmth against her skin. His hand was pressed over her own, a silent, grounding comfort.

"I'm fine," she said. "Entirely well."

"Nonetheless," he said gently. "I am sorry that love is so often unkind."

There was a lump in her throat. He had lost people too. He understood.

"Just so," she managed to say.

They sat, silent for a long moment. At some point they had turned to face one another, still sitting on the roof's edge, unseen and alone, his hand warm upon her own.

"I know I have to do it," he said finally, into the quiet carved out by their grief. His voice was soft. "I have to go to Irinah. I have to seek the Maha's ash. And I will have to trust in the cunning and the strength of the Hidden Ones, and hope that their many voices are a better answer than the singular power an Emperor wields."

"You don't have to do anything," Arwa told him.

"But I want to. Arwa, all of this: the searching, the study, the deaths. Your deaths, and mine. They cannot be for nothing. I've set my feet on this path. I'll see it to the end." Faint smile. "Perhaps I'll even find my lamp of truth."

She swallowed. Ah, Zahir.

"Just...Promise me. Don't give the Hidden Ones the knowledge of what the Amrithi can be used for," she said. "If you find that the only answer in the Maha's ash is more enslavement, more killing, please. Don't give it to them."

"Enslaving the Amrithi caused the Empire's curse," he said quietly. "And it was monstrous. For that reason, and many others, I would not."

She should have agreed with him then. But she couldn't. She drew her hand back, and looked down at it, at the paling silver of her scar.

"And yet, maybe you'll discover in the Maha's ash that there is no other cure to the Empire's ills. Perhaps you'll look at the Empire, at people dying in droves, and convince yourself the Amrithi are an acceptable price to pay. A small handful of lives, sacrificed for the many." She let out a breath. "I would—understand the logic of it. But I am still asking you to promise me, Zahir. If the Amrithi are the price—if *enslavement* is the price—then let the Empire fall."

He was silent for a moment. His shoulders tensed, as if he could feel the burden of it upon them: the choice to see the Empire end.

"I promise. Some prices should not be paid." He shook his head, slow. "If the Empire falls—the blame lies at the Maha's door, and his alone."

"Good." She exhaled. "That's good."

There was something tentative, inquisitive in the turn of his head toward her then: The lick of black hair against his forehead, bare as it was of his turban. The line of his throat. In the daylight he was sharp and mortal and hurt, and yet her heart softened at the sight of his bared neck, all the same.

"Arwa," he said. He had not called her only *Lady Arwa* since the night they leaped from the dovecote tower and lived. "Will you come?"

Come with him to Irinah. To gold sand and a blaring white sky. To daiva and strange mirages that loomed from the sand. To the Maha's grave, and the heart of her own grief.

"You may not need Amrithi blood, in Irinah."

"I may not. Irinah may be a strong enough bridge alone," he agreed. "But you are not a weapon made of your blood. You are a scholar and a soldier who has not broken herself upon her cause—only grown stronger and stronger with every blow the world has dealt her. You have been my partner, my fellow mystic. You are my friend." His eyes blazed, as if he had trapped the sunlight in them, as if the force of his feeling could warm her skin and mark it. "You have sacrificed so much for this task. I would...it would be my honor to see it to the end together."

I can go home, thought Arwa. The idea cracked her heart open like an egg. *Home.*

When she thought of home, it was not her father's small haveli in Hara that came to mind. She did not think longingly of the sharp lashing smell of sea and citrus. She did not think of her marital fort, either: sticky, humid heat, books and soldiers. No. Instead, she thought of the cool marble corridors of the Governor's palace in Irinah. She thought of her old nursemaid, a gnarled old Irin woman who had treated her kindly and firmly. She thought of her sister holding her, telling her stories, her curling hair and warm voice, rich as honey.

Irinah was home, once. Somehow—despite all her years of trying to grow beyond her roots—it was home still.

"We're a mystic order of two," Arwa whispered. "Of course I'll come with you. I'll come to Irinah."

CHAPTER TWENTY-FIVE

The day before they left, Aliye offered Arwa her mirror.

"If you want to cut your hair, of course," she said.

"Why wouldn't I?" Arwa asked.

Aliye hesitated, almost imperceptibly. Her gaze flickered.

"I know many a woman who left her widowhood behind," she said finally. "Courtesans. And—wedded women. After all, my dear, if you travel far enough from those who know you, and allow your hair to grow, no one need know you were ever wed before. It is very simple."

A marriage made after a husband's death could not be a true Ambhan marriage, but Arwa could well imagine that any woman with the opportunity to begin again would put aside the poverty of her widowhood and embrace a new beginning.

But Arwa was not one of those women. She was not ready or able to put her life aside. She knew what she was, for good or ill.

"The mirror would be helpful," she said.

Aliye brought her the mirror and helped her set it against the wall of her sparse room. It was an old thing and traditionally wrought, no more than a great piece of beaten metal, polished until it shone. Arwa thanked Aliye for the metal and for the loan of a sharp knife, and Aliye let her be.

She thought of her Amrithi dead. They had never had to

contend with the strictures of a noblewoman's life, or of a noble-woman's widowhood. What would Nazrin have thought of her shorn hair, her unwillingness to loosen her grip on mourning, even now, when her noble life seemed like a distant memory?

This isn't the Amrithi way. We don't make vows. We understand the power of freedom.

Arwa turned her head to the left and to the right, cutting as neatly as she could. Then she froze.

It was a strange thing, to always need to be alert to wrongness in the air: the scent of incense, a too-long shadow, black ash rising in your blood. But vigilance had trained her body, which knew even before her mind did that something in her reflection was... off.

Those are not my eyes, Arwa thought.

But of course, they were. They were upon her face, so they had to be her own eyes. It was her reflection that was tricking her. After all, nothing looked quite correct in a mirror. On the polished metal, her skin was strange, silvery; her hair was too black, her eyes...

She leaned in closer.

Her eyes were gray as ash, far beyond the locus of each iris. Ash from end to end, swallowing the whites of her eyes.

She blinked. Her eyes were her own again.

She flinched back. Lowered the knife. She felt a horrible urge to smash the mirror flat to the floor, but instead she stood and walked out of the room, refusing to turn back.

She should have told Zahir. She knew it.

He had warned her of the dangers of consuming ash. He had stared at her, horrified, when she had forgotten herself after they fell and flew from the dovecote tower. She had brushed off his fears, and his grief had distracted him from pursuing the truth further, but that did not change the truth. The ash had done something to her.

She knew now that reaching for the ash repeatedly had consequences. She measured it with the care she used for all theories put to the test. Consequence one: Reaching for the ash risked making her forget herself.

Consequence two: Reaching for the ash had resulted in the realm of ash closing in upon her. The realm of ash was close to her all the time, now. In Jah Ambha, when Zahir had guided her through the city, she had slipped in and out of it as easily as one donned a veil. The taste of ash—smoke and dying—came to her mouth now and again, unbidden.

Consequence three: When she drew upon her ash, her eyes clearly altered, clouding with it. Was that a new development? She did not know. Could Zahir have missed the sight of it, in the dark of the tomb? Or were the consequences of the ash growing worse with time?

She fretted, examined the problem, and fretted some more. But she did not tell Zahir.

If she told him, what would he do? What could he do? He had none of his books, and no time for study and contemplation. No firepit, no opium-laced tea, no sister with financial and political clout to protect him. He had nothing but his keen, clever mind and his bare-boned hopes of finding something— *anything*—in Irinah that could save the Empire from its painful stumble toward death.

She vowed to herself that she would simply stop reaching for the ash. No more sigils. No more rites. No more recalling memories that were not her own. She would, in short, avoid plunging to her death by sensibly avoiding the cliff edge before her.

Instead she focused on practicalities. She dressed as a pilgrim—face uncomfortably bare, a shawl drawn over her short hair—and tied a pack of supplies to her back. She waited until dawn had almost arrived with a quiet Eshara and Zahir, and then bid farewell to Aliye. The older woman led them out of a servants' exit from the pleasure house, which was still full of music and bursts of laughter.

"You're so like her," whispered Aliye to Zahir, clasping his face between her hands as they stood, all four of them, in the corridor, huddled uncomfortably close together. "Go well, dear heart. May the lamp burn for you."

Zahir murmured something in response, and Arwa looked away.

No, she decided. She would not tell him.

The homes of respectable men and women were still closed for the night's rest, but despite the hour—and the unease brought on by the Emperor's death—the streets were crowded. Young men and old, women in huddled groups, wealthier women on horseback in saddle palanquins that wavered unevenly—they were all pilgrims and mourners, ready to begin their dawn journey to the Maha's grave.

"It's busier than I thought it would be," murmured Eshara, neck craning as she strove to keep an eye on all of them and the crowd simultaneously, still a guardswoman to the core. "The Emperor's death has made everyone more pious, I think. Good for us."

"I doubt Parviz's hatred of heresy helps," murmured Zahir, and Arwa nodded in agreement. Traveling to Irinah was not an entirely sanctioned act, and no one yet knew what this new Emperor would decide to do with the mourners his father had tolerated. But there was an answer, of a kind, on the city's walls, where heads of the heretic mystics were still hung, reduced now to gristle and bone.

Although there were soldiers on the streets in significant numbers, soldiers at the city's walls, none looked their way. They were far more concerned with inspecting new arrivals to the city for sickness. For now, at least, Akhtar's policies of cleansing against the nightmares remained. The three of them passed makeshift tents and great drums of water, huddles of merchants and farmers with their carts, waiting to be assessed, and—Gods be praised—passed by them all unseen, carried by the mass of pilgrims out of Jah Ambha, and onto the first steps of their journey to Irinah's sands.

CHAPTER TWENTY-SIX

In mere weeks, they would reach Irinah. But Arwa could not imagine it. Irinah felt like a place that lived in her childhood memories alone. Irinah was the Governor's palace: great marble corridors, and the flickering candlelight on the pillows in her own nursery; her father's footsteps, firm and sure, and the whisper of her sister's voice, murmuring stories in her ear. It was like the realm of ash, gossamer and strange but not a thing of the world.

Appropriate, then, that their journey was a tough and slow thing, a true test of her will. Arwa had traveled long distances before. She'd had to, as a commander's bride. But she had traveled in the relative, if nauseating, comfort of a palanquin. She'd been tended to and guarded. Now she was a pilgrim, unveiled, her shawl knotted over her hair, walking. And walking. And walking.

Every painful step—beat of the sun on her forehead, sweat sticky at her neck and her back, her leg muscles aching—felt as if it were building the realness of Irinah. The desert was the thump of her heart and her parched throat and the hungry twist of her belly. It was a place that demanded body and bone to be reached, no different than traveling to the realm of ash.

Zahir—still recovering from his wound—could only walk

slowly. Eshara was solicitous of him. She slowed her pace so she could remain at his side, talking about life beyond the palace, about Aliye and her pleasure house, about Hidden Ones whose names Arwa had never heard before but clearly meant something to Zahir, who lit up at their mention. Arwa walked a little behind them on aching feet, and tried not to think too much on the way Eshara carefully avoided looking at her, her shoulders always turned, her back a forbidding line.

It was easy enough to do so. The journey was a new world, one very unlike any realm Arwa had walked in before. The pilgrimage route was well-established, the earth shaped by thousands of footsteps, which had killed the vegetation and worn the way smooth. The pilgrims traveled largely on foot, but there were a few notable wealthy travelers, in bullock-drawn carts or on horseback, their women concealed in swaying veiled side-saddles or separate palanquins. The sheer press of people made Arwa feel like a speck of dust, insignificant, carried on a strange wind quite beyond her control.

They stopped, now and again, at the roadside stalls that had been established to cater for the wave of travelers. They drank tea, rich in mint and cardamom, heaped with honey. At night they tried to sleep far from the other travelers, beneath the vague cover of sparse trees, a small fire lit for warmth. Sometimes, Arwa would wrap herself in a thick over-shawl and sit and stare out at the dark, seeking daiva in the shadowy flicker of their camp's flames. But she saw nothing. They were alone.

She woke early one morning, dawn barely breaking the sky. Zahir was asleep propped against a tree, his robe wrapped tight around him. But Eshara was awake, tending to the fire, warming flatbreads over the flames so that their doughy surface blistered with heat. She raised her eyes and gave Arwa a flat, unfeeling look.

"Ah. You're awake."

"Yes." Arwa watched Eshara lower her eyes, saw the tic in Eshara's jaw, as she ground her teeth. "Can I help?"

"Can you cook?"

"I'm teachable."

Eshara plucked the bread from the flames. Neatly flicked it onto a cloth.

"No, then," she said. "Quicker for me to do the job myself."

Eshara kept on working, as Arwa straightened, rolling her shoulders to erase the stiffness of a night's rest. She couldn't look away from Eshara. The woman's shoulders were hunched, her jaw still tight with feeling.

A voice, very like her mother's, whispered a warning in her skull.

Don't say a word. You don't need any more trouble than you've already earned.

"You do not like me very much, I think."

Eshara's jaw only seemed to tighten an increment further. Then she huffed out a sigh, and visibly forced herself to relax.

"I am not required to like you. You are not my mistress. Nor are you a sister in my order. You are just . . . a set of characteristics that have utility. To Zahir. To the cause."

"A tool, you mean."

"I have seen you, Arwa," Eshara said. "Servants see a great deal more than people think we do. *Yes*, you are a tool, shuttled about for the purposes of people greater than you." A beat. "No offense meant, of course."

"And how exactly," Arwa said, "am I not meant to take offense at that?"

"Oh, Princess Jihan said worse to you, I'm sure," Eshara said. "And no doubt you smiled and accepted her words without argument. But when I speak—well. I was just a function in your life, and my opinion is accordingly worth little."

There was no spite in Eshara's voice, which was somehow worse than if there had been. Instead her tone was weary and matter-of-fact. She dampened the fire, movements pointed but not hurried, then folded the cloth around the bread to keep it warm.

"I understand the need for you, and I appreciate you being here," Eshara added, in a tone that suggested she did not in fact appreciate Arwa being here at all, "but I trust in Zahir's dedication, and my own. Yours?" She shook her head. "You were not born to the Hidden Ones. You never earned our secrets. You haven't proved your worth."

Arwa clasped her hands tight, nails digging into her own skin. In a controlled voice, she said, "I've walked the realm of ash. I have chosen this path."

"You've walked the realm only because of your blood," Eshara said dismissively. "But for all your blood, Lady Arwa, you're no different from the rest of them."

"Them?"

"The noblewomen. The widows. The ones who smoke their pipes and drink their wine and lament their fate, even though they have nothing to lament. No hunger, no strife, no real suffering to speak of." Eshara shrugged then. "You've lived an easy life, Lady Arwa. You have no place on a journey this vital. And yet—here you are."

Her words were a knife twist, turning in Arwa's chest. Arwa sucked in a sharp breath, straightened her spine, and did not respond.

They sat for a long moment in silence. Then Zahir murmured and turned in his sleep. Arwa rose to her feet.

"May I borrow your bow?"

"If you like," Eshara said, not looking up. So Arwa took it from where it rested against their packs and walked away.

*   *   *

Ah. Truth was a sharp knife, wasn't it?

Eshara had a neat, serviceable bow and a handful of arrows. They were tools—*as I am a tool*, thought Arwa bitterly—and not a frivolous way to release her rage. So she made a focused effort to hunt for an addition to their morning meal, and didn't solely waste her arrows on venting her feelings, as she sorely wished to. But there were no animals in sight, no birds, no deer, only one hare that darted swiftly away from her, leaving her arrow to thud in the dirt. With nothing worth killing in sight, she allowed herself the indulgence of taking the used arrow and nocking it once more. She could already feel the soreness of her fingers, without a thumb ring to hand to hold the string steady, the tension of the bow mirroring the tension in her arm.

She heard footsteps behind her.

"Are you truly hunting this early?" Zahir asked.

"Leave me be," she said.

"I'll take that as a *no*."

"I was hunting," she acknowledged, through gritted teeth. "But as I'm clearly having no luck, I'm hunting my rage instead and—skewering it through."

"Ah."

"It is a thing that Gulshera taught me."

The thought of Gulshera—maybe dead, maybe gone, Arwa did not *know*—only wound her feelings tighter.

She let the arrow loose. It buried itself in the bark of the tree. She released a breath.

"Do you know what Eshara said to me?" said Arwa.

"No." Crunch of his boots. He stood beside her. "Did she say something that made you angry, by any chance?"

"I'm not angry with her," Arwa said. "I am just—angry."

Angry with her own choices and her own nature. Angry with a world that had told her that to be worthy she had to be a proper noblewoman, no more and no less; angry with herself for *believing* it. Angry that she had not been better, more, with what she'd been given.

Eshara had not been wrong. That stung.

When you strip everything away, Arwa thought, *there is nothing in me but raw feeling: rage pulsing free like the blood of a thing unskinned.*

I have to be more than this.

Zahir walked past her. He wrenched the arrow free; he touched a finger to the wound in the bark.

"A hare," he said regretfully, "would be more edible."

"Any more comments like that and you'll be the one on the end of my arrow," Arwa said. But there was no real ire in her voice, and Zahir smiled—a pale half smile—in response.

"I can still run if I must," he said. "I expect I'd survive."

She thought of how Gulshera had named archery a kind of alchemy for her grief: a way to give her hungry grief direction and discipline. She thought of the ache of her limbs, the way the journey was tiring and strengthening her, and the taste of ash.

Something alchemical was happening to her too. For good or ill.

She licked the salt of sweat from her lips. Shook her head.

"I suppose we should go back."

"Is your rage suitably quenched?" he asked.

"No," she said. "But it matters little. The bow would be of better use in Eshara's hands anyway."

As they traveled farther, the rest stops established for the pilgrims became more elaborate, and makeshift settlements began to crop up. Caravanserais, Eshara called them, these temporary towns of low mud walls that surrounded the tents and carts of travelers. Zahir found them fascinating. Whenever they reached one he would stare about them, clear-eyed and unblinking, taking in the sights around them with quiet hunger.

Arwa was not half as curious. But the widows and beggar

women who congregated in the caravanserais drew her eyes, always. They crouched in shadows with their faceless effigies and piles of ornate grave-tokens for sale, sticks of incense clouding the air around them. On a day when they had stopped to rest in a particularly busy caravanserai—and Eshara had gone in search of supplies—Arwa walked away from Zahir and kneeled down by one of the widows.

The woman straightened, adjusting her shawl. Her eyes brightened at the possibility of a sale.

"Take one of these fine items with you as an offering," she said quickly, "and the Maha's spirit will bless you. I can promise it."

It was a false promise, that Arwa didn't doubt, but still her curiosity was piqued. She felt, rather than saw, Zahir step behind her, tilting his head in the inquisitive way he often did.

Close now, she could see that the grave-tokens were not made of grass and earth as she'd first thought, but were shaped from clay and decorated finely with paint and small, pale facets of glass. She touched a fingertip to one, admiring.

The woman peered at her more closely.

"A fellow widow," she said knowingly. "Well, you'll know the benefit of my wares. Why, when you reach the House of Tears—"

"Arwa." A hand clamped on her arm. "We need to go now."

Eshara's voice. Arwa looked up.

"What is it?"

"Come with me now," hissed Eshara, grip tightening. "Or I swear—"

"Eshara," said Zahir sharply. "Let her go."

Eshara froze. She was breathing hard. Zahir stared at her. Said, in a careful voice, "You're hurting her. And you're drawing attention."

Eshara must have realized he was correct, because she released Arwa.

"Come on, then," she said, and turned and strode away.

Zahir turned to look at Arwa.

"Did she—?"

"I think we should follow her now, Zahir," Arwa said.

"Of course," he said, but his mouth was still a thin line, his brow furrowed.

When all three of them were alone, far from the crowd of pilgrims, Eshara said, "Zahir. Your tale has spread. That—worries me."

"Surely that was Aliye's intent," he said.

"It was a bad decision," snapped Eshara. "And I hoped the tale would stick to the cities. But it's worse than I thought. The story has *changed*. There are soothsayers and false mystics speaking of a blessed heir who rose from the dead, slithering out from between the corpses of his dead kin. A tea seller farther in the caravanserai told me that the Maha's heir has come to cleanse the Empire of the worst of its heathens. Amrithi, adulterous women, thieves." She paused, and said pointedly: "Kin killers."

"That's very—dramatic," said Zahir.

"It's all propaganda against the Emperor," Eshara said, with emphasis. "The tale's spun free of everyone's control, and you are at the heart of it. Parviz has put his faith in might and his own righteousness, but he's also placed himself squat in the center of a very ugly rise to power. People don't like it. And *I* don't like the danger swirling around your name. We need to travel more swiftly. Avoid the caravanserais, if we can. There is a Grand Caravanserai ahead of us, but if we travel a lesser-known road..."

"We'll be more exposed on less traveled roads," Arwa pointed out. She kept her voice even. Eshara was panicked, that was clear, wound tight with fear. Arwa had never seen her so. "At least here, we're easy to miss among the crowds."

"The crowds are the problem!" snapped Eshara. "So many eyes and so many whispers—I can't keep us safe here. What if—"

"Eshara." Zahir's voice. "We trust your judgment. We'll do as you suggest."

Eshara stopped, falling silent. She nodded.

"Well." A breath. "Well. Let's go, then."

Over the next few days they relied on Eshara to guide them as they walked through the rich vegetation of undisturbed green, far from the worn-smooth familiarity of the pilgrimage route. Arwa found she missed the noise and the throng of people. Eshara and Zahir were far too quiet. Arwa could not help but prod him with questions, uneasy with the weight of his silence and Eshara's combined.

"Does it worry you?" Arwa asked him. "These tales?"

"What led you to that conclusion?" Zahir said tiredly. Eshara did not even look back. She was striding forward, utterly focused and determined.

"Zahir," she said. "Please."

"Fine. Stories of the Maha's heir? Of course they worry me. It means Parviz will look for us, whether he believes I live or not. It will be enough that others do."

"You truly think he will care what ordinary people say?" Arwa asked.

"I think we both know that stories grow," said Zahir. "They swell and they spread swiftly, like sickness. And this story..." He was silent for a moment. Then he said, "I can see the appeal of it. It offers... hope. An alternative. That is dangerous to him."

Arwa thought of the story Aliye had told her, when Arwa had recovered in the safety of the pleasure house, under the shadow of the tree-carved lattice. There was a tale of sacrifice and love woven into the very fabric of Ambhan society: in its widows and their hermitages, its courtesans and their pleasure houses. A tale unspoken but *known*, in the bone and the blood. The Maha was a myth embedded in the skin of the Empire, deeper than any arrow. His death had left a void behind, waiting to be filled. All the Empire needed was the right tale. The right man.

Of course a legend was growing around Zahir. Not around Zahir himself, exactly—sharp-boned and exacting and hungry for knowledge as he was—but around what he represented. Emperor's blood. Not-prince. Blessed. He was a symbol around which the growing fear and discontent of the people could focus, a shining light of possibility in a world that stumbled, stricken by ill luck.

He was the promise of a miracle.

But the miracle had been Arwa's miracle, of course, a thing born of daiva and Amrithi blood.

What room did the Empire and its people have for that?

Arwa opened her mouth to speak, when Eshara stopped abruptly in front of them. In the blink of an eye she had her scimitar in her hand, free from its careful concealment under her robe.

"Eshara," Zahir said. Soft.

"The cart ahead," Eshara said. "*Look.*"

Through the shadows of trees, an overturned cart was just visible. One of its sides was splintered through. Now that Arwa was paying attention—as she should have been all along—she could hear the wet buzz of flies, and smell more than vegetation sweetness in the air.

She could smell *rot*.

There was a body there. She knew it. Her own body remembered the scent. She drew her shawl over her mouth and nose, straining to blot it out.

Bandits had attacked the cart, perhaps. Or animals.

Or something else.

"Someone," Zahir said, "may still be alive."

"No one is alive," Arwa whispered. "You can be sure of it. Whoever died has been there for some time."

"What do you know of death?" Eshara said. There was no sharpness in her voice; instead it trembled as if on a knife edge.

Arwa crumpled her hand tight into her shawl. Breathed deep and slow.

"I was at Darez Fort, Eshara," she said. "You know that. Surely you guardswomen gossiped. But look, if you like."

They all walked forward together, in the end.

Later, as Eshara retched against a tree, Arwa felt Zahir press his shoulder against her own. He did no more than that, but it comforted her more than she could say. She realized she was trembling, from her lips to her toes.

This was natural fear. Natural fear, only, and natural grief too, born from unnatural circumstances. She told herself that. Clung to the thought, as if releasing it would drown her.

Death. Everywhere she went, death seemed to follow her, and Arwa felt strangely exhausted, as if her heart had no more room for further mourning.

It was easy to forget, sometimes, what darkness lay over the Empire. She'd grown adept at folding away all her griefs. And then suddenly, such a moment came, and it was impossible not to remember.

Eshara walked back over to them. Refreshed her mouth with water.

"We need to return to the safety of the main path," she said grimly. "Tales aren't as great a risk as—*this*."

They walked until it was deep night, until there was nothing to guide them but a sliver of the moon, and then they curled up together, all shame and animosity forgotten.

Arwa finally slept with her head against Eshara's shoulder and Zahir's back to her own, in brief snatches fractured by fear. She dreamed, over and over again, like the turn of an inexorable wheel of worlds, of daiva skin peeling back to reveal a nightmare's terrible, chalky bones. She dreamed of her mother's hands washing her own clean, scrubbing until all the lines and whorls and scars had smoothed away from Arwa's flesh and she was marble pure. She dreamed of her father weeping. Dreamed that she walked across the floor to him, and pressed away his tears with her fingers. They burned her fingers blood red.

Why did you say Mehr is gone? she asked him. *Why gone, and not dead? Why only gone, Father? Where has my sister gone?*

She woke sharply, repeatedly, scent of incense in her nose, ash in her throat, and was grateful beyond words when dawn finally came.

CHAPTER TWENTY-SEVEN

The Grand Caravanserai resembled a military fort.

Long before they reached it—when it was only a miniature in the distance, an image wavering in the heat—she saw great watchtowers and high walls, clearly built to mimic the shape of a great Chand fort. If her blood had not already been frozen by the carnage in the forest, it would have grown cold at that sight.

She stopped for a moment, sucked in a sharp breath between her teeth, then continued to stride forward. She'd seen real horrors that night. She would not be shattered by a memory. Not today.

As they grew closer, she was comforted to see that the walls were simple mud and far lower and simpler than a fort's, the watchtowers unmanned. There were only surly guards at the caravanserai's entrance, collecting toll—*for the Governor*, they claimed—who waved them in once Eshara had pressed a suitable bribe into their hands.

A courtyard vaster than any belonging to caravanserais they had passed through before greeted them. There were stalls for tea sellers and food sellers; shrieking children and men and women shoving their way past one another. Newly constructed buildings were set back against the walls. Within those buildings—or so their banners and shouting voices of their owners suggested—were prophets and mystics, and pilgrims returned from Irinah's sands with precious relics, for sale at the right price. Scraps of genuine Saltborn mystic robes. The hem of the Maha's robe, preserved beneath glass.

Arwa stopped dead. "Did that man say he has the Maha's shin bone?" she said, incredulous.

"What?" Zahir stopped too. He craned his neck, turning. "Where?"

"I swear," Eshara said, aggrieved, "I am sick of both of you. *Sick*. And I am going to get some rest if it kills us all."

Limited though their coin now was, they found a place to sleep for the night. It was no more than an old storeroom divided into separate rooms by curtains affixed to the ceiling on hooks. Arwa could hear voices, someone snoring loudly. It was the cheapest accommodation available to travelers, but it was a blessing after their night of horror.

Eshara curled up almost immediately on the ground, cushioning her head on her arm. She looked shaken, face gray with exhaustion. She might have claimed she was sick of the both of them, but she leaned against Zahir easily enough when he kneeled down on the ground beside her and placed his hand on her shoulder, concern furrowing his brow.

"Eshara," he said. "You must rest."

"We need food," Eshara said tiredly. "We have only a little left, we'll need the bread for the desert, we're going to need something else for tonight."

Zahir raised his head, meeting Arwa's eyes.

"Let me go and buy a meal," Arwa said. "It's a simple enough task," she added, when she saw doubt cloud Eshara's eyes. "You can trust me with this."

"I'll stay with you and keep watch," Zahir said to Eshara, his eyes still on Arwa's.

Eshara visibly hesitated for a moment. Then exhaustion won out.

"There's coin in my pack."

It was a peace offering of a kind, so Arwa took it, curling her fingers around the coins, rising to her feet. She did not want to care for Eshara's well-being and yet...

Eshara was curled up fully, long braid of her hair drawn over her face. Zahir met Arwa's eyes. They shared another look, long and unspoken, and she thought of his fever-bright eyes when they jumped from the dovecote tower. The feel of him watching her, in the dark of the tomb.

"You both rest," she said. "I'll be back soon."

A woman ladled rice onto banana leaves and began to fold them shut for neater transport. As she worked, Arwa looked around idly, across the stalls, until her gaze was caught by a building in the distance, set back against the walls of the caravanserai.

The building should not have caught her attention. It was no brighter than the ones that surrounded it, but it was large, and upon its surface was a large painting in rich greens and browns. A tree with a vast canopy and great snarled roots, that curled in streaks of paint across the ground beneath the building's wall.

Arwa thought of the hermitage. Thought, too, of Aliye's tale, of a doe that was a woman, who died so Ambha could live. A story that lived in the blood, the air, the bones of the Empire.

"What is that place?" Arwa asked the woman. "With the tree."

"The House of Tears," the woman said. Her gaze flickered to Arwa's shorn hair. "They give widows a home there," she added. "Not a bad place to be, if you have no family to care for you."

The House of Tears.

With a murmur of thanks, Arwa paid her coin and tucked the parcels into a sling made of her shawl. She turned to return to their makeshift room. Then stopped.

She could not pretend that she didn't know how to resist her impulses. She'd learned to be whatever was required of her. But she did not want to resist this impulse. Her heart was singing in her chest. She turned on her heel and walked—slowly, deliberately—toward the House of Tears.

There was a pool of silence around it. The only person she could see was a short-haired widow in a pale Chand sari, cross-legged in the shade of the roof, filling small clay lamps with clarified butter. The widow did not look up as Arwa crossed the building's threshold, stepping into the cool dark of the interior.

She walked forward. Unexpectedly there were steps leading down to a room below the ground. She thought of Zahir's tomb enclosure, and kept on walking. Heavy doors at the base of the stairs were open. She passed through them, and the sight that greeted her stole her breath.

Lanterns upon the walls. Flames in miniature clay lamps, set upon the floor. And before her: an effigy. Maha and Emperor both.

The statue of the Maha was carved from grief itself. Pale as ivory, pure and austere. The world in its palm was a liquid sheen of silver and gold in the flickering light.

Arwa took a step toward it.

The ground was covered, from end to end, with grave-tokens made of green and also of clay. The clay tokens glimmered in the faint light, dusted with paints and fragments of mirror, ceramic and silver.

The widow at the last caravanserai they'd visited had been right: She would have benefited from having a grave-token to hand. Her palms felt empty, graceless at the sight before her.

She was kneeling. She hadn't intended to kneel.

All the Maha has done, she thought, *and yet the awe and adoration wells up in me like blood still.*

How terrible to have the Empire she'd lived in and loved be a thing born from such darkness. To be born from a person she had been inculcated to love, and couldn't let go of, in her bones and heart.

She looked at the Maha's statue, fear and grief buzzing at the back of her skull; then she stood and walked up the stairs, back into the blistering light.

The widow was no longer alone. She had a companion. The two of them looked at Arwa as she passed.

"Where are you going, sister?" one widow yelled. She rose to her feet, striding over to Arwa. "Where's your offering? Don't you know it's bad luck not to make an offering at a grief-house?"

She took hold of Arwa's arm. Turned her.

"Stop, stop," said the other widow. "Look at her hair."

The widow lifted Arwa's face to the brash daylight with a wrench of her fingers against Arwa's chin.

"Ah," said the widow. Her eyes narrowed, calculating, thoughtful. "Are you here looking for a home, sister?"

For a moment, Arwa could not talk. The House of Tears had stoppered her throat.

The moment was enough.

"Come with me, then," said the woman. She led Arwa around to the back of the House of Tears, despite Arwa's ineffectual protests, where a large group of widows sat under an awning. One, older than the rest, was holding court, seated on her own chair and smoking a pipe.

"Aunt Madhu," said the woman. "There's a new widow."

Madhu beckoned them closer. Puffed out smoke.

"She's young," Madhu said shortly. She leaned forward, placing her elbows on her knees. "There are worse places to stop than here," she said to Arwa. "We're established. Oh, there are plenty of charlatan visionaries here, but they keep the Governor's soldiers distracted."

"Do they," Arwa said faintly.

"You're young. Pretty. Can you cry on command? Never

mind." A waved hand. "You can learn. Show the pilgrims a sad face and they'll give you any gift we ask for."

"But you wouldn't be expected to whore," the first widow piped up.

"An added benefit," agreed Madhu. "The House of Tears has a good reputation for a reason."

"That is—I did not think—"

"You did not?" A grin. "My, you are a sheltered one."

"I." Arwa shook her head. "I am sorry, Aunt. I don't think I should be here."

Madhu pursed her lips. Sucked her teeth. Then she said, "Well, think on it. The world is becoming unsafe for women like us. We all feel the terror in the night. But widows have currency in such times. The world is mourning, and who knows better how to mourn than we do?"

Without conscious thought, Arwa removed one of her packages and placed it in the woman's hands.

"This is all I have to offer as a pilgrim. I..." Words failed her. She did not know how she felt. "I am sorry, Aunt. I have to go."

And she turned and fled.

Arwa returned to their makeshift room and handed out the food as Eshara dragged herself sluggishly to her elbows and began to eat. Zahir left his food untouched, a frown creasing his brow.

"You took a long time," he said.

She didn't want to explain where she had gone, or why she had given the widows her food. She didn't want to explain how she had felt in the House of Tears: the way those bright candles had moved her heart like a star across the heavens. She did not want to tell them how the old widow had reminded her of Gulshera, and made her wonder what had become of Gulshera. Of Jihan. Of Bega. Of all the women, left in the massacre.

"I lost my way," said Arwa. That at least was believable.

"You brought nothing for yourself?"

"I..." She shook her head, trying to clear the haze of grief and exhaustion. "I'm sorry. I am—tired, I think. That is for you." She gestured at the parcel. "I misplaced my own food, not yours."

"We can share, Arwa," he said. His gaze was steady, assessing her. "There's no need for sacrifice."

She nodded, truly too tired to argue, and ate a little, chewing on spongy rice and gram flour, the sharp tang of chutney. Then she drank a little water and curled upon herself. Head on her arm. Comforted by the sound of humans—living, breathing humans—around her.

"We leave in the morning," said Eshara. And Arwa, blackness already pulling her into sleep, did not respond.

CHAPTER TWENTY-EIGHT

She was in Kamran's study.

Papers lay before her. Dozens of missives. She sifted through them by rote, as was expected of her. She raised her eyes carefully to gauge his expression. He was seated in the corner, face resting on his knuckles, body in shadow.

"Husband," she said. "What am I to do with these?"

He was silent. Biting her lip, she lowered her eyes once more. Perhaps he did not want to be disturbed.

She read the next page; neat script, terrifyingly small. She knew this hand.

A chill ran through her. She raised her eyes once more, and stood.

"Husband," she said. Silence. Then: "Kamran."

She stepped over to him. Stopped.

Dark dust in the shape of an arm. The turn of a head.

He was dead. She remembered now. All that lay before her was ash.

She walked over to the window. A storm of ash raged outside.

Arwa swallowed. Placed her hand—the wrist heavy with a tangle of bloody roots—against the lattice.

The light poured through it.

Ah, she thought, her distant heart beating fast in her chest. *I'm here again. I should have known.*

The dream disintegrated around her, ruined as easily as wet paper. There was ash everywhere. Ash upon her hands, her face. She felt a memory rise in her mind that wasn't her own, fresh fear mingling with the horror of Darez Fort, the dead maidservant at the imperial palace. She felt cold, brittle fingers set themselves on the back of her skull—a terrible, familiar sensation. She opened her mouth, breathless, struggling to scream—

Woke.

Zahir was kneeling beside her. Light broke into the darkness of their makeshift room as the curtains wavered around him. People were walking, moving. She heard voices.

"Do you know yourself?" he asked.

A strange question. And yet…

Jah Ambha after the royal massacre.

Who—who am I?

"Yes," said Arwa, sitting up, throwing her shawl hastily over her hair. "I had a nightmare. What's going on?"

"Get up," hissed Eshara. She'd pulled the curtain of their makeshift room to the side and was peering outside. "Something's happening."

All three of them left the room, walking between the rows of curtains, out into the courtyard. They found a crowd already standing there, huddled together. Arwa couldn't see over their heads, but she could hear their voices, mingled together.

"…came and surrounded the walls last night, no way in or out. Not even if you have gold…"

"…bandits, they say, but you know that's just an excuse to root out the rest of us…"

"I've been speaking to people," Eshara said in a low voice. "And listening. The local fort commander has sent some men here. They're trying to weed out bandits and murderers. Apparently."

Arwa peered between the sea of bodies. She could see a man shouting at the soldiers. One of the sullen guards who had waved them into the caravanserai was slumped on the ground, unmoving.

One of the soldiers backhanded the man around the face. He fell to the ground. She heard a woman shriek, and looked away.

"Come back inside," urged Zahir. She felt his hand, a gentle touch at her back, and followed him. The press of people forced her to.

"It's a small group of soldiers," said Eshara, once they were back inside. "One patrol large, at most." She shook her head. Huffed out a breath. "I don't understand this," she said. "If they're searching for bandits, as they claim, this is a poor way to do so."

"They may have gone rogue," suggested Arwa. "Defied orders."

"And what do you know of it?"

"Come now, Eshara, you know how she knows. Her husband was commander of a fort," Zahir said. His expression—his voice—were grim. "Arwa, why do you think they would be here?"

Arwa shook her head.

"Men desert their duties for all sorts of reasons," she said. "I couldn't say."

"If they're here for me..." He paused, jaw tight. "Well," he said. "There's no need to place you both in danger."

"There is no reason to believe they're here for you," Arwa said sharply.

"They could be," Eshara said. "We heard tales in the last caravanserai. Too much interest in Zahir's fate was bound to draw the Emperor's attention eventually."

"Regardless," said Arwa, "we're not leaving you, Zahir. And you're not leaving us." *Me.* She took his wrist. Held tight. "You stay," she said. "Promise it."

Zahir met her eyes. His own gaze was startled, expression strangely raw. He nodded. She could feel his pulse against her palm.

"I promise," he said.

Eshara was looking at them both.

"Well," she said. "I suppose we wait."

The three of them sat and waited, as the sun rose in the sky. They waited to see if anyone would come for Zahir.

No one did.

If the soldiers were looking for him, they were doing a poor job of seeking him out. Instead they seemed content with keeping the pilgrims penned up and wound tight with fear. Sometimes they heard shouts from outside. Then silence. Eventually Eshara rose to her feet. She tucked a dagger into the sash of her tunic, and drew on a robe, to conceal it. When Zahir rose to his feet too, Eshara shook her head.

"No, you're staying here."

"Eshara—"

"Zahir," Arwa cut in. He went silent. Looked at her.

She said no more. She didn't need to. Her face said enough. His mouth thinned, and he sat.

"I'll be back soon," said Eshara. And she strode off.

She returned an hour later, no worse for wear.

"They've taken some of the traders," she said. "The ones selling talismans and relics. The ones who claim to be visionaries."

"I thought they were here in search of bandits," said Arwa.

Eshara smiled thinly.

"I expect the bandits are just an excuse. It's the heretics they're after."

"Parviz hates his heresy, true enough," Zahir said quietly. "And yet, I hoped the Hidden Ones would succeed. I hoped the disquiet surrounding his rise to the throne would—delay him."

"That was optimistic of you," said Eshara. She sounded bitter. "He is still the Emperor. He still has more power than any of us."

Zahir said nothing to that.

"We can't remain here hiding," Arwa said, filling his silence.

"No," Zahir said then. "I don't think we can. But what do you think we should do, Arwa?"

"Why do you assume I have a plan?"

The partition curtains wavered around them as a child ran between them.

"You were gone a long time yesterday," Zahir said.

So he hadn't accepted her excuses at face value after all. Or perhaps a night's rest had sharpened his mind. Arwa gave him a look, which he returned unblinking, something fierce in the furrow of his brow.

"Your secrets are your own, Arwa," he said. "But if you know something that may help..."

"If you have any ideas, Arwa, tell us," said Eshara impatiently. "Or simply stare at one another, if you prefer."

Zahir blinked. Looked away.

"Go on, Arwa," he said. "Please."

She looked at Zahir. The flush of his cheekbones, the curl of his hands. She was not sure if she was angry at him or...something else. She swallowed, and looked away from him.

"I do think I know where we might get some information," Arwa admitted. "But I'll need to go alone."

The walk to the House of Tears was tense and silent. There were pilgrims hiding in the stores that lined the courtyard, peering nervously through windows, and huddled under awnings and in shade, trying desperately to vanish from sight. Walking across the courtyard made Arwa feel horribly exposed, her skin hot with sweat, as she skirted close to market stalls and tried to ignore the fear pressing down on her skull.

There was a young widow outside the House of Tears, weaving a grave-token, her shoulders hunched and tense. She wore her shawl low over her face, but when she raised her head it tipped back, revealing a line of smooth hair and sharp eyes.

"I am sorry to disturb you, sister," Arwa said.

"I know you," said the woman slowly. "You're the widow that Aunt Madhu offered a place here."

"She did."

"You gave her an offering of food. But we could have bought better on our own."

"It was all I had," Arwa said.

"Well." The young widow shrugged. "Are you here to beg a place after all?"

Arwa shook her head.

"My name is Arwa, sister. And what is yours?"

"Diya," the widow said shortly. "What do you want?"

"I was hoping for information. Please. For the sake of my kin. We're... afraid."

"Aren't we all," said Diya. "And what do you think a few old widows know?"

More than I do, thought Arwa. *And that will have to be enough.*

"Can the guards be bribed?" Arwa asked.

"You think we widows have the money to bribe guards?" Diya laughed. "Don't be foolish."

"I'm not speaking of money only, sister," Arwa said, trying to keep her voice even, trying to think only of necessity. "So: Can the guards be bribed?"

Diya's eyes narrowed.

"Aunt Madhu told you. We aren't whores."

The silence grew. Then Diya huffed out a breath.

"No. They can't be bribed. They're too afraid of their captain."

"Captain?"

"Capitan Argeb. He serves under the commander at Demet

Fort, to the northeast," Diya said, picking at the edge of the grave-token until it frayed. "He's good at dealing with rebels, the commander keeps him busy, traveling the pilgrim roads, plucking out the worst heretics like weeds."

Arwa did not ask how Diya knew such things. The widow was not looking at her, shoulders tense and defiant, head bowed.

"If I wanted to meet this captain..."

"You don't."

"If I did," Arwa went on, "how would I arrange to do so?"

Diya stared at the ground in stony silence. Arwa took a step closer. The caravanserai was far too quiet around them. It was a waiting silence, tense, breath held.

"Please," Arwa whispered. "I'm sorry I have nothing to offer. But I'm desperate. I can't stay here."

"You think any of the other pilgrims want to be trapped here either?" Diya shook her head. "No, sister. Go and hide with your kin. This will be over soon enough, I'm sure."

There was a firmness to Diya's voice and to the line of her mouth that suggested she would not easily be swayed. And Arwa did not have ease with honeyed words. She had nothing to bribe the widow with. Nothing, in fact, to offer at all.

What could Arwa say? What could she do?

She closed her eyes. She could feel the heat of the sun on her face. Hear the silence around her, a painful stillness born from fear. She sucked in a breath. Released it.

Spoke.

"I dreamed last night of a monster. It had a face like bone that had never known flesh, and when I looked at it I felt fear. Nothing but fear, pure and uncomplicated and...terrible. I dreamed that it placed its hands on the back of my neck. And then I couldn't breathe, sister, through the fear. A fear that sat in my skull. Just so."

"You had a nightmare," Diya said. Her voice was shaking faintly. "That's all."

"Yes," Arwa agreed. "Perhaps. But I am still afraid, sister. I can feel its head, even though I am awake. And I am afraid..."

She placed her own fingertips lightly to the back of her neck. She saw Diya's fingers, still upon the edge of the grave-token, twitch.

Arwa had her. And oh, how she wished she didn't. Darez Fort was close, far too close.

"I am afraid that something worse than heresy waits within this caravanserai. And if we cannot leave..."

Arwa allowed her words to trail off.

Diya swallowed. Laid the grave-token down on the ground.

"Come closer," she said, and Arwa did, crossing the dust of the courtyard and kneeling down by her.

"There are soldiers you can speak to," said Diya. "If they're here, they'll take you to him. If you can convince them, of course."

"Convince...?"

"They're nice boys," snapped Diya. "A tall one. Bald. The other will be with him. They're called Aran and Sohal. Their patrol comes here often. They always bring offerings, they know the way things should be. But they know their captain, they won't want to take you."

Arwa's stomach roiled. They knew their captain.

"Their captain," she murmured. "What is wrong with him?"

"He does what his commander tells him."

"Some would say that is positive."

"Well," Diya said, "It isn't. He *enjoys* it. The capturing of heretics; the killing of them. We're lucky Demet's commander usually sends his other patrols around here. Most soldiers can be bribed to leave pilgrims alone, if you know their price. But him..." Diya leaned forward. "Once, he caught a man who claimed the Maha spoke to him in his dreams. Oh, lots of men claim foolish things, sister, and soldiers know when to ignore the sick. But Argeb—*he* didn't ignore it. He had the man's tongue out, and then had his head staked outside the caravanserai. It was a blessing when an animal finally took it."

Arwa shuddered. Drew her shawl tighter around herself, despite the heat of the day.

She thought of the men who had served under Kamran, at Darez Fort. She had only ever seen them through the lattice of her quarters' windows. They hadn't been quite real to her. Only Kamran's stories had given them flesh. But he'd told her of one patrol captain who had committed crimes against the women of a local village. He had only alluded to the crimes, of course—he would not have dreamed of soiling her ears with the full, unvarnished truth—but Arwa had understood.

The fool. What can I do with him now? Kamran had said, gruff and irritated.

It had not been a real question, of course. Arwa had known what was expected of her. To soothe him. Eyes lowered. Demure. *Whatever my husband wills, will be for the best.*

Send him away, she'd said instead. *He has betrayed your trust, husband, and betrayed his duty.* A beat. Fear a sudden flutter in her throat. *That is, if you so will it . . .*

And Kamran . . .

Kamran had looked at her as if he did not know her, looked at her with fresh, uncomprehending eyes.

My wife is wise, he'd said eventually—always so achingly formal, this man who shared her soul, whose marriage seal she wore around her throat. *I will see him gone.*

And he had. He had.

"Maha save us," she whispered.

"Aunt Madhu doesn't extend an invitation to join us to just anyone," Diya said then, sudden and sharp. "We have a good arrangement here. We're safe, we have enough food and coin, we can protect each other. You may be usefully young and pretty, sister Arwa, but our aunt also worries for your safety as a woman, with things as they are now. Think on her offer, will you? If the soldiers decide to make things difficult, if their captain..." Diya huffed out a breath, nostrils flaring. "Well. At least they pity us widows. They will not pity all the pilgrims, or all other women who carry out their business along the road. Think on it."

Diya grabbed the frayed grave-token. Held it out to Arwa as if it were a weapon, precious and fierce.

"For luck," she said. "Take it with you when you go back to your kin. We'll be waiting for you."

Arwa took it. Clutched it tight. Felt the crumbling dirt on her hands.

"Thank you, Diya," she said. "I will."

CHAPTER TWENTY-NINE

The itch of fear at the back of her skull. The tension in her chest, a band steadily pressing the air from her lungs. These were signs and omens, of a kind. She should have recognized them. She should have known.

She had felt this before, in Darez Fort, on the day of the massacre. Felt it as she'd touched her fingers to the window lattice and watched the soldier throw back his prisoner's hood.

Fear. Unnatural fear.

It can't be happening again. It just can't.

There were differences. She looked at them for comfort. In Darez Fort it had risen with awful swiftness. Here, in the caravanserai it moved slowly, building within her. Within all of them.

She thought back to Eshara's fear that the crowds upon the pilgrimage route were dangerous—the keen edge of her fear, too sharp by far. She thought of the way they had all stumbled and trembled, huddled together like children, after finding the bodies of the dead. She understood now: There had been a ghost of unnatural madness, crouched in the dust of the pilgrimage route. There had been one among the trees. There was one here now too.

The madness was an invasive crop, a blight that had taken

root and spread across the Empire. Darez Fort—and the sheer, bloody scale of its savagery—had only been the start. The death Zahir had predicted, the price of the Maha's ill magic, was now suffused in the Empire's soil, and here in the Grand Caravanserai it was near full bloom.

When it flowered, they would all die.

The knowledge filled her with a feeling of suffocation. Screaming babies. Wide-eyed children. Groups of men hunched together, and women curled against walls, already staring at nothing. Market stalls with cooking fires and sharp knives and vats of hot oil. Pilgrims with daggers and bows and scimitars at their hips. Sharp fingers for gouging. Teeth for biting. Bodies, vulnerable and vicious by turns. Their lodging was full of the presence of people. As Arwa passed through the curtains, she felt as if she were slipping between a dozen shrouds, waiting to be laid.

The fear in the Grand Caravanserai was like rainfall on bitter earth, seeping into the soil, rising out of it so insidiously that a person would only realize too late that a flood had come, and they were caught within it. No escape.

There were so many people here, and so many weapons they could turn on one another.

Part of her—the part that had splintered from her the night of the Emperor's death and remained still in the realm of ash—had known the curse was here. She'd fallen into the realm. Half dreamed, half walked. She'd seen that familiar face of bones. The realm had *warned* her.

Diya had felt the fear too. Eshara had trembled, unwilling to be alone. Someone had died beyond the caravanserai's walls, left to rot. All these were entangled together, a great skein of terror.

They needed to get out, no matter what it took.

"Talking to the soldiers," Zahir said flatly. They were sitting across from one another, face-to-face in their makeshift room, and his displeasure was impossible to miss. "That's what you've decided is best?"

"What else can we do?"

"I understand taking risks. Reasonable, measured, calculated risks. This is not one of them, and you know it. What do you think you'll accomplish?"

"The widow told me who to speak to," Arwa said determinedly. "I'll find the two soldiers she suggested—I'll plead with them, convince them. I have to try."

"Don't you think your widow friend would have spoken to them herself, if she thought they could help her escape?" Zahir asked.

"Perhaps Arwa does stand a chance," Eshara interjected.

She was sitting with her back to the curtain, slowly sharpening the edge of her scimitar. The hiss of steel on stone cut through the air. She had begun sharpening the blade the very minute Arwa had warned her of what the widow had said about the captain, as if a blade would be anything but a detriment, as if the hiss of metal didn't sharpen the edge of leashed violence in the air to a terrible point. "Their ilk listen to well-bred women, sometimes. Something about *treasuring* them." She shrugged. "She's a noble and pretty. She might be able to sway them."

"Or their captain may cut off her head and place it on a stake outside the caravanserai's walls," said Zahir. His eyes were keen blades, his voice equally sharp. Everything was sharp now. Even the thud of Arwa's own heart in her chest. Even the breath in her lungs. "Isn't that what your widow friend said he does to heretics?"

"He may also cut out my tongue," said Arwa. "You forgot that."

Zahir swore an oath.

"Arwa, you're cleverer than this."

"And what do you think we should do instead?" she threw

back. "This captain cannot be bribed, and we have little coin left anyway. We can wait here until we're freed—but when will that be? Will we be freed at all?" Arwa threw her hands wide, all feeling. "There are no clever options available to us. There's only this."

"There's no reason it has to be you," Zahir said. "I could speak to them."

"You're mildly less pretty," Eshara said, squinting down at her blade. Zahir gave her an irritated look and Eshara added, "And I've never cajoled anyone. It isn't my nature."

"We can go together, then," Zahir said. "All three of us, if need be. Arwa. Please. See reason."

She shook her head wordlessly, and Zahir leaned forward, clear light blazing in his eyes.

"You can't truly think they're going to let us go," he said. "You can't. Please. Be honest with me?"

It was hard to be barbed or secretive in the face of that naked *want*—that hunger for knowledge and truth that blazed in him always, like a great light.

She looked away.

"No," Arwa admitted. "But I…"

Truth. Give them truth.

What else could she do, after all?

"I had a dream," she said.

"Oh, a dream," Eshara said flatly. "Wonderful."

"You don't understand. The realm of ash, I…" She curled her hands, tight, tighter. "I have entered it. In my dreams. And sometimes—when I'm awake. When we fell from the dovecote tower, it wasn't my ash that made me forget myself, alone. Reaching for the ash made me fall into the realm."

Silence. Then Zahir's voice, tightly controlled:

"You should use ritual to enter the realm of ash. Opium. Blood."

"I can't entirely control it," admitted Arwa.

"You told me you were well, in Jah Ambha. And I..." He exhaled. Squeezed his eyes shut. "I should have questioned you more. I shouldn't have trusted you."

Arwa wanted to recoil, at those words. Something dark squirmed at the back of her skull.

"Because of my ability to slip into the realm," she said slowly, forcing herself to go on, "I think I was able to feel the danger here, in a way I could not if I walked only in one world. I saw something that I've seen before, at Darez Fort. Something that filled me with unnatural fear then and fills us all with it now. A nightmare, Zahir. I saw a nightmare. And I am more afraid of it than any soldier. Because... because I know what it can make a soldier *do*."

"I should have known," he said to himself. "I should have guessed."

"Are you listening to me at all? Eshara—"

"Don't involve me," Eshara said. She wasn't sharpening her scimitar anymore, but she was staring down at it with great single-minded intensity, as if the sight of the blade could keep the fear at bay.

"Zahir, then," said Arwa, turning her attention back to him. "There is no soldier in the Empire who doesn't fear being at the heart of the next Darez Fort. Perhaps if I warn the soldiers, they will release us, before the nightmare can consume us all." Even to her own ears, it sounded like a weak possibility. "We can hope."

"You and your foolish hopes," he said.

"They haven't failed us yet," she replied.

"What a fine time for them to do so, then," he said grimly.

"I need to see if the nightmare is in their eyes," she said, pressing onward. "I need to see it, because I will recognize it. I know the nightmare in all its forms. It haunts me. And I hope—my truest, strongest hope—that if I stare the nightmare in the face, the ash will show me a way to dispel it. And if it does not, and if the soldiers do not let us run for our lives... well." She swallowed. "We're all going to die anyway."

He leaned forward. Touched the ground before her hand, as if he wanted to grasp her but wouldn't. Couldn't.

"Don't do this," he said. "Stay here. Think. If the answer lies in the realm of ash, then Eshara and I are well placed to help. We can study, we can enter the realm more safely, together—"

"How long until the captain takes another head, kills another heretic?" snapped Arwa. "How long until the nightmares make us turn on one another in a blood frenzy?" Neither of them looked at Eshara, though it was a near thing. "And where will we perform a ritual, in this place? I won't live through a Darez Fort again, Zahir. I won't. I can't."

She was the one who breached the gap between them, who grasped his wrist, holding him fast. She felt the beat of his pulse against her fingers and saw something in his face—something strange and raw and lost.

"Arwa," he said.

"I saved our lives, Zahir. And all we had then was foolish hope. I think..." An exhalation. "There is more in me than either of us knows. There is more in me than *me*. My ancestor's ash may give me the answer to save this place. It may not. But when the nightmare came to Darez Fort, I hid and wept as my husband and his men died. Now the nightmare is here, now I know what it is and what it can do, now I have a second chance to be strong, how can I not try to save us?"

"She's already speaking like a thing cursed by fear," muttered Eshara.

"This isn't right," Zahir said. "You can't do this."

"I will. I can."

"It places you in terrible danger, you *know* that."

"We're already in terrible danger. Just this once—"

"The *risks*, Arwa—"

"We have a mission, Zahir. And the safety of these people—"

"It is not your responsibility to die as your husband died," he said sharply. "You lived through Darez Fort once, you owe no one anything—"

"Don't you care?" she asked, knowing even as she spoke that her words were unfair, untrue. "Do you truly want the nightmare to take us, without hope, without a fight?" She swallowed. Tried to soften her voice, feeling the trembling heat of his hand in her own. "I am sorry, Zahir. But if you're afraid, I—"

"I am afraid for *you*!" His voice was vicious. His pulse burned beneath her hand. "If anything happens to you here and I live, I will read every book, every tome, I will trick death itself to bring you back. I will become something terrible, not for your sake, but mine, because I *cannot* live in a world without you in it."

"You don't feel so much for me," she whispered.

He blinked. Blinked again. It was as if clouds parted upon his face.

"No. I don't. I." He shook his head. "Something is wrong."

He pulled away from her grip. He touched his fingers to the back of his neck. Shaken.

"Fear," he said. "This is my fear. And yet it isn't. We are— none of us—acting like ourselves."

Eshara had lowered her blade to the ground. Her face was gray. Distantly, Arwa could hear someone weeping.

"No," Arwa agreed. "We're not. You called me your partner, Zahir. Do you remember?"

"I do."

"Then trust me," she said softly. "Allow me to take a risk. At the very least, accept that I have the right to risk my life on my own terms, when death waits for us here, no matter what we do. Let me have that."

Zahir closed his eyes. Opened them.

"Arwa. I can't even think."

"I know. I'm sorry for it, Zahir."

"For what it's worth, two women will be considered less threat than even one man," said Eshara. "I'll go with her."

"You'll have to leave your blade behind," said Zahir.

"Ah." Eshara looked down. "I'll still go with her."

"Fine," said Zahir. "But if you don't return I will follow you both. I hope you understand that."

"Zahir."

"I have a right to risk my own life."

"It isn't fair to throw my own words back at me."

"Ah. Well." He smiled tightly. There was still fear in his eyes, still something tight and dark and blood bitter. "When is life fair?"

Eshara and Arwa left their lodgings. They stepped into the light, into air that swarmed with fear and heat, that lay heavy on Arwa's shoulders, and held her fast.

Eshara rolled her shoulders. Cracked her neck, and gave Arwa a level look.

"Well," she said. "Let's go to die."

Together, they crossed the courtyard. The soldiers were encamped, largely, near the main gate. They'd commandeered some of the largest buildings and stalls, which had been stripped of their signs and wares. Despite the dangers—the man who had been struck down for confronting the guards, and the palmful of fools who had followed his example—there were people begging for escape. Many women, a number clutching small children, begging for mercy. Arwa's heart twisted at the sight of them.

"I'm looking for someone in particular," she murmured,

searching the guards for the man Diya had described to her. "Do you see a soldier—bald, tall?"

"They're wearing helms."

"Not all of them," said Arwa. "And...ah. There."

Two soldiers were standing in the shade before an elegant storefront. They weren't mobbed—the shade provided them cover, and their lack of helmets and lighter clothing made them resemble the pilgrims more closely than their fellow soldiers. Arwa, at least, recognized their clothing and knew their bare heads were a sign of their status. They were still green recruits, perhaps no more than a palmful of years in service, barely full-grown men with thin limbs and awkward faces that weren't quite yet honed by time. One was bald, the other round-faced and softer looking for it.

She approached them, Eshara at her side. Stopped and waited, head lowered deferentially but eyes still fixed on them both, as they straightened up at the sight of her.

"I am sorry to disturb you, my lords," she said. "But I am looking for Sohal."

The bald one shifted his weight from one foot to the other. Uneasy.

"That's me," he said. "What do you want?"

"A friend gave me your name," said Arwa. "I was hoping for your help."

Sohal and his friend exchanged a look.

"You shouldn't be here," Sohal said finally. "Go on now."

"Lords," Arwa murmured, tilting her head down demurely, drawing her veil carefully over her face, without concealing the short cut of her hair. "I was told that you're...not unkind."

"I'm sorry," said the round-faced one, voice very soft, as if he were afraid of being overheard. "You—the other widows. We can't help you. We have our orders. Our captain has been very clear. No one may leave."

"He's not—he. Wouldn't respond well. If we were to help." The bald one—Sohal's—gaze flickered to the crowd of pleading people, then back to Arwa once more.

Arwa heard Eshara exhale, felt Eshara's hand touch her arm.

"As you say, my lords," said Eshara. "We'll go."

But of course, they couldn't go. Not yet.

Arwa raised her head and looked at them properly, tracing their faces with her eyes.

There was no evil living in them, not that she could see. Nothing unnatural rooted inside them, nothing like what had haunted Darez Fort. Their eyes were clear, their faces burnished by the sun; Sohal's nose was faintly peeling. They were just boys. No more.

But the nightmare was here.

There was a trick to this: to being soft enough to arouse sympathy, sweet enough to reel them in. But Arwa used none of it, only stared at them, demureness forgotten, and said, "Darez Fort."

Eshara hissed through gritted teeth.

The men stared at her with wide eyes. She'd spoken the name of a tragedy and pinned them with it. Good.

"My lords, in Darez Fort a commander serving the Governor of Chand and all his men and all their servants perished. Behind barred doors a curse consumed them, and they died, to the last man." A slow inhalation. The two men waited, silent before her. "Some say the Empire is cursed. That our crops die and our people sicken. But in Darez Fort, the curse wore a face. It made them murder one another. Every one."

She took a step closer.

"I am afraid something similar will happen here. Don't you feel it? The fear? Don't you feel something terrible growing within your skull with no way to leave it?"

She drew the memory of the dream close around her. The storm. The face of white bone. Kamran's dust—and all the memories his death brought with it—hovering half-formed in the air before her.

"I know you do," she said, letting her voice soften not with the gentleness expected of a noblewoman, but with the rasp Zahir's voice sometimes held when he showed the sharp edge of his curiosity. "Please, my lords, you must help us."

Sohal leaned forward. Like a tree swayed by a great wind.

"Your eyes," he whispered.

Her eyes. Panic clamored up within her. Had she reached for the ash? Were her eyes full of gray-white light? She blinked, breathed, hoping it would fade away.

Sohal cleared his throat, and turned away. "By the Maha's blessing," he said, "you believe we need to warn our captain? That everyone will die?"

"I know it."

"You can't," said the soft-faced guard. He lowered his voice. "That's heresy."

"I'm no heretic," Arwa said, even though it was a lie. She stared at him full in the face, holding her knowledge around herself like a fierce armor all of her own. "I *know* it."

Sohal shook his head. Took a step back. The spell was shattered.

"Go," Sohal said abruptly. "Go now, lady. And keep your foolish thoughts to yourself."

"Come on, sister. Let's obey," Eshara said tightly. Arwa could hear the fear tucked in her voice.

She felt Eshara grip her tight and knew her time had run out.

"Sohal." A voice, deep from within the storefront. "He heard voices. He's asked for you to bring him the women at the door."

Sohal closed his eyes. Opened them. There was sweat on his forehead.

"My apologies, young widow," he said. "You have your wish after all."

*   *   *

They stepped into the store. Arwa assumed it must have been used for selling medicine, once. The air smelled of spices and herbs; jars of turmeric and honey and stoppered clay containers lined the walls, on cramped shelves. Some of the jars were broken, their contents spilled across the floor. Seated slumped against the wall, surrounded by shattered jars, a carafe of wine before him, sat the captain.

His helm was on the floor, but he wore his status in the fine fabric of his tunic, visible through his half-assembled armor, and the bands of decorated metal encircling his wrists. He had a cluster of men with him. One, old and grizzled, helm still on his head, was kneeling and speaking to the captain in a low voice. The older soldier rose when Eshara and Arwa entered, gave them a grim look, and stepped back into the shadows, where the captain's other palmful of men stood in uneasy silence.

Captain Argeb raised his head. He gave them a smile that was unexpected in its openness: mouth curling, teeth faintly bared, eyes crinkling with joy.

"So much useless chattering," he said by way of greeting. There was a faint slur to his voice. "Ladies, come and sit."

Arwa and Eshara kneeled down across from him.

He placed his own cup on the ground.

"Wine," he said, pushing it toward Arwa, keen light in his eyes. "Drink."

"I am a widow," Arwa said softly, scrabbling for decorum in the face of the captain's drunken joy, the nervous and fearful silence of the soldiers. "My lord, I will not imbibe with men."

"Your honor, is it?" Lips peeling back from his teeth. "As I see it, a respectable widow wouldn't be flirting about with my men at all. A respectable widow would trust the Governor's men to protect the caravanserai as they see fit. She would have faith."

He turned his gaze onto Eshara.

"And you, I think, are not a widow. Too much hair, for one."

"No," Eshara said shortly.

"Then you can drink for the both of you," he said.

"I think we'd best leave," said Eshara.

"No," said the captain. "We haven't talked yet. Drink."

Eshara took the cup. Drank a sip. Lowered it. Satisfied, Argeb picked up the cup, placed his mouth pointedly where hers had rested on the rim, and drank deep and fast. When he'd finished he lowered the cup. Poured again.

"I can forgive your behavior, widow. People are so desperate to leave that they'll do anything, it seems. Why, a man tried to climb the walls an hour ago. He's being made an example of; of course, we can't treat men the way we do women. Has it been done, Giresh?"

"Sir, I, well…" The soft-faced soldier, Giresh, stopped and swallowed. Then he said, "I will check. My lord."

"Do."

Giresh vanished.

"I am not just rooting out bandits, you see," the captain said. "I am rooting out all sorts of things."

He leaned forward, conspiratorial, and she smelled his breath, sweet with wine, bitter with something that was not wine. *Not just drunk*, she thought.

How long had he been sitting here drinking, imbibing, even as his men stood apart from him in nervous, fearful silence? The oldest of them was watching the captain like a hawk. This was his patrol. No doubt they knew his moods well.

"I heard you speak, widow," he said. "You spoke of Darez Fort. Said we could end up like that place. You verged on heresy."

"Not heresy, my lord," Arwa said, even as her heart pounded in her chest. "Only a mere woman's fears."

"*I know*, you said. *I know.*"

He leaned in even closer. Arwa felt the back of Eshara's hand against her leg, grounding her, helping her avoid the desire to wrench herself away.

"I see it in your eyes," he whispered. "Something...inhuman. Your eyes are not a natural color. They are like..."

Ash, Arwa thought.

But he did not finish his statement. Instead his smile twitched, spasmodic.

"You hear it too," he said. "Don't you?"

He did not say, *the nightmare*. But she understood. She knew.

She nodded. Careful. She had to be careful. The wrong words would see her and Eshara dead.

"It whispers to me," she said.

"It whispers in my ears too," he said. "Constantly. I hear it waking. I hear it in my sleep. I gave it so many gifts, and yet it follows me."

"Gifts," she echoed.

"You know how it hungers."

She thought of the bodies on the road. Her stomach twisted.

Could the men around the captain hear him? Eshara certainly could. But they were silent, no words, barely breathing.

"I have studied Darez Fort. I have been to it, can you imagine that?"

"No, my lord. I can't imagine such a place."

"I made a special visit of it. The blood has never been cleared, you know. You can still see the shadow of death..." Argeb trailed off. Lifted his cup. Drank deep again. Refilled it. "The place was cursed, widow. Oh, that I don't doubt. But the death!" He leaned forward. "The death," he said, "cleansed it."

Images flickered through Arwa's mind's eye. What she had seen at Darez Fort had not been cleansing. But she bit her tongue. Silent. For once, she would be silent.

"I'm no weak-willed creature," he said. "Oh, it speaks, but I question it. It wants butchery, it knows killing can be sweet. But I speak to it in return. And I have come to understand it. It has taught me the truth. The Empire is cursed. Saving it demands a price. And the terror, its voice. I think..." Voice trembling with joy. "I think it is the Maha's voice. The Maha's will.

"Butchery is disrespectful," he continued. "Untidy. What I do here will be a purification. Perfect. Precise. When I am done everything will be pure. The Governor is wroth with me *now*, but he won't be. He won't. The Emperor will be glad. Everyone says he desires above all things to blot out heresy. These caravan-serais, these pilgrims, are a part of the Empire's curse. They must be cut away, as infected flesh must be."

One heartbeat. Two. Eshara's hand on her leg now, gripping tight. Hold fast.

The ash had no answers for her. The nightmare was in him. The nightmare would see them all dead.

And she could not stop him.

"My lord is wise," Arwa managed.

With a sense of dull dread, Arwa felt the inevitable occur: The captain's hand gripped her shawl, drawing it away from her shorn hair, baring her. He gripped her face. Sweat-damp fingers, his hold too firm, his face far too close.

"Yes," he said satisfied. "You hear it too."

"Captain." Sohal's voice from the entrance. Shaking. "May I speak to you? Giresh has news of the latest heretic's punishment."

For a moment, the captain continued to hold Arwa's face in his grasp. She waited, feeling Eshara's nails against her knee, the sheer tension in the air. Then the captain exhaled, released her, and slumped back against the wall.

"Come in and speak," he said.

"Let me refresh your carafe, Captain," said the older soldier. He leaned down, blocking the captain's view. He gave Eshara a look.

Eshara tightened her grip. Released it.

"We go," she whispered. "We go now."

Arwa fumbled to her feet. None of the soldiers stopped them as they stepped carefully away. At the door was Sohal, arms crossed, face gray. He stepped aside to let them pass, and then stepped into the interior.

"Walk faster," Eshara said in a low voice, and Arwa obeyed.

CHAPTER THIRTY

Eshara walked faster, still gripping Arwa's arm.

"That man," she said tightly, "was cursed."

Arwa's own throat felt terribly tight.

"Yes," she managed. "He was."

"We're in the shit," Eshara said grimly. "It was a miracle we left that room. It'll be an even greater miracle if we make it to Irinah. Keep walking. Don't look behind us."

"He may be following us," said Arwa, breathless, struggling to keep up with Eshara's brisk pace. "Or his men, he may—"

"Keep. Walking."

They made it across the courtyard, nearly to their sleeping quarters. Then Eshara dragged Arwa into the shadows of a stall and leaned forward, breathing unevenly.

"Eshara..."

"Get Zahir," she said. "We can't stay here now. *Your eyes*, they couldn't stop speaking of your damnable eyes. What is wrong with them, anyway?"

"Ash," Arwa said tightly. "It doesn't matter."

"They look almost normal now at least," Eshara said. "Better for us. Those men will be looking for us soon enough, after all. When the drink and— whatever that captain was suffering— wears off." Eshara pressed a hand on her face. She swore violently.

Arwa didn't move. She stood still, day's heat around her, fear curling unnatural fingers along her spine. She knew Eshara felt it too. She could not blame her for shattering. But she also couldn't ignore Eshara's strength, the curl of her fists...the memory of the men of Darez Fort turning on one another, as the fear ate them whole.

"I hate being this afraid," Eshara said suddenly. Her voice was savage.

"All is well, Eshara."

"Don't tell me what's well. It isn't."

Arwa swallowed.

"Fine, then," she said. "It isn't."

Deep breaths. Eshara straightened.

"You must think I am easily cowed," said Eshara, clenching and unclenching her fists. "The bodies we found sickened me. I can't sleep alone. But I'm not afraid of death or of killing. I was a guardswoman. I knew my duty, and there's no shame in death. It's what I was trained for. But what was done to Reya, to my fellow guardswomen..." Eshara shook her head. "She was loyal. They were all loyal. We deserved better. It has...shaken me. And the damnable curse on this place doesn't *help*."

Eshara began to pace, for all the world like a creature caged.

"Perhaps you think because I am a Hidden One that I wasn't truly loyal," Eshara said, suddenly savage.

"I know you were loyal," said Arwa. But Eshara was not listening.

"Zahir's mother," said Eshara, "offered her skills to save the Empire. She did more than simply cajole the Emperor with soft words and flattery. She took a risk. The others hated her for it, but I thought it was brave. I still do. How much can you really do to save an Empire from the shadows?" She made a vague, fierce gesture with one hand. Kept on pacing. "I protect him because I believe in his purpose, in the power of knowledge, of *truth*. But I protected the imperial women because I am loyal to the Empire, and to everything it offers us. Safety. A future. A purpose."

"You think noblewomen are pampered fools," Arwa said, because ah, she had no *sense*.

Eshara looked at her.

"The Empire," she said, "is not a group of pampered women. It is not the Maha. It isn't even an *Emperor* anymore." She spat the word *Emperor*, heavy with all her hate for Parviz. For what he had done. "But all of those elements maintain the Empire, and I do my part to ensure that the structure of our world does not shatter. I do my part to keep it whole so we can make it better." She stretched out her hands. "And yet here we are. The world breaking around us. Isn't it?"

Sickness. Terror. Dead imperial sons. Failed harvests. Hunger stretching its hands across the provinces.

"That's what the curse on the Empire is, I suppose," said Arwa. "All the ways the Empire is fragmenting. Turning to dust."

Eshara had stopped pacing. She stood now, wavering on her feet.

"We are better than this," she said numbly. "Stronger than this. More glorious than this. We have to be."

"We need to get Zahir," Arwa said, with more gentleness than she thought herself capable of. "We need to take him and hide, and do our best to ensure he survives and reaches Irinah. Hold on to that, Eshara."

"Yes," Eshara said. "Yes. All right. I will."

Eshara looked at Arwa then, not as if she were seeing her with new eyes, but as if she had come to the end of the world, and no one was left but Arwa, so Arwa would have to do.

It was hardly complimentary. But it was something.

★   ★   ★

Zahir was waiting for them. She could see the relief on his face, splintered all through with fear.

"Good," he said. "You're still alive."

"We need to go."

"Oh, I'm aware of that," he said. "But where do you suggest? And what happened when you spoke to the soldiers, exactly?"

"I'll tell you as we walk," said Eshara. "Just hurry up. We've wasted enough time coming back for you."

They left their makeshift room and walked across the courtyard, Eshara speaking to Zahir in a low, hurried voice. The open space was still full of milling people, but it was silent. People were staring up at the walls.

Arwa raised her own head. Something was staked on the walls. In the light she couldn't quite see.

"Don't stare," hissed Eshara. Her own voice trembled on a knife edge.

But Zahir had paused too, raising his own face up, and said nothing when Arwa stopped alongside him and blinked through the glare of the sun. She saw what was there. Swallowed the bile that rose to her mouth.

Corpses upon walls. Ah, Gods save them.

At least she knew what the punishment Argeb had spoken of was.

She tugged Zahir's sleeve. Understanding, he followed her.

The House of Tears had shut its doors. Eshara strode forward and rapped on them sharply. She knocked harder still when there was no response.

Arwa pressed her own hand to the wood.

"Sisters," she shouted. "Aunts. Please. If you recognize my voice, or not—I am a fellow widow. You offered me sanctuary once. I beg it of you now. Please. Answer me."

Silence. Then:

"We're not allowing anyone in, widow or not." The voice was a woman's voice. Trembling. It was painfully close, just beyond the wood.

"Please," Eshara said, pressing her hand flat to the door alongside Arwa's. "We only want—"

"We do not care what you want," another voice said. How many women were pressed close to the door, huddled tight together? "We will not open the door."

"They're killing a man," said Zahir. His voice was devoid of feeling. "Out in the open. They're making a spectacle of it."

Eshara turned. Swore again. But Arwa did not turn.

"Please," she said. "You offered me safety once. Please offer it again."

"We don't owe you anything, woman," snapped the widow. "Not safety. Not entry here. Is this how you repay our kind offer? By placing us all at risk by asking us to open our doors to chaos?"

"You have wooden doors," Eshara said bluntly. "Cheap. They won't hold for long. And I know how to gut a man from groin to neck. Do you?"

"At least one of us does," another widow said guardedly.

"Horse shit," said Eshara. "You need us."

"Let us in, Aunt, or we will die out here," said Arwa, trying a softer tack. "I know you are good hearted. You offered me shelter when you believed I had none. I beg you now: Do not rescind your offer. Do not allow us to die."

"All of you?" said the first voice. Hesitant. "I heard a man's voice, sister."

"You do not need to take me," Zahir said. "Only take them."

"We survive together or not at all," said Arwa. "Please."

Silence. Nothing. Nothing.

Somewhere, distantly, she could hear wailing.

The door opened.

"Quickly now, before I change my mind."

They needed no further encouragement. The three of them tumbled in, and the doors of the House of Tears closed behind them.

CHAPTER THIRTY-ONE

As soon as they were through the door, Arwa felt as if she could breathe more easily. The terror eased, just enough for her to take in the sight before her with clear eyes. The widows were all crowded at the top of the stairs, which led to the prayer room. They had no proper weapons—no scimitars, no bows, no hand-held daggers—but they had makeshift tools of defense. Cooking knives. A broom, broken, the end sharpened. One was holding, of all things, a bucket.

Zahir lowered his head and made a gesture of respect.

"You have our gratitude," he said. "My apologies for intruding."

Eshara didn't bother with such niceties. She gave the door a critical look and said, "Do you have any more wood? Any more brooms like that one?" She gestured at the broken wooden shaft in one woman's hands.

"Yes," the woman said cautiously. "Some."

"Bring it here, then," said Eshara. "We're going to strengthen this door."

As a few of the women moved to obey, Arwa crossed the room. Aunt Madhu was seated in the corner, wrapped in a thick shawl. Her mouth was pursed. Diya stood beside her, arms crossed. She gave Arwa a curt nod.

"Aunt," said Arwa. "Thank you for giving us sanctuary."

Aunt Madhu snorted. "What else could we say to all that groveling?" She turned her gaze on Eshara. "Your friend. Can she really protect us?"

Arwa could hear Eshara ordering the widows about.

"She'll certainly try," said Arwa. "She told no lies."

"And the man. Can he fight?" A frown. "He's pretty enough, but he doesn't look like much."

Arwa thought of the night at the imperial palace when Zahir had cut a man's throat. Absurdly, she found herself smiling.

"Oh, he can," she said.

"And you," one of the widows said shortly. "What good are you?"

"I do what I can," Arwa said.

She helped Eshara and Zahir and the widows try to secure the door, but it was a futile task. The House of Tears was far more ramshackle than Arwa had realized on her first visit, when it had been cloaked in careful candlelit darkness. Without the careful veil of shadow and oil lamps, under the blaze of fully lit lanterns, the state of disrepair the grief-house was in was readily apparent.

She and Diya stood together under a hole in the roof. When Arwa tilted her head just so, she could see the sky.

"This may be a problem," Arwa said.

"We do well here," Diya said defensively. "But we cannot afford better than we have. Besides." Voice lowered. "I'm not convinced the door will protect us. I think your friend is merely trying to make us feel better."

Arwa had thought the same. But she didn't want to say so.

"You must have had more generous donors, once," she said instead. "You may yet again."

Diya snorted. "No. Why on earth would you think that?"

"Your grave-tokens. Clay and lacquered—"

The widow waved a dismissive hand. "Prayers from visitors,

no more. We prefer coin. It's truly the hawkers who benefit from selling them, preying on pilgrims and mourners. If anything, we should be the ones selling such things..."

As she spoke, Arwa felt a terrible pressure build behind her eyes. This was not the unnatural, clawed thing resting at the base of her skull. No. It was only natural, dawning understanding, and terrible for it.

"Your holy effigy," she said haltingly.

"What of it?"

"It is expensive. Isn't it? Marble or—ivory."

Diya gave her a perplexed look, frown line forming between her eyebrows.

"It is wood, girl. Plain wood. Your eyes must have deceived you."

Flesh like white bone. A faceless thing. No, Arwa's eyes hadn't been deceived. Not at all.

She swallowed. Said, "Diya. Sister. Why are all sitting up here? Why is nobody hiding in the prayer room?"

Diya gave her an odd look. Blinked, as if confused. Then haltingly she said, "I...I don't know."

Arwa nodded. She rose to her feet, walked over to Zahir, and placed her hand on his shoulder. He looked at her.

"Tell me," he said.

"Please come with me," she said. "I know where the nightmare is."

They left Eshara behind to watch the widows—and the door.

"If you're not back soon, Zahir," Eshara said, voice low, "I'll follow. The fact you're leaving me here..."

"I know," he said. "But needs must, Eshara."

She gave him a narrow-eyed look, but said nothing more.

They walked down the stairs, a lamp in Zahir's hands. The prayer room was not entirely dark. Some of the clay lamps on the floor were still giving off a faint light. But the dark around the light was somehow too rich, and far too alive.

"It feels wrong here," Zahir murmured. "The air is too heavy. My skin...my body knows something isn't right. And yet, I'm not as afraid as I was, beyond the grief-house's walls."

"Please don't tell me you find this fascinating," Arwa murmured in return.

"I won't, if that's what you wish."

"But you do. Don't you?"

"Fear and curiosity can coexist," he said. "You know that very well."

He raised the lamp. In the flickering light, the effigy was clearly visible. Its surface was still smooth ivory, inhumanly pale. It remained faceless, palm upraised with the world grasped inside it. Awe flickered to life inside her. She resisted the urge to fall once again to her knees.

"Strange," whispered Zahir. He lowered the lamp carefully to the floor, and moved to stand beside her.

"Do you feel it?" she asked. "The—awe?"

"Of course."

She released a breath. Steadied herself, grounding herself as if she were beginning a rite. Held her hands before her. Stopped.

"What is it?" Zahir asked. He turned to her, shadow and light reflecting in his eyes.

"There are daiva here," said Arwa. She swept one hand through the air. "*Look.*"

The rich darkness—too rich, too complete, she'd been right to think it was—was moving. Eyes flickered in and out of sight, mingling with the light of the lamps. They were not bird-spirits, nothing akin to animals. They were amorphous darkness.

The effigy glowed all the brighter between them.

Her hands were shaking. She lowered them.

She could think of nothing but the spirit she'd seen at Darez

Fort. Cloaked in shadow. Darkness peeling away to reveal its face of white bone.

"Ah, Gods," she whispered. Shaking. She'd thought herself prepared for this, willing to be brave, to try, no matter the consequences. She'd thought she knew what she was facing. But of course, she did not.

"Nightmare," she said. "I know you. One of your kind nearly murdered me. I can't witness this again." A pause. She heard the gentle, measured cadence of Zahir's breath. "As a fellow daughter of an immortal lineage, as kin of a kind, I ask you—please. End this."

The air shuddered, light rippling like liquid.

The statue didn't change. Nonetheless, the nightmare *moved*.

Arwa heard something within her skull, her hindbrain—a scraping, screaming thing, noiseless and yet furiously loud. She saw Zahir clutch the back of his head, swearing. The fear poured through her again with a sudden vengeance. The awe was gone. The clarity of her mind was shattered. There was nothing but fear in her now, pure and clean and thick with rising blood.

The shadows clasped closer to the effigy, crawling across its surface. The nightmare was unmoving, was still faceless, still a hollow simulacrum of holiness. Arwa shaped a sigil on trembling hands, demanding its name. It did not flinch. Did not respond. In fact, it showed no recognition at all.

Around it the darkness of the daiva moved, shifting in understanding. But it wasn't enough.

Fear had a way of stripping everything from a person. It denied even dignity. She could feel her eyes, her nose, streaming. Blinked hard. She could not move. Could not think. She could barely remember her own name.

As the fear wiped her clean, she felt something rise to fill the void. The taste of ash filled her mouth, clouded her skull.

The realm of ash was here. Just beyond her skin.

She leaned into the feel of it, ash rising ferociously through her mind. When she did so, the light altered. She saw the nightmare's blank face shift.

Saw the serrated curl of lips. Teeth.

In the realm of ash, the nightmare wore a face. In the ash, where the dead lived, it walked. And somewhere, deep within the storm waiting upon her path, she heard its voice, a cool and terrible thing.

You called me. Kin.

She touched her hand to Zahir's. He took it. But the touch of his skin didn't make the presence of the realm fade. The ash surrounded her still, formless white air, a rain of dark dust. It was calling to her, unmooring her from her skin.

"Can you see it?" she asked.

Zahir gripped her hand tighter. Looked at her. She could see his struggle to remain calm and conscious. His jaw was tight; thoughts flickered across his face like winged things.

"I can see the—nightmare," he said carefully. "The daiva. I can feel the fear. Is there anything I'm missing?"

She wet her lips. "The realm of ash," she said. "Its voice. I can hear it in the realm. I think if I enter I can...communicate with it."

He stared at her.

"Arwa," he said. "No."

There was a crashing noise from above them. A sharp breath. Arwa turned. There were women on the stairs; Eshara behind them, face gray.

"What—" choked out Diya.

"Don't let them come down here," snapped Zahir. He hadn't looked away from Arwa. "It isn't safe. *Eshara.*"

"I won't," she said thickly. Raised her voice. "Step back. *Now!*"

The nightmare shifted forward. The shadows of daiva whirled

around the nightmare like a great cloak, following it, coiling around it. One of the women shrieked, and together they stumbled back.

"I can feel it," Arwa said. "The realm."

"You'll lose yourself," Zahir said urgently. "It's too dangerous."

"I need to understand it," she said. "I need to stop it."

"It doesn't have to be you."

She swallowed. Throat dry.

"I think it does."

"I have flame," he said. "I have a dagger. At least let us go together. Let us do this *properly*."

"Nothing to make you sleep, though," she said. "And it's here. It's here now." Her voice wavered. "Zahir, I was not lying. I can't live through such death again."

"Arwa," he said. Eyes wide, his face an open book. "Please don't."

She did not need a fire, an opiate, a sleeping mind, a closed set of eyes. She had been carrying the realm of ash since the moment she leaped from the dovecote tower, the daiva's great wings around her. It rested in her eyes; it was in her skin. It had been waiting for her patiently. It was time to meet it.

She felt Zahir's hand on her wrist, heard him bite out her name, all sharp edges to its usual soft syllables.

"Arwa, don't—"

She released a breath and—fell.

She opened her eyes.

She was still in the House of Tears, slumped over, Zahir whispering her name desperately as he held her and lowered her carefully to the floor. But she was also in the realm of ash. The clay lanterns flickered on the floor before her, even as the world unfurled, vast and gray. Memories swam about her. Great forests carved of shadow. Lakes of pearlescent black. A familiar desert roiled beneath her feet as a storm howled over her head.

She rose from the bed of her blood roots, and looked at none of it.

The nightmare stood before her.

It was all sharp skeletal lines, white and brittle. Its eyes were silver, flat and inhuman. It was no longer faceless, and it was no longer still: its head was all shifting angles. Curve of a jaw, sharp knife of a nose. Bones likes blades. Around it moved a sea of daiva, silent, clinging to its flesh.

She heard its whisper again. Sibilant. Soft.

Kin. How pleasing, to speak to someone worthy of my voice.

Her dreamed flesh shuddered. Her true flesh recoiled, distant echo of her racing heart, her tense limbs.

"I hear you in my skull," said Arwa.

Fear belongs to the flesh and soul both.

It did not walk toward her. Instead, the realm seemed to... contract. It was suddenly before her, loping around her, its footsteps the sound of snapping limbs. She felt her distant lungs expand and contract. The nightmare circled Zahir as he held her body, as he controlled his own breath. Fear belonged, too, to the worlds of the living and the dead. She saw that now.

Breathe. Breathe. Just so.

The daiva know your blood.

"I am Amrithi," said Arwa, even though it felt far from the full truth. "Old one, I am Amrithi through my birth mother. That is why the daiva recognize in me."

No. It is your blood the daiva know. They broke oaths upon it. They remember.

"Broke oaths," she echoed.

It smiled. The surface of its face was a dozen fragments, moving unevenly, scraping against one another. She saw teeth like points of light.

The one who holds you has old blood of the Empire. His bloodline know a great deal of oaths. Shall we speak to him of it?

"You don't touch him," Arwa said sharply. "He is mine."

The nightmare cocked its head.

Yours.

"Mine," Arwa said firmly, feeling the burn of the words distantly, the hunger in them, and the fear of them too.

I suppose I cannot take what belongs to my kin. Wet, strange curl of its mouth, pale flesh peeling into a simulacrum of lips. *So, kin: Shall I tell you what you could be? Shall I tell you the tale your fear spins?*

"As you told Captain Argeb? No, old one."

It placed the cold points of limbs against her dreamed flesh. Its face shifted once more, forming into something almost human.

You fling yourself into fears, it crooned. *Death. Service. Your Amrithi blood.*

"I am not afraid of such things."

The nightmare's face, for a glimmer of a moment, was her mother's—fierce and furious, ashamed. Then it was broken once more.

You can't lie to your own dark blood. You are always afraid. And yet you throw yourself into the things you fear. As if choosing the knife will make the pain less. So, my kin, let me tell you the truth.

Its face changed once more. Mehr's face. Throat oozing great black pearls of blood.

It doesn't, said the thing wearing her sister as a mask.

She was frozen. Her insides were ice. She could not even weep.

"No," she managed.

Her sister's face, wrought in ivory and bone, smiled once more.

She held her courage close. She forced herself to ignore her sister's face, the awful whisper of the nightmare's voice reaching into her skull. She met its flat silver eyes and said, "How can I convince you to let this caravanserai live?"

I have done nothing, it said. *You have no need to convince me.*

"What has been done to the captain's mind is not nothing," Arwa said, clinging to the dregs of her strength. "What has been done to pilgrims he calls heretics is not nothing."

That was done by men.

"You whispered in the captain's ears."

That is merely my nature. Your bird-spirits fly. Your death-spirits kill. I am part of the balance, my kin. I speak, and sometimes mortals listen.

Argeb. Hungry for purity and purpose. He must have been easily swayed.

Arwa swallowed.

"Everyone died, at Darez Fort."

Ah.

The daiva whirled around the nightmare like a crown. Her sister's face peeled at the edges; she saw the bones of a jaw, shaped into a permanent smile.

The daiva control us. Bind us. Slow, they say. The world must change slowly or it will shatter. But sometimes...

The face peeled away. All bone again.

Sometimes they lose their grip, and we are entirely free.

"You are a curse," Arwa whispered.

It laughed. She had not expected it to be capable of such a noise.

We are not a curse, it said. *We are balance. You think your Empire's glory was natural? Built upon the backs of the dead? No. Your Empire is a blight. But now the Maha is dead, the dreams he crushed using Amrithi gifts are free. Ill dreams. Death. Disaster. Ruin. They must shape the world, as they always should have.*

"Darez Fort wasn't right," she said, sickened. "No matter what the Maha did, Darez Fort wasn't balance. It wasn't just."

Justice is the business of mortals. It is no concern to us.

"How can I beg you to set this place free?" Arwa asked again, knowing her voice was pleading, knowing she was full to the

brim not with nameless fear, but with true, solid terror, shaped
by the knowledge of what was happening within the caravanserai's walls.

*You cannot. We are like the tide. Slow. The daiva make us slow, but
we will reach the shore of all mortal minds eventually, all the same. That
is our purpose. The fear. The knife in a mortal's hands. The pleasure of
blood.*

"I understand." Her voice did not shake. "I saw what was happening beyond the walls of this grief-house. I saw your hands
upon those minds. But please, my kin, help me understand this:
Why do the widows not turn on one another? Why are they less
afraid here, nearly in your grasp, than those out in the open and
far from you?"

The nightmare tilted its head. She heard the click of its verte-
brae. She followed the turn of its head. Looked down.

She was staring at the grave-tokens.

*They showed us respect. As the daiva are shown. As the Gods are
shown.*

They worshipped us.

No. They had worshipped the Maha. But by accident or
design, the daiva had trapped the nightmare within the Maha's
effigy, where all unwitting the widows had offered it grave-
tokens and flowers and prayers and soft awe, bloody and heart-
sweet. And in return, they stood in the House of Tears above the
trapped nightmare, and did not flay one another alive.

Arwa shuddered, and kneeled.

"Then let me worship you also," she whispered. She pressed
her face to the sand of her desert, glittering and cold. "Let me
pray that you will leave the people of this caravanserai unharmed
and untouched. That you will not ask for the knife or the pleasure of blood. *Please.*"

As she spoke, as she began to recite a mantra, she felt her mind
sharpen and the fear peel away from her. Prayer had power. Oh,

it did. But the nightmare was moving, prowling on its sharp bones, and it crooned to her, *Perhaps you will live. My kin.*

But we will have our due.

Her prayer was not enough. Of course it was not.

She thought of the inevitability of the tide, and the way it could turn any stone to the finest dust. Perhaps if she had a little more time, she could seek out the widows, and ask them to pray with her. They could clasp hands, worship the nightmare until its terror was small and its power broken. Perhaps together they could beg some benevolence from the nightmare. *Pass over this caravanserai, kin. We beg you: Do not bring the dark here.*

But she had no time. She was, in fact, running out of time. There were screams beyond the walls of the House of Tears. Her voice faltered. She raised her eyes. A howl, unfurling once more, at the base of her skull. And the nightmare was watching her, all flat and smiling malevolence, its mouth a rictus.

You cannot reason with a nightmare. You cannot cajole fear or make it serve your will. The nightmare was a thing born from horror and history, and Arwa could not destroy it.

But the nightmare had given her a key, nonetheless. Something to fuel the hope that had sustained her ever since Kamran's death.

Prayer. There were many ways to pray.

She remembered a memory that was not her own: of dancing an Amrithi rite upon Irinah's sands, and the way the daiva had moved with her. For Amrithi, their rites were worship. Every sigil shaped by a hand, every stance. Worship.

Worship had power. And Amrithi worship had power over the daiva.

She remained kneeling upon the desert, as if overcome.

Around the nightmare, the daiva shifted in a black corona. They clawed at its arms. They struggled to hold it. Balance. In Darez Fort, the nightmare had been surrounded by a daiva's flesh. It was only when the flesh shattered that the nightmare had flown free. The daiva sought balance. She had begged them so many times to save her, and they had done so. But there was a price. She knew there was a price. At the dovecote tower, she'd been forced to use the ash she'd consumed and she'd almost been destroyed by it.

Who am I?

Beat of her heart. One, two.

Losing herself was a risk she would have to take.

This was her realm. Her path. The place where the echoes of the dead lay within her soul, still.

She remembered the bodies of the Amrithi dead upon her desert. Her desert, which lay beneath her. She pressed her hands deep into the sand, lowered her head, and breathed in.

The ash rose from the desert to meet her. Filled her dreamed lungs, her soul's flesh.

Dozens of memories. Thousands. The nightmare skittered toward her, with a menacing click of its limbs. She was screaming, somewhere where she was flesh. Footsteps pounded on the stairs. Zahir was holding on to her tight, fumbling for something on the ground. Ceramic shattered.

She was—

She was not—

"You're stubborn," Ushan said. "Just like your mother."

Hands clasped on his knees. He was leaning against a rock, sun blistering overhead. "But you need to learn, Iria. You'll thank me one day."

She rose up onto her elbows. Spat out sand.

"Why," she said, "is it always you?"

He was silent for a moment. The memory wavered. Then he straightened, and stood.

"One day," he said, "you're going to understand that not all daiva are as benevolent as my progenitor."

"They've made vows," Iria said. "I don't see why—"

"Iria," he sighed. "Darling. Not all people are blessed as we are."

"I don't see why that matters."

"It matters because they matter," he said gently. "If not to you, then to someone. And they need someone to help them survive when a death-spirit enters their village, or when a daiva takes more than people can bear to give. You will be needed then to protect them. And you'll need a powerful rite. Something old and strong."

"I don't know see why it has to be me."

"It may not be. Consider this a . . . broadening of your options."

He kneeled down beside her.

"Father," she said. "Must I?"

"It's a simple rite," he said gently. "Not difficult at all. Now, Iria. Let's begin."

She sat up. "Fine," she said. "I'm ready, Father. Show me."

"Its name," he said, "is the Rite of the Cage."

She rose out of the memory, was dragged, red roots drawing her home. She sucked in great gouts of air. The world spun around her, half-ash, half-mortal, but Zahir was holding her, clasping one of his hands tight against her. She realized he'd cut his hand and her own and clasped them together. The feel of their shared blood was terribly hot.

"I'd hoped it would be enough to draw you back somehow," he said raggedly. "Blood and flame, if not—sleep."

"Zahir," she said shakily. "There is too much in my head."

"I know."

"No, you don't. I keep forgetting. Forgetting who I am—"

"Arwa," he said softly. "You are Arwa." He held her tight, drawing her hand against his chest. "I'm holding you. My roots to yours. I'm trying to take some of the burden from you. Can you feel it?"

She nodded silently. The realm of ash was still so terribly close. In her mind's eye she could see the way their roots were tangled together. Stronger than they would be alone. Between them the ash moved, flickering at the edges of his mind even as it filled her own, filtered through the conduit of their roots.

They were a mystical order of two. They *were*.

"Good," he said. Smiled. He was sweating. Even in the dark, she could see how wan he was. "Because I certainly can."

She blinked up at him. Ash. She could still feel the ash.

"Help me up," she said hoarsely. "I need to perform a rite."

He asked far fewer questions than she expected, helping her to her feet. He supported her body, holding her steady as she breathed deep and held her arms before her.

"What do you need from me?" he asked.

"Keep holding me up," she said. "I know what I need to do."

Once, long ago, Ushan had gripped his daughter's forearms. Lifted them.

"Remember," he'd said. "Back straight and strong. Legs at an angle—"

"I know."

"Holding firm will be important, Iria," he'd said patiently. "You must understand this rite isn't—easily done."

Arwa held herself as firm as she could, relying on Zahir's strength. She held out her arms. Shaped sigils. One. Then another.

Hold. Strong.

"I need to move," she said. "Just—don't let me fall."

He said nothing, but he held on as she moved, his breath sharp against her hair.

Blood.

Hands circling, mimicry of a knot.

Bind.

Fingers fanning. Arms shaping a winding circle, her thumbs catching together.

Lock.

"The daiva won't thank you for demanding they cage one of their own," said Ushan. "But they'll do what's needful. And that will give you time."

"Time for what?"

"To tell people to run, of course. What else?" He shook his head. "Don't let anyone tell you that you can fight the child of a God."

The nightmare was not a daiva, to be caged by its own so that mortals would have time to flee. But it was an immortal creature, God-born, as immortal as a daiva, and daiva had the capacity to contain it. Or so Arwa hoped. She only had hope, and a theory. But Arwa had learned the value of testing a theory, and what better time than now, when lives depended upon it?

Hands interlocked. Fingers interlocked. Brought back against her chest, to her heart.

Cage.

There was a sound—awful, screeching, racing through her skull—and then—

Silence. Darkness.

The pale light of the nightmare had been snuffed out. Arwa heard Zahir release a ragged breath.

"The fear," he said. "It's gone."

"The daiva will hold the nightmare for a while," she slurred, crumpling. He held her steady, whispering an apology as he steadied her.

"How long?" he asked.

"I don't know. Not long, Zahir. Balance. It will need to—let go. For balance. We need to get out while we can. Can you...?"

"Anything," he said.

"Lower me," she said. "My head. It hurts."

He lowered her down. The world spun her, in lazy and vast circles.

"The captain may still not let us pass," she said. "But now we…"

"Stop talking, Arwa," he said softly. "Please." He touched a hand to her face. "Your eyes…"

She wanted to laugh. "I know."

The worry on his face only made her try to stand up once more. Her legs crumpled. *Fool.*

"We have a chance," she said. "We have to take it."

"We will. I promise it."

CHAPTER THIRTY-TWO

There was a pointed noise from the staircase. Arwa turned her head, as Zahir turned his. The widows were on the stairs once more. Eshara was in front of them, arms outstretched protectively, her mouth a thin line.

"For clarity, Zahir, these fine ladies just watched the Maha's strange white effigy vanish into the air, consumed by dark spirits," Eshara said tightly. "They'd like an explanation. You will remember, of course, that they have weapons."

Arwa could not help him. She was exhausted beyond words, shaking with the weight of the realm of ash still clinging to her mind.

What had they seen? Zahir holding Arwa; the shadow of hands moving. The darkness swallowing the effigy—and the fear racing through their minds and their dreams—whole.

"What witchcraft was this?" one widow asked shakily. Another adjusted her hold on her weapon, knuckles visibly white.

"This was not witchcraft," Eshara bit out. Then, "*Zahir.*"

He was looking down at Arwa, head bent, gaze thoughtful. Fool boy, her not-prince—as if he had time to think, now. She saw his eyes close, and a fine crease form between his brows.

There were no lies readily at hand that would explain what had happened before the widows' eyes. She knew he was considering falsehoods, one by one, and discarding them. And he could not tell them the truth either. Not the whole of it: not what lay in Arwa's blood, the spirits she'd called to her, the paths of death and ash they had walked together.

There was only one tale that would do. A tale that had grown into its own beast. A tale that would draw Parviz's ire and drag Zahir out of hiding and into the blazing, dangerous light.

A tale that—once invoked—would set its teeth around his throat and never let go.

She saw him think. And she saw him make his choice.

He opened his eyes and his face smoothed. Before her, she saw a Zahir she both knew, and did not. His expression was serene, his eyes full of a cutting light.

"You don't need to be afraid," he said. His voice, ah—it was a rasp of silk, his father's voice, rich enough to stop the heart. He raised his head. In the light, she saw that bringing her back from the realm of ash had marked him, at least for the moment, as it had marked her.

His eyes were gray from end to end. Liquid silver.

They had barely looked at him, these widows, when he'd first entered the House of Tears.

They looked at him now.

The lantern light flickered across him, framed the sharp loveliness of his bones. She remembered how she'd hungered when she'd first seen him, and was glad. There was power in that. He stood.

"My name is Zahir," he said. "Son of the courtesan Bahar. Blessed scion of the departed Emperor. Brother of murdered princes. I have walked the Empire as a pilgrim. I have mourned and feared with you, I have saved this caravanserai from the Empire's curse, and I . . ." He tilted his head back, haughty and pure, an effigy given flesh and face. "I am the Maha's heir."

★   ★   ★

It was Zahir who led the way, out into the courtyard.

In his pilgrim's robes, his hair uncovered, no turban to give him status, he should not have been imposing. But he was impossible to ignore. For all that he was a bastard, a blessed, disgraced and hidden, he was still the Emperor's blood. He'd been raised knowing what grace lay in his bloodline. He had seen the utter ease with which his siblings had held power. He wore a stitched costume of their confidence now—wore it as if it were his own.

The crowd responded to it. The widows had been shaken by fear, but now they were fierce with hope. They had witnessed a miracle. They would not be easily shaken, now.

She walked close to Zahir, mere footsteps behind him, Eshara holding her steady. Eshara kept grinding her teeth. Arwa didn't have the heart—or the energy—to tell her to stop.

"I can't believe this," Eshara said, not for the first time. She kept her voice low. "Does he really believe they'll simply let us leave?"

"What else can we hope for?" Arwa whispered in return. "You think we can fight imperial soldiers with broom handles?"

Eshara ground her teeth again, and said nothing more.

We could still die, Arwa thought. She did not say it. She knew Eshara thought it too. The guardswoman was holding her fast, staring unblinking at Zahir and the soldiers ahead of him.

The soldiers were at the gates. A crowd still stood about them, tense and silent. But they parted when the widows approached, and Arwa could not blame them for it. The widows were an eerie, silent sea of white, their heads covered with their shawls, their hands full of grave-tokens.

The grave-tokens had been Aunt Madhu's suggestion. Gimlet-eyed, hands shaking as she ordered her women around her.

We need to remind them of what we are, she'd said.

"Let us go." Diya's voice. Clear as a bell. Her head was raised, her hands before her, full of soil and grief. "We are widows, my lord. Not heretics or bandits. We mourn the Maha's memory. We are keepers of the Empire's great grief, just as we keep our own. Let us go free, or may the Maha's heir remember your ill deeds, and strike you down."

Let us go. Let us go. Maha's heir.

The call was taken up by the other widows. The chant spread from them to the watching pilgrims, who stood under the walls, their voices growing and swelling until Arwa could hear nothing but a press of noise, taste nothing but iron and ash and foolish, foolish hope.

Before them all, Zahir stood silent and unblinking. Eshara had once feared that his name had become a locus for all the Empire's rage and hope. In that moment, his body was a talisman, a shield. They surrounded him and believed they would live, that he was their hope and their future, their Maha's heir, and so he was.

He did not tremble. That was all right. She trembled enough for him.

Sohal stepped forward from the line of soldiers. She recognized his bald head; his tense shoulders. He walked slowly, shivering like a newborn animal. But his expression was resolute as he met Arwa's eyes—one long, unblinking look—then bowed his head. Slowly, deliberately, he lowered his scimitar to the ground. Reached into his sash, removed his dagger, and lowered that too.

There was no falter in the chanting, which grew and grew; against the tide of noise came another soldier, walking steadily forward. This one was a stranger to her, older and helmed. He lowered his weapon too. Placed a hand on Sohal's arm.

The rest of the soldiers did not move.

"This will end in a bloodbath," muttered Eshara.

It certainly will if we're not free before the nightmare is, thought Arwa. She gripped Eshara tight in return, heart in her throat.

"Open the gates." A voice, gruff with command. It was a leader's voice: loud enough to echo through the air and cut through the desperate fury of the crowd. The chanting faltered. "Let them out."

It was the old soldier Arwa had seen in the store. He walked slowly, with a pronounced limp she hadn't seen before. Behind him was another soldier, cleaning a blade upon a rag.

"Where is the captain?" one soldier asked.

The older soldier said nothing. Arwa noticed—as surely the soldiers also did—that his sword wasn't entirely clean either.

"Open the gates," he repeated. His gaze was flat. "Now."

There was a moment—a long moment—when Arwa was sure the men would not obey. But then she saw one move, then two. She heard the creak of gates being drawn wide, and felt the press of people surging forward around her.

"Don't fall, now," Eshara said, gripping her. "I've got you."

They stumbled forward, following the pilgrims, and finally left the Grand Caravanserai—and its nightmare—behind.

CHAPTER THIRTY-THREE

"I don't think there's any doubt now," said Arwa. She had one hand raised to shade her face, squinting against the fading sun. "We have a proper retinue."

"Stop staring at them," Eshara said, aggrieved.

"Do you think if I stop they'll go away?" Arwa asked.

"Don't joke with me," said Eshara. "I am still not your friend, *Lady* Arwa."

Despite her words, she guided Arwa forward gently, supporting Arwa as she walked onward and onward on shaky legs. The worst of her fall into the realm of ash had faded, like a dream, to dust. For two days they'd walked from the Grand Caravanserai, Eshara and Zahir in turn holding Arwa steady, near carrying her as they'd followed the pilgrim route toward Irinah. At first Arwa had struggled to walk at all, but her strength was returning. She only saw the realm of ash when she slept; when she closed her eyes for too long, red roots bloomed.

But she was going to be fine. She told herself this. There was no option but for it to be true.

When they'd first left the Grand Caravanserai many of the pilgrims had dispersed. Some had chosen to travel to Demet Fort, to the relative safety of the local commander's care. Others had turned home, or made their way to Irinah on more commonly used paths. Eshara had directed Zahir and Arwa on a lesser used, winding route. For concealment, she'd said.

But there were pilgrims who followed them. Two days on, and they were still following. There was a distressingly large handful of strangers, who murmured of the Maha's heir and watched Zahir with hot, hopeful eyes; Sohal and his fellow soldier, the helmed one that had lowered his weapon; and a cluster of widows, noticeable in their widow whites.

A proper retinue indeed.

Zahir had only called himself Maha's heir in the presence of the widows. Only in that dim prayer room, with Arwa on the floor beside him and a nightmare chained behind him. But tales had power, and this one had spread on swift wings.

"You know what I think," Eshara muttered. "They make us too visible. Parviz is looking for us, that I don't doubt. If we could just convince a *few* of them to leave, that would be something."

"I don't think we can control the pilgrims, or Zahir's lie, or what the Emperor does or does not learn. We can only…keep on going."

"Zahir's lie," Eshara muttered. Trudged forward. "I'm not sure I would call it a lie."

"He's nothing like the Maha," Arwa said sharply. "He would hate to be called the Maha's heir by you. You know he only claimed the title to save us."

"It doesn't change the truth," Eshara said. "Miracle after miracle—"

"They're my miracles," said Arwa. "Born from my blood. My ash." Arwa shook her head. "But ah, I know. You think I'm just his tool."

But even that wasn't true. It was not her knowledge that had saved them—not rites hard-won through years of study. She'd begged and scraped and stolen everything that had kept them alive, from the dark of her own soul, from the strength of her own ancestors. She was a hollow woman, a conduit for people of greater grace and strength than she possessed.

And yet in her heart she rebelled at the idea of being nothing but a puppet. She had made a tool of her own gifts; she was not one herself. She . . .

She did not know what she was.

"Those pilgrims can believe Zahir saved them," said Arwa. "And they are not wrong, Eshara, I know that. Zahir is . . ." She paused, breath in her throat. She had no words for what he'd done, drawing her back from the realm of ash, walking to the caravanserai gates, head held high. *I am the Maha's heir.* "Zahir is Zahir," she said finally. "I don't care what they think of me, only what they think of him. But what you think . . ."

"You don't care what I think," said Eshara flatly.

"Believe what you like," said Arwa. "But somewhat against what little good judgment I have, I do. You faced the captain with me. You risked your life for me."

"For Zahir's sake, Arwa."

"As you say," Arwa said softly. "Just as you say."

Zahir approached them then. His face was burnt dark by the sun; his brow was furrowed. He looked between them—clearly thought better of speaking—and placed his arm on Arwa's.

"I'll help her now, Eshara,"

Eshara let Arwa go.

"Best walk fast, if you can," she said. "We need to stop soon. Night's falling."

Then she walked off.

"Where were you?" Arwa asked.

Zahir shook his head.

"It doesn't matter," he said. "Lean on me properly."

She locked her arm with his. Leaned against his shoulder, and kept on walking.

* * *

The pilgrims created a fire and sat close to its flames, as the bitter night's chill crept in. As they neared Irinah, the weather had begun to alter. The days were hotter, the nights colder. But here, near a copse of trees and a thin river of running water, they had fish and birds to cook, and water to boil.

"There isn't life like this in Irinah," a pilgrim was telling some of the others. "It's an arid place. Except when you move deep—which isn't easy, of course. Then you can see strange things. Mountains and palaces growing out of the sand. Great monsters..."

Arwa walked away from his tale.

The widows sat farther back from the fire, clustered close together. Arwa drew her shawl tighter around her head and shoulders and walked over to them. It was Diya who caught sight of her first, and rose to her feet.

"Sister," Diya said by way of greeting. "Are you going to tell us to leave?"

"Me? No." Arwa looked at the other widows. Huddled. Straight-backed. Defiant. "Eshara spoke to you?"

"The tall woman you travel with? Yes."

"You needn't come with us, Diya. You, or any of the others. But you needn't go either," Arwa said, looking over Diya's shoulder at the defiant gaggle of women behind her. "I am just..."

"Yes?"

"Sorry," said Arwa finally. "That you have lost everything. The House of Tears. You, and Aunt Madhu, and all the others. It was—a good place."

Diya's mouth twisted into a strange smile.

"You have no reason to be sorry. And Aunt Madhu will start again, and she'll do well enough. We are survivors, sister. *You* should know that." Diya's hands clenched and unclenched on her shawl, held close to keep away the bitter chill. "When my husband died, his family cast me out. They called me cursed. They said they should not have to feed and clothe a woman who had lost her purpose and duty, a woman who was dead. But I lived, and I found a grief-house where my mourning would be holy. I am well. So I lost my home. What of it? I'll begin again. We all will. We are used to it."

She looked over Arwa's shoulder at the fire. At the men, at the other women. Then she spoke once more.

"The Maha's heir saved us all, when I feared we would all die. He gave us a gift. He made me hope." She gave Arwa a look that was all defiance. *Mock me if you like,* that look said. *I will not be swayed.* "No one else has offered that to us in a long, long time. What can we do but follow?"

"Nothing," Arwa said, voice coming out of her thin. She swallowed. Said, "Rest if you can, sister. The day will be long tomorrow."

With a nod of respect, Diya returned to the other widows. Arwa turned back to the fire.

There was no sign of Zahir. She heard prayers on the wind, pilgrims by the fire with their heads bowed.

She walked off into the dark of the wood.

She found Zahir hiding by the stream. His boots were on the water-logged bank, his arms clasped around his knees.

"You shouldn't sit here in the dark," she said. "There could be snakes. Leeches."

"I'm fine," he said, and he did seem so. He was staring out at the tranquil dark, water playing at his feet.

She sat herself down beside him.

She heard him exhale.

"Finally," Zahir said. "A little peace."

"It's almost as if you don't enjoy being worshipped."

He gave her a displeased look. She smiled in return, and

brushed her shoulder against his, the barest touch of cloth against cloth.

He was tense, for a long moment, his body knotted with feeling. Then she heard him exhale once more, and felt his shoulder come to rest against her own.

"What a time we've had," she said softly. "Can you believe we're still alive?"

"No," he said. "I truly can't." A pause. "When you entered the realm of ash, when you chose to face the nightmare alone—for a moment I thought you were lost. I do not know what I would have done, if you had been."

I cannot live in a world without you in it.

She shivered a little, remembering his words. The fierce rasp of his voice.

"You would have died too, I expect," she said. "And the rest of the Grand Caravanserai with you."

"You saved us," he agreed, faint smile on his lips as he looked at her. "The pilgrims should be calling you their savior."

"I'd rather they didn't," said Arwa. "You don't look like you're enjoying it very much."

His smile faded, abruptly.

"There is something—unpleasant—about lying to people, I find," Zahir said. "But I suppose facing their worship is a small price to pay for our survival. And soon enough it will not be a lie."

There was a thread of something dark in his voice, in the tilt of his head, as he looked carefully away from her and looked at the water once more. She thought of his fear of being the Maha's heir in truth, a creature fed by prayers and adoration. She thought of what waited for them both in Irinah.

Her stomach felt suddenly leaden.

"Speaking of worship," Arwa said, with false lightness, "the nightmare told me something of its secrets, in the realm of ash."

She told him of its vulnerability to prayer: how worship could weaken its power, soften its influence. How it had saved the widows in the House of Tears. As she'd hoped, his eyes brightened. He turned toward her, jostling their shoulders, the water splashing against the bank.

"Arwa. Do you know what this means?"

"I do," she said. "We have a tool to use against the nightmare."

"A shield," he said. "Limited, and no cure in truth, but a shield against the dark and death regardless."

"We have the Rite of the Cage too," she reminded him.

"We do," he said. "We do." And he smiled at her, nothing worn or faded about the look this time; he was brilliant and soft-eyed and oh, her breath caught in her throat at the sight of it. "And it's all your doing."

His face was more familiar to her in near darkness than light. She'd grown to know who he was—pedantic, idealistic, clever, alone—when he lived in constant darkness, in the tomb enclosure on the palace grounds. She'd thought he wasn't quite real then. Too pretty, too strange, too cut off from the world.

She didn't think he was unreal now. His hair was growing longer. His jaw was stubbled, his mouth chapped. His nose was faintly burnt. He was so familiar to her and yet still so strange.

She wanted to unravel him.

She wanted to place her fingertips against his burnt nose. She wanted to smooth his hair.

She wanted to put him back together.

Fool, she thought. *I am a fool. I throw myself into my fears as if I have control—*

"Zahir," she said. Heart a cold patter in her chest. Breath blooming in fog before her lips. "I...I told the nightmare that you were mine."

Breathless silence. Then, "Why?"

"Why what?"

"Why did you tell it that I'm yours?"

"To protect you," she said. "Because it wanted to—never mind. You know why, Zahir. Surely you must."

"Tell me," he said softly.

She could have refused. But she had already opened the door on her hunger, on the thing that twisted like a viper in her chest. She had already bound herself to him with a terrible tangle of ash and blood and roots that bound flesh and soul tight.

She could throw herself to the wolves of her fear one last time.

"Because," she said, "I have always made myself into what was required of me. I have always belonged to someone else. My father, my mother, my husband. And I think I want something—someone—that is mine." It felt like a terrible confession, like a thing she had ripped out of herself, a thing she'd revealed in her usual impetuous way, always seeking harm. She was not meant to want such things. Her wants were meant to be small, they were meant to adhere to specific parameters. "I look at you, Zahir, I speak to you and I know you and I *hunger*."

"Arwa," he said.

He had not moved away from her. That was good at least.

"Arwa," he said again. "I belong to no one."

"I know." Rush of shame in her belly. Heart flayed open. "I know, I—"

"No," he said. Strange, almost hurt, twist to his mouth. "I don't think you do. Why do you want me?"

"Zahir—"

"Humor me."

Exhalation. Ah, how her face burned.

"Because of your curiosity. You do not know when to stop asking questions, except—you do. You know pain, and fear, and what it is to be used. You know some things shouldn't be known. You are a pedant, exacting, and you're an idealist, you..." She swallowed. "Because your face is my lamp," she said finally; *ah, fool, fool, to talk like a silly child in love.* "Because this world is so dark, Zahir, and yet you—shine." She shook her head. "You could hurt me in so many ways with what I've told you."

"You think I will?"

She gave him an incredulous look. "It's as if you haven't listened to me at all. Have you?"

"I have. Arwa." The way he said her name—ah. "Show me," he said.

"Show you what?"

"If I were yours, what would you do? If I said, *You have me.* What would you do?"

"Your damnable curiosity," Arwa muttered.

"It is not just—curiosity," he said.

She looked at him. There was a challenge in his gaze and—something else. Something wanting.

Something vulnerable.

"Say it, then," she said. Voice lower than she'd thought herself capable of. "Go on."

He swallowed.

"You have me, Arwa," he said. "And now?"

For a moment, she did nothing. Only looked at him, his face, the turn of his shoulders, the ink dark of his hair. Then she reached up a hand, and settled her fingers, as she'd so longed to, against the nape of his neck. His skin was warm, his hair soft.

She drew his head down to meet hers. Pressed their foreheads together, so their breath mingled and their eyes closed, and there was nothing between them but the way she clasped his throat still, holding him fast.

"Arwa," he whispered.

She could see ash still beneath the closed lids of her eyes. But his skin was warm.

"Shall I kiss you, Zahir?"

"You have me," he murmured. "Do what you will."

She pressed her mouth to his. He tilted his head as her fingers tangled in his hair, and met her.

He kissed as if he had never kissed anyone before—clumsy, curious, learning as she guided him with the curl of her hand, following the touch of her mouth as if it were language, as if she were the mentor and he the apprentice. It was true, perhaps.

But she had never kissed like this before either.

They were both dirty from their travels—from blood and from dust, burnt from the sun, exhausted by dreams and by horror. When they broke apart, he stared at her. He touched his fingertips to the shell of her ear, and she shivered, and laughed.

"That tickles," she said, and he touched her face instead. He touched her like she was a mystery he wanted to unravel and make whole.

"Arwa," he said softly. "I'll be yours, if you'll have me."

I'll be yours.

Her breath stuttered in her throat.

She was a widow. A noblewoman. She had no right to make vows to Zahir, or take vows from him, no matter what she wanted.

She had no *amata*, but she still felt those words, *I'll be yours*, hovering over her skin like a brand. If she took his vow—if she let one pass her own lips—she would not be the woman she was any longer. She would be fundamentally altered.

And yet it had already happened, hadn't it? Oh, she wore her hair widow short, but her heart had already changed inside her. She was no longer folded small, no longer humble and soft, no longer a woman terrified of her own blood. She was fierce and foolish, brave and not yet broken upon her cause. She was a scholar. She was a mystic, who had her lamp of truth before her. Zahir, before her.

I'll be yours. What did those words mean for an Amrithi-blooded widow who could not wed again, and for an Emperor's blessed son and uneasy heir to the Maha himself?

She did not know what the words meant. And surely neither did he. And yet they were both still holding one another—her hand in his hair, his fingers on her cheek—and for all the world she could not think of anything she wanted more.

"I'd like that," she whispered. "I'd like that very much."

CHAPTER THIRTY-FOUR

If the world were just by nature, then after the horrors of the Grand Caravanserai, after holding one another in the dark and *hoping* like the fools they were, their journey would have been entirely straightforward. But the world was not just, of course.

A pilgrim woke the sleeping camp in the pale gray predawn light. He carried his lit lantern, woke the men first, then the women, and bowed his head to Zahir as if he were afraid.

"There is something out among the trees, great one," he said. "Something that—frightened me."

"Ah, Gods, not again," muttered Eshara. Then, louder: "We can move on. Pass it by."

Like many of the pilgrims, Arwa turned and fixed her gaze upon Zahir. Only hours ago, he had been bright and laughing, his mouth soft on her own. Now he stood, all pale stillness in the dark, listening to the fear ripple through the retinue around him. His expression was remote. Then he gave Arwa a sidelong glance. Soft.

She nodded in return. Drew her veil close over her hair.

"There's no need for that," said Zahir. His voice quelled the noise of the crowd, held it in a silence like a closed fist. "Please. Show me the way."

★   ★   ★

Zahir asked if any of the pilgrims would follow him. "It may not be safe," he said. "But I seek a way to weaken the curse's strength, and I believe that power lies in your hands." A pause. He softened his voice. "I will not make you follow. You all paid a high price, in the Grand Caravanserai."

No one refused.

It was terrible, the power he had over them, this vise of love and hope and faithfulness. And he knew it. She could see it in the thin line of his mouth, in the tight curl of his hands against his sides. But he walked into the dark of the trees regardless, into the faint grasp of an unnatural terror that hung soft in the air.

It reminded her of the fear they'd felt when they'd found the cart of corpses, an echo that turned her knees to water and made her stomach roil. Perhaps a nightmare had passed through these trees. Perhaps a little farther into the jungle lay bodies gone cold. Still, the ghost of it remained, setting its claws insidiously into their skulls.

Zahir stopped, and turned. The light of lanterns flickered over his face.

"Pray with me," he said. And when one man began immediately, stumbling through an old mantra dedicated to the Maha, Zahir shook his head. "Not to me," he said. "Pray to the terror in the dark. Pray for it to leave us be."

The pilgrims hesitated.

"Trust me," he said gently. And how could they not, when he looked at them with soft, steady eyes and his palms outstretched, as if he trusted *them*, utterly and completely?

The pilgrims began to pray.

They were not all Ambhan. They were from Chand, from the east and the west, from Numriha's mountains, from Hara's fields of gold and green. They had different prayers. Their litanies and mantras and songs jumbled together in a great cacophony of noise. Arwa squeezed one of her hands tight, nails marking her palms with grooves, and used the other to grip Eshara's hand.

Eshara gripped back.

Their prayers grew louder and more confident, tangling together in a great river of noise, a snarl of words that melded like magic. Arwa prayed with them, words pouring from her lips. Noise, noise, rising and rising, like a storm's howl, like a cry against the void.

This was nothing like praying alone before the nightmare's face of vicious bones. This felt intense and fierce and *powerful*. They grew louder still, and Zahir stood before them all, and met her eyes once more. And stopped.

Their prayers faded away. There was silence.

The fear remained but it was...quiet. So very quiet. Arwa thought again, of a tide against the shore, of the way a river of voices could wear a nightmare's bones smooth, given time.

"The nightmare cannot harm us any longer," said Zahir. Quiet, hope like light in his face. He met Arwa's eyes. "And I thank you."

Arwa breathed once, and again, and once more after that.

The sun was rising on the horizon.

A week passed. Arwa had begun to recognize Zahir's followers, to know their names, even as she marveled at the strangeness of the way they looked at and listened to Zahir. They looked at him with awe—read wisdom into his every act. In turn, he was more measured, and quieter than he'd ever been in the past.

She hadn't realized how much he usually talked—about their studies and the world around them, drinking everything in— until he stopped, and focused instead on appearing quiet and aloof and appropriately beyond reach.

Only in the early mornings, before dawn's light woke the

camp, could Zahir act more like himself. Sometimes he and Eshara would sit and talk, as she whittled the points of her arrows,
or cleaned her blade. But often he would look at Arwa, and she
would get up, and the two of them would walk off into the gray
light, stand very close, and not think about hunger.

One of the pilgrims had a snore that carried. The noise certainly helped to stop Arwa's mind from straying.

"You're still so quiet," she said to him.

He shook his head.

"I'm worried about our retinue. Taking so many people into
Irinah's capital is going to draw attention. That's unavoidable."
He paused, then said, quietly, "I'd hoped more would leave."

"They won't. Not now."

"They have a way to protect themselves."

"That you gave them," Arwa pointed out, as they crossed scratchy
undergrowth away from the camp. There were plants with sharp
thorns on the ground, interspersed with brilliant orange flowers.
She walked carefully between them. "They believe in you."

"They believe in the Maha's heir," said Zahir. "Well. Their
version of the Maha's heir. Certainly not the one my father
hoped for. I am just the body pinned to the tale."

He stopped and bent down. He'd crushed a flower with his
boot, and he plucked it now, smoothing the bruised petals with
his thumb.

"It isn't enough," he said abruptly. "The prayers. The rite. The
curse on the Empire is spreading so *fast*. We need the Maha's ash.
And yet..." He swallowed. "I still do not want to be his heir, in
truth."

Leaden weight in her stomach. Her heart a knot.

"I know," she said.

She did not want to think of the Maha's ash, of curses and
consequences, any longer. The thought of what could happen to
Zahir...

Her insides felt sharp with it.

To distract herself, she took the flower from his hands. Soft petals, but it was still whole. She placed it behind his ear. She combed her fingers gently through his hair. She felt the curve of his skull under her palm, the warmth of him as he pressed his cheek to her arm, trusting her utterly.

"There," she said. "No one will mistake you for the Maha's heir now. I doubt he ever wore flowers behind his ears."

"Perhaps if you make me a crown of them the pilgrims will be convinced," said Zahir.

She looked up at his face, the tentative smile that curled his mouth. She ignored the ash falling through the dawn-gray sky behind him; ignored the tug of the realm of ash, winding sinuous through her own skull. Instead she brushed the hair back from his face, and said, "Let's get back before the others wake."

One of the pilgrims had a mule, a soft-eyed thing that was much more obedient than its kind usually were. He offered it to Zahir—*for the widow's sake*, he'd said—and Zahir had accepted on her behalf. Although she found that riding on a mule made her nearly as sick as riding in a palanquin once had, she appreciated the rest it gave her weary legs.

Sohal often left his fellow soldier and led her mule for her— an act she appreciated, as she was unused to traveling on a mule's back, and didn't know how to direct the damnable thing.

"I'm good with animals," Sohal told her, early on, guiding the mule gently. "My parents were farmers, in Chand."

As they grew nearer to Irinah the days grew even warmer, until the heat was blistering.

"Your head will burn," said Arwa. "At least wear a robe."

"I don't have anything of that sort," said Sohal.

If Zahir asked the pilgrims for one, no doubt Sohal would have an array to select from. But Zahir asked for nothing; he was maintaining his aura of holiness through the judicious use of silence and far-eyed stares.

"Share my shawl, then," she said, and draped the long end over his head.

"But—"

"Just the edge of it," she said. "You won't be exposing me, don't fear. And don't argue, I can see you thinking of it."

He laughed—a shy, awkward thing—but shared it with her as they continued moving.

Time passed. Nauseous, Arwa climbed down from the mule, and walked alongside it with Sohal for a time, drawing her shawl fully back over her head and her shoulders.

"I'm not following for his sake," said Sohal, eventually. "I thought you should know."

She looked at him, his bare head, his hunched shoulders.

"Why are you here, then?" she asked. "Leaving your captain I can understand. But you could have returned to Demet Fort."

"Likely the commander would have executed us. Argeb led us very astray." Sohal swallowed. "Our patrol was only meant to pass through the Grand Caravanserai, as usual. But he told us to stay and we did. We were...afraid. Of the evil in the air, of the Empire's curse. Of Argeb. It's no excuse, but it's true."

You killed people on his command, thought Arwa. She didn't say so. That, after all, was what soldiers did.

Her husband had done the same.

In a very quiet voice—so quiet she realized even before she understood his words, that he feared being heard—he said, "Were they the cause? Of what happened in the caravanserai? The...daiva?"

She froze then, stumbling to a stop.

Sohal gave her a tremulous smile. "I'd hoped you'd understand. When I saw your eyes, I thought—that widow. Whatever she is, she isn't entirely human."

"I am human," Arwa said. "Entirely, utterly."

Sohal nodded, but he didn't look convinced.

"My great-grandmother," said Sohal. "She was from Irinah. But she...well. She wasn't Irin. You understand? You can be honest with me."

She did. Oh, she did.

Sohal was Amrithi. A part of him, at least.

"I'd visit the House, when we passed through. Take the widows offerings. I thought I imagined them the first time, but later I was sure that the dark was...not simply dark." He shook his head. "I thought they were there for me. For—family. But now I wonder if they were just there to curse us. Were they?"

He was Amrithi enough that he'd recognized the daiva, in the dark of the House of Tears. Enough that he'd looked into her ash-blown eyes and not thought of witchcraft or of heresy, but of daiva, and of people with immortality in their blood.

He was as Amrithi as she was.

And yet he looked as much part of the Ambhan Empire as she did.

She felt strangely shaken.

"No," she said. "They were trying to save us."

"Ah." He breathed out. "That's good, then."

She looked ahead, at all the pilgrims—young and old—following a foolish hope. At the turn of Zahir's head, in the distance—the way he looked back at her, searching for her face.

"Sohal," she said. "We're alike. At least in this."

"I thought so," he said, and there was something eager and lonely in his voice. "Hoped so, maybe."

"How much do you know of being Amrithi?" she asked him, a strange yearning in her belly. "Do you know of—rites? Sigils?"

He shook his head.

"Food? Or—traditions?"

"My family didn't want me to know anything," he said. He

spoke the words as if they shamed him. "They thought the less I knew, the less likely it was that anyone would ever know the truth. But sometimes my grandfather would speak about his own mother and his childhood and I listened." There was yearning in his voice.

"My mother hoped the same. But I know—a little—of what being Amrithi means. I have a little knowledge of rites and sigils, and history. And yet..."

She stopped, abruptly. *And yet.*

She could not articulate it, could not put into words how not having something nonetheless left a void with a history inside it—a void that reshaped the rest of her, all the Ambhan parts of her that were incomplete without the lost pieces of her that would have made her feel whole.

She recognized the yearning now. It was hunger for a thing she had never had.

Sohal was nodding. There was recognition in the shape of his mouth, the tilt of his head. "I know," he said. "It is hard, knowing other Ambhans would hate you for the Amrithi blood in you. Knowing you've forgotten something of who you are. Isn't it?"

She nodded in return, wordlessly.

"The other pilgrims follow *him* now because of what the widows said. Because they think he is the Maha's heir, or failing that, that he has power to keep them safe." Sohal hesitated. Looked up at her. The sound of the mule's hooves clipped the air. "But me, I follow because of you."

"Oh," she breathed. She did not know what to say to that. "And your friend?"

"He follows because I follow. Because we shouldn't have obeyed, in the caravanserai." Sohal looked away. Swallowed. "I think Aran is looking for the Maha's forgiveness."

Arwa did not know if such forgiveness existed. So she merely nodded once more in acknowledgment, and listened to the huff of the mule, the chattering of pilgrims' voices.

There had to be others like both of them in the world. Others with Amrithi blood, denied anything but fractures of part of their lineage; others with a gift often named a curse hidden within them.

Sohal had little knowledge of being Amrithi. Arwa had once been in the same position. But now she had one thing he did not: a mind full of ash and memories, a fractured knowledge dredged up from the dead.

And she had the Rite of the Cage.

She was no longer ignorant, she realized. No longer a woman shaped only by the emptiness within her history. She had her ash, and the knowledge it gave her was a gift.

"I have something more than prayer," she said. "If you're willing to learn from me, then I can teach you a rite. A way to hold the nightmare at bay for a time, if you encounter it again. If you feel that fear again, Gods forbid—if you sense it clawing at your skull too swift for shared prayers to quell it—the rite may save you. It will be swifter than prayer alone, and allow you time to flee."

He gave her a wide-eyed look.

"You would teach me that?" he said wonderingly. "Me?"

"It is yours by right," she said gently. "Just as much as it is mine."

"Then yes," he said. "Yes. I want to learn. Please, teach me. Can we begin now? Or—no. We can't begin now. We're walking."

"We can begin now," she said. She would have to teach him the movements later: the steady stances of the rite, hands to sky, feet ground to the earth. The sigils that would shape his hands and draw the daiva to his bidding.

But for now she would rely on words, simple and unvarnished words. She would give him a piece of himself back.

"We can start with history. This rite is called the Rite of the Cage," she said. "And once, our Amrithi ancestors used it to keep people without the blood of daiva in them safe..."

Arwa saw the great city of Jah Irinah and realized that they must have been in Irinah for hours. Strange. She'd thought she would feel it, somehow know it, when they entered the desert province of her birth. But the sun was still hot, the ground still parched, and nothing had changed but the sight on the horizon.

She saw small households and settlements, set against the edges of the city. Within it, she knew, were grand havelis of honeyed sandstone, and mosaic-lacquered fountains along the roads that ran between the houses of the wealthy. She also saw, towering above it all, the Governor's palace. The place where she'd lived the first nine years of her life.

She walked by Zahir's side this time, Eshara to the left of him. Now that they were rejoining the larger throng of travelers, Eshara was on the alert, her hand moving constantly to check the hilt of her blade. But Arwa could not be so alert. She was afraid, certainly—she had a great deal to dread about their arrival in Irinah—but she was also *home*.

"The last time I saw that palace I was a small girl," said Arwa to the both of them. "My sister watched me go. From there." She pointed a finger to the roof. "She stood there. My mother thought I wasn't looking. But I was."

"What a lovely childhood home," Eshara said, in a voice that was only mildly acerbic. "So many rooms to run about in, I imagine. Was it in better condition when you lived in it?"

Arwa squinted through the sunlight up at the Governor's palace. Even from here she could see the decay of the walls. Great chunks had been removed. One of the gates was splintered.

"Yes," she said slowly. "It was."

* ⋆ ⋆ ⋆

Jah Irinah was a city abandoned.

Not abandoned by people. No, the streets were still full of stalls and hawkers and houses of widowhood and houses of prayer. The sandstone havelis were open-doored, full of people. But the roads had not been cared for, and rubbish and human waste were gathered in dark corners, where people did a good job of ignoring them. The fine fountains were bone dry. Most of the tiles had been ripped away from them, leaving them gray-white and bare and useless. The havelis were houses of prayers and shops, now. Arwa looked into one and saw a statue of the Maha, wreathed in incense. She looked away.

Even as the mourners and pilgrims had claimed it, the Empire had abandoned Irinah.

"There are boarding houses where we can stay tonight," said Eshara.

"Entering the realm is better done at night," Zahir said. "But Arwa needs time to recover. Best if we find a place."

"I don't need to recover," Arwa said. She was not entirely lying—the realm of ash was with her always now, and she was not convinced that was going to change. "Besides, do we have money for proper rooms?"

"Aliye's money is running short," Eshara acknowledged. "But one of the pilgrims offered to pay."

"And you think we should *accept*?" Zahir said, incredulous.

"I'd like a real bed," said Eshara. "Besides, what else are they good for? Go and offer them your blessings, Zahir. They'll think that's a fair exchange."

Zahir gave her a complicated frown, and walked off.

"You probably shouldn't share with Zahir," said Eshara, after he was gone, "even though you no doubt want to. It would tarnish his image, and then we'll have no one to pay for our beds."

Arwa gave her a sharp look.

"Of course, it would tarnish your image much more than his," Eshara added. "In fact, they'd probably forgive him and insist we leave you behind. But when he refused we'd end up in the same mess, so what it does matter?"

"*Eshara.*"

"I'm not stupid," Eshara said. "And you two have never hidden your feelings well. But this won't end well, Arwa."

"I think we have greater things to concern ourselves with than this," Arwa said.

"Oh, we do," said Eshara. "But that doesn't make either of you less foolish."

Arwa knew they were foolish. She was a widow. He was a blessed. They had no future, and only a thin scrap of hope to sustain them.

But he was hers. And she was—

"Let's find this boarding house," Arwa said. "And never speak of this again. Does that bargain suit you?"

"That's not a bargain of any kind," said Eshara, rolling her eyes. "But fine."

A pilgrim paid for rooms in a boarding house, in the end. When their companions fell swiftly into sleep, Arwa took Zahir's hand and said, "Do you think there's a way onto the roof?"

"Most likely," he said.

"Well, let's find it. I want to look across the city."

They climbed a ladder to the roof. Then they stood at its edge and stared—between the buildings—at the true Irinah that lay beyond the borders of the city.

The desert.

In the dark it was almost blue-gold, great rolling waves as night-dark as an ocean. The sky above it was a deeper black, and beneath it the desert seemed to shine.

This was the true Irinah. Not the dilapidated, half-abandoned city of Jah Irinah that pilgrims had populated, walking its ruins like bright ghosts. Irinah *was* the desert.

"My father's armies were all driven away from this desert," Zahir murmured, staring out at the waves of darkness with something like awe. "By daiva, by the very sand—they said it flung them back, and those that weren't flung were consumed."

He leaned forward, dangerously close to the edge. He stared at the sand.

"Arwa," he breathed. "I have never seen anything like it."

The wind caught her shawl, ruffled her hair. She held her shawl still.

"I have something to tell you," said Arwa. "While we're alone."

He dragged his gaze away from the desert. Took a step back, giving her his focus.

"Go on."

"I taught Sohal a rite," said Arwa. "The rite I used in the House of Tears. He's..." She hesitated. "Zahir. He's like me."

"How so?"

"In the way of blood, Zahir," she said sharply. Then she bit her lip. Ah. She hadn't meant to snap so. "It isn't an easy thing for me to say. It is a sign of my trust in you that I am. Being part Amrithi—well." She curled her fingers tighter in the cloth. "When I was small...once, my mother took me in the palanquin to watch an Amrithi family being driven from the edges of our hometown in Hara. The family had traveled far. They were just a mother and father—two children. They had their heads shaved and were beaten. And then they were driven off with sticks. And that was considered *kind*.

"She wanted me to see," Arwa went on, "so I would understand why I had to be better than my mother's Amrithi blood. Only barbarians, she told me, scrape at the edges of the civilized world. Only heathens are not allowed *in*."

He touched a hand to her sleeve. She took it. Held it tight and turned to him, resting against him. She felt him exhale and wrap an arm around her, ever so gentle.

"Sometimes those who love us harm us," he said. "I am sorry for it, Arwa."

"Don't be. I'm well enough."

"Who am I to argue?" He pressed his face to her hair. "It is only that—well."

Only that she was so visibly in pain. Only that her mother's love was both a comfort and a forever wound.

"I know," she said. "But I am glad I have met Sohal. I've given him what little knowledge I can. Of—nightmares. Of a rite to manage them. I am glad that...I am not alone. I knew there had to be others like me in the world, Zahir. Other Amrithi living and thriving in the Empire. But to meet one—to truly know, with your own eyes and your own heart, that you are not alone—it's beyond words. There are others like me, Zahir. Somewhere. Everywhere. I am not *alone*."

He said nothing, only held her against the brush of the wind, the ash raining behind the closed lids of her eyes. The distant glow of the desert welcoming her home.

CHAPTER THIRTY-FIVE

After a night's rest, they decided they would enter the desert proper at sunset. Enough time to obtain something to help them sleep, and something akin to a firepit.

"There's a guide who claims to be Amrithi," said Eshara. "He said he can get you safe into the desert to the Maha's grave, for a price. He's taken plenty of people before."

"You believe him?"

Eshara shrugged.

"Believe or not, I have a very sharp and convincing sword, if he tries to trick us."

"We can go alone," said Zahir. "We don't need to find the Maha's exact resting place, after all. It's Irinah's nature that is the key to our work, not his physical remains."

"The desert can be a dangerous place, or so people say," said Eshara. "I've heard all the tales from your worshipful retinue."

"We don't need to go far," Zahir said firmly. "And this is—personal. We don't need a guide present."

"If we're lucky," Arwa said, meeting Eshara's eyes, "whatever makes the desert dangerous will avoid harming me, and will avoid harming Zahir too because he's in my company."

Eshara's mouth thinned, but she didn't argue further.

As night fell, they donned thick robes, bought from one of

the local stalls. They were a pale gray, heavy and hooded, well suited to the sudden storms and bitter night cold of the desert.

Eshara donned her own, her scimitar in the sash at her hip, bow slung over her back. As Zahir prepared their supplies, Eshara turned to Arwa.

Arwa braced herself, expecting more criticism. Instead Eshara took her hood. Held the edge of it with great care.

"I don't hate you," said Eshara. "I thought you should know that." She met Arwa's eyes. "You remember, I called you a puppet."

"I don't need to be reminded," Arwa said.

Eshara shook her head. "I'm not sorry," she said. "But, I will say, I don't know what you are anymore, Arwa. I don't think you're a puppet any longer. And I've found I care, somewhat, whether you live or die."

She adjusted Arwa's robe.

"So try not to die."

"I'll do my best," said Arwa.

They left the boarding house in the dark of night, she and Zahir and Eshara. They walked through the littered streets toward the desert.

"Where are you going, then?"

Arwa knew that voice.

Diya strode toward them. She had another widow with her and a couple of pilgrims, looking equally determined.

"You're walking into the desert," she said, looking between them, "the three of you, all alone?"

"We have work that must be done in isolation," said Zahir, voice even and smooth. "Eshara will protect us. You have no reason to follow us or fear."

"You and her?" Diya said, looking between Arwa and Zahir. "A widow can't be alone with a man, oh great one," Diya added, striding forward determinedly. "We will accompany you in order to protect her honor."

"I'm already there to do that," Eshara said dryly.

"There's strength in numbers."

"Sister," said Arwa, "my honor isn't at stake."

"Well, we're coming anyway," said Diya.

When Zahir gave Eshara a helpless look, she shrugged and said, "They know the risks. They've come here to see the place where the Maha died, but I suppose they'll settle for watching you perform a miracle."

"It won't be an impressive miracle," Zahir said, looking hunted.

"I'll make them keep their distance," Eshara said, amused.

They walked out onto the sand.

True to her word, Eshara kept the watchers a respectful distance back. Zahir and Arwa made their way down into a valley in the sand, a basin surrounded on all sides by faint outcroppings of rock and vague, wizened trees. It felt like an appropriate place to begin.

Zahir kneeled down to start a fire. He began setting it in place. Paused.

"Arwa," he said. "Look down."

She looked.

The sand had flared out around them, gleaming like it was full of jewel-toned flame. They stared down at it in awe. She kneeled beside him and pressed her hands into the sand, sifting it between her fingers. It fell like an outpouring of light.

"Gods," she breathed. She felt shaky. He was staring at the earth, eyes wide and wondering.

She touched her hand to his. Felt the blood roots, distant, ash-blooded, pulsing between them.

"Start the fire," she said. "I have my dagger."

She removed her dagger from her sash. It was the dagger her sister had given her so long ago, when she was just a girl. She made a cut, adding her blood to the flames. He did the same.

Here in Irinah—the desert where the worlds of the living, dead, and immortal touched—they placed their blood in the flames. It took no more than that. The realm of ash dragged them in.

And it was nothing like it had ever been before.

The realm unfurled around them, melding with the mortal world. The sand lost its color, fading to rich silver. The sky darkened further, ink black, pricked with glaring white stars. This was Arwa's path of ash and the true desert of Irinah entwined into one. In snatches she saw the storm of her path, carving the air with winds that turned like white blades in the air. Around them she saw Zahir's ink-black trees unfurl, their great grace of branches curling against the air.

Irinah was a gate binding three worlds. Arwa should not have been surprised by the sharpness of the realm around her— the sheer richness of it, as if it were a place of flesh and not echoes. But she was.

She looked at Zahir's face. All the hewn, glittering edges of it, the way it tilted toward her.

He offered his hand. She took it.

"Let's find the Maha," he said.

They stepped away from the flames. Their flesh remained where it was, slumped by the fire. But their souls walked. Beneath their feet the sand shivered and settled and turned, as if it lived and breathed, marking the way in rippling waves before them.

"I think this is my path." He paused, silent for a moment, then said, "I suppose we follow it."

Arwa squeezed his hand.

"Lead the way," she said.

They walked and walked, through the shadows of trees that sprouted from nowhere, through the strangely real hills and eddies of the desert. They walked a familiar path, passing the shadows of the dead, the stars stitched upon a ceiling, the ink of lost books.

They walked through Arwa's own dead. She felt the roiling thud of her own heart and stomach, a deep reflexive grief, but this time she didn't let go of Zahir's hand, and she didn't look down.

"Do you feel any pain?" Zahir asked.

"No." She felt as if she could walk forever here, in a place that was mortal ash and immortal dreaming both, walk until the end of time, until she'd forgotten her flesh and her *self* entirely. The idea was both exhilarating and terrifying. "Do you?"

"No," he said. He was staring forward. Through his glass skin, she could see the dark of the night, and glow of the sand, far brighter than it should have been, and far too alive. Through his skin, she saw the shadows of the dead. "But I think we're nearly there. I can feel him."

They took a step forward. Another.

And there he was.

The Maha's ash stood at the end of his desert of dead. Beyond him was nothing but howling darkness, a storm without color, as if dreamfire had thrown a great shadow across the realm. But the Maha's ash glowed despite the dark, as if each inch of it were suffused with the desert, drunk with the magic of Irinah.

The lamp of truth, Arwa thought. Ah, how bitter truth could be. Awe and love and grief welled up in her, unbidden and unwanted.

Where the past figures of ash they'd seen in the realm had been fractured, only partial shadows of the people who had left them behind, the Maha's ash was eerily perfect. He was not unusually tall or broad, and not as old as she had thought he would be. His face was unremarkable, austere. His eyes were closed.

Zahir walked toward him. Arwa held tighter to his roots and her own, and followed.

The sand moved beneath them, wavering like water in the wind's hands, like a pale and cold fire. They crossed it. And Zahir stopped before the Maha and looked into his face.

They were the same height, he and the Maha. They had the same sharp bones. Everyone had told Zahir that he had his mother's look, but standing before the Maha's ash, it was as if Zahir stood before a dark mirror. His reflection, carved by the smoke of the dead.

Zahir reached his free hand out, nearly touching the Maha's. But not quite. Not yet.

"We look alike," Zahir said shakily. "I'd hoped we wouldn't."

"You look nothing alike," Arwa managed to say.

"Thank you," said Zahir, "for lying. I appreciate it."

His hand moved up, tracing the air around the Maha's ash. His arm. His shoulder. His close-eyed face.

"Here," he whispered. "Here at last."

He steeled himself, his face as resolute as it had been on the day he thought his father would strike him dead. Then, abruptly, he crumpled to his knees.

His head was bowed.

"Zahir," she said, alarmed. She kneeled down with him, their roots a great slash of red across the desert floor.

"I can do it," he gritted out. "I can. I am only afraid." Then he shook his head. "No. Not afraid." He looked at her, face fierce with feeling. "I told you, to fix a broken tool you must understand the intent of its maker. But he built with the purpose of breaking the natural balance for his own ends. He built with an unforgivable intent by unforgivable means. What can I take from his ash, but another way to break the world? But how can I leave his ash here, and say that balance is *enough*, and let the people of the Empire suffer and die?"

"You need not do this now," she told him. "We can stay in Irinah and consider what to do...or. Or we can try to find another way."

"And waste all our work, our sacrifice, on my cowardice, my fear of becoming too much the scion of my father's blood?" He shook his head. "I can't."

"Zahir." She spoke his name as if it would quell him, comfort him. She did not remind him of the price the realm of ash would demand of him. She did not tell him she feared seeing him lost. Her heart ached.

They both knew the risks that lay before him. They had come anyway.

She pressed her forehead to his. They remained like that for a long moment, no breath between the hewn glass of their souls, the Maha's silent ash towering above them.

She felt him freeze. Felt him pull back, just a little, eyes open.

"Arwa," he said. "Do you hear that?"

Her storm was wavering about them. Silent, wheeling. But...

Yes. She heard it.

"Is it the sound of the trees?" she asked.

"No," he said. He stood. "No. Those are voices. And I...I think I can hear my mother's, among them."

The wind was moving through the trees, setting the skeletal branches wavering. But the wind was not simply wind. It was a great, sinuous blade, paring the trees down to ribbons of darkness. The dark unfurled, liquid as water and just as river quick, streaming across the sand in great skeins of words that moved and whispered. Arwa recognized those words: They were poetry of the Hidden Ones. The poetry of a lineage that lived in Zahir's blood and in his soul.

Zahir hesitated for only a moment. Then he placed a hand to the sand. He raised his palm up, and watched the words slip between his fingers. The voices shimmered, sweet echoes that fell to the sand and curled into silence once more.

She stared. They had walked so often among the ink-dark trees of his path, his neem and peepal and ashoka. She had not realized, all this time, that they carried his grief within them, just as her desert carried her own.

"Of course I would find her here," he murmured. He raised his head, looking at the sharpened, richer beauty of the realm of ash in Irinah's palm. His smile was sad. "I hear so many voices, and yet I still recognize hers among them. I thought I had forgotten it, Arwa. But I remember now."

The voices whispered and shook and tangled about them. Words bloomed through the sand, and seeped like great pearls of sap from the trees of ink. The whispers rose and rose, the words spilled and unfurled, and Arwa and Zahir kneeled beneath the Maha at the nexus of it all, haloed by the roar of a thousand voices.

Voices. So many voices, and all of them like a single wave. Perhaps it was the voices that whispered in her ear, then. Perhaps not.

She thought of the tale of the Maha's heir: how it had slipped free of the Emperor's grasp, taking on a vicious life of its own, reared and fed by the faith and discontent of a thousand whispering voices. She thought of the widows and pilgrims who had softened a nightmare, saving themselves unwittingly with worship and grave-tokens alone. She thought of the prayers of Zahir's followers, their voices rising together and winding and winding into a sound greater than the sum of its parts.

Their voices had sounded like hope.

It hit her like a great fist to the stomach:

The flat, resigned acceptance of death in Zahir's eyes, when his father named him Maha's heir.

The leaden weight of her own heart, when she'd pressed a flower behind Zahir's ear, and tried to forget what was to come.

This is wrong.

Together, they rose to their feet. They had to rise together, bound as they were by blood roots, but Arwa rose numbly, helpless in the grip of her own thoughts.

Zahir, the first moment she'd seen him. Already entombed, his home wrapped around him like a promise of death, the moonlight a blade upon his neck.

Zahir standing before the pilgrims as they prayed, his hands in fists, his eyes fixed on her as if she were his guiding star, and without her he would be lost.

"Arwa," he said. Just her name. As if it would give him the strength to go on. Then he kissed her forehead, one brush of cold lips, and took a step toward the ash. "All will be well."

He reached out a hand. The Maha's ash was a reflection before him, deep and dark. One touch—the barest touch of his hand— and they would be joined.

There was no more time to be numb. She sucked in a sharp breath, her distant lungs aching, and wrenched at his arm. She pulled him back, throwing her own body in front of his.

Behind her, she heard the whisper of ash falling to the earth. Zahir hissed, startled.

"What—"

"*No.*" She hadn't known she could sound as she did in that moment: so furious and so very afraid. "No, you may hate me for it if you wish, Zahir, but you can't. You *can't.*"

"Arwa," he said. Tender, his voice was so tender, as if he understood. He gripped her arms. "Let me go."

"No." She tightened her grip on him in return. "Will you push me aside?" she demanded. "Will you let go of my roots, and break yourself upon his ash on your own? No, you need me. And I am not moving."

"You know this is necessary," he said, with that same terrible tenderness—as if he had expected this and was prepared to refuse her.

"I'm not sure that I do," she whispered. "I can still hear the poetry, Zahir. I can still hear your Hidden Ones. And I hear the tale Aliye told me. A tale of a doe and an arrow and a sacrifice for the good of love, because the story lives inside me. And in you."

The ink wrapped around their feet. Words upon words.

"We have been taught all our lives that we must destroy ourselves in order to be worthy. To have purpose. Have we not, Zahir?" She looked up at his face. The hewn glass of his soul, flayed open before her own. "Jihan taught you so. The Empress taught you so. Your mother. The Hidden Ones. So I was taught, by my mother too. But we don't. We don't. We do not have to lay ourselves at the Maha's feet."

He looked at her as if she had wounded him, as if she had his blood on her hands.

"There is no other way," he said. "Arwa. You know there isn't."

"There is," she said sharply. "There *is*. For all your logic and your precision, Zahir, you can't see beyond the Maha. He is like—the sun. All this time we have loved him and hated him and chased him because we have been told he lies at the heart of everything, that he is all light and without his knowledge we will be left to die in the cold. But he isn't the sun. He is dead, only dead, and we don't need him. We have prayer. We have Amrithi rites. We have knowledge enough, knowledge we can share, and with it we can save the world."

She stopped, her body's heart racing, the air wavering about her.

"People will die this way," he said, in a voice she did not recognize. Too hollow, too old. "The slow way may see so many, many people dead. We may fail them all."

"I know," she said. "And yet the slow way, perhaps, the world heals. Perhaps the slow way is the only way. The Maha broke the world. To heal the wound he made will take...time. And knowledge shared. And hope, even in the dark."

He tried to turn from her, to blot her words out. She gripped his face.

"You've searched so long for the Maha's ash. You listen to the Hidden Ones. You listen to your mother's ghost. Now, please, listen to me," she said softly, her fingertips points of light against his cheekbones. "You told me I have you. You gave yourself to me, Zahir. And I tell you now, if you walk this path you will not be mine anymore, and you will not be your own. You will be his creature, just as you feared, and I..."

She swallowed. It was hard. Hard to speak truthfully. Hard not to fear the effigy of ash behind her.

"You will think I am being selfish," she whispered. "But I see another path, Zahir, for the first time. And it may not be the wisest route, or the swiftest. But it is not *his* path. You asked me once if I could even dream another world. I couldn't then. But when I think of prayers and rites and the slow way through the dark, I *can*."

He stopped holding her. Instead he raised a hand to his face, and pressed it over her own fingers. Light and glass, and the gentleness of his eyes.

"Arwa," he said softly. "Let me go."

She shook her head, wordless now.

"Please," he said again. "Let me go."

She had no words left. She'd tried everything she could.

She released him.

He stood once more before the Maha. He stood in ink that unfurled like silk around him. Their blood roots, wound together, held them bound. She watched him. Waited.

"I am the Maha's heir," he said finally. "So my father named me, binding me to the tale, whether I liked it or not. I *am* the Maha's heir, and I cannot change that, but I..."

He faltered. He looked at the Maha. With hatred, with yearning. With knowledge of a fate he could not run from.

"I can decide what that means," he said. His voice was thin,
raw with feeling. "Because I am Bahar's son too. Because I am
myself. I know people will listen to the Maha's heir. If he tells
them, *Pray and the nightmares will fade and leave you unharmed*, they
will pray. And if the Maha's heir has the support of the Hidden
Ones...his message will spread, with certainty."

He turned to her.

"It will be a hard path. Parviz will hound me. He will want
me dead, and one day he'll no doubt succeed. But perhaps by
the time he murders me, people will know how to worship the
nightmares. That would be—enough."

If he tries to murder you, I will gut him first, thought Arwa.

"The Amrithi-blooded will know the Rite of the Cage,"
she said, with a tilt of her chin. "It belongs to them, after all.
I'll ensure it reaches their hands. We will save the world. And
I promise you, Zahir: Your brother will never sit easy upon his
throne."

"No," said Zahir grimly. "That, at least, I can make sure of.
My father's gift of a title gives me power enough for that, with
or without the Maha's ash. He has made an enemy of the Maha's
heir. He'll never own the tale again."

"You'll do this with me, then," Arwa blurted out. She curled
her hands into fists, hopeful and terrified in equal measure.
"You'll walk away from the Maha's ash. You'll choose another
path."

"Yes," he said. She saw the way the choice shattered something within him—and made him whole. His gaze was full of
light. He straightened his shoulders, as if some invisible burden
had been raised from them, as if he could breathe. "Yes. I'll walk
a new path with you."

She could have wept then. Instead she clasped her hands over her face, overwhelmed, and felt his forehead once more against her own, his voice whispering her name with utter softness. He pried her fingers away and kissed her.

It was—strange—to kiss without flesh. She felt the tingle of her lips, her body alive with it, but here in the realm of ash she was only light and glass, clear and pure, and she felt him like blood and life through the roots that bound them.

"We should leave here," he said.

"Yes," she murmured, relieved. "Let's go."

He turned to stare at the Maha's ash once more—the perfect shadow of it—before he let the blood roots take them home.

She returned to her flesh, gave a rattling gasp—and immediately spat out the sand she'd somehow swallowed while unconscious. She rose up onto her elbows. The fire was still burning strong. Beyond it, she saw Zahir raise his head.

Then she heard a voice—a scream that echoed through the air, high and sharp.

"Run!"

"Zahir," she said, scrambling to her feet.

"I hear it," he said grimly, rising with her.

But they had neatly trapped themselves. They had no vision within the valley they'd settled in. They were surrounded by sloped sand on all sides. They could not run easily. They did not know where—or what—the enemy was. They ran regardless—and immediately found themselves facing a line of soldiers, who surrounded the valley on all sides.

There was no sign of Eshara. No sign of the pilgrims.

The two of them stood frozen. The line parted, just enough to allow a figure to pass between them. The figure was robed and hooded, and carrying a bow. They lifted their head.

Pale eyes met Arwa's.

"Gulshera," she said shakily. Stumbled forward, even as Zahir gripped her wrist. "Gulshera? You're alive? You're well?"

"Lord Zahir," said Gulshera. "Your sister has been looking for you."

"Lady Gulshera." He cleared his throat, his voice shattered. "You—Jihan. Jihan is alive?"

"Come with me, and you can see her."

"And Nasir? Is he alive also? Is he with her, and well?"

"Come with me, and Jihan will explain everything," Gulshera said.

Zahir's eyes traced the line of soldiers.

"Why so many soldiers?" he asked. "And where have our friends gone?"

"Soldiers have a tendency to die in this forsaken desert," Gulshera replied. "I was required to bring spares. Now—come. We have little time."

Zahir remained silent.

Gulshera sighed.

"I don't have time for this, Lord Zahir."

"Parviz sent you," he said. "Jihan would have sent you alone. Or—a spy. She's no warmonger."

Gulshera shook her head. Took her bow from her shoulder, nocked the arrow, and raised it.

"I am sorry, Arwa," said Gulshera.

She let the arrow loose.

Arwa heard a thud. Felt a blow that flung her off her feet and back onto the sand.

The pain came a second later.

She couldn't scream. A thin, high wail escaped her mouth. The arrow—the arrow had hit her. She tried to reach for it. But her arm was numb fire, and she could not move it.

"Arwa!"

"Stay still, Lord Zahir." Gulshera sounded tired. "I have had a long journey, and I have little interest in a boy's hysterics. Come with us meekly, or the next blow will go through her leg. It's an easy target to miss, but I have excellent aim. I expect she would not walk again."

Pounding of her blood in her skull. She would not be able to stay conscious long. The air had gone white around Zahir, who loomed above her. White, and riven with ash.

He bowed his head.

"I'll come quietly," he said.

"Good," said Gulshera. "You, pick Lady Arwa up. *Gently.*"

It was all darkness, after that.

CHAPTER THIRTY-SIX

She woke in agony.

"Stay still," Zahir said in a low voice. "You have an arrow in your left shoulder."

"Really?" she gasped. "I hadn't noticed."

He brushed her hair back from her face. His fingers were blessedly cool.

"Don't try to move again," he said.

"Where are we?"

"A tent," he said. "We walked through the city. We're as far from the desert as one can be without leaving Irinah entirely."

It was larger than any tent Arwa had seen before, with a great domed ceiling and a lantern upon the table. Neither of them was chained, but Arwa supposed there was no need. Arwa could not run, not as she was, and Zahir would not leave her.

The tent flap was drawn back. A woman walked in. She wore a plain gown, but her shawl was richly beaded, her earrings heavy with pearls. She raised her head, looked at Zahir.

"Zahir."

"Jihan," Zahir said. "Ah, Jihan."

"You're alive," whispered Jihan. She crossed the room and cupped his face in her hands. She was weeping openly, her eyes red. "Ah, Zahir. I didn't know what had become of you. I saw…

I arranged Akhtar's funeral. They told me it was a brother's duty to bury a brother, but I did not care. I told them I cared for his household. That he was my dearest kin. So I buried him, Zahir, but you—I did not know what the Emperor had done with you, and he refused to tell me, no matter how I wept. I could not mourn you."

"Nasir, what of Nasir?"

"Masuma stole him away," said Jihan. "I know nothing more than that. But you, Zahir. What became of you?"

He stared up at his sister, and said, "Please, Jihan. Lady Arwa needs a physician. She's gravely hurt."

"Of course," Jihan said softly. "Of course, dear heart."

She kneeled down, her great skirt fanned around her.

"Where have you been?" she asked. "What became of you?"

"I survived," said Zahir. "And then you found me."

"That is no answer, Zahir."

"Forgive me," he said. "I am somewhat distracted by Arwa bleeding to death on the floor beside me. Perhaps if you find her a physician, I'll be more amenable to talking."

"I've just missed you," said Jihan. "Worried for you."

"Jihan." Tired. He sounded so tried. "I know Parviz sent you here."

"Don't call him that."

"His name?"

"He is the Emperor," Jihan said. "All old names discarded. He is Emperor as much as our father was Emperor. However he may have risen to the title, we must accept the way things are."

"You accept the man who killed your brother—your maidservants?"

"I don't have my birds or my letters or my women any longer," she said, voice taut. "He denied me all of that. Denied it wholly. What am I to do, but obey him and prove my loyalty? Prove my worth?"

"And you have proven it," Zahir said. "You have me. But please. A physician, Jihan."

"Lady Arwa will have a physician when I have the truth," Jihan said. Her voice was hard. "You entered Irinah. You went to the realm of ash. You returned. What did you find?"

"You could have captured us earlier," Zahir said. He lowered his head. "Of course. You *waited*."

"It is not hard to follow a tale," said Jihan. "Especially when it concerns a widow and a man who calls himself the Maha's heir. So what did you find, Maha's heir? Hm?"

A pause.

"Nothing."

"I cannot save you with *nothing*." She leaned forward, staring into his eyes fiercely. "The Emperor is furious, Zahir. He's heard all those tales about you. He wants to shame you before all his greatest lords and then kill you. He wants to make an example of you, which means a terrible death. Give me the Maha's knowledge, Zahir. I know you have it. Then, perhaps, I can save you."

"Or at least ensure me a swift execution?"

"I wish you'd had the good sense to fade away, Zahir," said Jihan. "After Father's death, after we buried Akhtar...I liked to imagine that you and Nasir were both safe somewhere. Living good, happy lives." She inhaled and exhaled slowly, deeply. "More fool me."

She leaned back and rose smoothly to her feet.

"The Emperor is coming," said Jihan, walking over to the table where the lantern sat. "I am glad I've wept today, Zahir. He will be pleased with me for giving you to him, and when he kills you I will be able to watch without weeping. My tears will be done. That will please him. Perhaps he will allow me some of my old privileges. Another opportunity to prove what Akhtar knew I could do."

"It is a pity you were not born a boy, Jihan," Zahir said. "We would have died peacefully in our sleep, every last one of us, before you wore our father's title."

She flinched.

"You think so little of me?"

"Ah, no. I think you love all your brothers fiercely." Zahir's voice was wretched with grief. "But I think you will always place the Empire first."

"Protecting the Empire is everything," Jihan said. "It is worth any price. Even love."

"Yes," Zahir said softly. "So you always taught me."

"So my mother taught me in turn," Jihan said sharply. Then her face crumpled into tears once more. "Zahir," she said. "Please. Do you have nothing I can take to the Emperor? No knowledge from the realm that could spare your life or grant you a merciful death?"

"I have nothing for him," Zahir said. "Nothing at all."

"Then he will condemn you as a heretic and take your head. You will condemn me to witnessing that." Jihan's face trembled. Then she tensed her jaw. She took a stoppered flask from the table and opened it. "Take this, at least," she said. "It is all I can offer you now."

"What is it?"

"Opium water," she said.

He shook his head sharply. "No, Jihan. So much of it—no."

She nodded. Then she said, "Guards."

Two guardswomen entered immediately. They pinned Zahir. Wrenched back his head. Arwa tried to scramble toward him—failed. As she lay gasping, Jihan walked over to him. For all her tears, her arm did not tremble as she poured the liquid down his throat. She stroked his hair, lowered him to the floor, and left him there. Arwa heard her footsteps. Then silence.

Arwa could not even go to him.

He barely moved, after that. Only lay still, where they'd let him fall.

She spoke poetry to him, the soft cadences of the Hidden One's poetry as he lay in a stupor on the floor, eyes glazed and distant.

Hours passed. Two guards entered and lifted Zahir up, dragging him away.

"Where are you taking him?" Arwa called out. "Please— please tell me!"

They didn't respond. She was alone.

She was hallucinating. She was sure of it.

Shadows flickered on the walls. The lantern was guttering. The pain was so constant that she was beginning to believe she had always been in pain, and always would be.

I am going to die, she thought. She squeezed her eyes shut. Felt ash upon her face. When she turned her head, she saw the arrow impaled through her shoulder. But her shoulder was all mirror and glass. Through it she could see the shaft of the arrow; upon it she could see the reflection of her pained face, surrounded by a halo of blood and black hair.

Then she opened her eyes and saw nothing but her own skin once more.

The tent flap opened.

Gulshera strode in, bow and arrow still over her shoulder. Gone were her widow whites, her veil. She was dressed like a guardswoman, with nothing but a shawl wound about her hair to protect her modesty.

"Come to kill me?" Arwa asked.

"I don't want you dead," Gulshera said. "I'm trying to convince Jihan to arrange you a physician. For now, you will have to be patient."

"I might...be dead. Before then."

"Try not to be," said Gulshera. She kneeled down. Offered Arwa a cloth. "Bite on this."

Arwa did not want to take it, but when she turned her head, Gulshera merely stuffed the cloth into her mouth. Then she took hold of the shaft of the arrow, and snapped it clean.

Arwa bit down hard, screaming. Gulshera waited a moment, then pulled the cloth from Arwa's lips.

"You should be a little more comfortable now, when the pain passes."

"You shot me," Arwa said hoarsely.

"I told you court had teeth and claws," Gulshera said eventually. "Well, now you have faced court's fury."

"You didn't...tell me," Arwa forced out, "that you were... the claws."

"I did not know I would need to be," she said.

Arwa forced herself into an almost seated position. For all it hurt, white-hot, it was easier to breathe like this. She dreaded looking at her shoulder, which still had the rest of the arrow embedded within it.

"What will happen to me?"

"If Jihan allows you a physician, you'll live," Gulshera said levelly. "Until the Emperor decides what best to do with you, of course."

"Death either way, then," Arwa said. "I see."

"She ordered me to shoot you if Zahir disobeyed," Gulshera said, no inflection in her voice. "She was testing me, as she does. I could not fail her." Gulshera reached a hand out to Arwa's face. Hesitated. Drew it back. "I tried to prepare you for this world, Arwa. I truly did. But my first loyalty has always been to Jihan. That has not changed. Your fate is in her hands now."

Gulshera stood and began to walk away. But Arwa could not, would not, let her go so easily.

"For a little while. In the hermitage. And in the palace." Gasp of breath. Gritted teeth. "I thought of you as—a mentor. As a— friend. I trusted you."

"Ah, Arwa." Gulshera shook her head. "There's no need for this."

"No. There is. I trusted you when I feared trusting. Trusting anyone. And now." Deep breath. "She'll turn on you too, one day. We are all—things. To people like her."

"I know what Jihan is," Gulshera said steadily, her eyes on Arwa. "Perhaps one day she will. And when that day comes I will accept my fate. Because she is the child I nursed—and because she is the only worthy child the late Emperor had." Gulshera bowed her head. A gesture of respect and farewell. "Emperor's blessings on you, Arwa. I promise you, although it may be little comfort to you now: Your fate will haunt me for the rest of my days."

Then the tent flap closed, and Gulshera was gone.

CHAPTER THIRTY-SEVEN

Hours and hours.

Hours and hours and hours.

No one was going to come for her. There would be no physician. No food. No water.

She heard the men and women in armor. The stamp and cry of elephants. Music.

The Emperor is here, then, she thought. She thought of Zahir and felt helpless, helpless.

She could not save him. She couldn't even save herself.

"Can't you?" A man's voice. Gentle. Patient. "Come now, Iria. *Remember.*"

With difficulty she raised her head. Through the flicker of ash and glass, as the world wavered, she saw figures of ash kneeling around her. No longer nothing but broken limbs, they were whole people, staring at her eyes like the palest clouds.

"You can't be here," she said, uncomprehending. "I am still Arwa. Still myself."

"Your mind is full of ash," Iria said. She was no child any longer. She was a woman grown, with keen dark eyes and a braid of curling hair thrown over her shoulder. Her face was a thing carved of dust. "We are with you. Within you. And you haven't the sense to keep us distant."

Were those Iria's words or Arwa's own? Now that she was paying attention, forcing herself to think through the pain, she could taste the ash through the iron of blood in her mouth. She could feel the tug of the ash clouding her mind, the way the memories of her long dead were unfurling within her.

"I suppose," Arwa gritted out, "that dying has made a fool of me."

"No," said Nazrin. Her ash was missing a great gout at the neck, leaving nothing but a void where her dagger had sliced her own artery through. "You simply don't want to die alone. There is nothing foolish about that."

Arwa swallowed. But she was alone. That was the truth.

"I don't want to be in pain anymore," whispered Arwa. "I don't."

The ash moved in her head. A great whirl of it.

"Then you know what to do," Nazrin said gently.

Yes. Arwa knew.

She needed to go to a place where she was not flesh. Where the pain would be a distant thing—bound to her only by thin roots of blood. She closed her eyes. Breathed deep and slow. She did not need anything but her own will.

She sank back into the realm of ash.

The tent still surrounded her. Her body lay still upon the floor. When she had entered the realm of ash in Zahir's tomb, she had entered another world entirely. But this was Irinah, where all realms met. The world of flesh lay against the realm of ash, one breathing with the lungs of the other.

She kneeled, free of her flesh. The pain was blessedly far away.

She could remain where she was and take comfort in the peace the realm had offered. She could wait, now, quietly for death. But when she'd entered the realm with Zahir in Irinah's desert, she'd felt as if she could walk forever. She felt the same now. Two worlds lay spread about before her. Her feet of mirror and memory could carry her.

She thought of remaining here, dying, inch by slow inch.

She thought instead of throwing herself into the abyss before her.

Always, when she had a choice, it was the danger she chose. She looked back at her body, at its bloody wound, at the way her chest rattled from the pain of it. She looked about—at the walls of the tent, at the ghosts around her—and took a step forward.

She walked through the canvas wall into the open. She saw the elephants, the soldiers, the glaring blankness of the sky. The realm of ash echoed with things still living. There was a tent in the distance, far vaster in size than the one she'd been contained in. Its surface glittered in the light, richly embroidered with either silver or gold.

So the Emperor was here, after all. She had not been wrong to think so.

Zahir, she thought. Walked on.

The realm unfurled a storm beneath her feet, carried her forward as if on a wave. She could feel Zahir's blood roots, still. His soul had walked with her own. Just as he'd found her in the realm of ash when she'd left him behind in the House of Tears, she found him now.

The large tent had a sumptuous carpet spread across the entirety of its floor. Great lanterns hung on stakes set in the ground. A select group of nobles lined the walls, their expressions blank, bodies tense. Behind a screen of fine netting were Gulshera and Jihan, the two of them seated.

Before them all, sat the Emperor. Parviz was cross-legged upon his throne, hands upon his knees, back ramrod straight. There was nothing opulent about his garb. He wore plain clothing once more, an unadorned turban and a tunic and trousers of plainest mourning white. There was something fierce and cruel about his plainness: about his military posture and the flint of his eyes as he stared down at the ground before him.

The ground where Zahir knelt. Hands chained, his head tipped forward, as if he could not hold the weight of it up. Perhaps he could not.

"Zahir," said Parviz. "You will look at me."

Arwa wondered how many times Parviz had asked. He was thin-lipped with fury, his hands curling into the threat of fists.

"Zahir," she whispered. "Look up."

"Zahir," the ash echoed around her. All her dead, speaking with her voice. "Look up."

With great difficulty, he raised his head. His eyes were bloodshot. His cheek bruised.

"Zahir." Parviz's voice was iron. Unyielding, and deadly for it. "Son of Bahar. Did you falsely call yourself the Maha's heir? Did you lead men and women of the Empire to heresy using my ancestor's name?"

"You'll give me the illusion of a trial, then?" Zahir asked. His voice was broken glass. His lip, too, she thought, was swollen. How long had he been gone from her? She didn't know. "I know—I know my fate. Already. There's no need for this."

"Did you use heretical arts," Parviz pressed on, "occult and barbaric, to speak with the dead, and to flee the palace and imperial justice?"

"Imperial justice?" Zahir echoed. A smile tugged his mouth. He was still drugged, she thought, although his eyes were bright, his words clipped and fierce. "Imperial justice...No. It was not that I fled from. And I used no heretical arts. The Maha's own heir surely cannot defy the faith he dictates."

"You admit your lies, then."

"I admit what our father and Emperor named me, upon his deathbed. Who am I to deny his will?"

"He was not your father." Parviz's voice was rumbling, deadly and soft. "Know your place. You are a traitorous whore's son. A bastard. And your actions have proved you barbaric as any black-blooded Amrithi heathen. My father never named you Maha's heir."

"You are Emperor now. If you say it, then it must be so." Zahir's head jerked, his gaze tracing the circle of noblemen around them. "Even if your court heard the truth from our father's own lips."

Arwa saw two of the departed Emperor's old council of advisers exchange glances, their faces carefully blank of feeling. The rest stood frozen and silent.

"The ravings of a dying man," Parviz said coldly, "who did not know what he was saying. He was not himself."

"Not himself, when he named me Maha's heir, and Akhtar his own," Zahir said. "I see."

"I saved the Empire from a dying man's feverish error." Parviz's voice was iron, a great weight forcibly reshaping the world to fit his vision of it. "The only worthy heir to the Empire is a powerful one. A strong one. And that," Parviz said levelly, "you are not. But I am."

There was a noise from beyond the partition veil, quickly hushed. Parviz did not move, but his expression seemed to darken.

"My sister's soft womanly yielding to your monstrous occult acts is *done*. You will plead for your false soul, heretic, and then you will be put to death. If you do not confess your crimes, your fingers will be cut from your hands. Your eyes will be gouged. Your teeth will be pried from your mouth. Your skin will be burned. These are the punishments the worst heretics suffered, when I quelled Durevi beneath my boot." He leaned forward. "Jihan pleaded for death by swift poison. I am inclined to indulge her soft nature, if you confess now, and beg me to be kind."

"Bastard, heretic, son of a traitor whore—you do not think much of me, brother." Head raised, eyes bright as new coins, mouth twisting into a smile. "And yet, that makes me no less the Maha's heir. It was those you call bastards who the Maha raised up and proclaimed as his mystics. The fatherless, the unloved, the children of traitors—he *loved* them. Who else would he choose for his successor, but a bastard of his own blood? The Maha's own spirit dictated our father's choice. I know it."

He spoke the lie with utter conviction. It lit him from the inside, and she saw his words fall on the nobles' ears like a blow.

They would remember this. When Zahir was dead, they would remember this. And they would doubt Parviz a little more, as each day passed, as the curse on the Empire sank its claws deeper and deeper into the bitter earth.

"You will be executed for your heresy," Parviz said. "And it will not be quick. I promise you that."

Beyond the screen, Arwa saw Jihan lower her head.

Arwa kneeled down beside Zahir. The world rippled around her.

He turned to her.

Looked at her.

"Arwa," he breathed.

"You fool," she whispered. "You utter fool. We're not dying like this, Zahir. Not like this."

She touched her glass fingers to his face. Drew back. The ash whirled through her, around her, so close.

She stepped back. Back.

"I need knowledge," she said. The grand tent around her wavered. Even Zahir was a smear of faint light.

"We are knowledge," the ash said.

"No," said Arwa. She felt her distant flesh—fading, suffering. And she was alight, furious. If she'd had blood in her, it would have burned. "I need all your rites. All your sigils. All your lost knowledge. I need to save us both. And for that, I need everything. Can it be done?"

"Perhaps," said Nazrin.

"Perhaps," said Iria.

"It will come at a cost," Ushan said. "You will go far deeper than any mortal woman should."

"You could lose yourself," said Nazrin. "The ash could carry away your name. Your nature. The weft of your soul."

"You could become trapped here, never able to return home," said Iria.

"Or worse, both," said Nazrin. "You could become lost, forgotten even to yourself. A ghost within a land of ghosts."

"I know," Arwa whispered. But of course she did. They were part of her. "And yet, I would rather lose myself than let them take me."

She turned to face her ghosts.

"Did you walk the world in the end, Iria? Did you save people from ill-starred daiva?"

Iria's ash turned to her. The answer rose to the lips of her ash, from deep within Arwa's own skull. From the wealth of memories she'd consumed.

"I did, for a time. But no one can protect others forever."

"No." Arwa said. "I suppose not. But I would have . . . I would have liked the chance to try."

Arwa gripped her courage—and her roots—tight. She turned from Zahir and began to walk her path of ash.

Deeper and deeper she went. Ink-black trees that had once been Zahir's surrounded her. The sand glowed, as rich and wild as the Haran sea. She was unraveling from her own flesh, step by step. The pain faded. She looked up at the sky, which was a lidless eye, blazing with fury and storm light.

She had walked Zahir's path. She had stumbled through her own out of desperation. But she had never walked it deliberately. The realm raged around her, sweetly familiar, a thing born from her own soul, and terrifying for it. Irinah unfurled itself beneath her feet, real and mortal and yet so far away. It shifted about her like a dream.

On her path loomed her past. Doors opening to opulent rooms. An overgrown garden. Blades and—

She stopped. Froze.

Around her loomed Darez Fort.

Before her were Darez Fort's great gates. And before them lay Kamran, all riven ash, slumped, a knife through his gut.

"You are not my blood," she whispered, gazing at him. "You should not be here."

But he had been her husband. She'd wed him in the Ambhan way: placed her marriage seal around his throat. Worn his, until his death. Vowed that her soul was bound to his, all through her mortal lifetime.

She walked toward him. Kneeled by him. His face was a void. His head thrown back, hand reaching for nothing.

"I wish you were here," she said. "And yet I don't. We should never have wed, husband. We were so ill-suited to one another. And yet I so desperately wanted to be the wife you needed. Did you know it, Kamran?"

He could not answer her. He was a shadow. If she touched his ash, breathed it . . .

"I do not want to keep you. I want to let you go." She would have wept, if she could have. "That is wrong, and I know it. But I do not want to mourn you forever. I do not want to be the silent widow you deserve.

"I'm sorry," she whispered, and pressed her hand to the gates. And pushed.

They were ash. No more than ash. They fell to dust around the press of her hand.

His dust crumbled behind her. She kept on walking.

A moon bloomed in the sky above her, opening like a flower.

The trees were melting around her, collapsing into reams of words, which spread their limbs across the sand. Poetry. A piece of the Hidden Ones lived in her too.

Her soul had traveled the breadth of Irinah. Her soul had traveled the breadth of the realm of ash.

The realm of ash wasn't always straightforward. It could be made of tales and of the dead. It could lead to your childhood. It would always pass through your greatest griefs. Arwa was beginning to understand the poetry of the Hidden Ones, all those many tracts of longing and loss, as she never had before.

The realm of ash contracted around her. She knew, then, that she had come near to the end of her journey.

Mehr waited, ahead of her.

Her sister was seated, cross-legged on the sand, with her back to Arwa. Her hair was loose, curling over one shoulder. Arwa could see the curve of her neck. Whorl of her ear. She was entirely still. It was as if she had been in the sand all this time, waiting for Arwa's end. Waiting for Arwa to find her way home.

Arwa took a step forward. Another.

There was a shout, and a screech of laughter and—a child. It ran up to her sister, flinging itself into her sister's arms. Mehr murmured something, and the child laughed again. It was a chubby thing, with big curls, babbling volubly away. But Arwa could not listen to it. She could only walk forward and stare at her sister, who was brown-skinned and smiling and moved as a living woman moved, lifted and lowered her shoulders, tilted her head to hear the child speak.

All the times she had seen Mehr in the realm of ash—in fragments, between the smoke of the storm, or standing lamp bright before the bodies of the Amrithi dead—Mehr had been too far to see clearly. But Arwa saw her now. This was not her sister as Arwa remembered her, with guarded smiles and wary eyes. This woman was older, softer in the face with skin darkened by sunlight, a grown woman with a fall of loose curls and a face that smiled easily.

This woman was *alive.*

Arwa felt as if she would shatter. As if she were truly a thing of glass, fragile enough to fragment. She could not hope. She could not *hope.*

And yet—

"Mehr." Her voice came out of her without her bidding. Thin as a reed. "Sister. It's me."

Mehr turned. Froze.

Arwa did not know what Mehr saw, what strange thing peered at her through the worlds, fleshless and terrible. But Mehr looked at her and looked at her, and began to shake.

"Arwa." She rose to her feet. "Arwa?"

The child murmured something in a small voice. But Mehr said nothing. She stared at Arwa with wide, stricken eyes.

"It can't be," Mehr whispered. "Little sister. What has become of you? Where are you?"

"I'm here," Arwa said. "I'm—home."

"I'm dreaming," Mehr said numbly. And yet she took a step forward, grief and yearning written into her wide eyes. "I'm dreaming you again."

"I'm the one dreaming," said Arwa. "You're dead and gone and yet I want you alive so much I sicken with it. But how can you be alive, when I've grieved you so long, and I stand in the land of the dead?"

Mehr made a sound—a wordless gasp, as if the air had been stolen from her lungs. She took a step forward, her hand before her, and Arwa stumbled back. Back.

"I can't," Arwa said. "I can't lose you again. I can't watch what will become of you, don't you *see?* I can't watch you leave me."

"Don't go. Arwa. My dear one. Don't go. Stay with me."

Mehr's hand was still before her. Held out like a hope. "Stay, my dear one. *Please.*"

Arwa stopped. The ash was quiet around her.

She held out her own hand.

Arwa braced herself for Mehr to turn to dust before her: for all Mehr's strange, bright ash to shatter and leave Arwa with nothing but grief and memory and the cruelly stolen promise of her sister, returned to her, whole and safe and alive.

Their hands touched.

Skin. Warm, callused. Grip of Mehr's fingers, reaching between two worlds.

Mehr met her eyes.

"I'll find you," she said. "Wherever you may be, Arwa. I will."

The worlds shifted. The wheel turned. She fell back into the cold of the realm.

She clutched her hand tight.

She could not think of whether her sister lived after all. She could not think of her parents, and the cruelty those who loved you could inflict, for the sake of that same love. She could not think of what she'd seen: the hope of it, too rich to be borne. She could not think of anything but reaching her ash.

She forced herself to keep on walking.

Finally, she came to it. Her sea of dead.

She kneeled upon the sand, between bones and limbs and shattered ghosts. The end of her path had come. Beyond it lay starry darkness, stricken with the shadow of dreamfire.

A world of the Gods, perhaps, or of the daiva. But Arwa would not walk there today.

Today, she pressed her forehead to the sand, a supplicant and a mourner. She could not weep here. Could not be as bodies were: soft and hurt and grieving.

She thought of how it had felt at the House of Tears, when she had opened the door to all the ash within her. How much it had hurt her and scared her.

She thought of the dovecote, where the fear had tasted sweet. Like fire.

At least we can choose the shape of our death, she'd told Zahir then. It was still true.

The choice of how she died—if that was all she had, then she would take it.

She parted her mouth. Breathed in.

She knew—everything.

A thousand voices whispered in her ears at once.

If we run fast they'll notice, better to be slow—

The same shape of a rite, raise your hands, here, just so—

—Rukhsar, Rukhsar, your daughter is a lovestruck fool—

hetookthebladehetookthebladehetook

She focused on her blood roots. On her flesh. She struggled to keep the ash at bay.

She still knew herself. That, at least, was a blessing. But the pressure within her skull was growing and growing, and soon enough what defenses her mind had constructed would shatter.

She had very little time.

Body and soul. For this, she needed both. She stood in the realm of ash. She stood on the solid ground of the tent, on legs that did not want to obey her.

She moved her feet into the first stance of a rite.

She had nothing to venerate the daiva with, as they deserved.

She had *never* shown them the reverence they deserved. She had no kohl for her eyes or red to stain her hands. Her dagger was gone. She had only the will to perform a rite that would save her and Zahir both.

And an arrow in her shoulder.

At least the wound gave her the gift of blood.

She forced her arms to move. White-hot agony in her skull. She gave a choked sob. Gritted her teeth. Kept on going.

Sigils and stances. Her body moved without grace. Sigils fell from her fingers like splinters. Sigils for beckoning. Sigils for fear.

Come. Kin. Blood.

A careful turn on her heel. She did not fall. Did not fall. In the realm of ash, the ash beneath her rippled, hard as a drumbeat.

Death.

Mercy.

She knew, now. There were rites of worship. And there were rites that were furious prayers flung into the abyss. This was one of them.

She was broken. She could not move as the rite deserved. And yet, she tried. And tried.

The flutter of wings touched her ears. A dark bird flew in through the tent wall—turning to coils of smoke when it met canvas, then becoming whole once more. Another followed. Another.

She gazed at the bird-spirits. They gazed back.

"Ah, you," Arwa whispered. Tears pricked her eyes. "It's been so long."

The bird-spirits fluttered around her head. They settled on the table. Melded into the shadows along the walls.

More shadows slithered toward her as she shaped sigils on her fingers. A new figure grew slowly from the ground beneath them.

It was…ancient, she thought. *Knew.* Her ash spoke to her, all its voices telling her this was an ancient daiva, its flesh almost mortal, its eyes keen and knowing.

The sigil for *time*. The sigil for *silence*.

Sigil for *life*.

Sigil for *fire*.

It had been so long since it had heard a voice calling in fury.

She clasped her hands together. Lowered her head. Gestures of respect and worship. Then with a rattling breath—with her blood roots wound about her soul self—she began to move.

Will you help me? she asked it, in the only way she could: a rite for mercy. A rite for justice. Her body was hollow agony. She stumbled. Pressed on. *Will you?*

The daiva's hand moved. One smooth arc.

Yes.

Then all the shadows converged, surrounding her in a great ring. And swallowed her.

Outside, under the glaring sun, the Emperor's retinue—his guardsmen, his attendants, his scribes, his soldiers—were calm.

At least until Arwa stepped out of the tent.

She flickered in and out of the realm of ash as she walked, as the daiva surrounded her like a skin. One of the guards tried to use his sword on her.

The daiva pointedly cleaved the blade in two.

How strange it must be, she thought distantly, *to see a woman walk surrounded by darkness, her eyes gray as the pyre, her hair a widow's shorn hair, a broken arrow in her shoulder.*

No wonder they ran so swiftly.

They must feel as if the curse has come for them.

Good.

Parviz's court did not expect her to rip through the canvas and cross the carpet. The nobles stumbled back, yelling in horror. The guards reached for their scimitars, terror in their eyes.

She raised a hand. The daiva flung them back.

Beyond the partition screen, Jihan and Gulshera were both standing, Gulshera's hand tight upon Jihan's arm.

On the ground, Zahir raised his head. He gazed at her not in horror but in heartbreak. He knew, as she knew, that she was already lost.

But he was alive, still alive, and she was glad of that.

"Zahir," Arwa said, smiling. "An old daiva has granted me a kindness."

"Arwa," he said shakily. His expression was shattered. "*No.*"

She shook her head. Felt darkness waver about her. Then she raised her eyes, fixing the silver of her gaze upon Parviz, who stood now before his throne, his own dagger in hand.

As if he could fight her. Fool. She had worlds within her.

"You were wrong to take him from me, Parviz," she said. She spoke in her own voice—soft and delicate, not a thing suited for instilling terror. And yet, Parviz recoiled as if she had struck him with it. "He is not yours to take. He is his own. And he is *mine.*"

She kneeled by Zahir. The lantern light wavered. Blotted by her darkness. The dark encircled his wrists. Broke his chains, and set him free.

"Monster," said Parviz, in a voice that shook with rage and fear. "I will not be frightened and cowed by *demons.*"

"I am no demon," Arwa said. "I am the consequence of your crimes."

He had tried to take back control of the Empire's faith by taking Zahir and the tale that surrounded him and putting them both to death. But he would not have Zahir's death. He would not have his Empire's heart.

Aliye had tried to ensure Parviz would sit uneasy on his throne. Zahir had done the same. But Arwa wanted *more.* He had killed his brothers. He had staked heads upon walls. He had tried to take Zahir, and take the world, and she was ash-fierce and hollow with the rage of the dead. She would allow him none of it. She was heir to an old injustice, and she would have her due.

"I speak for Prince Akhtar, the Emperor-who-should-have-been. I speak for the Maha's heir, who is. I speak for heretics falsely accused. I speak for the Empire that dies under your rule. I am grief, and I speak for the dead."

She looked at the terrified faces of the nobility. He would need them to rule—their loyalty, their obedience, their strength. And if they were not already lost to him, they would be now.

"I have a prophecy for you, not-Emperor," she said. "You stole what was not yours. Your reign will be a blight. When the nightmares come, your people will pray and they will be saved, but they will know you did not save them. You will find no love and no peace. You will be called Emperor, but the name will be ash in the mouths of your people, because it belongs to one who is dead. You will sit upon a throne of dust, and when your end comes—and it *will* come, Parviz, in ruin and shame—your legacy will be nothing but dust also. That is my prophecy, Parviz. My prophecy. And your curse."

The nobility recoiled. Parviz recoiled.

Her work was almost done.

Daiva birds flew in great circles overhead.

She took Zahir's face in her hands. He did not flinch at the feel of a daiva's sharp claws on his neck, or his brother's blood. He looked at her with grief and with utter trust.

"Will you come with me?" she said.

"I told you long ago," he said. "I go with you. Always."

She drew back from him. Held her hands before her. With great care, she shaped a new sigil. It was all she had left within her.

The sigil for *flight*.

As she felt the darkness unfurl and change around her, she embraced Zahir. Held him tight.

She thought how it must look to the nobles: the ghostly widow embracing Zahir, the great dark wings around him. They would remember the tale of how he flew from his father's palace. They would remember his power. And Parviz—cursed, weakened, sitting upon a dais in a shattered tent—would no longer have the power to see Zahir dead. She felt that in her bones. And she was glad.

"I love you," she said. "I thought, maybe, that you should know."

For the second time in their lives, they flew.

CHAPTER THIRTY-EIGHT

They landed on a vast expanse of sand beneath a blistering hot sky. Arwa felt the daiva release her and uncoil. She made a sigil of thanks on shaking hands—and collapsed to the ground.

The bird-spirits remained, circling overhead, uncomfortably reminiscent of carrion birds. Zahir said her name, his voice hoarse and shaken, and lifted her up in his arms.

"How—?"

"I didn't want to die there," Arwa said fiercely. Whispers were pouring through her. Whispers and ash. "Not there."

"You're not dying," he said. "You're not."

"I thought you hated—inaccuracy."

He made a choked sound. One breath. Another. He said, "You asked me not to make a sacrifice of myself. I expect you to extend me the same courtesy."

Then he was lifting her up, up. She bit off a scream.

"Your shoulder," he said.

"Just move me carefully," she told him.

"I will," he said. Slung her good arm over his shoulder, stooping to hold her weight. "We're getting help," he said. "I promise it."

She tasted blood on her lips. Ash. She nodded, and stumbled along with him.

He walked, and time moved strangely, swimming in and out

of focus. She dreamed a dozen dreams, that flickered through her mind, fractures of shadows.

"Arwa."

"Yes." She remembered. How strange, how the name fit. Her self fit her like an old familiar skin. "I am."

"Arwa," he said, aggrieved. He lowered her down. Collapsed beside her, flat upon the sand. She breathed in and out. The tide had ebbed. She knew herself again.

She was Arwa. She *was*.

"I am sorry," Arwa managed to say, "about Jihan."

"Don't be," he said.

"But you love her."

"I do," said Zahir. "But she's made her choice. And I, mine."

Arwa rolled her head to the side. She saw falling ash and a pale white sky.

"You should leave me," she said. "I won't... be me for long."

"Don't be a fool."

"Zahir..."

Zahir swore, hefting her up once more. "Come on now," he said.

They made it only a few steps before Arwa stumbled. Something had changed within her. Something had severed.

She raised her hurt arm. Slow.

"Arwa, please," he said shakily. "Stop trying to move it."

But she couldn't. She raised her hand to the light. In the realm of ash, she watched the glass of her skin cloud with darkness.

"It's too late," she told Zahir. Mouth moving. She remembered how flesh worked, still. "I'm losing myself."

She turned her hands once more. Her roots were withering, the bond between her and her flesh decaying to dust.

He lowered her once more.

It took her soul a second to follow her flesh back to the ground: a dizzying second of blankness, where her soul was suspended in nothing, a constellation of ash burning its edges smooth.

"The tale," she whispered, touching his flesh with her hands of mirror-glass, his soul with her trembling, bloodied fingertips. She did not know where she was anymore. She was undone. "Aliye's tale. Of the doe. I thought—I could escape it. But I took the arrow, I think. Does that make me the doe? The willing sacrifice?"

"Gods, Arwa. It is just a tale."

"They're never just tales."

"Look at me." He held her face in his hands. "I'm going to help you as I did in the caravanserai. Let me share the burden of your ash."

"It won't be enough."

"It can be. It will be."

"There's too much," she said helplessly.

He touched his forehead to her own. "You are in the realm of ash, even now, aren't you?"

Ash. Sunlight. The gold of sand. The black and white of an ash sky.

"Yes."

"Well then," he said. "Well. There must be a trick to it."

He closed his eyes, and then he was there in the realm with her, all gossamer and glass, holding her still. Expression grim, he wound his blood roots around her own, lifting them to grace her fingers, her ash-dark wrists.

"Let me take the weight of the ash," he said. "Let me share it with you again."

"It won't be enough."

"Arwa. Let me *try*."

She said nothing more, as he drew the weight of the ash between them, through the bond of their twined roots, said nothing as the clamor of voices grew and grew. But when she saw gray darkness begin to cloud his hands, his arms, she swore and tried to draw back.

He held her fast.

"Zahir, *no*."

"What are blood roots, Arwa?" he said softly. "We studied them together, didn't we? A bond between body and soul. A conduit allowing the one to feed the other. The soul is shaped by the realm of ash. The soul shapes the body. But when mystics enter the realm together, when they share the strength of their roots... Arwa, that *strength*. What is that strength?"

"Stop thinking," she told him. "Stop thinking before you get yourself hurt."

"That really isn't my nature," he replied.

"Zahir," she said. Winced, something climbing within her, a scream, a memory that wasn't her own. "Don't do anything foolish."

"I told you, in the caravanserai, that if you were taken by the realm I'd do anything to bring you back." He said it as if it were fact: a simple line from a book, indelible ink that could not be undone. "I told you it was fear that spoke, and it was. But it was true also, Arwa."

He was still close. Clouded with the weight of her own dreams.

"The roots," he said. "They share the body's strength. Blood, heartbeat, life. And through them, I can share mine with you." His hand curled tighter against her own, the roots furled between them.

"You *can't*."

"I can," he said. "If there is one thing I know, Arwa—one thing at all—it is the nature of the soul and of sacrifice."

"Those are two things."

"You already sound more like yourself," he said gently. He brushed his fingers over her face, the roots wavering between them.

"You don't know what it will do to you," she told him.

"Shorten my life, I imagine. We'll keep a record of the outcome."

"I saved your life," she said furiously, "and now you want to part with it?"

"We know better than most that death isn't an end," he murmured. "And no. I want us both to live. That's all." His voice was so soft. "Arwa, if I am yours, then don't leave me behind. Let me try to save you. If we are partners in this work, then trust me. Trust my will. Let us go together."

She stared up at him, thousands of voices pouring through her, wearing her thin. But it was a strange truth: as they wore her away, peeled artifice away from her, she found that all that remained was the softness of his eyes. The promise she had made him.

You are mine.

She nodded. "Do it," she said.

He closed his eyes then. Exhaled.

She had seen him consume ash. But she had never seen anything like this. She saw the surface of his skin shift, the facets of its glass surface moving. It reminded her of how the nightmare had moved—reworking its flesh in response to her fears, ferally clever.

But Zahir was not reshaping in response to her fears.

He was pouring his strength into her. His life. His blood.

The roots wound between them. Their hands—their dreamed skin—fused together. Beneath them the ground of the realm splintered and shifted. Their realms were melding too. Joining into one.

In the place where their realms were now joined she saw their roots coil and spread. He placed her against them, letting them bind her tight. Her soul was bound close to the mortal world, by his life and her own. Body to soul. Soul to body.

Just a tale, he'd called it. But she had seen this tree in the hermitage and the pleasure house and the House of Tears. Vast branches. Deep roots. A sacrifice written into the world.

She raised her hands to the sky, watching the light pour through them, dappled with shadow. She felt the roots, deep and strong, holding her steady: his heartbeat, his breath. His soul, his dreams.

He collapsed to the ground beside her. His distant lungs drew breath, and she called his name, and drew him into her arms. In the land of the dead, they were holding each other, and they were *alive*.

"Zahir," she said, her voice a fading echo. "I thought the dead had me."

"No," he said. He was beside her, his soul ashen and glass-cold, his skin burning with warmth. "The dead can't take you. Not while I am living. Not when I can guide you home."

CHAPTER THIRTY-NINE

She heard a lullaby.

There were other noises too. The sound of conversation, low and distant. Wind on desert sand. But it was the lullaby that surrounded her like a halo of comfort.

Soft, familiar voice. Fingers combing gently through her hair. She was dreaming of being a small girl again. Of a better time.

Her head hurt. She could feel the tumult of the realm of ash eddying through her mind. She could feel Zahir still, in her roots, an echo of his own heartbeat an ocean in her ear. He was near. She knew he was near, and alive. Her shoulder still hurt, still ached, but the pain had dulled. Eyes still closed, heavy with sleep, she moved her other hand carefully, feeling along her collarbone, toward the wound.

Fingertips touched her own.

"Careful," said Mehr. "You'll move the bandages."

Arwa's eyes snapped open.

Mehr was looking down at her. Mehr's eyes were damp and red; a faint smile curved her mouth.

"Ah, little sister," she said, brushing Arwa's hair back from her face. "My dear one. I have missed you."

Her hand traced Arwa's cheek. Her gaze took in Arwa's ash-clouded eyes, her face, her shorn hair—and Arwa looked at her in return. She took in the softness of Mehr's face, the redness of her eyes, the curl of her hair. Alive. She was alive.

Wound be damned, Arwa flung herself into Mehr's arms. Mehr held her carefully, murmured that she should be careful, but Arwa did not care about pain. She wept noisily, fiercely. She wept like the child she hadn't been for a long, long time, clutching her sister who was alive and whole and safe, and was not a ruin of limbs lost in a desert of dead. Her sister murmured to her, attempting to quiet her. *Calm, Arwa, calm, all's well.* And then, abruptly, she realized Mehr was crying too, miserably and quietly as her shoulders and her voice shook, as she ran a tender finger over Arwa's shorn hair, as if she could not bring herself to believe that Arwa was here before her at all.

"I thought you were dead," Arwa wept. "Father told me, he told me you were gone and he—he wept for you. Grieved for you, but then he would not speak of you. I thought you had no grave, I could not *mourn* you."

Mehr tensed, just a little. She wiped her tears from her eyes with her fingertips, then laughed weakly, and shook her head at her damp hands.

"No, Arwa. I'm alive and well." Even though her voice trembled, it was as soothing as the desert at moonrise. "I'm not hurt. I'm safe and I am *happy*. I have a good life here, Arwa. A good life among our mother's people."

"You live with Amrithi?"

"Yes."

"It's all you ever wanted," Arwa whispered, feeling small and flayed. Mehr's hand stroked her again.

"Not everything," she said. "But you're here now."

"How did you survive? You—the Maha took you."

"He did," Mehr said quietly. A faint shudder crossed her skin. "Ah, it is a long story, Arwa. But he died, and I'm free. I owe you the full tale. But not now. Not yet."

"Did you ever look for me?" Arwa asked.

"Oh, Arwa. Yes." Her tone was emphatic, gaze suddenly fierce. "I couldn't leave Irinah. After the Maha...No." She put a hand to her chest, as if she could press something brittle to stillness in her heart by touch alone. "But one of my clan—he searched for you. He carried letters. For you, and for Father."

She remembered her father at her bedroom window. Hunched. His eyes wet, his face stricken, a letter crumpled in his fist. She remembered her mother, forbidding her questions, telling her they would only cause her hurt.

Arwa knew then. She knew what her mother and father had done. A part of her had known for a long time.

"Tell me," she managed to say. "Please, Mehr. I need to hear it from you."

"He found Father," Mehr said, voice careful, weighing each word as if she knew the wound she struck. "The member of my clan. He gave Father my letter. And Father wrote to me. He told me he loved me. He told me he was—sorry he couldn't save me." Here, her voice wavered once more. "And he told me he would keep you safe, as he'd promised me, before the Maha took me. And he told me..."

Arwa knew. She knew.

"He thought I couldn't be Amrithi and be safe. He thought I couldn't have you and be safe. Not in the Empire. So he—lied to me. He lied to me."

Mehr was silent. Arwa swallowed, and thought of how hard she had fought to be a worthy daughter. To build her parents a future. She thought of how impossible it had been for her to dream of another world, one not shaped by the Empire she had grown up in. She thought of her father, who had fought to save his daughters, and been broken by the Empire for it. Even sick, even disgraced, he and her mother had tried to carve a space for her in the Empire. A future. It had been cruel of them. They had probably thought it a kindness.

"He was trying to protect me."

Then her sister said, gently, "Yes."

She looked away from her sister, then almost immediately looked back, afraid that Mehr would vanish like ash before her. But Mehr was still there, whole and dark-eyed and a woman grown.

He wanted you to be safe.

She had been molded and erased and silenced for safety. She had been denied the truth for safety. Her history had been cleaved in two, for safety. They had almost broken her, for the sake of making her safe, for the sake of their love for her, and she would carry the wound of it all her life.

Love was not always kind.

She curled her own hand against the beat of her heart against her ribs. The heart Zahir had saved; the life he'd bought with a piece of his own.

"Arwa," Mehr said quietly. "I cannot put right the past. I cannot change the forces that have shaped us both. Whatever horrors you have been through, I cannot wash away. But I can offer you a home here. I can offer you time. I can tell you that I will defend you with every breath in me." She cupped Arwa's face, utterly tender. "I have family here," she said. "And you do too. If you will meet them, they are yours. And if you will not, then know that I have loved you and missed you every day since we were parted. I have always been your sister, Arwa—no distance, no time, no grief, has changed that."

They were both weeping again; both wiped tears from their faces in the joyous, ugly, miserable way of people who hadn't planned to cry and didn't care for it.

"Mehr," Arwa said shakily.

"Yes."

"I lost your blade."

Mehr laughed through her tears.

"It doesn't matter," she said. "Oh, Arwa, it doesn't matter at all."

The tent canvas—and they were in a tent, Arwa realized now—rustled. Drew back a little. She saw the shape of a man, silhouetted to shadow by the sun behind him.

Mehr curled her hand over Arwa's, salt-damp, then released her.

"We'll talk more," she said. "Of everything. I promise it. But now I should let you rest."

"The man I came with," Arwa said. "Zahir. Will you send him to me?"

"Yes," Mehr said. "Of course."

She saw Mehr touch her hand to the man's wrist, saw her lean against him, as if he could hold the weight of all her feeling, her joy and grief alike—and then they were gone.

"Well," Zahir said. "We're not dead."

"Hello to you too," Arwa said.

He exhaled. He was bruised, sunburnt, and—in the realm of ash—a thing run through with dazzling light. His eyes were gray as ash, deep and endless dark, no matter what realm she looked at them in. He kneeled down beside her bed and she placed her fingertips against his cheek. Their roots were no longer twined, but one seamless weft of lace, a whorl of rose without end.

"Did my sister treat you well?"

"She saved our lives out in the desert, she and her clan, so yes. Well enough, although her men were suspicious of me, and wouldn't allow me near you until you asked." He kneeled down. "I love you too," he added. "In case you were wondering."

"Oh no," she said, curling her fingers around his. "I knew. Why else would you have given up part of your life for me? *Fool.*"

"I don't regret it," he said. "I have no interest in being a mystic order of one."

"Very funny."

He smiled faintly. Then the look faded to something...lost.

"In truth, Arwa, I don't know what will become of us. I have been exactly the kind of fool I loathe. We may die early, or not. We may always walk in the realm of ash and the mortal world at the same time or...we may not. It will be telling, when we leave Irinah, and see what becomes of us without its power."

"You think the bond between us may break?"

"No, Arwa. But I think we may feel a little more—human."

"Really?"

He paused, but only for a moment.

"No," he admitted. "I think we're—changed." He held his hands before him, pale brown, knuckles bruised. Dazzling white glass, fingernails like points of light. "We walked too far. I am sorry, Arwa. I wish I could have saved more of you."

"You saved all of me that matters," she said. "And I regret none of it." She could feel the realm of ash within her and without her. Iria, Ushan, the daiva with their great wings—they whispered within her. Her family of the dead.

She had the possibility of a family of the living now too. Amrithi who were not decimated. Amrithi who had their own clans, and lived within Irinah's desert, and carved out a life from the Empire's control. This was her heritage.

"Perhaps one day we'll simply walk into the realm of ash together," she said quietly. "Step into the realm, walk to the end of the path, and see what lies beyond even ash." She sat up, wincing a little. "But not now. Now we have a plan, and I'd like to see it through."

"Of course."

"But I would like to stay for a time. To recover. To know my sister," Arwa admitted. "And...there are other Amrithi. Here. In her clan. Perhaps they know everything I gleaned from the realm of ash. Perhaps. But I would like to return the knowledge regardless. It's their own, after all. And then..." She looked at him. "I'd like to see what we could do, you and I. I'd like to bargain with the Hidden Ones. I'd like to teach others like me the Rite of the Cage. I'd like to spread the knowledge of prayer, and grind Parviz's reputation to dust, as I promised him. I'd like to walk the breadth of the world, before I walk deep into the ash again. Zahir, would you join me?"

He looked at her and smiled—a true, real smile that blazed on him like light.

"Arwa," he said. "I'd like nothing more."

Her marriage had been a heavy thing, a yoke of hurt and unknowing and duty, and it had smothered her. She hadn't thought she would ever want anything like it again. But this, hands upon hers, the curve of his smile, the trust of him.

That, ah. That she would have. A lifetime of bravery. A lifetime of this.

All the rest, she thought, could wait.

Two days later, Eshara arrived. She limped into the tent after Zahir, her face bruised and swollen, gait heavy. When she saw Arwa, her face—ah.

Arwa worried, for a moment, that Eshara would weep.

"Don't feel sorry for me," Eshara snapped by way of greeting. "I tripped trying to get your damnable retinue to safety. I would have stayed to protect you, but it seemed pointless for all of us to die. Sohal was angry about it, though. He said he would have stayed and protected you, when the widows started blubbering at him."

Her tone was light enough. Still, there was a shadowed, haunted look to her face that belied her words. She looked at Arwa's shoulder. Looked up. "You're still alive, then?"

"I told you I'd try my best," said Arwa. "I'm glad you left, Eshara. I wouldn't have wanted to mourn you."

Eshara lowered her eyes. Zahir kneeled by Arwa's side. She felt the roots between them, the sureness of him in two worlds, and held out her hand. He took it.

Eshara began to speak once more.

"After we made it to safety—after a full night hiding in the desert, by the way, and wasn't *that* a thrill with a handful of hysterical pilgrims—we made it to Jah Irinah. The locals were restless, saying soldiers had angered the daiva, driven the spirits into frenzy. They said anyone who walked into the desert would be ripped apart. I tracked down the Amrithi guide we'd been recommended. I offered him all the money I had to take me back to where we'd last been. I thought at least I could..." She swallowed. "Well, I thought they might have killed you there. I thought I'd see you buried. He refused."

Eshara bent forward. Tucked Arwa's blanket around her legs, not looking up. "He came and found me this morning. Said his Tara had told him to find me, whatever that means." She lifted her gaze. "I think your sister might be important, Arwa."

Of course her sister was important. The other Amrithi deferred to her. She had *amata*. She'd survived the Maha's service. She'd seen Arwa somehow in the space between worlds, in ash and dreams and desert, and reached for her. And she was Arwa's family. That was enough.

"A Tara is an Amrithi clan leader," Arwa said simply.

"Well, I'm right, then." She hesitated. "I assume—you haven't found the Maha's ash?"

A pause. Then Arwa shook her head and Zahir said, "No. There was nothing to find. He's beyond our reach."

Eshara cursed, and Arwa met Zahir's eyes.

She had asked Mehr to bring Eshara here not for affection alone. Eshara had risked her life for their task—for the bare scrap of hope the Maha's ash offered.

"The world can still be saved," Zahir said slowly. "And Arwa and I, we have a plan for how to do it. If the Hidden Ones are willing to help us."

"We have a rite that will hold the nightmares, after all, and prayer," Arwa said. "We have a path into the realm of ash. And we have...a hope. It will not be easy or quick or without danger. It will be the slow way toward the Empire's survival. But it is still a way. Will you help us, Eshara? Will you ask any Hidden Ones you trust if they may want to ally with us, and share our knowledge and our purpose?"

Eshara looked between them for a moment. Then she scowled and rubbed her knuckles between her eyes.

"You two," she said. "As if I haven't almost died for the both of you." She sat down. "Tell me what you want from the Hidden Ones, and I'll see what I can do."

That evening, still weak, shaking, Arwa walked out into the desert. The members of Mehr's clan who had been tasked with guarding Arwa's tent didn't stop her, though they protested. Only Zahir nodded and said he would wait for her with Eshara.

Arwa walked out into the black of the desert, the cold sky above her. Arwa walked the realm of ash, crossing eddies rich in colorless light. She walked in two worlds now, held steady by deep roots, by the beat of two hearts.

She felt Zahir behind her. Her blood and life. He did not need to fear for her. He knew her like she knew him. It was like knowing the shape of your own breath.

She would learn how to survive here, in two worlds, in two skins. She would learn how to be more than a noblewoman, with more than her own foolish, fierce bravado to fuel her. And if her life would be cut short, if the sacrifice Zahir had made of his own strength would only sustain them so long—well. What a glorious life it would be.

She would bring Sohal here, if he wanted to be brought. She

would show him how the desert moved, and teach him what she knew.

She would tell the truth to Diya. The widow had a right to that too. After all, she had faced an army with the strength of hope alone, with hands full of grief and her voice full of fire.

She and Zahir would leave the desert. They had nightmares to face. They had the teachings of the Maha's heir to share: teachings of the power of prayer and grave-tokens against the dark. Perhaps she would go and see her mother and her father then. She would face them as the person she was now, with her ash eyes, her full heart, her spirit that walked two worlds, and see if they had the strength to understand her, and she the strength to forgive them.

She would seek out the nightmares with Zahir at her side. She, the widowed witch who was Amrithi and Ambhan both, who knew the secrets of the dead, and he the Emperor's blessed son, who was called Maha's heir by those who spun their hopes around him, and wore his knowledge like a blade. They would save what they could, she and him, one nightmare at a time. And they would see what new world awaited at the end of their path.

But first...

She stood still.

She waited.

A breath or two passed, and then the bird-spirits landed, surrounding her. Their eyes were bright in the dark. Careful of her shoulder, Arwa drew her hands together. A sigil for *respect*.

"Spirit. I've long wondered why you protected me, of all Amrithi-blooded people in this world. I have heard the whispers of the dead and now I think I know why you defend me." She looked at it, soft-winged, dark and bright. "You were in Darez Fort with me, weren't you?" she said, holding her arms out, her scarred hands outstretched, forming a question in her stance, a sigil on her hands. *Follow?* "You were there when the nightmare almost killed me. You were controlling it. You were its balance."

Nightmare.

Lock?

A susurration of wings.

"The soldiers frightened you," said Arwa. "Or perhaps the sight of me, at the lattice, shocked you. I only know you let the nightmare go, and very many people died."

Hands turning. *Unlock. Free.*

"You made a vow to my birth mother's people," said Arwa. "To my sister's people. And yet I was harmed. However unwittingly, you broke your word."

Vow.

Hands against one another. Abrupt turn of them. Just so.

Broken.

The daiva splintered about her, smaller and smaller still, until the birds were like bursts of shadow against the greater night's dark.

"Is that why you followed me from Darez Fort? Why you protected me there, and protect me still?" She shaped nothing. "Please," she said. "Tell me."

The birds wavered, drew together into one formless many-eyed being, as they had on the dovecote tower once before.

It shaped arms—hands like clawed spindles. The sigil for *forgiveness* formed in the air before her. There was a question in its stance, the wavering turn of its shadow.

It splintered back, once more, into birds.

It was like a creature cursed, she thought. Under a spell of its own grief, it could not leave her, and it could not be as it once was: ancient, child-shaped. A daiva of strange strength.

"You gave me wings at the imperial palace," Arwa said, voice thick. "You saved my life time and time again. Of course I forgive you."

How could she prove it? The whispers of the ash ran through her, roots and all. She swallowed. Steeled herself against the inevitable pain, as she aggravated her wounded shoulder once more.

The Rite of the Cage reversed. She would never be truly graceful, never truly know the rites in her bones. But she had learned them. She had thieved back from the abyss, and paid in blood and spirit and the life she'd been raised for. Every sigil she turned on its head, binding to freedom, hold to release.

When she reversed the lock the daiva chirruped. All its small birds chorused—then flew together, a flock that became a shadow, a shadow that became a child.

The child-daiva looked at her. Its eyes were soft prayer flames. Its hair curled around its face.

"Go," she murmured. "Go with my love."

It changed once more—this time into a bird of vast size. It rose into the air.

Arwa watched it. Her heart felt too big for her skin, at the sight of it.

Behind her waited her sister. Behind her waited Eshara, worn out and bruised, and almost-strangers who could become more in time, if they chose to.

Behind her waited Zahir. Her clever not-prince, her idealist, her fool. Her future.

She watched the daiva fly away, greater than any bird she'd ever seen, its great wings spreading shadows across the sand. Then she turned back, back across sand and ash, back to all her people, and began following the path that led her home.

Acknowledgments

Everyone told me that writing your second book is harder than writing your first. They weren't lying. Thank you to my family for giving me endless, unflinching support despite the fact that I spent the better part of the year as a hissing gremlin hidden behind a laptop. Special thanks goes to my mum and to Carly, who had to suffer through living with me. I love you both. Also, thank you to my cat, Asami, who slept curled up next to me on the sofa every night that I stayed up late writing. When cats finally learn to read, I'm sure you'll find this and appreciate the sentiment.

To my agent, Laura Crockett: thank you for being such a champion. You're the absolute best. Thank you also to Uwe Stender, the entire team at Triada US, and also to Tori Bovalino, my agency sister, who read an early draft of this book and helped me find my way through.

Sarah Guan, my editor—thank you, from the bottom of my heart, for making this book shine. Thank you also to the wonderful team at Orbit: Tim Holman and Anne Clarke; Paola Crespo, Laura Fitzgerald, Stephanie Hess, and Ellen Wright for all their work on publicity and marketing; Kelley Frodel and Bryn A. McDonald for their fantastic editorial insight; and Lauren Panepinto for another stunning cover. Big hugs to the glamorous UK Orbit team, too—my UK editor Jenni Hill, and publicist Nazia Khatun.

And finally, my warmest gratitude goes to the readers and bloggers who supported my first book and this one. I literally wouldn't be writing this without your generosity, enthusiasm, and support. If I could hug you, I would, and if we've met in person, I probably have.

extras

orbit

meet the author

Photo Credit: Shekhar Bhatia

TASHA SURI was born in London to Punjabi parents. She studied English and creative writing at Warwick University and is now a cat-owning librarian in London. A love of period Bollywood films, history, and mythology led her to write South Asian–influenced fantasy. Find her on Twitter @tashadrinkstea.

if you enjoyed
REALM OF ASH

look out for

THE THRONE OF THE FIVE WINDS

HOSTAGE OF EMPIRE: BOOK ONE

by

S. C. Emmett

Two queens, two concubines, six princes.
Innumerable secret agendas.
A single hidden blade.

The imperial palace—full of ambitious royals, sly gossip, and
unforeseen perils—is perhaps the most dangerous place in the

*empire of Zhaon. Komor Yala, lady-in-waiting to the princess
of the vanquished kingdom of Khir, has only her wits and her
hidden blade to protect herself and her charge, who was sacrificed
in marriage to the enemy as a hostage for her conquered people's
good behavior, to secure a tenuous peace.*

*But the Emperor is aging, and the Khir princess and her
lady-in-waiting soon find themselves to be pawns in the six
princes' deadly schemes for the throne—and a single spark could
ignite fresh rebellion in Khir.*

Then, the Emperor falls ill—and a far bloodier game begins…

Little Light

Above the Great Keep of Khir and the smoky bowl of its
accreted city, tombs rose upon mountainside terraces. Only the
royal and Second Families had the right to cut their names into
stone here, and this small stone pailai[1] was one of the very oldest. Hard, small pinpoints about to become white or pink blossoms starred the branches of ancient, twisted yeoyans;[2] a young
woman in blue, her black hair dressed simply but carefully
with a single white-shell comb, stood before the newest marker.
Incense smoked as she folded her hands for decorous prayer, a
well-bred daughter performing a rare unchaperoned duty.

---

1. A single family's tombs.
2. A tree similar to a cherry.

Below, the melt had begun and thin droplets scattered from tiled roofs both scarlet and slate, from almost-budding branches. Here snow still lingered in corners and upon sheltered stones; winter-blasted grass slept underneath. No drip disturbed the silence of the ancestors.

A booted foot scraped stone. The girl's head, bowed, did not move. There was only one person who would approach while she propitiated her ancestors, and she greeted him politely. "Your Highness." But she did not raise her head.

"None of that, Yala." The young man, his topknot caged and pierced with gold, wore ceremonial armor before the dead. His narrow-nosed face had paled, perhaps from the cold, and his gaze—grey as a winter sky, grey as any noble blood-pure Khir's—lingered upon her nape. As usual, he dispensed with pleasantries. "You do not have to go."

Of course he would think so. Her chin dropped a little farther. "If I do not, who will?" Other noble daughters, their fathers not so known for rectitude as the lord of Komori, were escaping the honor in droves.

"Others." A contemptuous little word. "Servants. There is no shortage."

Yala's cloud-grey eyes opened. She said nothing, watching the gravestone as if she expected a shade to rise. Her offerings were made at her mother's tomb already, but here was where she lingered. A simple stone marked the latest addition to the shades of her House—fine carving, but not ostentatious. The newly rich might display like fan-tailed baryo,[3] but not those who had ridden to war with the Three Kings of the First Dynasty. Or so her father thought, though he did not say it.

A single tone, or glance, was enough to teach a lesson.

---

3. Carrion-eating birds with bright plumage, often kept as garbage-eating pets.

461

Ashani Daoyan, Crown Prince of Khir newly legitimized and battlefield-blooded, made a restless movement. Lean but broad-shouldered, with a slight roundness to his cheeks bespeaking his Narikh motherblood, he wore the imperial colors easily; a bastard son, like an unmarried aunt, learned to dress as the weather dictated. Leather creaked slightly, and his breath plumed in the chill. "If your brother were alive—"

"—I would be married to one of his friends, and perhaps widowed as well." *Now* Komor Yala, the only surviving child of General Hai Komori Dasho, moved too, a slight swaying as if she wished to turn and halted just in time. "Please, Daoyan." The habit of long friendship made it not only possible but necessary to address him so informally. "Not before my Elder Brother."

"Yala..." Perhaps Dao's half-armor, black chased with yellow, was not adequate for this particular encounter. The boy she had known, full of sparkstick[4] pride and fierce silence when that pride was balked, had ridden to war; this young man returned in his place.

Did he regret being dragged from the field to preserve a dynasty while so many others stood and died honorably? She could not ask, merely suspect, so Yala shook her head. Her own words were white clouds, chosen carefully and given to the frigid morning. "Who will care for my princess, if I do not?"

"You cannot waste your life that way." A slight sound—gauntlets creaking. Daoyan still clenched his fists. She should warn him against so open a display of emotion, but perhaps in a man it did not matter so much.

"And yet." *There is no other option*, her tone replied, plainly. *Not one I am willing to entertain.* "I will take great care with your royal sister, Your Highness."

---

4. A handheld firework.

Of course he could not leave the battlefield thus, a draw achieved but no victory in sight. "I will offer for you."

"You already would have, if you thought your honored father would allow it." She bowed, a graceful supple bending with her skirts brushing fresh-swept stone. "Please, Daoyan." Her palms met, and her head dropped even farther when she straightened, the attitude of a filial daughter from a scroll's illustrations.

Even a prince dared not interrupt prayers begun before a relative's tomb. Daoyan turned, finally, boots ringing through thin snow to pavers she had not attended to with her small broom, and left the pailai with long, swinging strides.

Yala slipped her hands deeper inside her sleeves and regarded the memorial stone. Bai, of course, would have sniffed at the prospect of his little sister marrying a man with an honorless mother, no matter if he had proven himself in war and the Great Rider had legitimized him. Bai would also have forbidden her to accompany Mahara. He was not the clan-head, but since he came of age their father had let him take heavier duties and listened to his counsel. Bai's refusal would have carried weight, and Yala could have bowed her head to accept it instead of insisting upon her duty as a noble daughter must before a distinguished parent.

Perhaps that would have been best. Was the cringing, creeping relief she would have felt cowardice? The other noble families were scurrying to keep their daughters from Mahara's retinue, marriages contracted or health problems discovered with unseemly haste. The Great Rider, weakened as he was by the defeat at Three Rivers and the slow strangling of Khir's southron trade, could not force noble daughters to accompany his own, he could only...request.

Other clans and families could treat it as a request, but Komori held to the ancient codes. It was a high honor to attend the princess of Khir, and Yala had done so since childhood. To cease in adversity was unworthy of a Komor daughter.

Burning incense sent lazy curls of scented smoke heavenward. If her brother was watching, he would have been fuming like the sticks themselves. A slow smolder and a hidden fire, that was Hai Komori Baiyan. She could only hope she was the same, and the conquering Zhaon would not smother her *and* her princess.

First things first. You are to pay your respects here, and then to comfort your father.

As if there could be any comfort to a Khir nobleman whose only son was dead. Hai Komori Dasho would be gladdened to be rid of a daughter and the need to find a dowry, that much was certain. Even if he was not, he would act as if he were, because that was the correct way to regard this situation.

The Komori, especially the clan heads, were known for their probity.

Her fingertips worried at her knuckles, and she sighed. "Oh, damoi,[5] my much-blessed Bai," she whispered. It was not quite meet to pronounce the name of the dead, but she could be forgiven a single use of such a precious item. "How I wish you were here."

She bent before her brother's grave one last time, and her fingers found a sharp-edged, triangular pebble among the flat pavers, blasted grass, and iron-cold dirt. They could not plow quite yet, but the monjok[6] and yeoyan blossoms were out. Spring would come early this year, but she would not see the swallows returning. The care of the pailai would fall to more distant kin from a junior branch of the clan.

Yala tucked the pebble in a sleeve-pocket, carefully. She could wrap it with red silken thread, decorate a hairstick with

---

5. *Khir. Affectionate.* Elder brother.
6. A small, slightly acrid fruit.

falling beads, and wear a part of both Bai and her homeland daily. A small piece of grit in the conqueror's court, hopefully accreting nacre instead of dishonor.

There were none left to care for her father in his aging. Perhaps he would marry again. If Bai were still alive...

"Stop," she murmured, and since there were none to see her, Yala's face could contort under a lash of pain, a horse shying at the whip. "He is not."

Khir had ridden to face Zhaon's great general at Three Rivers, and the eldest son of a proud Second Family would not be left behind. The battle had made Daoyan a hero and Bai a corpse, but it was useless to Khir. The conquerors had dictated their terms; war took its measure, reaping a rich harvest, and Zhaon was the scythe.

Khir would rise again, certainly, but not soon enough to save a pair of women. Even a cursory study of history showed that a farm could change hands, and he who reaped yesterday might be fertilizer for the next scythe-swinger. There was little comfort in the observation, even if it was meant to ease the pain of the defeated.

For the last time, Yala bowed before her brother's stone. If she walked slowly upon her return, the evidence of tears would be erased by the time she reached the foot of the pailai's smooth-worn stairs and the single maidservant waiting, holding her mistress's horse and bundled against the cold as Yala disdained to be.

A noblewoman suffered ice without a murmur. Inside, and out.

Hai Komori's blackened bulk rested within the walls of the Old City. It frowned in the old style, stone walls and sharply pitched slate-tiled roof; its great hall was high and gloomy. The longtable, crowded with retainers at dinners twice every tenday, was a blackened piece of old wood; it stood empty now, with the lord's low chair upon the dais watching its oiled, gleaming surface. Mirrorlight drifted, brought through holes in the roof and bounced between polished discs, crisscrossing the high space.

Dusty cloth rustled overhead, standards and pennons taken in battle. There were many, and their sibilance was the song of a Second Family. The men rode to war, the women to hunt, and between them the whole world was ordered. Or so the classics, both the canonical Hundreds and supplements, said. Strong hunters made strong sons, and Yala had sometimes wondered why her mother, who could whisper a hawk out of the sky, had not given her father more than two. Bai the eldest was ash upon the wind and a name upon a tablet; the second son had not even reached his naming-day.

And Komor Madwha, a daughter of the Jehng family and high in the regard of the Great Rider and her husband as well, died shortly after her only daughter's birth.

Komori Dasho was here instead of in his study. Straight-backed, only a few thin threads of frost woven into his top-knot, a vigorous man almost into the status of elder sat upon the dais steps, gazing at the table and the great hearth. When a side door opened and blue silk made its subtle sweet sound, he closed his eyes.

Yala, as ever, bowed properly to her father though he was not looking. "Your daughter greets you, *pai*."

He acknowledged with a nod. She waited, her hands folded in her sleeves again, faintly uneasy. Her father was a tall man, his shoulders still hard from daily practice with saber and spear; his face was pure Khir. Piercing grey eyes, straight black hair topknotted as a Second Dynasty lord's, a narrow high prow of a nose, a thin mouth, and bladed cheekbones harsh as the sword-mountains themselves. Age settled more firmly upon him with each passing winter, drawing skin tighter and bone-angles sharper. His house robe was spare and dark, subtly patterned but free of excessive ornamentation.

He was, in short, the very picture of a Khir noble—except he was not, as usual, straight as an iron reed upon his low backless chair with the standard of their house—the setting sun and the komor flower[7]—hung behind it.

Finally, he patted the stone step with his left hand. "Come, sit." His intonation was informal, and that was another surprise.

Yala settled herself, carefully. With her dress arranged and her feet tucked to the side, she lowered her eyelids and waited.

Lord Komori did not care for idle chatter.

The great hall was different from this angle. The table was large as it had been when she was a child, and the cavernous fireplace looked ready to swallow an unwary passerby whole. The braziers were blackened spirit-kettles, their warmth barely touching winter's lingering chill. Flagstones, swept and scrubbed even when winter meant the buckets formed ice which needed frequent breaking, stared blankly at the ceiling, polished by many feet. Yala stilled, a habit born of long practice in her father's presence.

The mouse that moves is taken. Another proverb. The classics were stuffed to bursting with them.

As a child she had fidgeted and fluttered, Dowager Eun despairing of ever teaching her discretion. In Yala's twelfth spring the weight of decorum had begun to tell, and she had decided it was easier to flow with that pressure than stagger under it. Even Mahara had been surprised, and she, of all the world, perhaps knew Yala best.

After Bai, that was.

---

7. A native, very hardy Khir plant with seven petals on its small highly fragrant flowers; the root is used for blue dye.

"Yala," her father said, as if reminding himself who she was. *That* was hardly unusual. The sons stayed, the daughters left. An advantageous marriage was her duty to Komori. It was a pity there had been no offers. *I wonder what is wrong with me*, she had murmured to Mahara once.

I do not wish to share you with a husband, Mahara answered, when she could speak for laughing.

"Yes." Simple, and soft, as a noblewoman should speak. She wished she were at her needlework, the satisfaction of a stitch pulled neatly and expertly making up for pricked fingers. Or in the mews, hawk-singing. Writing out one of the many classics once again, her brush held steady. Reading, or deciding once more what to pack and what to leave behind.

She wished, in fact, to be anywhere but here. After a visit to the ancestors, though, her presence at her father's wrist was expected. Brought back to endure scrutiny like a hawk itself, a feather passed over her plumage, so as not to disturb the subtle oils thereupon.

"I have often thought you should have been born male." Komori Dasho sighed, his shoulders dropping. The sudden change was startling, and disturbing. "You would have made a fine son." Even if it was high praise, it still stung. A formulaic reply rose inside her, but he did not give her the chance to utter as much. "But if you were, you would have died upon that bloodfield as well, and I would have opened my veins at the news."

Startled, Yala turned her head to gaze upon his profile. The room was not the only thing that looked different from this angle. The thunder-god of her childhood, straight and proud, sat beside her, staring at the table. And, terrifyingly, hot water had come to Komori Dasho's eyes. It swelled, glittering, and anything she might have said vanished.

"My little light," he continued. "Did you know? I named you thus, after your mother died. Not aloud, but here." His thin, strong right fist, the greenstone seal-ring of a proud and ancient house glinting upon his index finger, struck his chest. "I knew not to say such things, for the gods would be angry and steal you as they took *her*."

Yala's chest tightened. A Lord Komori severe in displeasure or stern with approval she could answer. Who was *this*?

Her father did not give her a chance to reply. "In the end it does not matter. The Great Rider has requested and we must answer; you will attend the princess in Zhaon."

This much I knew already. The pebble in her sleeve-pocket pressed against her wrist. She realized she was not folding her hands but clutching them, knuckles probably white under smooth fabric. "Yes." There. Was that an acceptable response?

He nodded, slowly. The frost in his hair had spread since news of Three Rivers; she had not noticed before. This was the closest she had been to her father since . . . she could not remember the last time. She could not remember when he last spoke to her with the informal inflection *or* case, either. Yala searched for something else to say. "I will not shame our family, especially among *them*."

"You—" He paused, straightened. "You have your *yue*?"

Of course I do. "It is the honor of a Khir woman," she replied, as custom demanded. Was this a test? If so, would she pass? Familiar anxiety sharpened inside her ribs. "Does my father wish to examine its edge?" The blade was freshly honed; no speck of rust or whisper of disuse would be found upon its slim greenmetal length.

"Ah. No, of course not." His hands dangled at his knees, lax as they never had been in her memory. "Will you write to your father?"

"Of course." As if she would dare *not* to. The stone under her was a cold, uncomfortable saddle, but she did not dare shift. "Every month."

"Every week." The swelling water in his eyes did not over-flow. Yala looked away. It was uncomfortably akin to seeing a man outside the clan drunk, or at his dressing. "Will you?"

"Yes." *If you require it of me.*

"I have kept you close all this time." His fingers curled slightly, as if they wished for a hilt. "There were many marriage offers made for you, Yala. Since your naming-day, you have been sought. I refused them all." He sighed, heavily. "I could not let you go. Now, I am punished for it."

She sat, stunned and silent, until her father, for the first and last time, put a lean-muscled, awkward arm about her shoulders. The embrace was brief and excruciating, and when it ended he rose and left the hall, iron-backed as ever, with his accustomed quiet step.

He is proud of you, she had often told Bai. *He simply does not show it.*

Perhaps it had not been a lie told to soothe her brother's heart. And perhaps, just perhaps, she could believe it for herself.

if you enjoyed
REALM OF ASH

look out for

THE SISTERS OF THE WINTER WOOD

by

Rena Rossner

In a remote village surrounded by vast forests on the border of Moldova and Ukraine, sisters Liba and Laya have been raised on the honeyed scent of their Mami's babka *and the low rumble of their Tati's prayers. But when a troupe of mysterious men arrives, Laya falls under their spell—despite her mother's warning to be wary of strangers. And this is not the only danger lurking in the woods.*

As dark forces close in on their village, Liba and Laya discover a family secret passed down through generations. Faced with a magical heritage they never knew existed, the sisters realize the old fairy tales are true . . . and could save them all.

1

Liba

If you want to know the history of a town, read the gravestones in its cemetery. That's what my Tati always says. Instead of praying in the synagogue like all the other men of our town, my father goes to the cemetery to pray. I like to go there with him every morning.

The oldest gravestone in our cemetery dates back to 1666. It's the grave I like to visit most. The names on the stone have long since been eroded by time. It is said in our *shtetl* that it marks the final resting place of a bride and a groom who died together on their wedding day. We don't know anything else about them, but we know that they were buried, arms embracing, in one grave. I like to put a stone on their grave when I go there, to make sure their souls stay down where they belong, and when I do, I say a prayer that I too will someday find a love like that.

That grave is the reason we know that there were Jews in Dubossary as far back as 1666. Mami always said that this town was founded in love and that's why my parents chose to live here. I think it means something else—that our town was founded in tragedy. The death of those young lovers has been

a pall hanging over Dubossary since its inception. Death lives
here. Death will always live here.

2

Laya

I see Liba going
to the cemetery with Tati.
I don't know
what she sees
in all those cold stones.
But I watch,
and wonder,
why he never takes me.

When we were little,
Liba and I went to
the Talmud Torah.
For Liba, the black letters
were like something
only she could decipher.
I never understood
what she searched for,
in those black
scratches of ink.
I would watch

the window,
study the forest
and the sky.

When we walked home,
Liba would watch the boys
come out of the *cheder*
down the road.
I know that when she looked
at Dovid, Lazer and Nachman,
she wondered
what was taught
behind the walls
the girls were not
allowed to enter.

After her Bat Mitzvah,
Tati taught her Torah.
He tried to teach me too,
when my turn came,
but all I felt was
distraction,
disinterest.
Chanoch l'naar al pi darko,
Tati would say,
teach every child
in his own way,
and sigh,
and get up
and open the door.
Gey, gezinte heit—
I accept that you're different, go.

And while I was grateful,
I always wondered
why he gave up
without a fight.

3

Liba

As I follow the large steps my father's boots make in the snow, I revel in the solitude. This is why I cherish our morning walks. They give me time to talk to Tati, but also time to think. "In silence you can hear God," Tati says to me as we walk. But I don't hear God in the silence—I hear myself. I come here to get away from the noises of the town and the chatter of the towns-folk. It's where I can be fully me.

"What does God sound like?" I ask him. When I walk with Tati, I feel like I'm supposed to think about important things, like prayer and faith.

"Sometimes the voice of God is referred to as a *bat kol*," he says.

I translate the Hebrew out loud: "The daughter of a voice? That doesn't make any sense."

He chuckles. "Some say that *bat kol* means an echo, but others say it means a hum or a reverberation, something you sense in the air that's caused by the motion of the universe— part of the human voice, but also part of every other sound in the world, even the sounds that our ears can't hear. It means that sometimes even the smallest voice can have a big opinion." He grins, and I know that he means me, his daughter; that my opinion matters. I wish it were true. Not everybody in our town sees things the way my father does. Most women and girls do not study Torah; they don't learn or ask questions like I do. For the most part, our voices don't matter. I know I'm lucky that Tati is my father.

Although I love Tati's stories and his answers, I wonder why a small voice is a daughter's voice. Sometimes I wish my voice could be loud—like a roar. But that is not a modest way to think. The older I get, the more immodest my thoughts become.

I feel my cheeks flush as my mind wanders to all the things I shouldn't be thinking about—what it would feel like to hold the hand of a man, what it might feel like to kiss someone, what it's like when you finally find the man you're meant to marry and you get to be alone together, in bed... I swallow and shake my head to clear my thoughts.

If I shared the fact that this is all I think about lately, Mami and Tati would say it means it's time for me to get married. But I'm not sure I want to get married yet. I want to marry for love, not convenience. These thoughts feel like sacrilege. I know that I will marry a man my father chooses. That's the way it's done in our town and among Tati's people. Mami and Tati married for love, and it has not been an easy path for them.

I take a deep breath and shake my head from all my thoughts. This morning, everything looks clean from the snow that fell last night and I imagine the icy frost coating the insides of my lungs and mind, making my thoughts white and pure. I love being outside in our forest more than anything at times like these, because the white feels like it hides all our flaws.

Perhaps that's why I often see Tati in the dark forest that surrounds our home praying to God or—as he would say—the *Ribbono Shel Oylam*, the Master of the Universe, by himself, eyes shut, arms outstretched to the sky. Maybe he comes out here to feel new again too.

Tati comes from the town of Kupel, a few days' walk from here. He came here and joined a small group of Chassidim in the town—the followers of the late Reb Mendele, who was a disciple of the great and holy Ba'al Shem Tov. There is a small *shtiebl* where the men pray, in what used to be the home of Urka the Coachman. It is said that the Ba'al Shem Tov himself used to sit under the tree in Urka's courtyard. The Chassidim here accepted my father with open arms, but nobody accepted my mother.

Sometimes I wonder if Reb Mendele and the Ba'al Shem Tov (*zichrono livracha*) were still with us, would the community treat Mami differently? Would they see how hard she tries to be a good Jew, and how wrong the other Jews in town are for not treating her with love and respect. It makes me angry how quickly rumors spread, that Mami's kitchen isn't kosher (it is!) just because she doesn't cover her hair like the other married Jewish women in our town.

That's why Tati built our home, sturdy and warm like he is, outside our town in the forest. It's what Mami wanted: not to be under constant scrutiny, and to have plenty of room to plant fruit trees and make honey and keep chickens and goats. We have a small barn with a cow and a goat, and a bee glade out back and an orchard that leads all the way down to the river. Tati works in town as a builder and a laborer in the fields. But he is also a scholar, worthy of the title Rebbe, though none of the men in town call him that.

Sometimes I think my father knows more than the other Chassidim in our town, even more than Rabbi Borowitz who leads our tiny *kehilla*, and the bare bones prayer *minyan* of ten men that Tati sometimes helps complete. There are many things my father likes to keep secret, like his morning dips in the Dniester River that I never see, but know about, his prayer at the graveside of Reb Mendele, and our library. Our walls are covered in holy books—his *sforim*, and I often fall asleep to the sound of him reading from the Talmud, the Midrash, and the many mystical books of the Chassidim. The stories he reads sound like fairy tales to me, about magical places like Babel and Jerusalem.

In these places, there are scholarly men. Father would be respected there, a king among men. And there are learned boys of marriageable age—the kind of boys Tati would like me to marry someday. In my daydreams, they line up at the door, waiting to get a glimpse of me—the learned, pious daughter of the Rebbe. And my Tati would only pick the wisest and kindest for me.

I shake my head. In my heart of hearts, that's not really what I want. When Laya and I sleep in our loft, I look out the skylight above our heads and pretend that someone will someday find his way to our cabin, climb up onto the roof, and look in from above. He will see me and fall instantly in love.

Because lately I feel like time is running out. The older I get, the harder it will be to find someone. And when I think about that, I wonder why Tati insists that Laya and I wait until we are at least eighteen.

I would ask Mami, but she isn't a scholar like Tati, and she doesn't like to talk about these things. She worries about what people say and how they see us. It makes her angry, but she wrings dough instead of her hands. Tati says her hands are baker's hands, that she makes magic with dough. Mami can make something out of nothing. She makes cheese and gathers honey; she mixes bits of bark and roots and leaves for tea. She bakes the tastiest *challahs* and cakes, *rugelach* and *mandelbrot*, but it's her *babka* she's famous for. She sells her baked goods in town.

When she's not in the kitchen, Mami likes to go out through the skylight above our bed and onto the little deck on our roof to soak up the sun. Laya likes to sit up there with her. From the roof, you can see down to the village and the forest all around. I wonder if it's not just the sun that Mami seeks up there. While Tati's head is always in a book, Mami's eyes are always looking at the sky. Laya says she dreams of somewhere other than here. Somewhere far away, like America.

4

Laya

I always thought
that if I worshipped God,
dressed modestly,
and walked in His path,
that nothing bad
would happen
to my family.
We would find
our path to Zion,
our own piece of heaven
on the banks
of the Dniester River.

But now that I'm fifteen
I see what a life
of pious devotion
has brought Mami,
who converted
to our faith—
disapproval.
The life we lead
out here is a life apart.
I wish I could go to Onyshkivtsi.
Mami always tells me stories
about her town
and Saint Anna of the Swans
who lived there.

Saint Anna
didn't walk with God—
she knew she wasn't made
for perfection;
she never tried
to fit a pattern
that didn't fit her.
She didn't waste her time
trying to smooth herself
into something
she wasn't.
She was powerful
because she forged
her own path.

The Christians
in Onyshkivtsi

built a shrine
to honor her.
The shrine marks a spring
whose temperature
is forty-three degrees
all year,
rain or shine.
Even in the snow.

It is said
that it was once home
to hundreds of swans.
Righteous Anna used to
feed and care for them.
But Mami says the swans
don't go there anymore.

There is rot
in the old growth—
the Kodari forest
senses these things.
I sense things too.
The rot in our community.
Sometimes it's not enough
to be good,
if you treat others
with disdain.
Sometimes there's nothing
you can do
but fly away,
like Anna did.

Follow us:

f **/orbitbooksUS**

𝕏 **/orbitbooks**

▶ **/orbitbooks**

Join our mailing list
to receive alerts on our
latest releases and deals.

orbitbooks.net

Enter our monthly
giveaway for the chance
to win some epic prizes.

orbitloot.com